The Color of HEAVEN

Kim Dong Hwa

ELK GROVE VILLAGE PUBLIC LIBRARY
1001 WELLINGTON AVE
ELK GROVE VILLAGE, IL 60007
(847) 439-0447

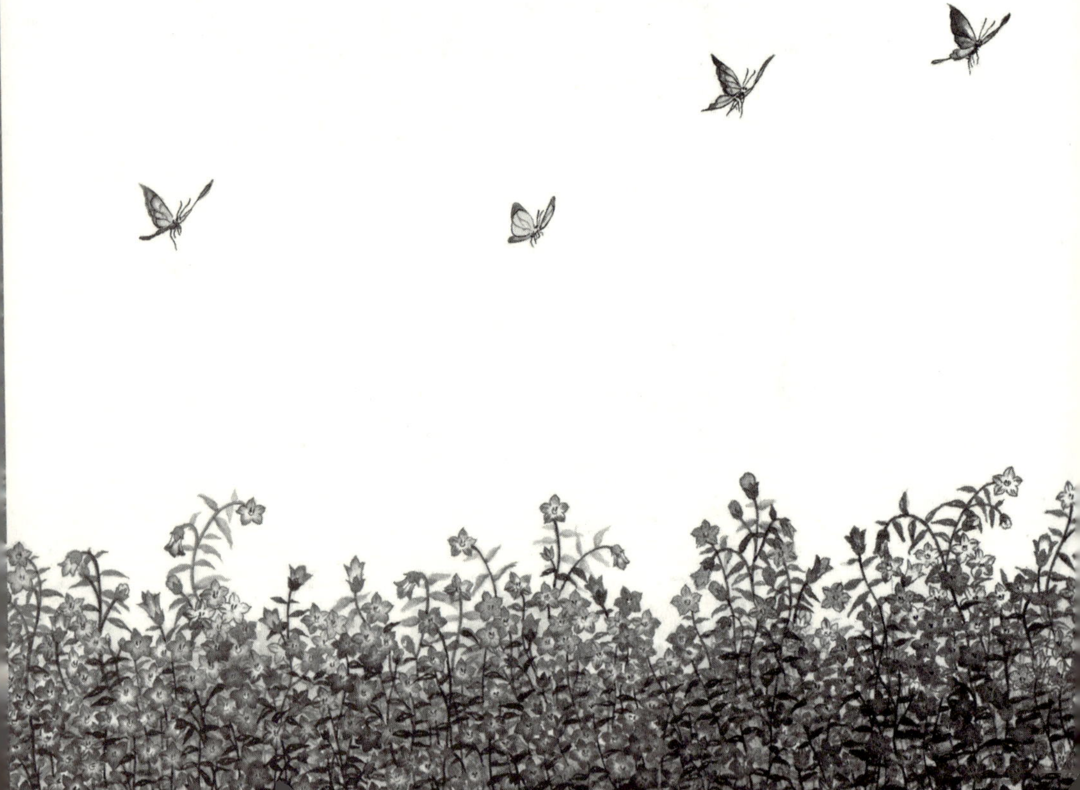

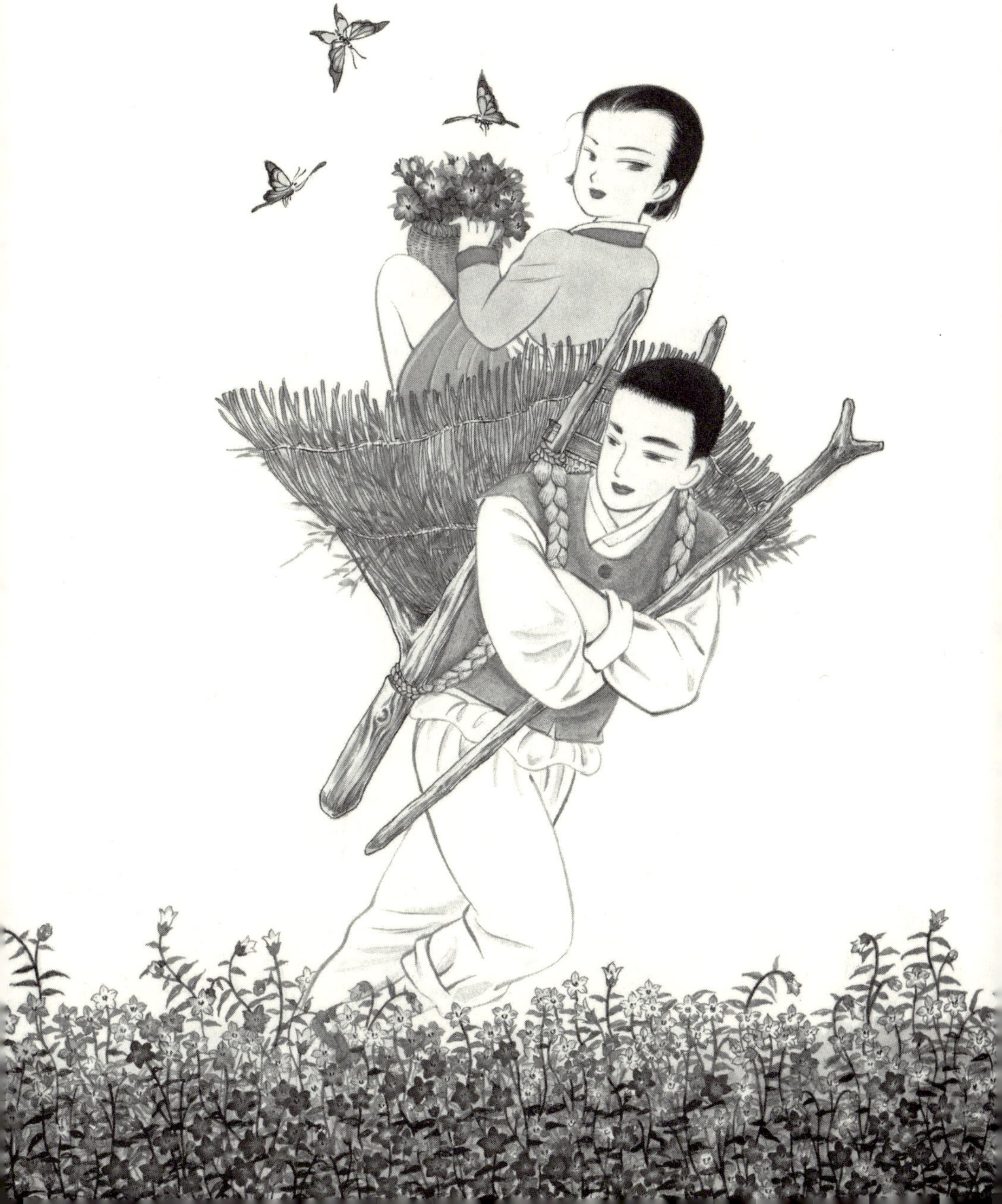

:01
First Second

New York & London

The Story of Life on the Golden Fields Vol. 3 © 2003 by Kim Dong Hwa
All Rights Reserved
English translation copyright © 2009 by First Second

Published by First Second
First Second is an imprint of Roaring Brook Press,
a division of Holtzbrinck Publishing Holdings Limited Partnership
175 Fifth Avenue, New York, NY 10010

All rights reserved.

Distributed in Canada by H. B. Fenn and Company Ltd.
Distributed in the United Kingdom by Macmillan Children's Books,
a division of Pan Macmillan.

First published in Korea in 2003 by Kim Dong Hwa
English translation rights arranged with Kim Dong Hwa through Orange Agency
English edition © 2009 by First Second

Cataloging-in-Publication Data is on file at the Library of Congress.

ISBN: 978-1-59643-460-8

First Second books are available for special promotions and premiums.
For details, contact: Director of Special Markets, Holtzbrinck Publishers.

FIRST
EDITION

First American Edition September 2009
Printed in the United States of America
1 3 5 7 9 10 8 6 4 2

BY ART WE LIVE

황토빛이야기

The Color of HEAVEN

Kim Dong Hwa

Translated from the Korean by Lauren Na

:01

First Second

New York & London

My beloved has arrived, but rather than greeting him,
All I can do is bite the corner of my apron with a blank expression-
What an awkward woman am I.

My heart has longed for him as hugely and openly as a full moon
But instead I narrow my eyes, and my glance to him
Is sharp and narrow as the crescent moon.

But then, I'm not the only one who behaves this way.
My mother and my mother's mother were as silly and stumbling as I am
       when they were girls...

Still, the love from my heart is overflowing,
As bright and crimson as the heated metal in a blacksmith's forge.

Deeply etched on my mother's face are wrinkles as fine as the strands on a spider's web. As I remove these threads, one at a time, I see her transform into a blushing sixteen-year-old girl.

Now, open for you to read, is the tale of this clumsy sixteen-year-old girl. From an era where time stood still, her story is revealed in bits and pieces, a tale that slowly escapes from the past.

Little gems from my mother's life at sixteen...

Ochre-colored earth stories...

From the West Bridge–
Kim Dong Hwa

CONTENTS

Little gems from my mother's life at sixteen...

Chapter One	The Butterfly Flew Over the Mountain	11
Chapter Two	South Wind	41
Chapter Three	Fire Butterfly	71
Chapter Four	Paper Moon	101
Chapter Five	Naked Lady Lily	131

Chapter Six	First Snow of the Season	161
Chapter Seven	Guest	191
Chapter Eight	White Hair	221
Chapter Nine	Ehwa is Getting Married	251
Chapter Ten	The Bridal Night	281

Chapter One

THE BUTTERFLY FLEW OVER THE MOUNTAIN

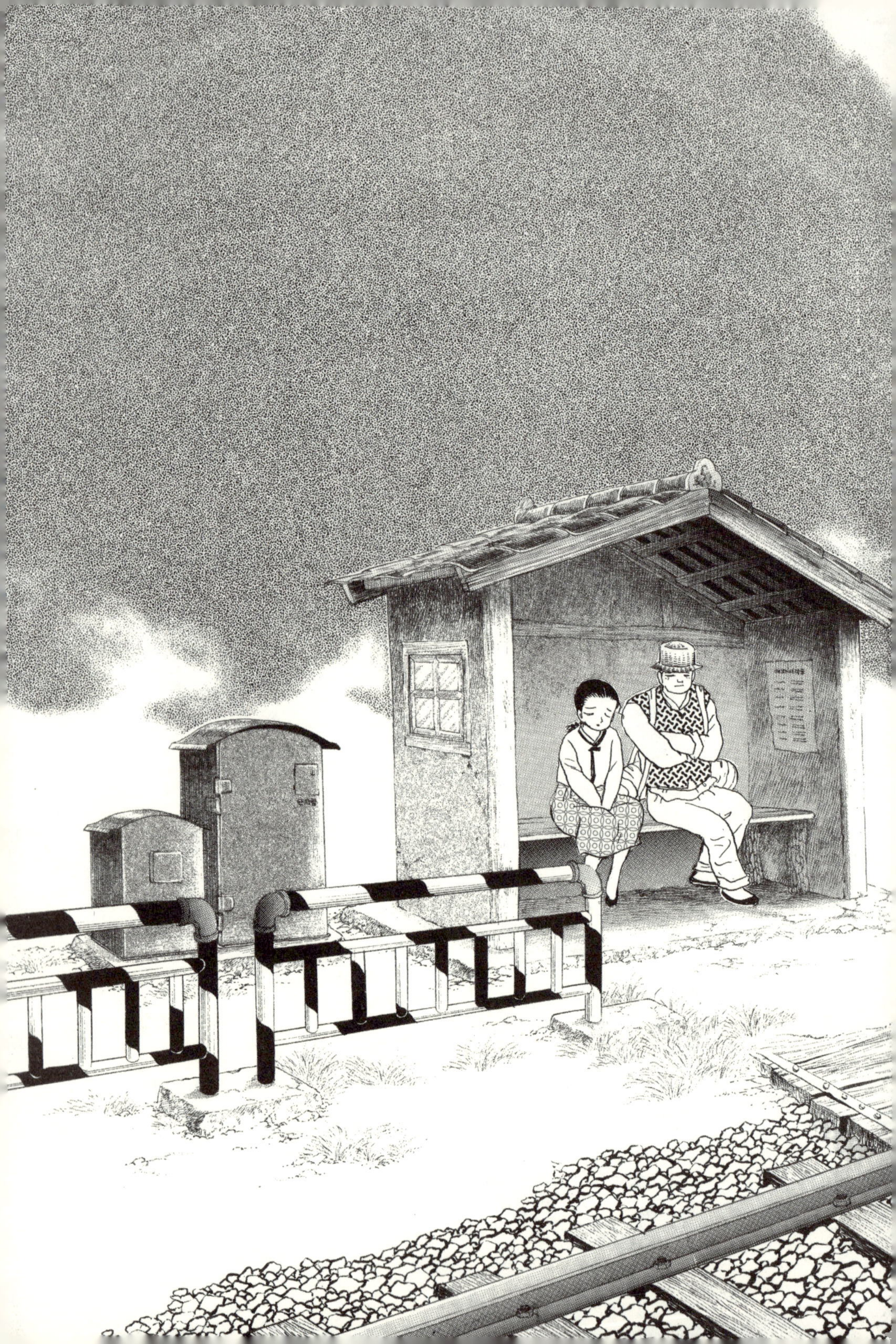

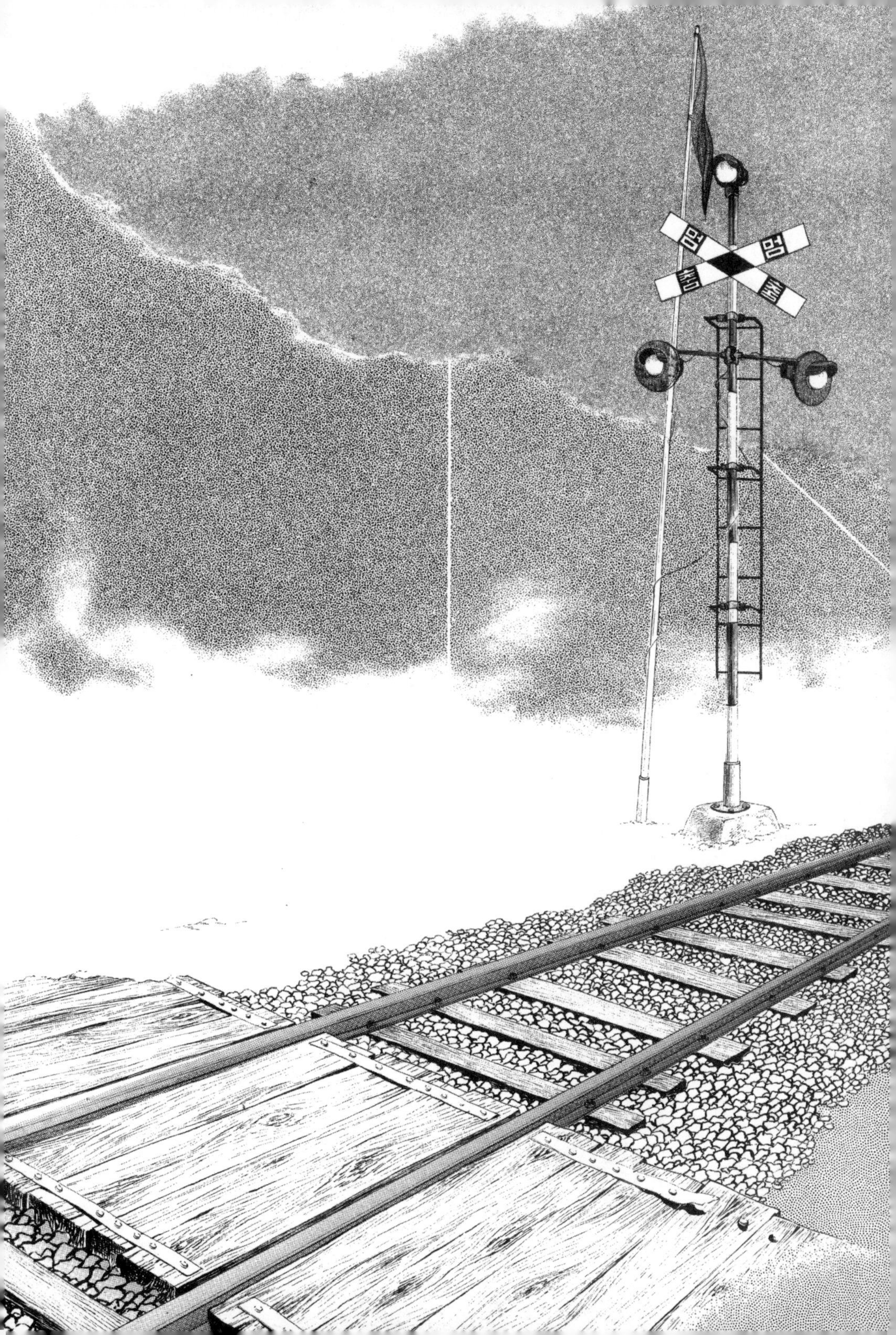
멈춤
멈춤

WAITING AREA

FIRST TRAIN 06:00
LAST TRAIN 23:30

Do you really have to go?

14

Yes...

How can you say that so easily? You're leaving your home town.

I can make a living just about anywhere, and it'll be just as good, if not better, than I had it here. If I become fond of a place, wherever that may be, it can become my hometown.

Well then, I guess you're fine.

You can go anywhere and make it your new home... I didn't realize that's how you were thinking, and here I was all worried for no reason.

Wherever you go, you will be able to find a girl in a braid... You can pour water over her hair, begin to love her, and then finally marry her.
You can call anywhere your home, and you can choose any girl as your wife.
It must be great to be a man. You can up and leave as you please.
Just like a butterfly, you can fly from one flower to another, and when you're dissatisfied, you can fly over the mountain and go away...
I feel sorry for women. All a woman can do is look at the sun and let her petals fall off as she waits. It's so sad.
WAITING AREA
FIRST TRAIN 06 : 00
LAST TRAIN 23
Yes, it's true that no matter where I go in this land, it will always remain my country. But it's not like that for people.

Because no matter whom I meet out there, she couldn't be my wife.
The face I met one day by chance has now become such an important part of my life that it ties my feet to this place.
No matter where I search, I will not be able to find that face anywhere else but here, and that face, right now, is cutting my heart into pieces.
Leaving you is the scariest thing I've had to do in my life, and it's made my feet hesitate.
Then don't go.
Do you think I'm going because I want to? I'm running for my life.

I'm sure by now, Master Cho has sent out men to search for me.
If they catch me, I'll be lucky if they spare my life. That's why I have to leave.
Also, leaving is the only way to make sure I can see you again.
That I can come back to get you.
I understand what you're saying, but it doesn't make things any easier. I wasn't prepared for you to leave so suddenly like this.

I wasn't even able to give you a hot meal or some warm clothes...
I wish I had something to give you.
You have. You've given me your face.
I'm going to remember your face so vividly that I will be able to recall it a thousand—no, ten thousand times at any given moment.
I'm going to take your fragrance with me, and no matter what happens, it won't fade away.

CHOoo

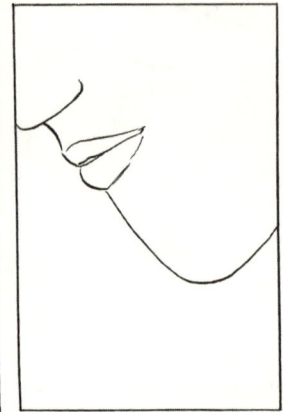

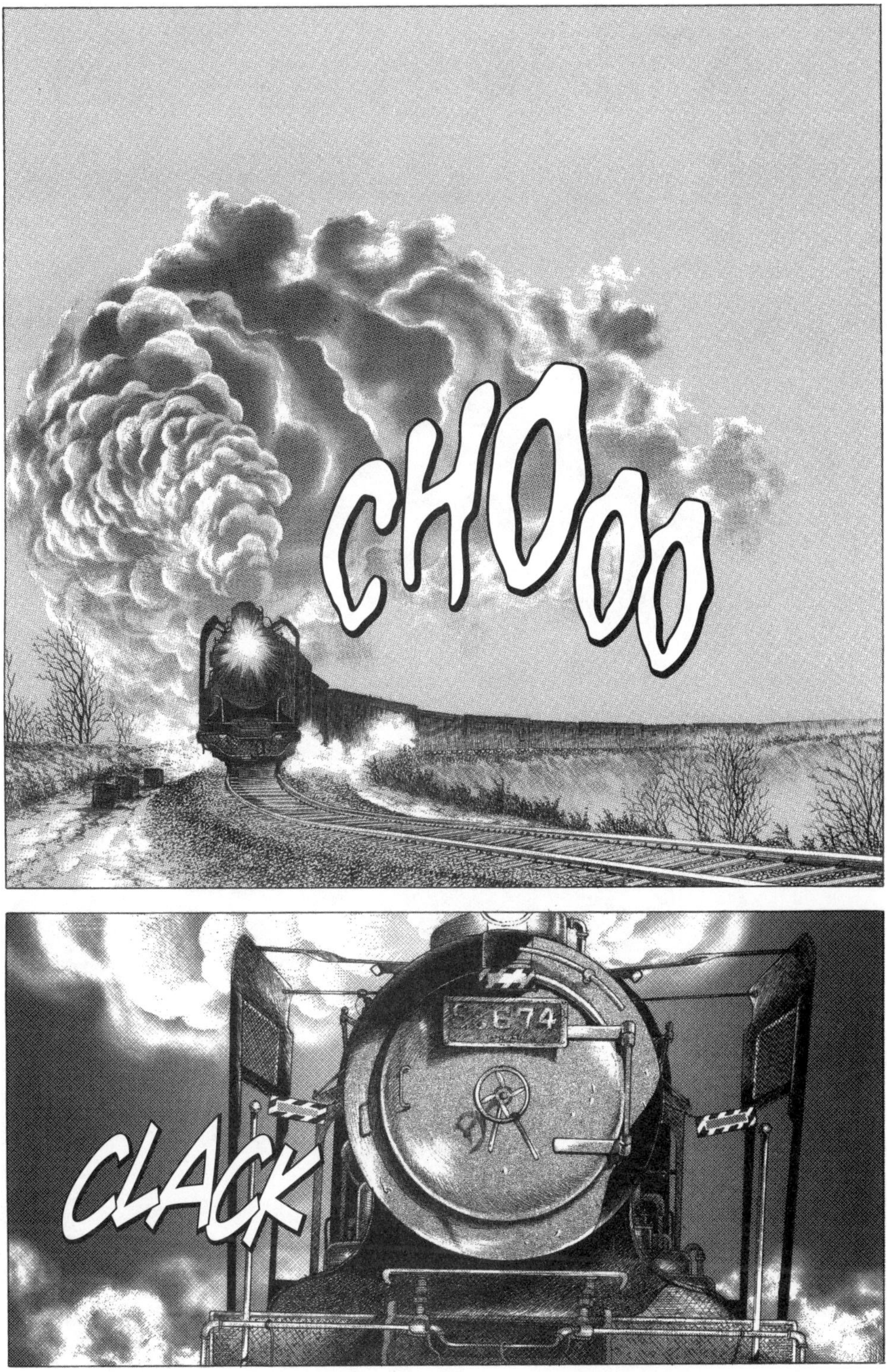
CHOOO
CLACK

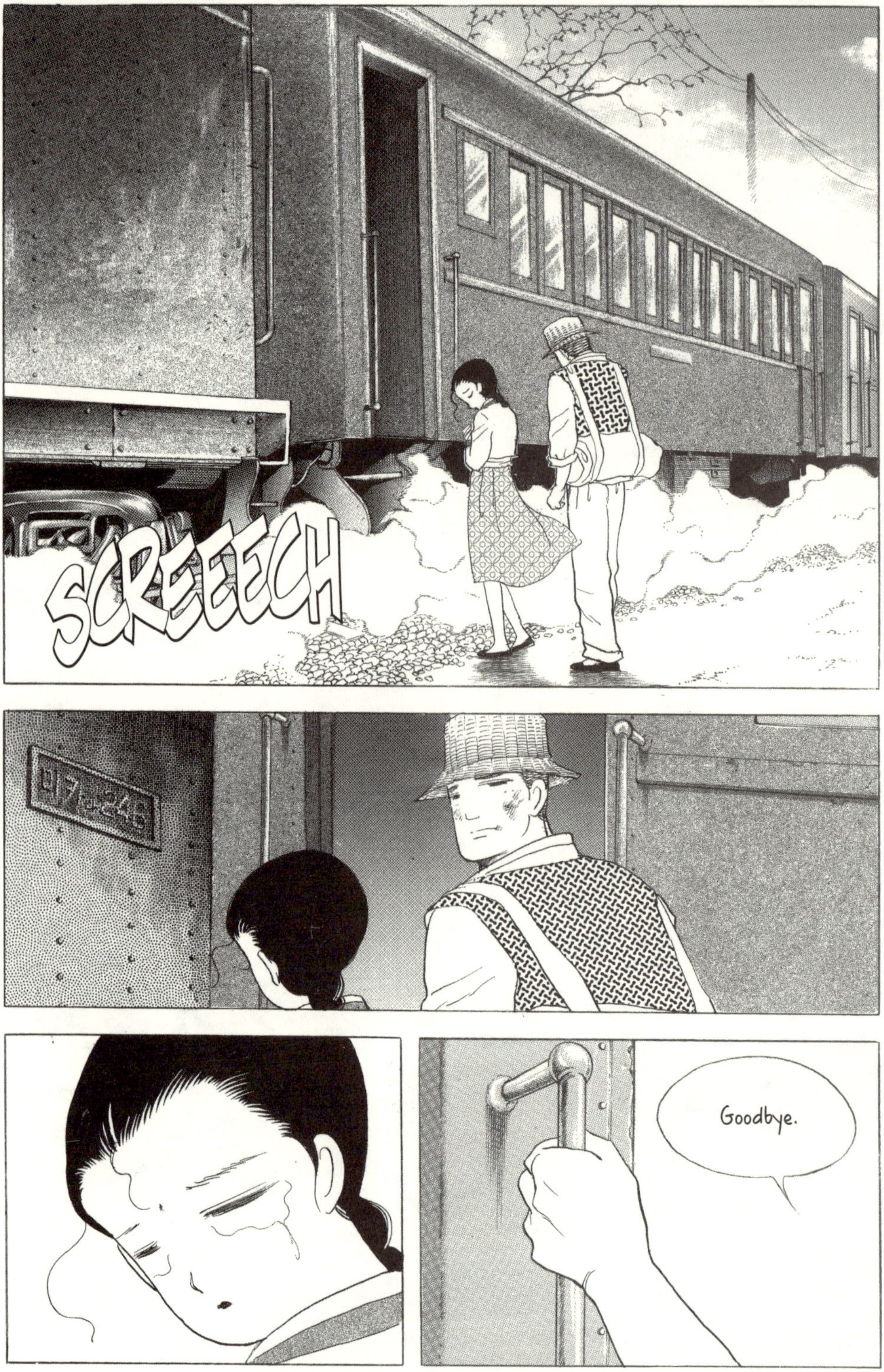
SCREEECH
Goodbye.

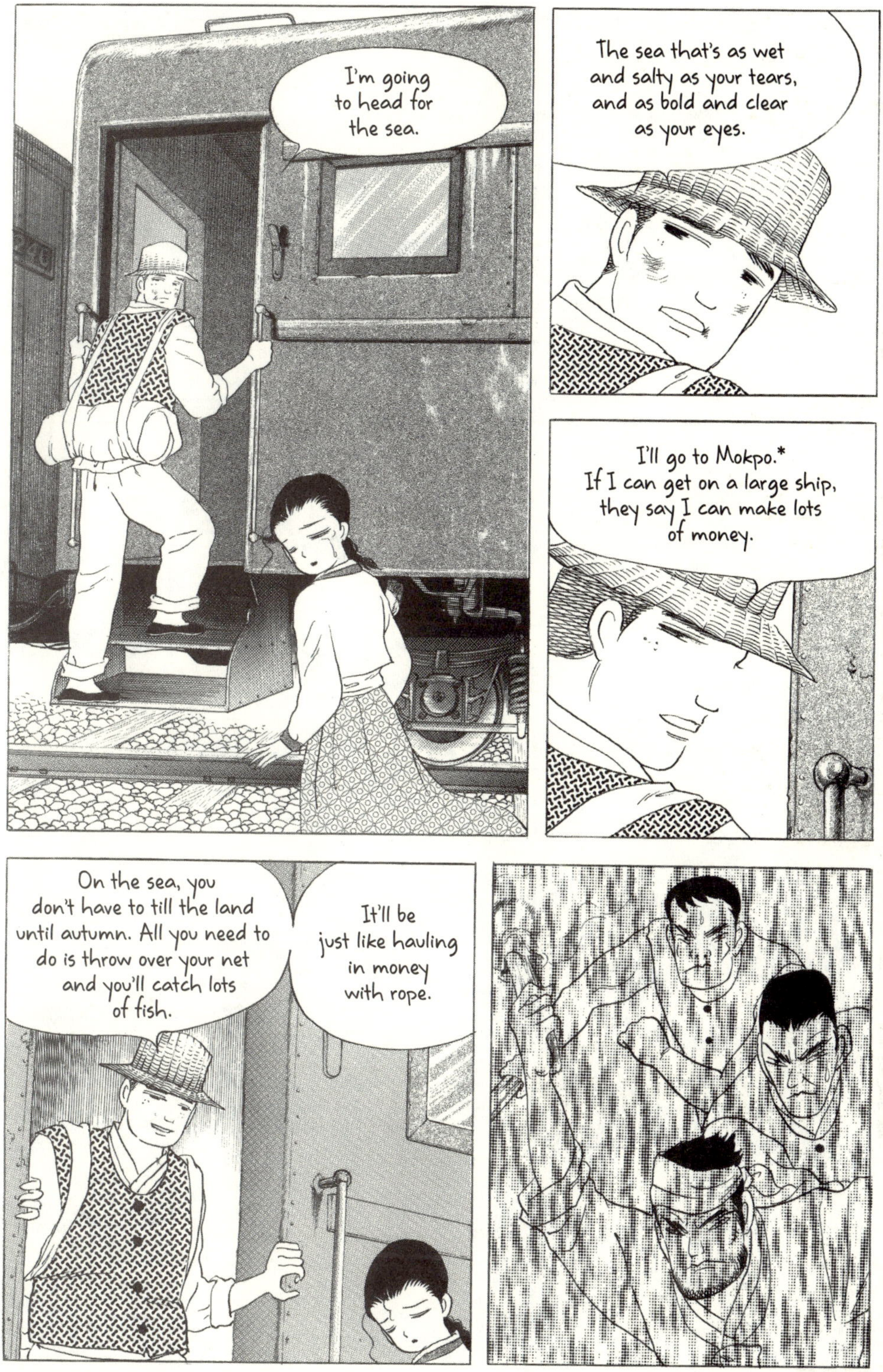
I'm going to head for the sea.
The sea that's as wet and salty as your tears, and as bold and clear as your eyes.
I'll go to Mokpo.* If I can get on a large ship, they say I can make lots of money.
On the sea, you don't have to till the land until autumn. All you need to do is throw over your net and you'll catch lots of fish.
It'll be just like hauling in money with rope.

*A port city located in southwestern Korea.

It'll be hard work and even harder being apart from you, but we can get married once I make enough money to support us, Ehwa.

When that time comes, I will come for you. I'll come with a flower palanquin, and a gold and silver cloth to wrap you in.

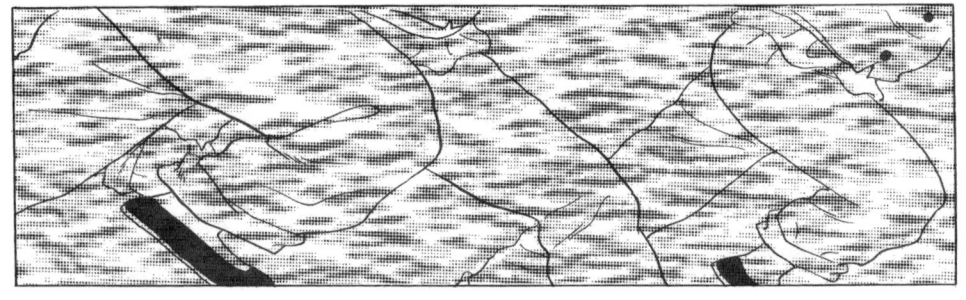

CLICK

I'll come get you when the hollyhocks are in season.

CHOOOK   CHOOOK   CHOOOK

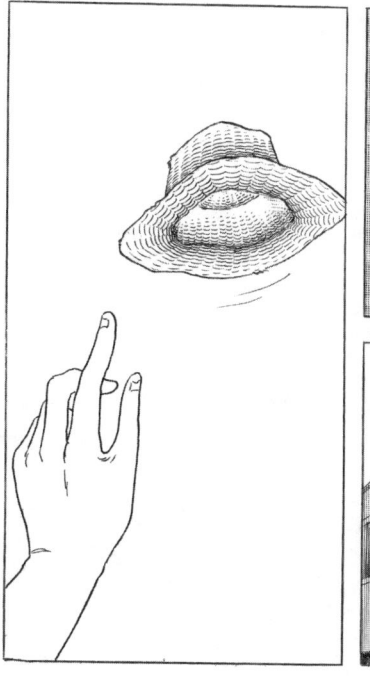

I'm sorry! I'm sorry I'm leaving you with tears on your face, and that I won't be able to wipe them.

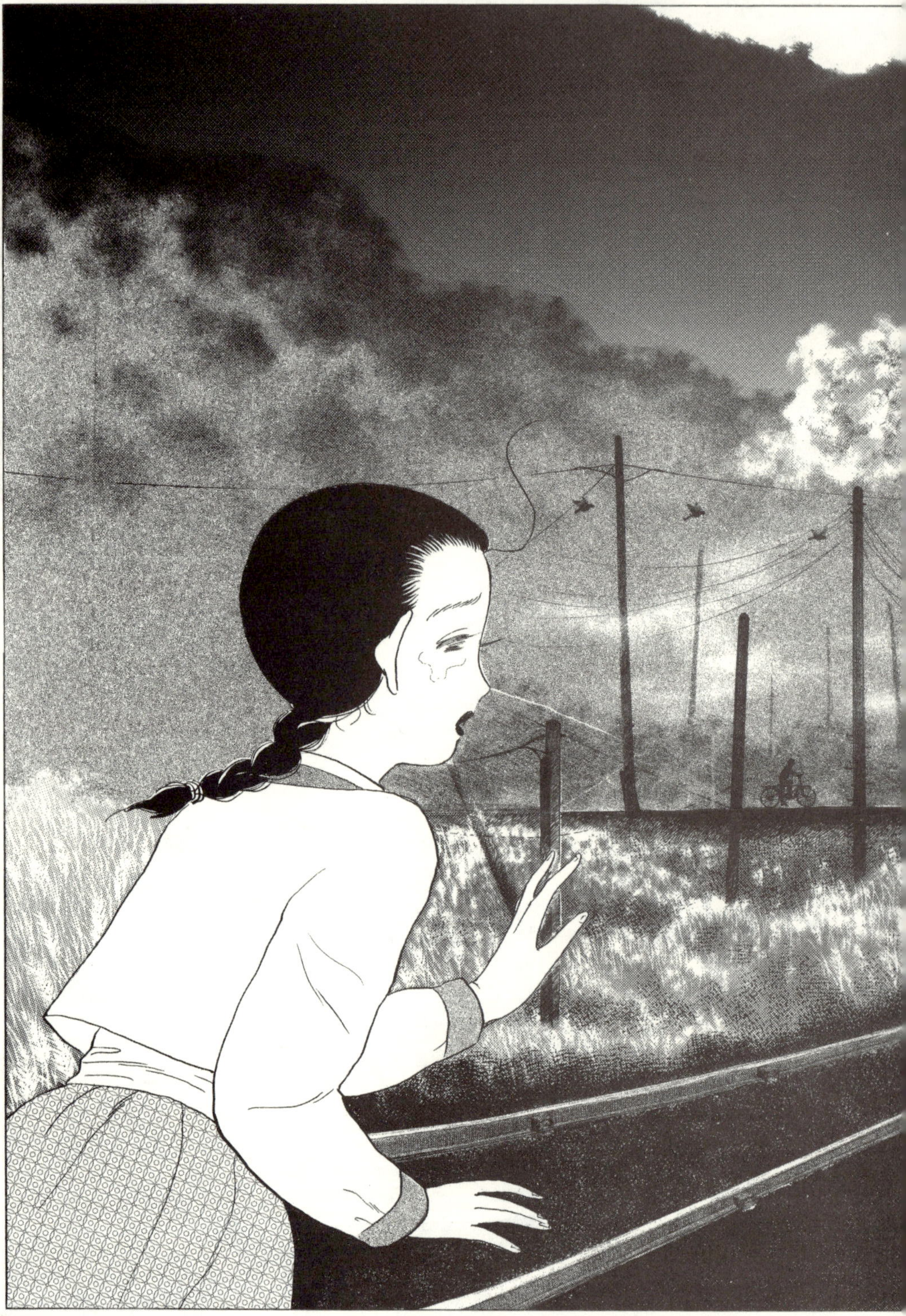

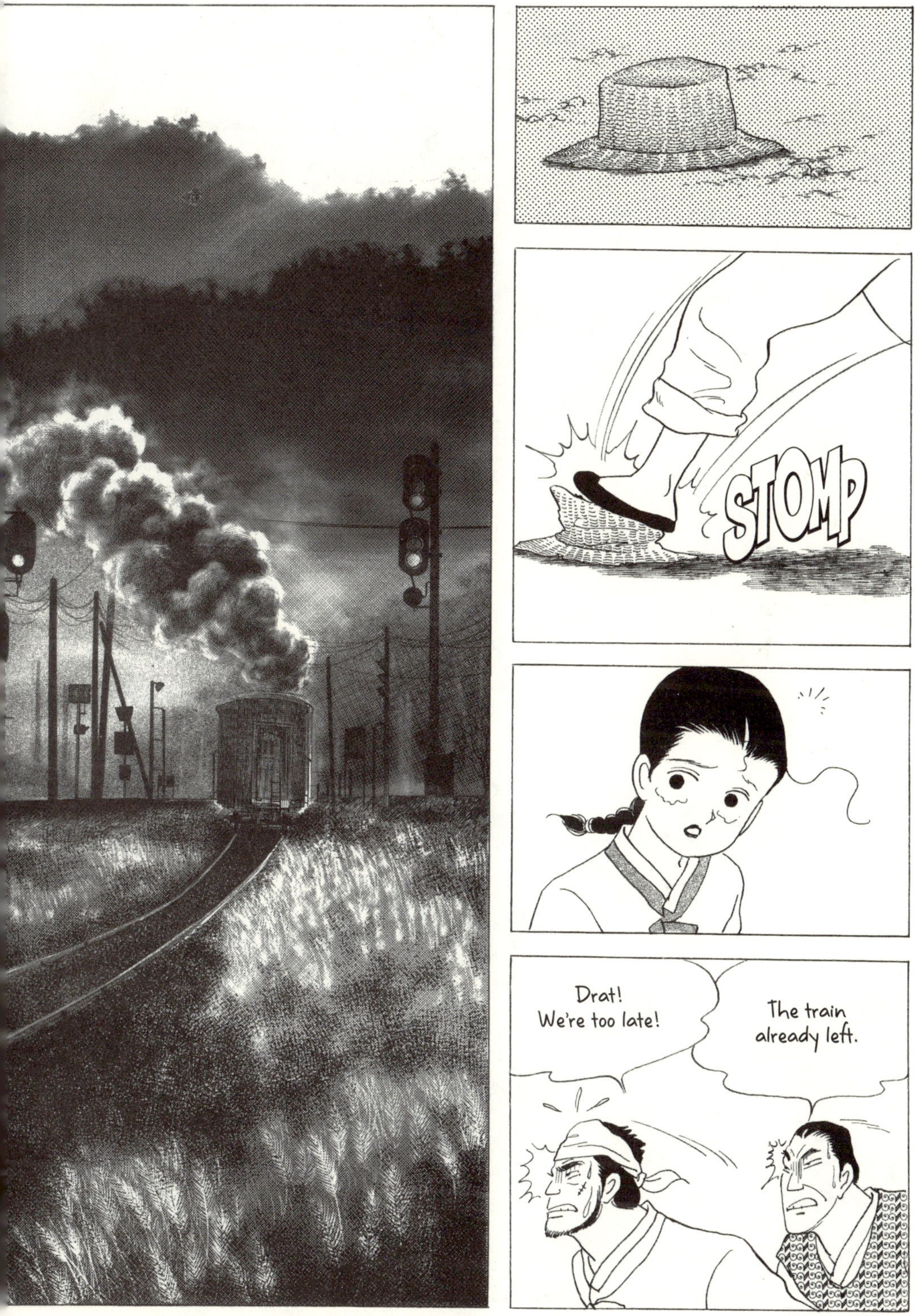
STOMP
Drat! We're too late!
The train already left.

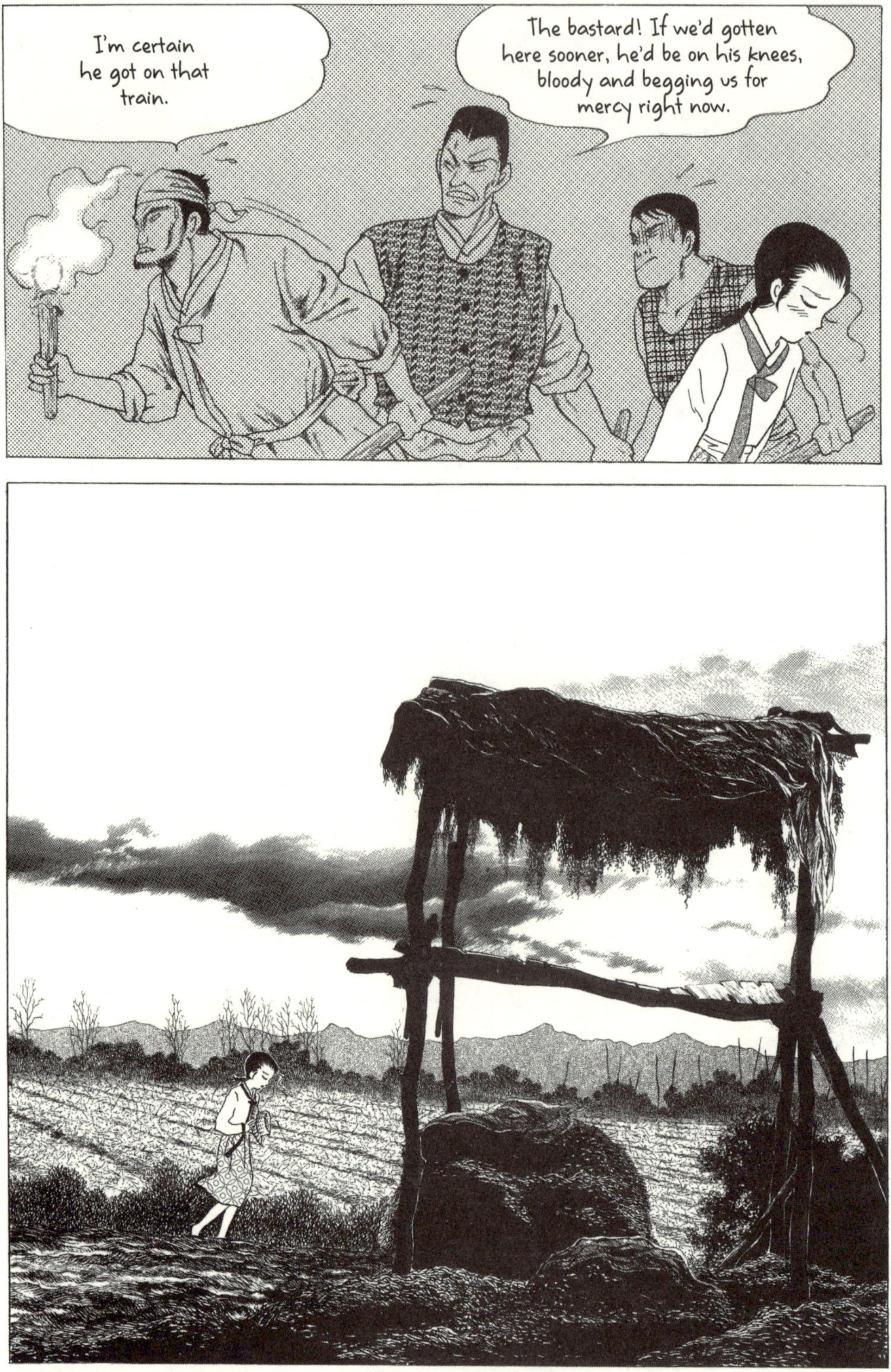
I'm certain he got on that train.
The bastard! If we'd gotten here sooner, he'd be on his knees, bloody and begging us for mercy right now.

What's going on?

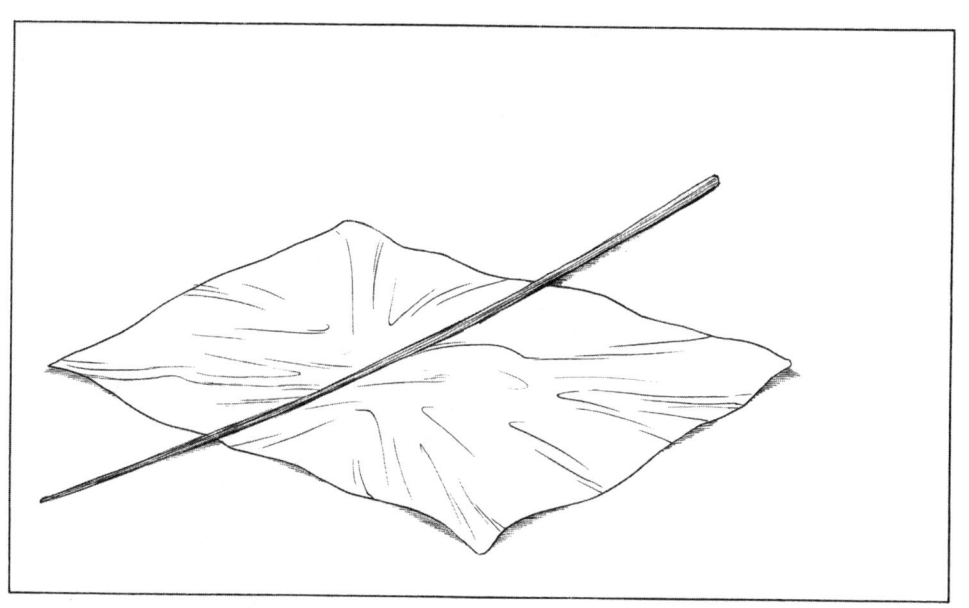

.....

Why aren't you saying anything? You left the house in the middle of the night and came back at the crack of dawn.
You said you were going out to pee. Was the outhouse miles and miles away? Is it so far that it took you all night to come back?
.....
Where did you go?
Why haven't you said anything?
Did you get enchanted by a hobgoblin? Who's the creature that entranced you with this flimsy straw hat?

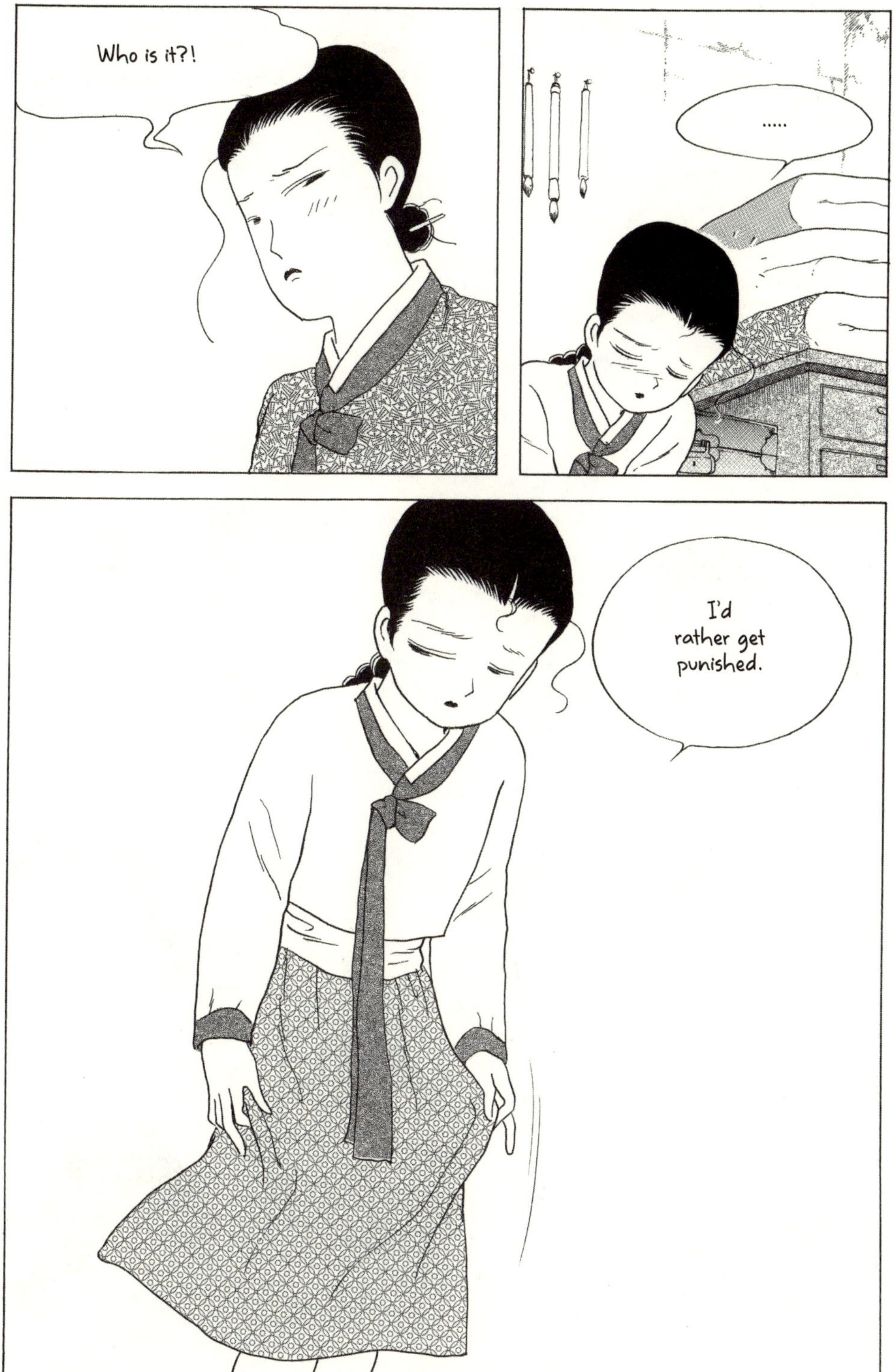
Who is it?!
.....
I'd rather get punished.

But just so you know...

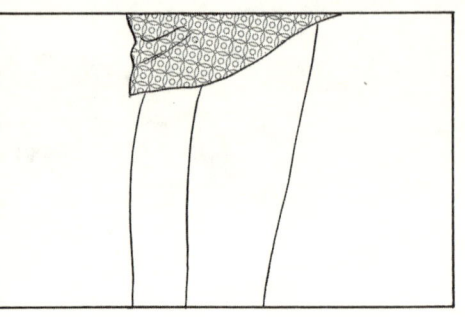

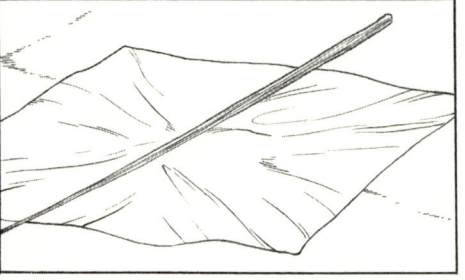

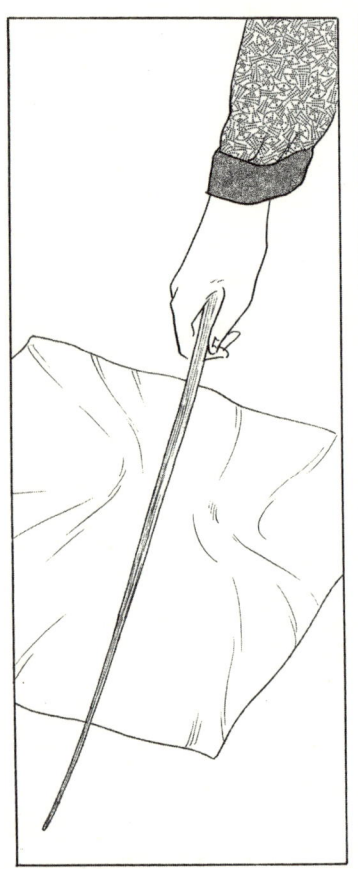

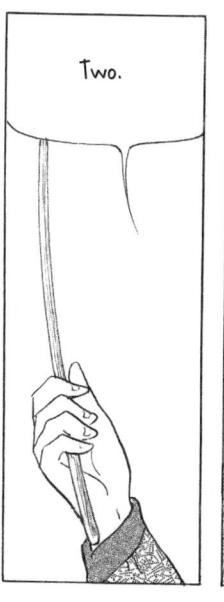

...whether I came back in the morning or ten days from now, nothing happened or would ever happen.

I swear on the name of the gods.

One.

Two.

You made me search the garden, all around the house... And across the entire village...

SMACK

SMACK
SMACK

...but you came back home without a single hair astray or corner of your dress out of order so I know nothing happened!
SMACK
SMACK
SMACK
SMACK
SMACK

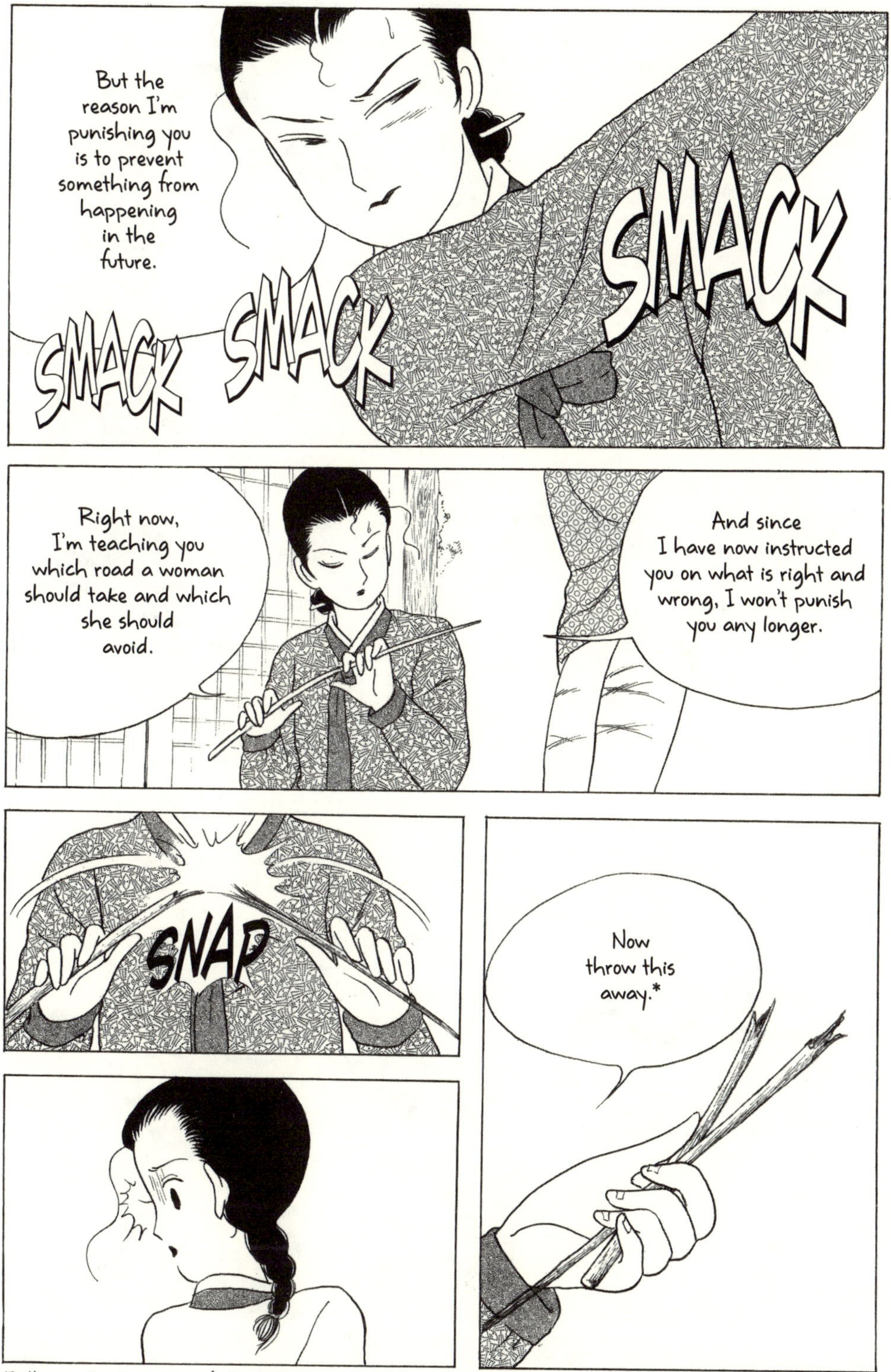

But the reason I'm punishing you is to prevent something from happening in the future.
SMACK
SMACK
SMACK
Right now, I'm teaching you which road a woman should take and which she should avoid.
And since I have now instructed you on what is right and wrong, I won't punish you any longer.
SNAP
Now throw this away.*

*In Korean culture it is customary for the child to discard the rod that was used for discipline. It's symbolic of recognizing one's error and discarding the wrongdoing, never to make that mistake again.

Ehwa...
...on a day like this, wouldn't it be nice if rain just poured down from the sky?
You can cry to your heart's content in the rain and no one would know you're upset.
A wound on your skin can be easily healed with ointments, but a wound of the heart needs a good cry to start healing itself.
So why don't you go for a walk to the spring and wash your face while you're there? A face that's swollen from oversleeping is not a pretty sight, but a face that's stiff from trying to hold in the tears is even worse. You need to let those tears out all at once.

I don't know who he is, but he sure was in a hurry.
He calls her out in the middle of the night and leaves a tattered straw hat as a keepsake...
Take this.
What is it?
These are gourd vine seeds. Keep them close to your heart and then find a place to plant them.
If you're waiting for someone, you need to plant a gourd vine. The gourd flower is the only flower that lights up the night and sends its fragrance to the far off corners of the earth.

I am a cruel mother. Of all the things I could pass down to you, it had to be "waiting"...
I can't believe I'm telling you to plant the gourd flower, out of all the pretty flowers out there...
I only need to wait, but it's the one who must leave and come back that has it the hardest...
You're saying you're all right with waiting?
Would you rather wait a year? Or would you rather leave for ten years? If I had to choose between the two, I'd choose to leave rather than wait.
I would rather crawl on my knees, searching, than sit and wait, or lie down and wait.

"You don't know how hard it is to wait. You don't know how painful it is. As seasons pass and you see the rains come and the trees grow taller, you feel yourself withering as you wait and wait."

"Even if that's true, I still plan on waiting."

"Even if it's that painful, the fact that you have someone to wait for is happiness itself."

"That's true. No matter how painful it is, you still wait because of the longing you have for that certain someone."

"Even though I say that counting the gourd flowers in the night is a lot sadder than getting drenched by rain, it must not be true because I can't bring myself to uproot the gourd vine and throw it away. Instead, I carefully collect the seeds to plant them again."

From now on, you and I will be sighing together while we look toward the village entrance.
Then do you want to make a bet over who will hear the footsteps first?

Why you saucy little girl!
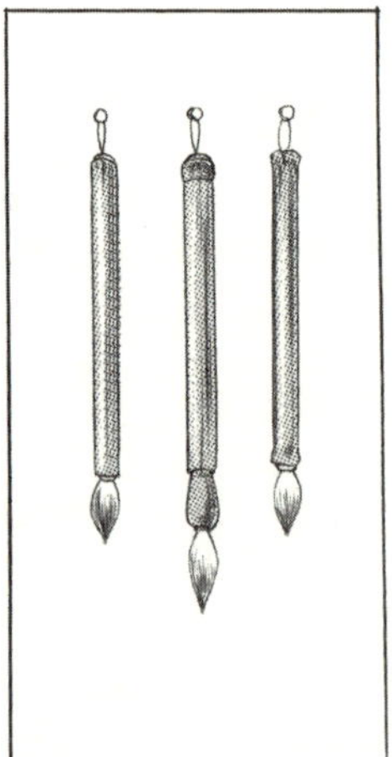

Chapter Two
SOUTH WIND

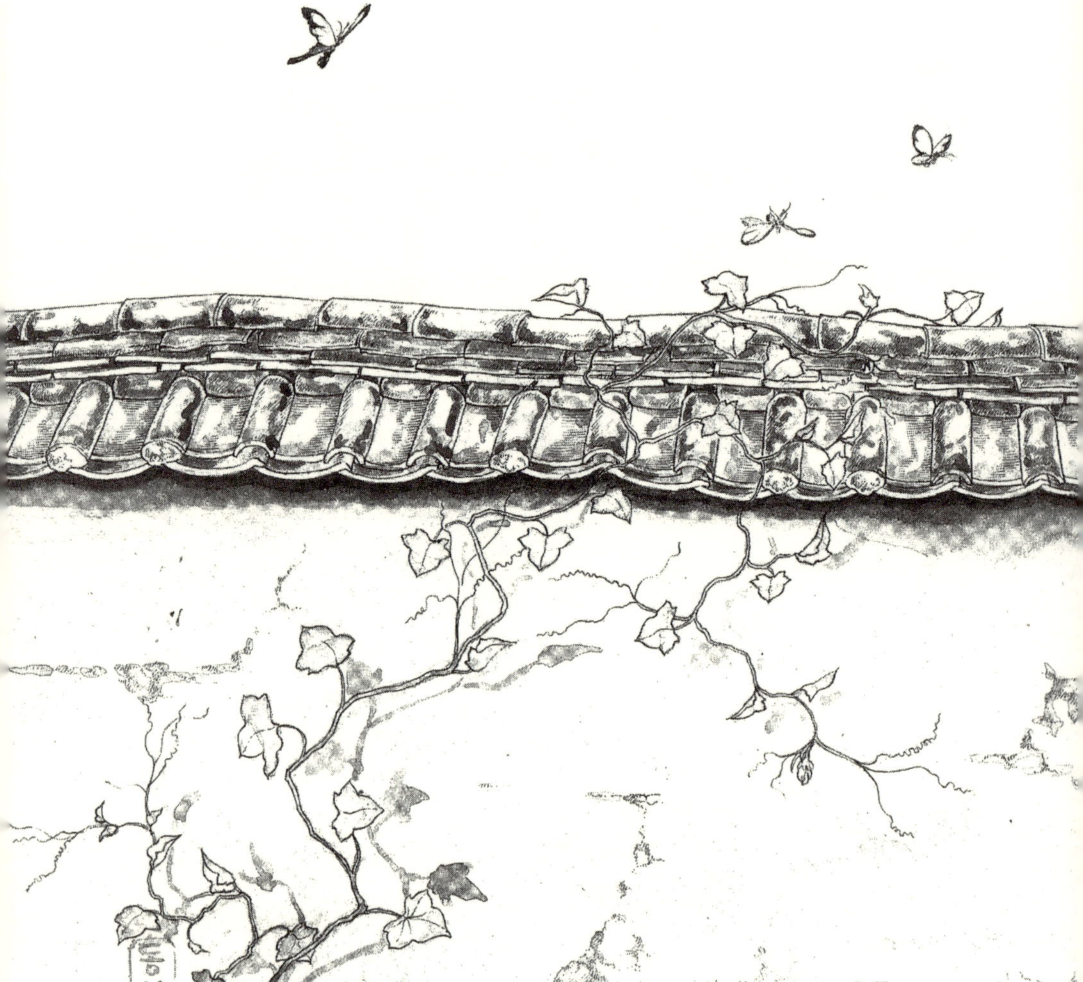

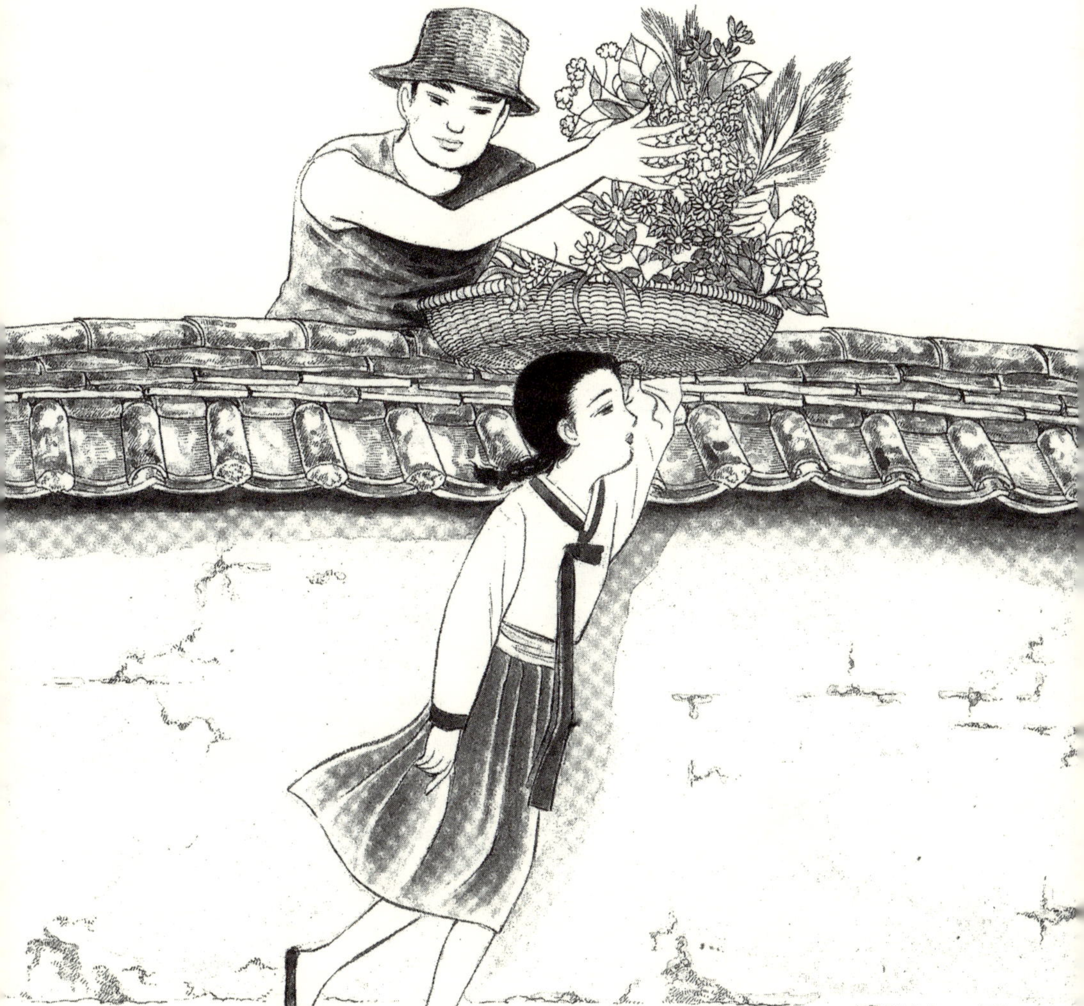

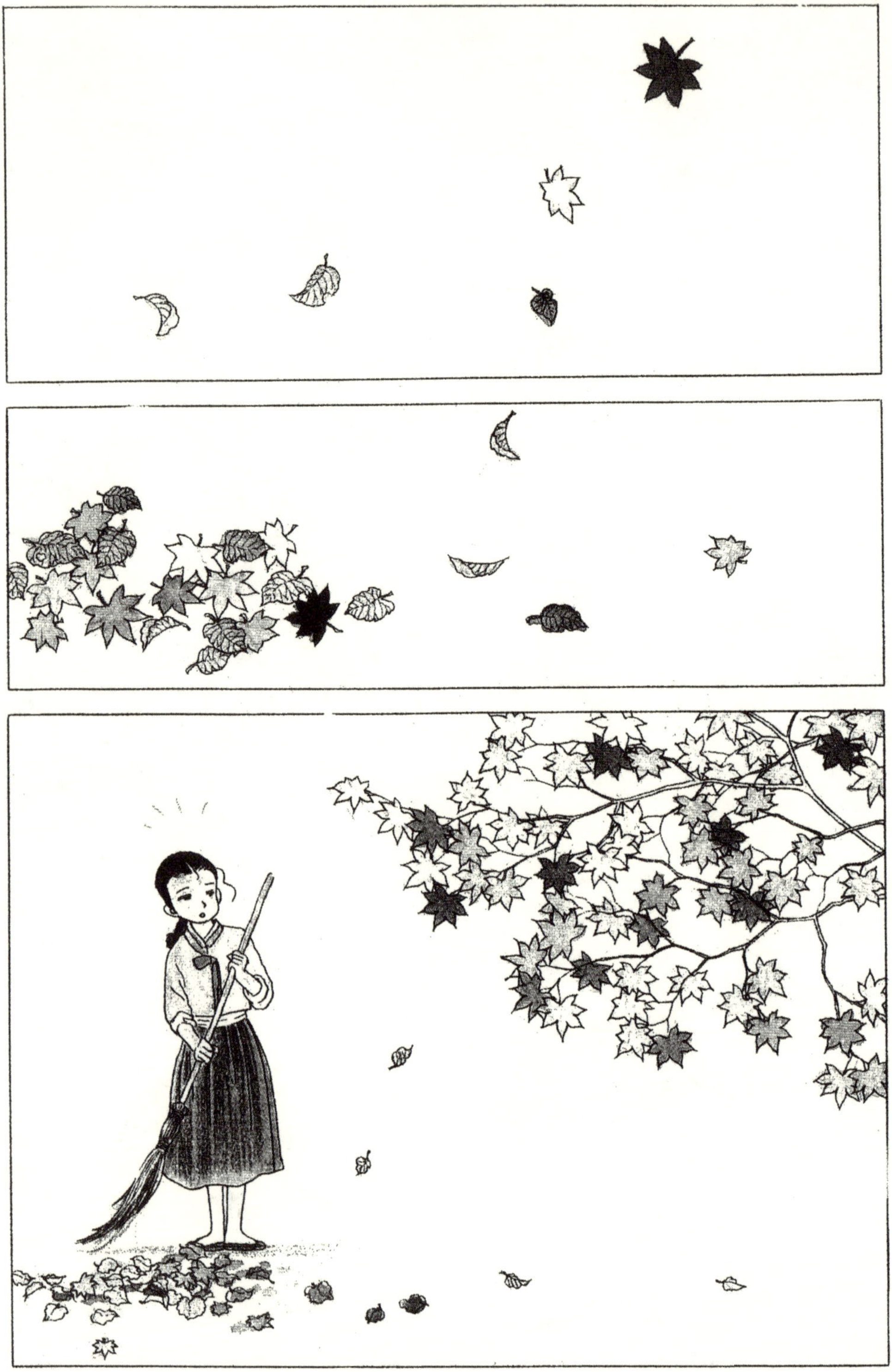

What's so interesting that it's keeping you from sweeping the yard?
I'm waiting for a message, and all that comes are piles of leaves.
No news is good news.
I remind myself of that all the time, but I still long to hear from him.

I'm sure that he's somewhere, absentmindedly and peacefully working away, but for some reason I can't stop feeling anxious about him.	What did I tell you before? I told you that waiting for someone is harder than anything in the world.

After waiting and waiting, you begin to lose track of whether it's the moon or the sun in the sky, and that's when he comes in with a smile on his face. As soon as you see that face, all is forgotten and you begin chasing after his footsteps once again. That is the heart of a woman.

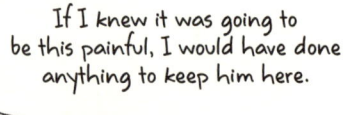

That is the karma of women. It's our punishment for planting love in our heart and carefully watering and tending to it.

I didn't know.

If I knew it was going to be this painful, I would have done anything to keep him here.

And if he still insisted on leaving, I would have gone with him.	I can't believe you're saying that in front of your mother.

A man escapes from his hometown in the dead of night, and you talk of following him? You speak as if you're a mistreated widow.

It's because waiting's so hard.

Are you saying you'd leave me behind to wait not only for the picture man, but you as well?

If you did that, I'd die of exhaustion.

It was just talk. I didn't really mean it. I just said it because I'm sad.

Well, the autumn nights have a way of making people feel restless.

If you're all done sweeping, put the leaves in the stove and burn them. With each leaf you add to the stove, include a bit of your pain as well.

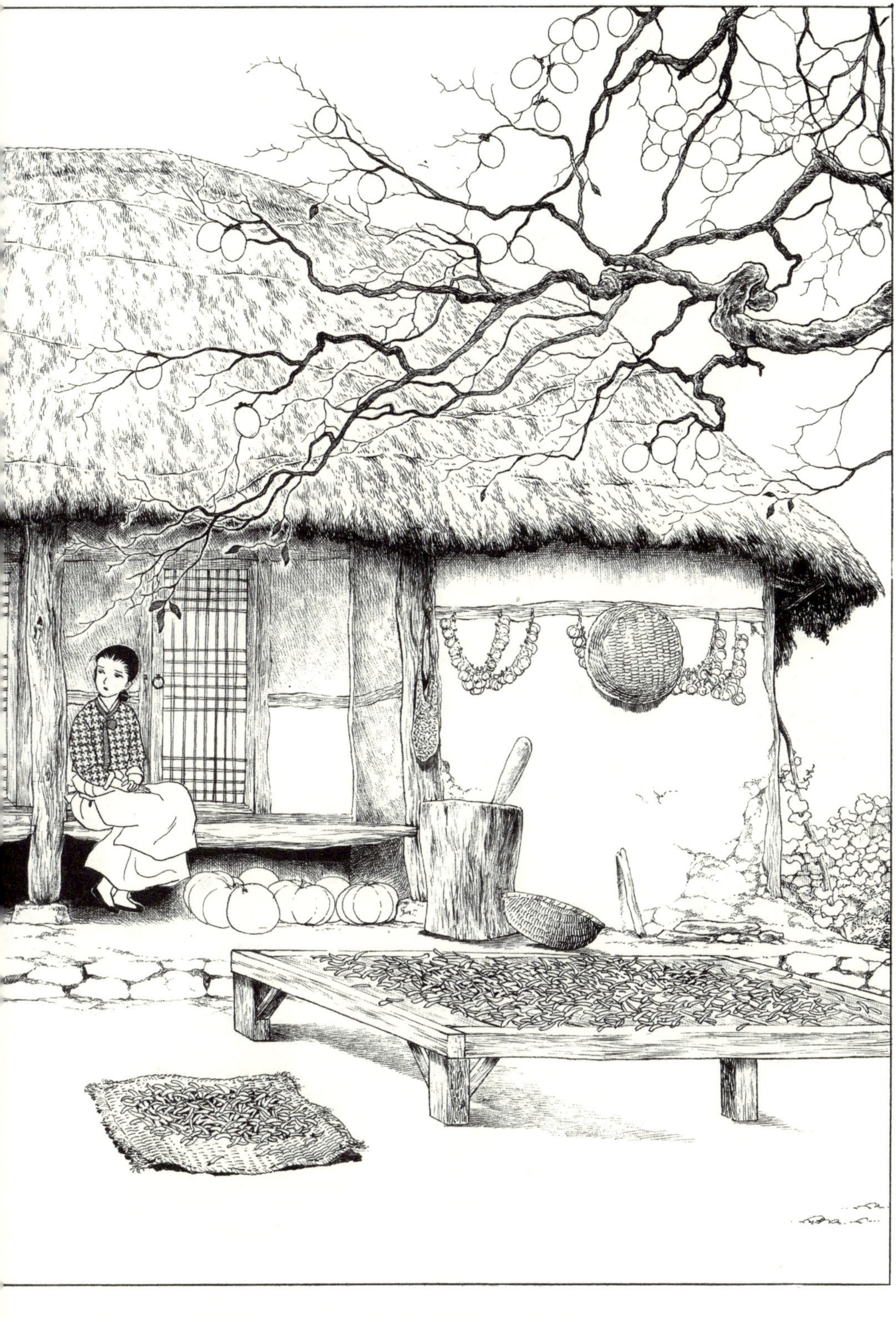

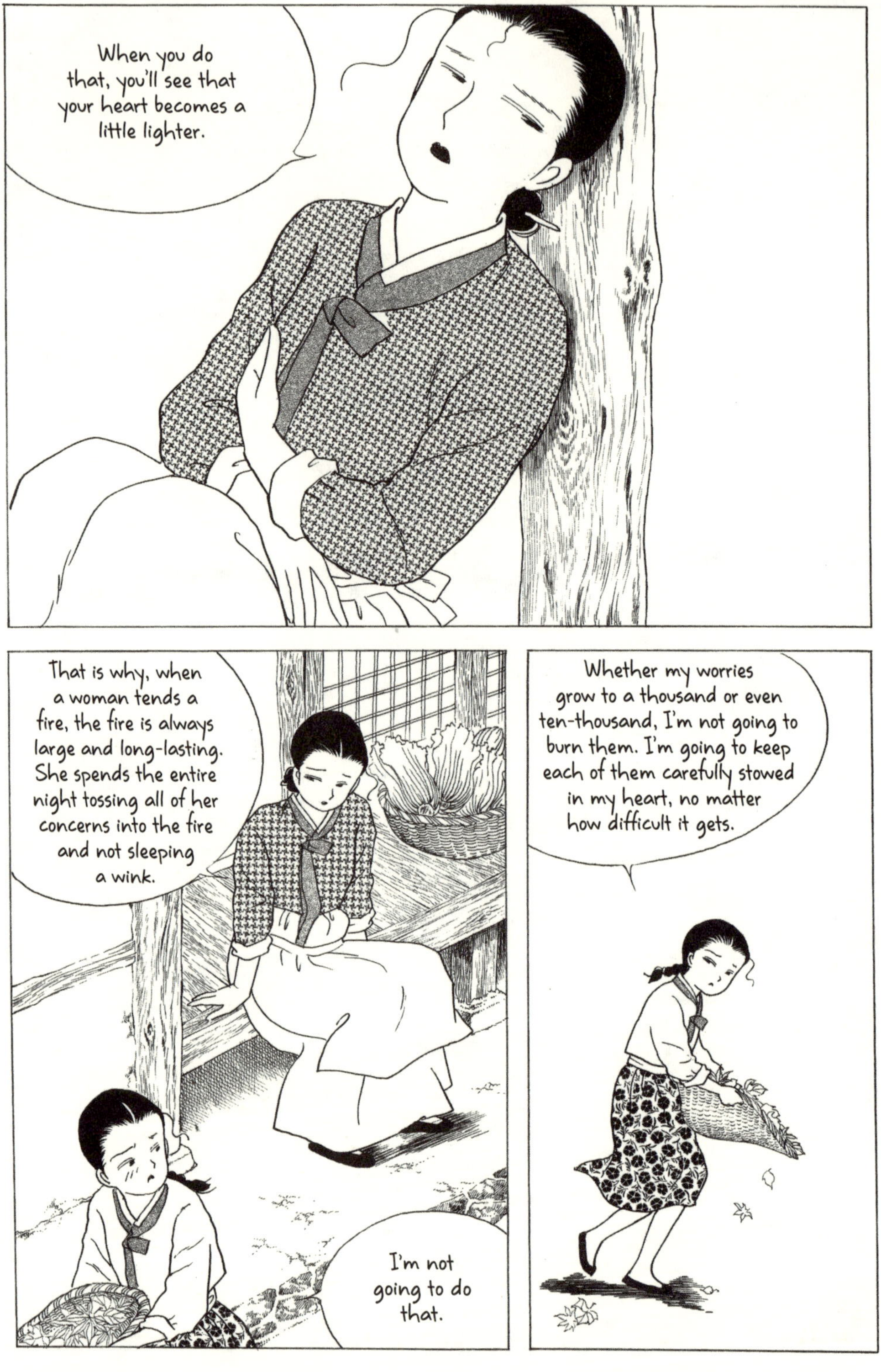
When you do that, you'll see that your heart becomes a little lighter.
That is why, when a woman tends a fire, the fire is always large and long-lasting. She spends the entire night tossing all of her concerns into the fire and not sleeping a wink.
I'm not going to do that.
Whether my worries grow to a thousand or even ten-thousand, I'm not going to burn them. I'm going to keep each of them carefully stowed in my heart, no matter how difficult it gets.

If only these leaves were a message from Duksam.

With each leaf I place into the stove, I would read another word.

If these were words written by Duksam, then this letter would be so long that it would take all night to read it.

What are you doing?	I'm burning the leaves.

What's the point of sweeping them up? As soon as you're done, dozens more have fallen.

Anyway, where are you headed off to with that basket?

Chestnut picking! They say the winds knocked a bunch down.

I wonder if other people have already gathered them all.

Even if they have, at least we could have a nice a nice afternoon out.

It was so dull and stifling at home that I wanted to scream. As soon as I heard about the chestnuts, nothing could keep me away!

"How can leaves be so beautiful?"

"Even with the most exotic, beautiful dyes in the world, I doubt we could ever do as good a job coloring them as nature."

"The red leaves remind me of the lips of a bride on her wedding day."

"It's not just the lips that are similar. The body is like that too."

"What are you talking about?"

"When the husband begins to take the bridal clothes off of the wife, one garment at a time, she becomes so shy that her face turns all red."

The leaves turn from green to red because the trees are embarrassed that they're being undressed one leaf at a time.
What?
Whether it's a person or a tree, they're both embarrassed when they're unclothed.
Bongsoon, you're too much! Making things up as you go.
I think trees are very impatient! Instead of waiting for their husband to unclothe them, they just begin taking everything off by themselves.
A woman doesn't only take off her clothes in front of her husband, you know!

"She can take off her clothes to take a bath!"

"What do you mean?"

"What are you really talking about, Bongsoon? It sounds like you're referring to somebody."

"And here I thought you were talking about the beetle, and how it just latches on to anyone it sees."

"You're a terrible girl. I shouldn't have told you about those beetles."

"No...not at all. There's no hidden meaning to what I was saying."

Wait a minute... What's that?
What?
It looks like a pair of men's trousers.
Trousers? Then there must be a skirt nearby, too.
?
Let's go! It'll be a fun sight to see.
I don't want to.
Stop being so shy! You need to learn to live a little, Ehwa!

For me, there's very little I love more than catching a couple in the act. It's more delicious than a table set with the finest desserts!
?
?

Is...is that you, Dongchul? What are you doing here, all by yourself, without your pants on?
Can't you tell just by looking? I'm drying my gochoo.

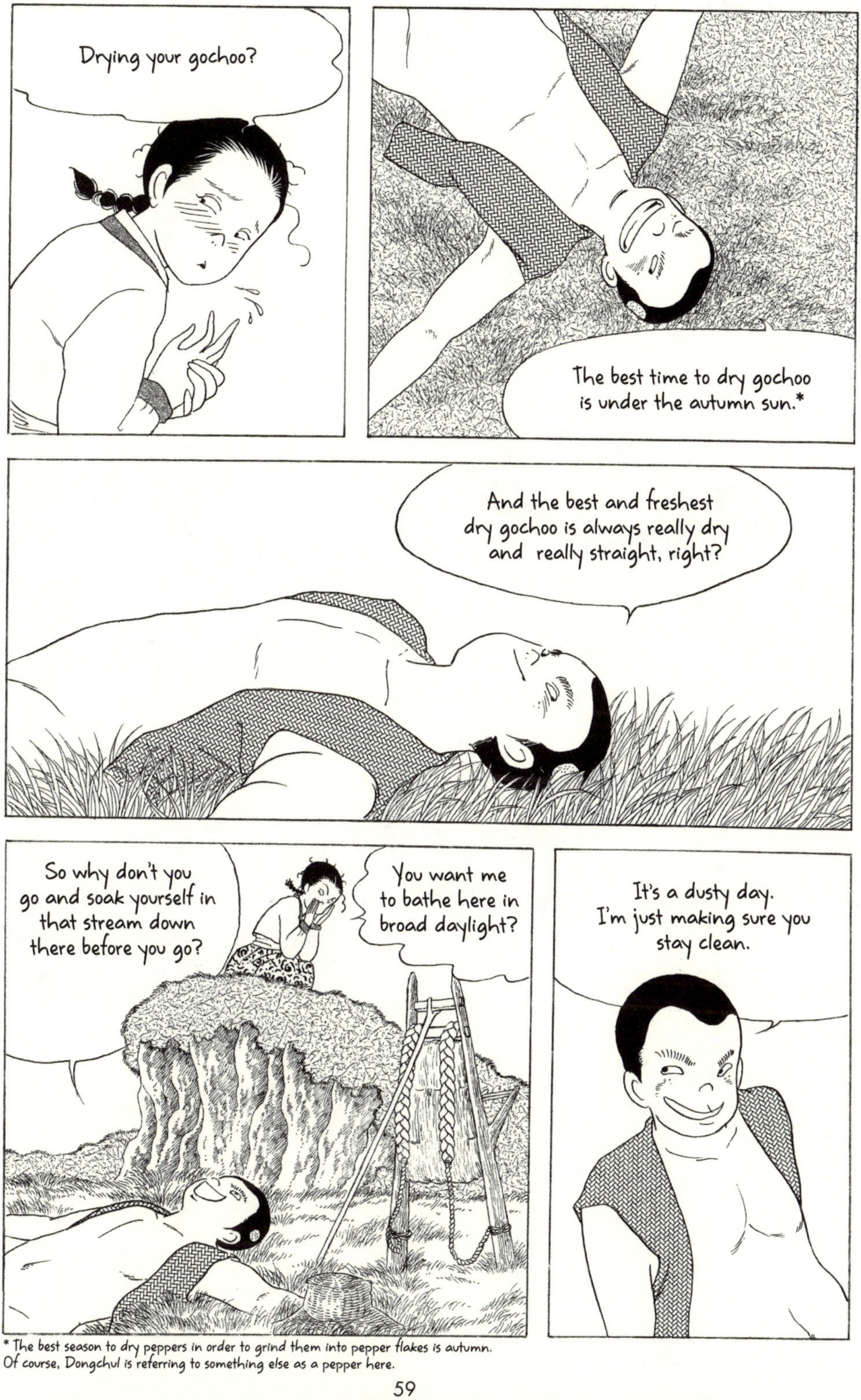
Drying your gochoo?
The best time to dry gochoo is under the autumn sun.*
And the best and freshest dry gochoo is always really dry and really straight, right?
So why don't you go and soak yourself in that stream down there before you go?
You want me to bathe here in broad daylight?
It's a dusty day. I'm just making sure you stay clean.

* The best season to dry peppers in order to grind them into pepper flakes is autumn. Of course, Dongchul is referring to something else as a pepper here.

You're just saying that because you want to see me naked, aren't you?
Just because my gochoo is dry now doesn't mean it needs to stay that way.
Thu-Thump
Thu-Thump
Eeeek!
.....

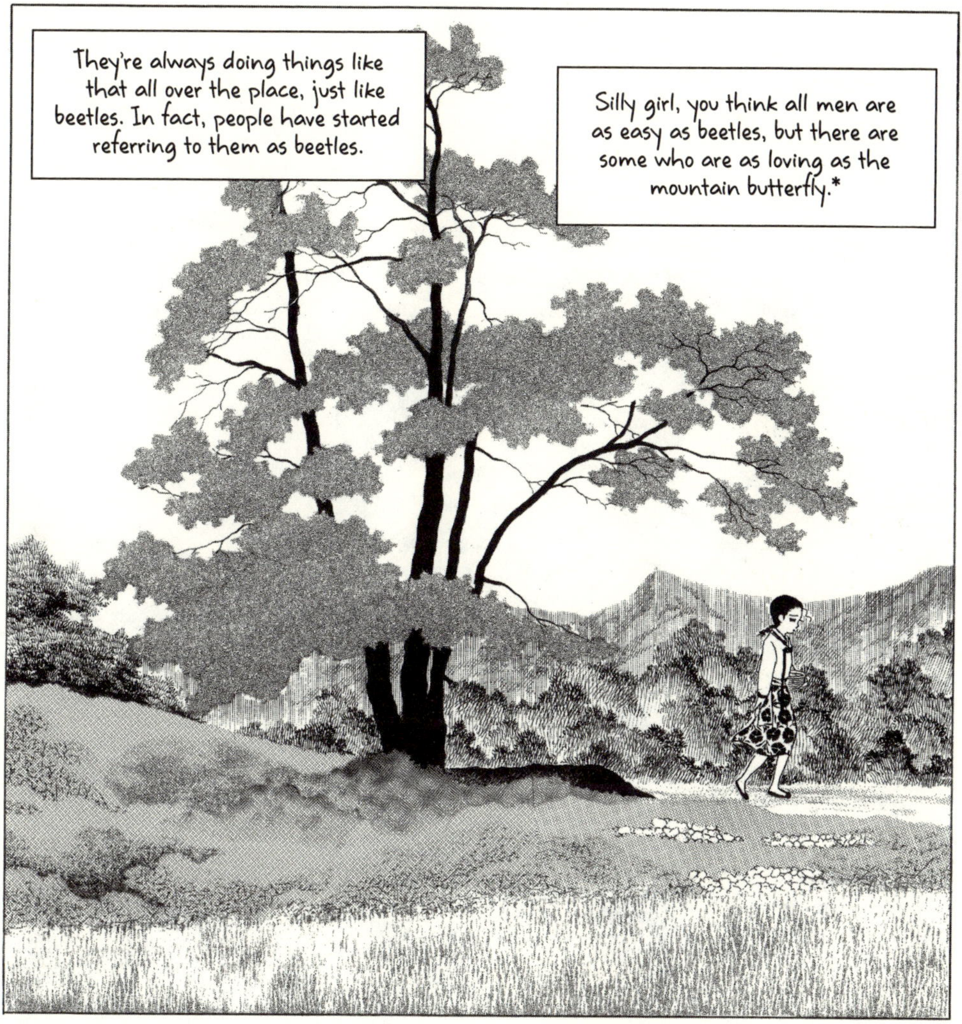
They're always doing things like that all over the place, just like beetles. In fact, people have started referring to them as beetles.
Silly girl, you think all men are as easy as beetles, but there are some who are as loving as the mountain butterfly.*

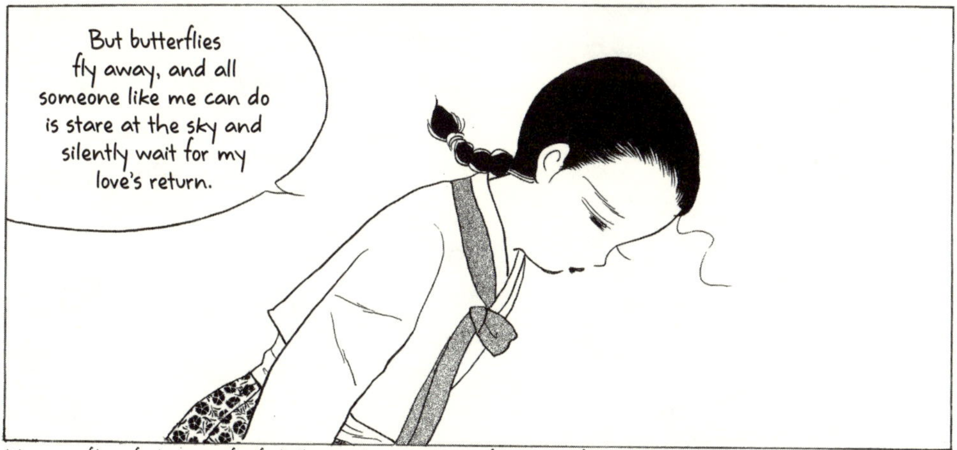
But butterflies fly away, and all someone like me can do is stare at the sky and silently wait for my love's return.

* A species of butterfly that mates for life. To Koreans, the mountain butterfly symbolizes fidelity, and is associated with love.

We work all summer, and by the time we get to sample the wine, all that remains is a sip.
After the seaweed dries and we finish harvesting the field, all that's left is a handful. Then, when we're done at the mill, all that remains is one small spoonful.

So, my old friend, this wine we're drinking isn't really made from rice, but gold.
If we sweated and labored while mining gold, like we do with farming, that's all the gold we'd get, too.

So now that all the rice paddy and field farming is done, what are we gonna do?
Bed farming, of course!

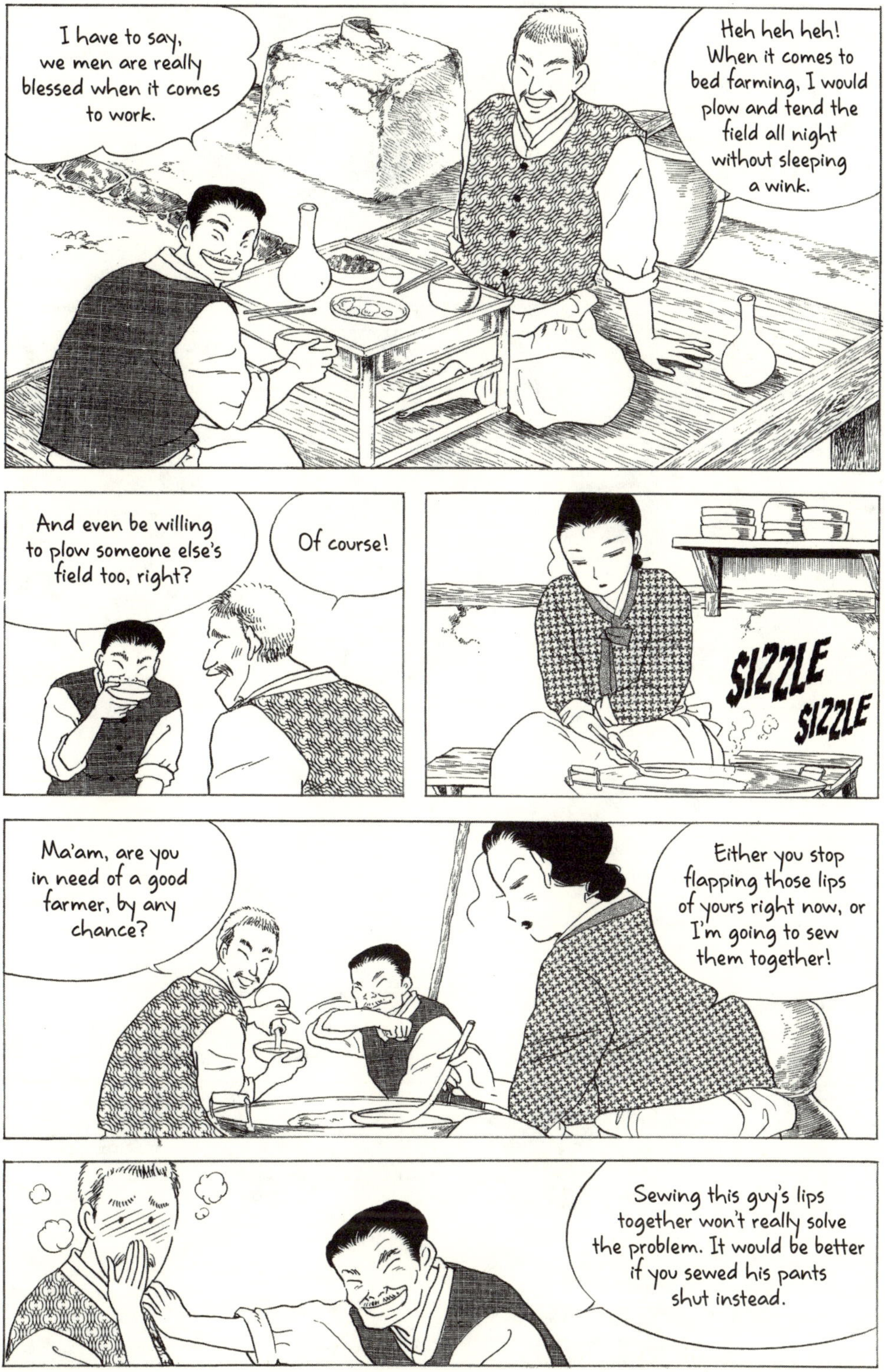
I have to say, we men are really blessed when it comes to work.
Heh heh heh! When it comes to bed farming, I would plow and tend the field all night without sleeping a wink.
And even be willing to plow someone else's field too, right?
Of course!
SIZZLE SIZZLE
Ma'am, are you in need of a good farmer, by any chance?
Either you stop flapping those lips of yours right now, or I'm going to sew them together!
Sewing this guy's lips together won't really solve the problem. It would be better if you sewed his pants shut instead.

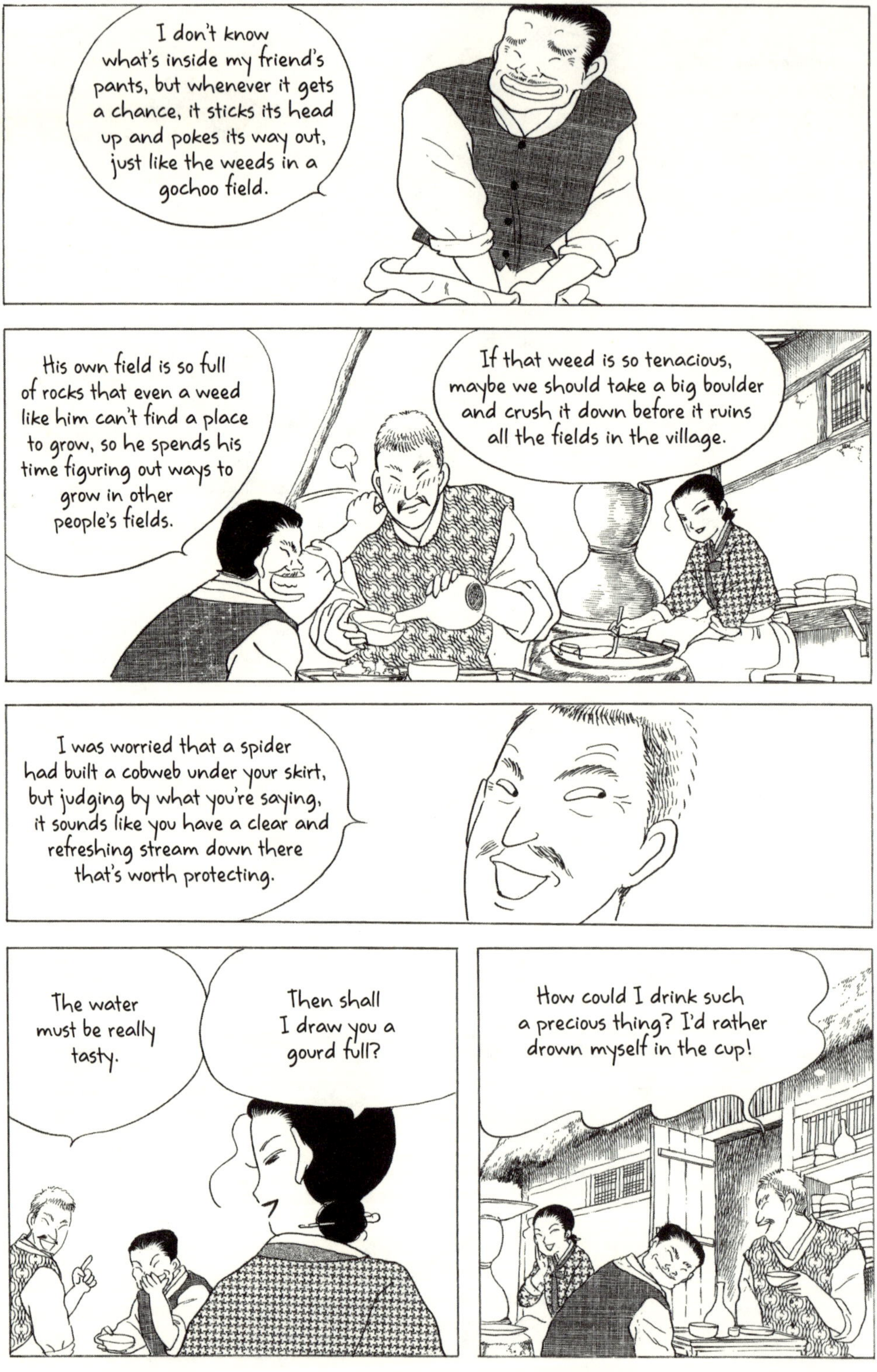
I don't know what's inside my friend's pants, but whenever it gets a chance, it sticks its head up and pokes its way out, just like the weeds in a gochoo field.
His own field is so full of rocks that even a weed like him can't find a place to grow, so he spends his time figuring out ways to grow in other people's fields.
If that weed is so tenacious, maybe we should take a big boulder and crush it down before it ruins all the fields in the village.
I was worried that a spider had built a cobweb under your skirt, but judging by what you're saying, it sounds like you have a clear and refreshing stream down there that's worth protecting.
The water must be really tasty.
Then shall I draw you a gourd full?
How could I drink such a precious thing? I'd rather drown myself in the cup!

| | Mom, do you enjoy talking to those two useless drunkards? | How can I ignore them when I make a living selling food and alcohol to people like them? |

I talk for the sake of talking and not because I enjoy their company.

| Even though they behave that way here, I'm sure they act quite differently when they're at home. | Instead of finding fault with others, think about yourself. You shouldn't be eavesdropping on adults, young lady. | I wasn't eavesdropping. They were talking so loud, I couldn't help hearing them. |

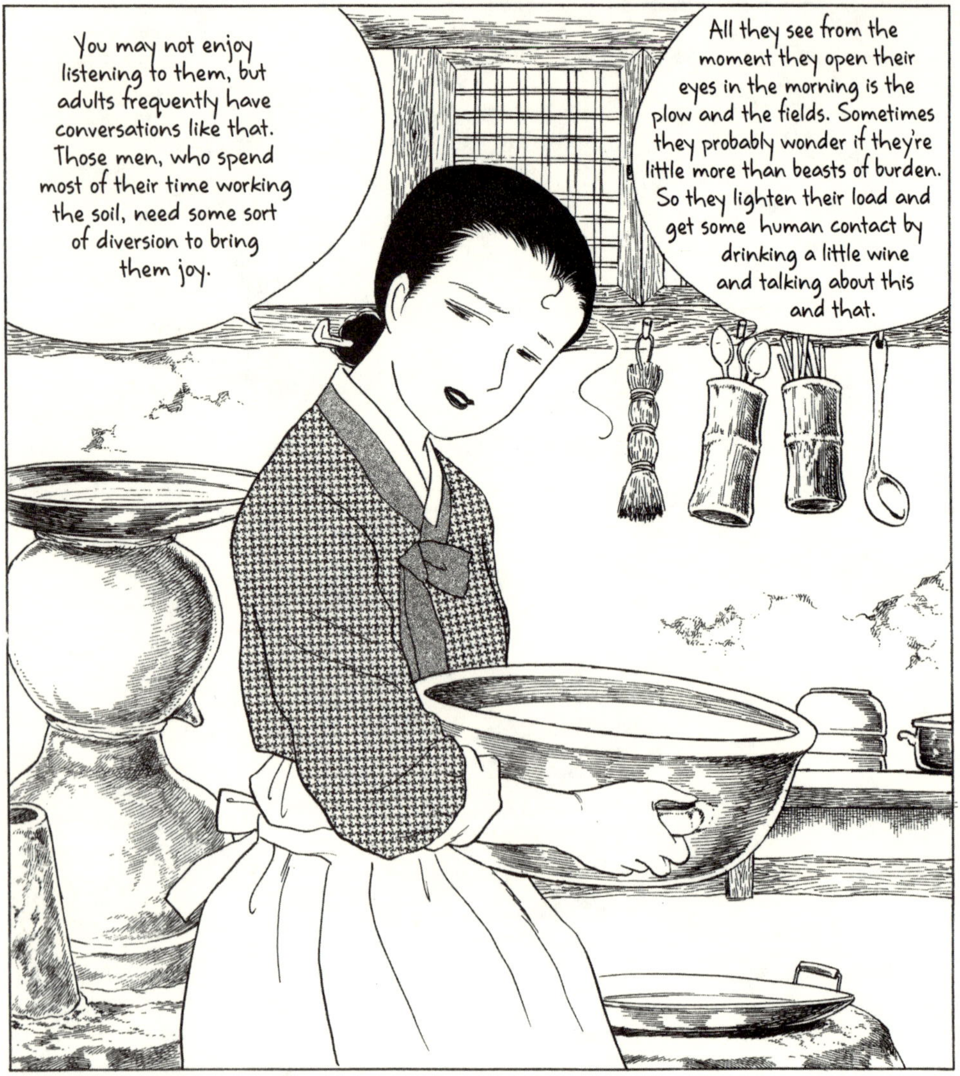
You may not enjoy listening to them, but adults frequently have conversations like that. Those men, who spend most of their time working the soil, need some sort of diversion to bring them joy.
All they see from the moment they open their eyes in the morning is the plow and the fields. Sometimes they probably wonder if they're little more than beasts of burden. So they lighten their load and get some human contact by drinking a little wine and talking about this and that.

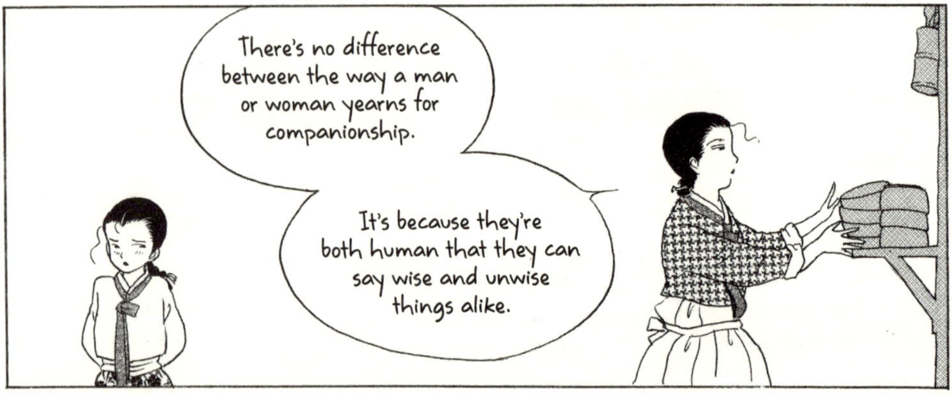
There's no difference between the way a man or woman yearns for companionship.
It's because they're both human that they can say wise and unwise things alike.

Ah!
WOOOSH
The south wind is blowing!
I wonder if this means that some good news will be blowing in from the south?
Is there supposed to be good news if the south wind blows?
I think so! Especially since he's down south.
RINNNG
?

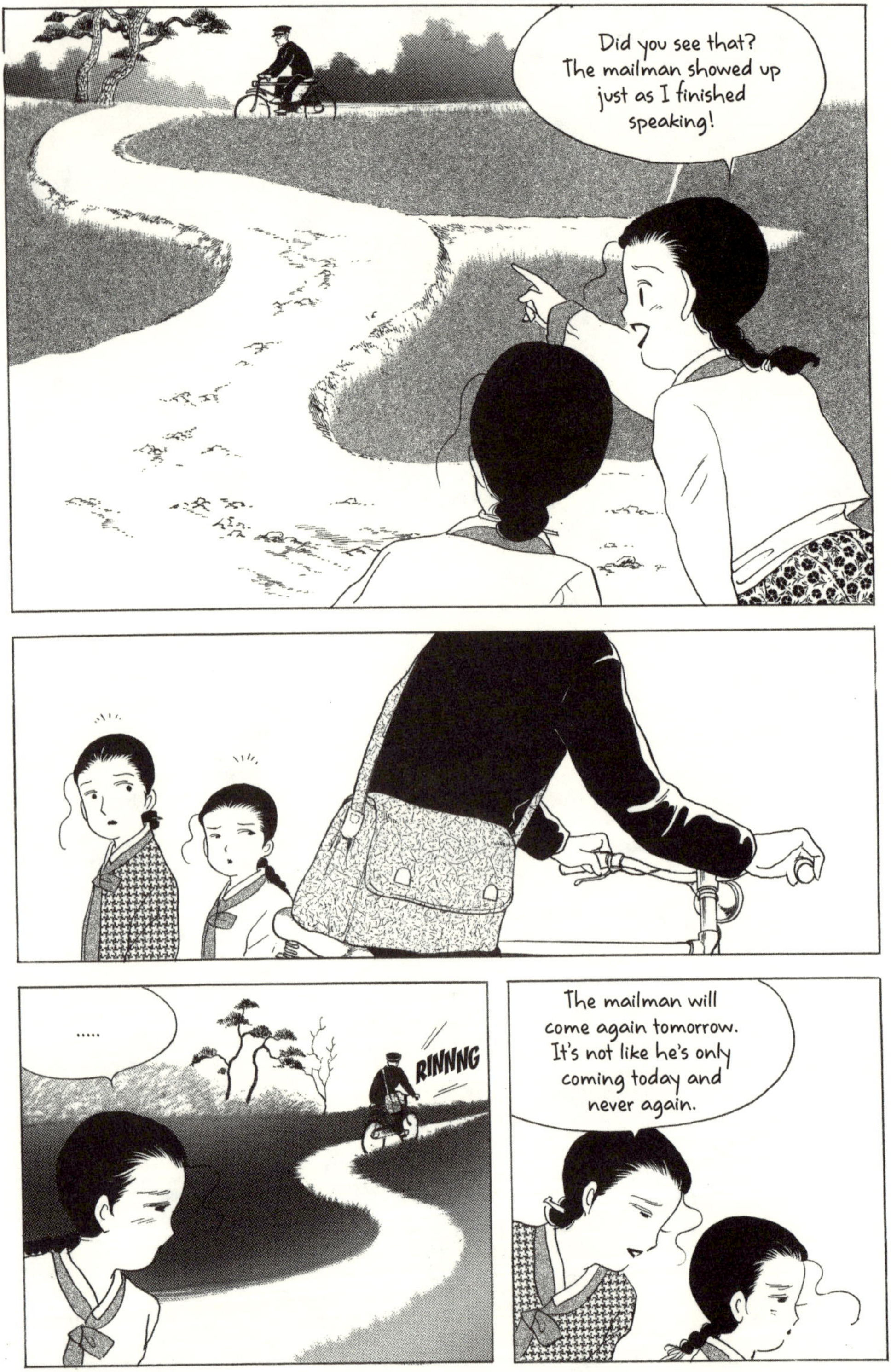
Did you see that? The mailman showed up just as I finished speaking!
.....
RINNNG
The mailman will come again tomorrow. It's not like he's only coming today and never again.

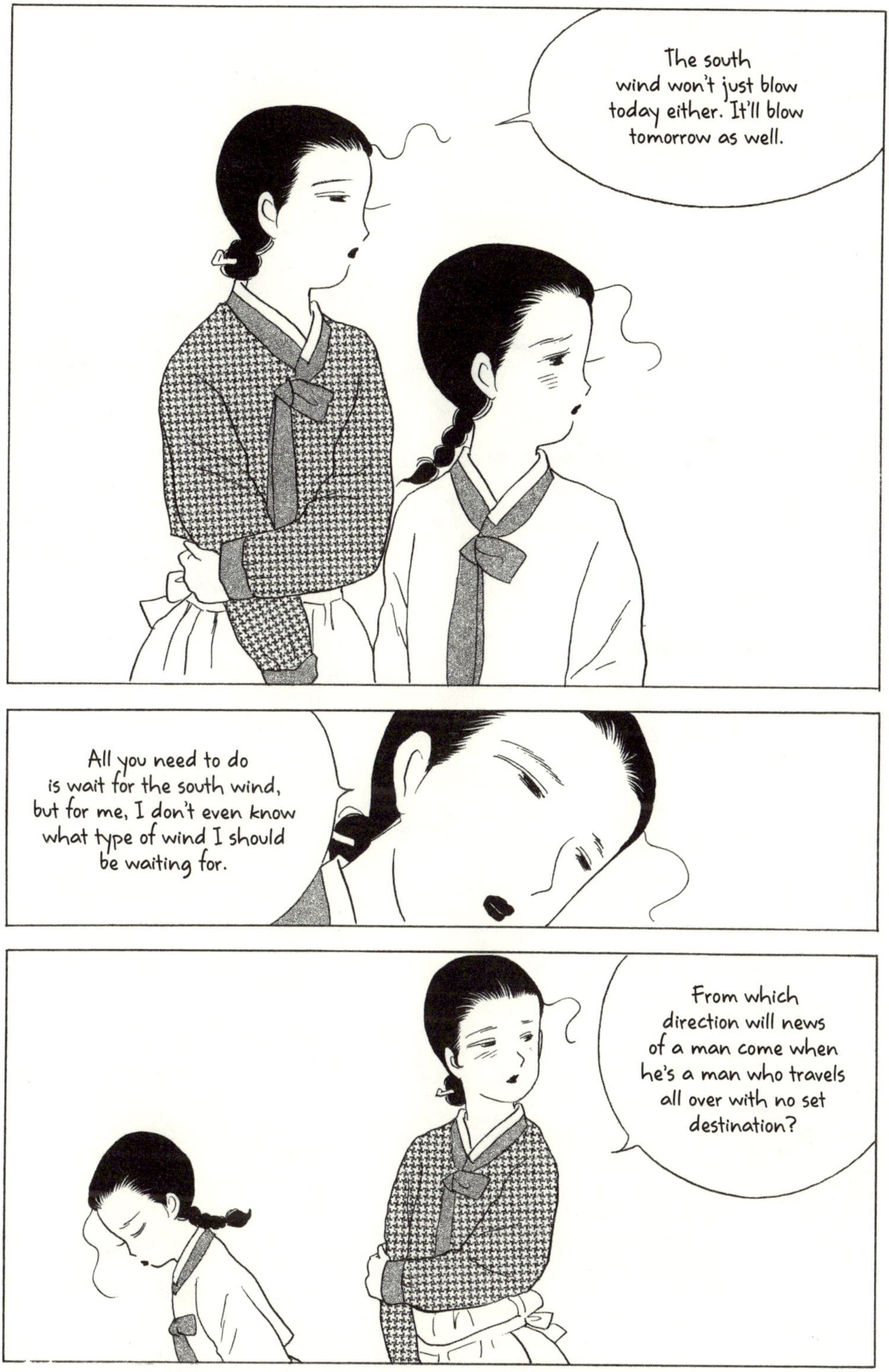
The south wind won't just blow today either. It'll blow tomorrow as well.
All you need to do is wait for the south wind, but for me, I don't even know what type of wind I should be waiting for.
From which direction will news of a man come when he's a man who travels all over with no set destination?

That's why I'm looking toward the village entrance, waiting to grab hold of any wind that passes by, just to ask it for news about him.

Chapter Three

FIRE BUTTERFLY

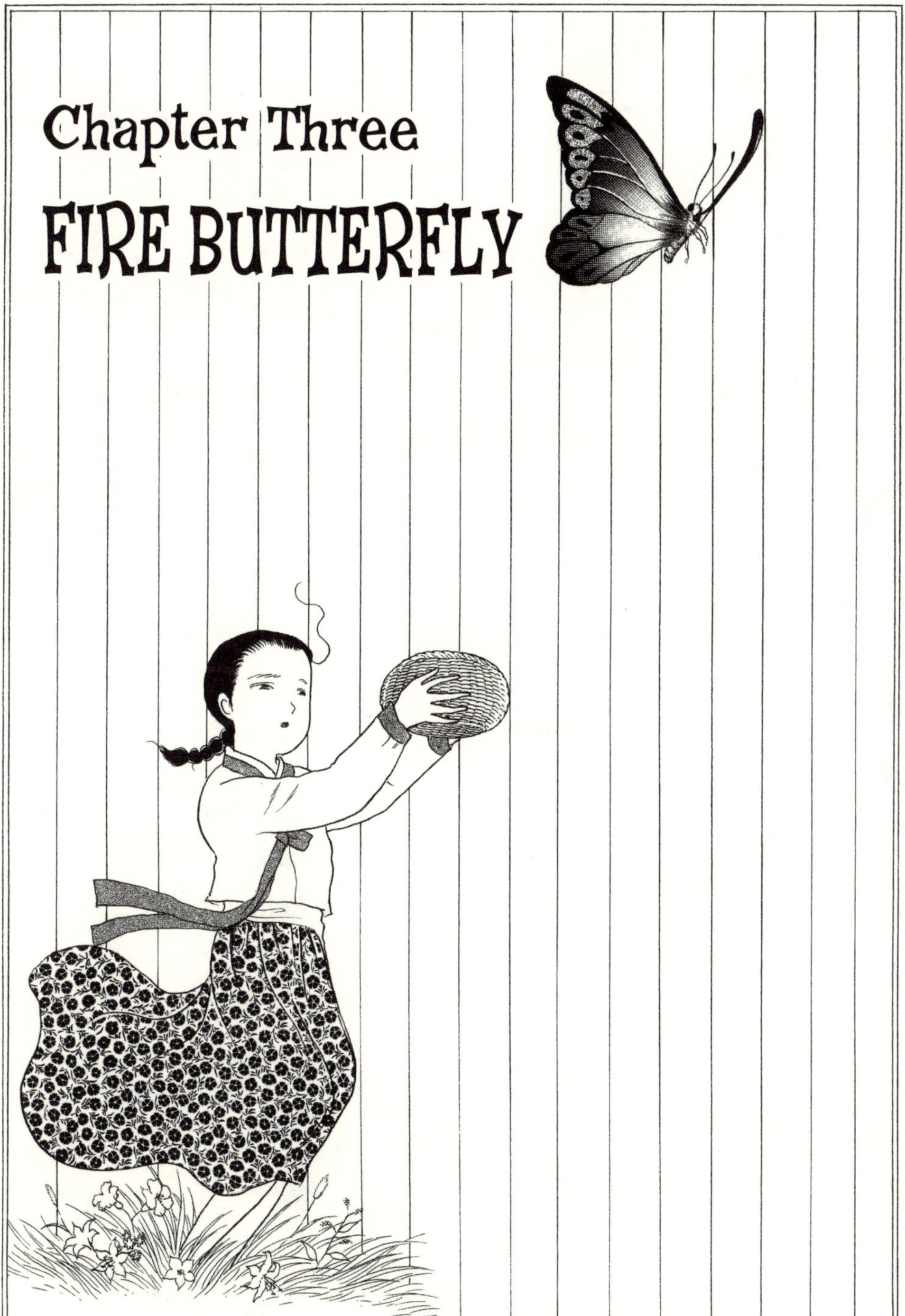

Hmm? Hmm... What's this smell coming from you?

Did you put on more of that cream from Europe? You know I've been trying to save it!
I only used about the size of a mosquito bite, Mom. There's going to be a lot of people there, so as your daughter, I have to look my best.

Those people aren't there to see you, you know! They're at the market to buy and sell things.
Still, you never know! There might be a young man somewhere in the market whose heart trembles at the sight of me.

Stop talking nonsense and come back before it gets dark.
And make sure you remember to buy every item that I asked you to buy.
I'll be back.
Does going to the market really make you that happy?
Well, I suppose that for a woman, market day can be a nice change.
Wait a minute...
Where did I put yesterday's earnings?

I'm positive I put it in the money belt, and I put the belt in here, but now I can't seem to find it.
Did Ehwa take it without asking me?
Or did someone break in here and steal it?

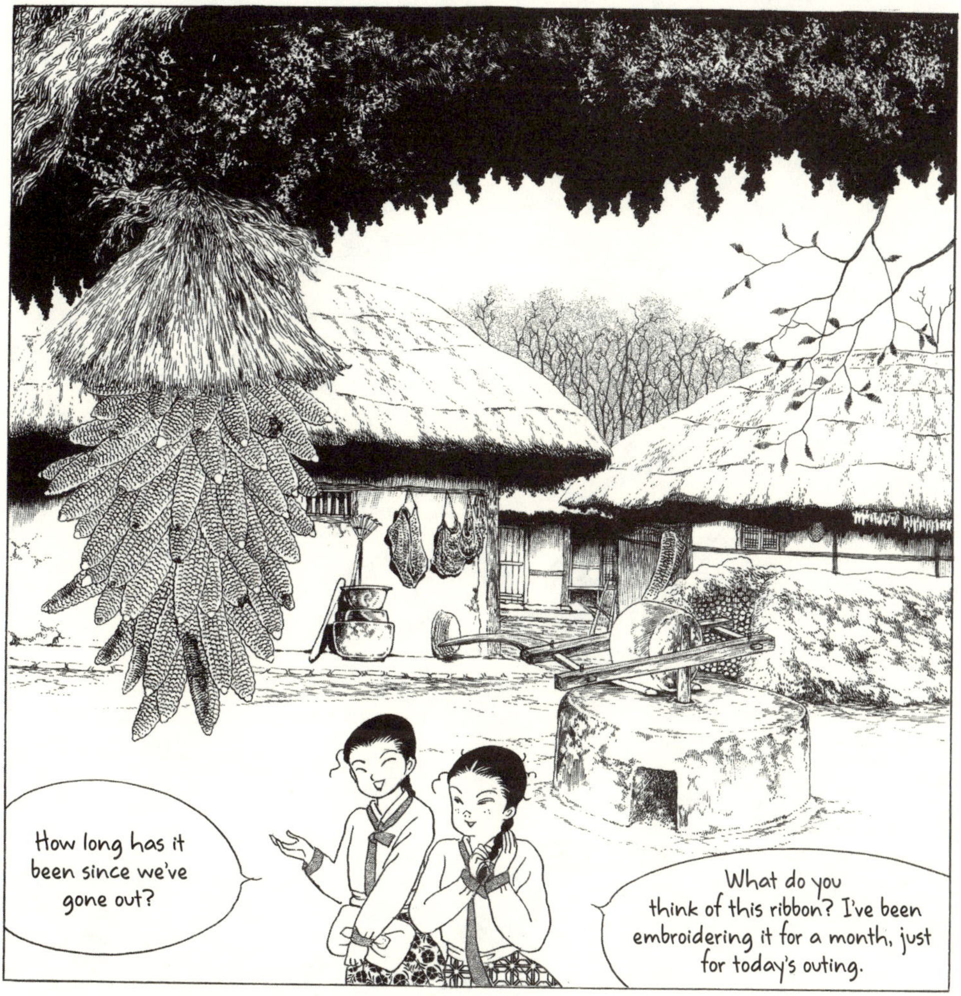
How long has it been since we've gone out?
What do you think of this ribbon? I've been embroidering it for a month, just for today's outing.

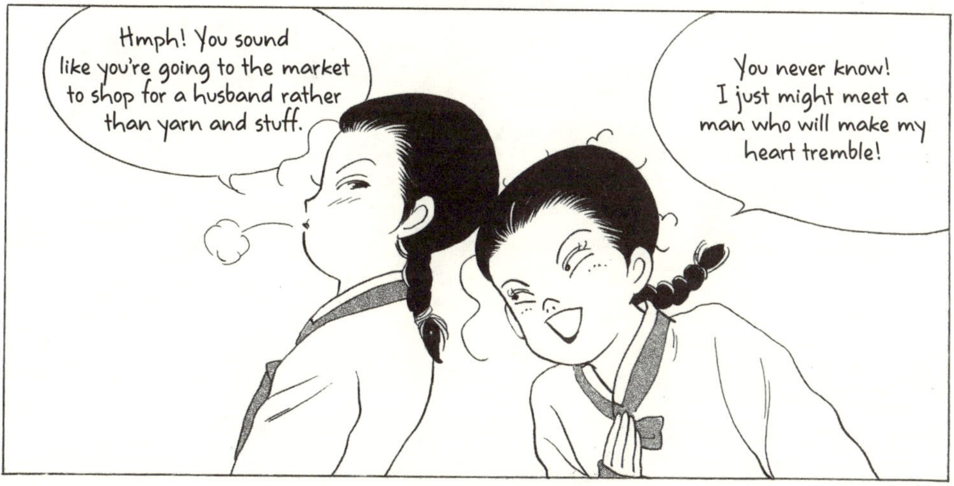
Hmph! You sound like you're going to the market to shop for a husband rather than yarn and stuff.
You never know! I just might meet a man who will make my heart tremble!

I wonder why our hearts become so restless every time we head for the market, even though we've been there many times before.
Ahem.
Ah...
Hello, elder Lee.

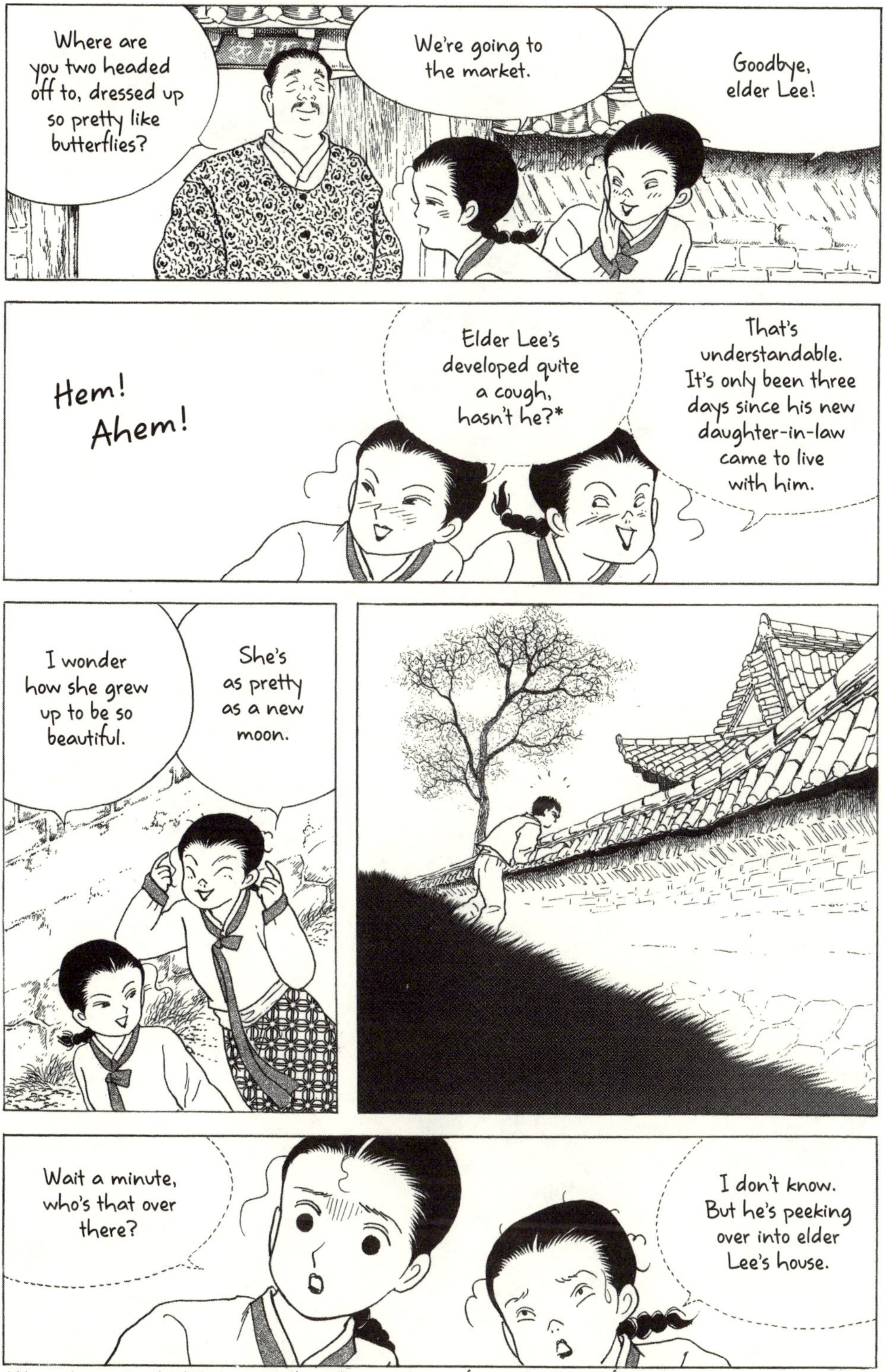
Where are you two headed off to, dressed up so pretty like butterflies?
We're going to the market.
Goodbye, elder Lee!
Hem! Ahem!
Elder Lee's developed quite a cough, hasn't he?*
That's understandable. It's only been three days since his new daughter-in-law came to live with him.
I wonder how she grew up to be so beautiful.
She's as pretty as a new moon.
Wait a minute, who's that over there?
I don't know. But he's peeking over into elder Lee's house.

* Ehwa isn't insinuating that Elder Lee is sick. His cough is simply his way of getting the attention of passersby so that he can brag about his beautiful new daughter-in-law.

Do you think he's a thief trying to steal the new bride's jewelry?
Maybe! There have been quite a few strangers wandering through the village lately. The villagers have been talking about it.
What should we do?
I'm sure it's nothing. It's the middle of the day!
It's night when we need to make sure our gates and doors are locked.

Oh my! Just look at this hand mirror. It's small enough to fit in a pouch around your waist!
How can it be possible to make such wonderfully small mirrors?
Looking for someone?
Ah... No, it's nothing.
I guess the picture man couldn't make it to this market this time around.
I wonder how it would feel to meet him in a place like this?

Fresh caught knife fish, here!
Lively flipping mackerel, here!
Where was this mackerel caught?
Where do you think? It was caught right off the shore of Mokpo.
From Mokpo!
Duksam might have caught this fish.
I'll take two!
Excellent choice. Of the mackerel, these here with the blue back are the best.
Sniff, sniff... I think I can smell a little of Duksam on them.

It's as if these fish are bringing news that Duksam is doing well.

Now that I've bought this hand mirror, I feel like the most beautiful girl around.

I bet you're the only girl who has a hand mirror like that in the entire village.

Next time I'm going to buy some of that cream from Europe. The smell was absolutely wonderful.

I wonder where *this* lovely smell is coming from?

Let me see. Sniff... Sniff...

I only smell those stinky fish of yours.

Stupid! That hand mirror must have plugged up your nose!

81

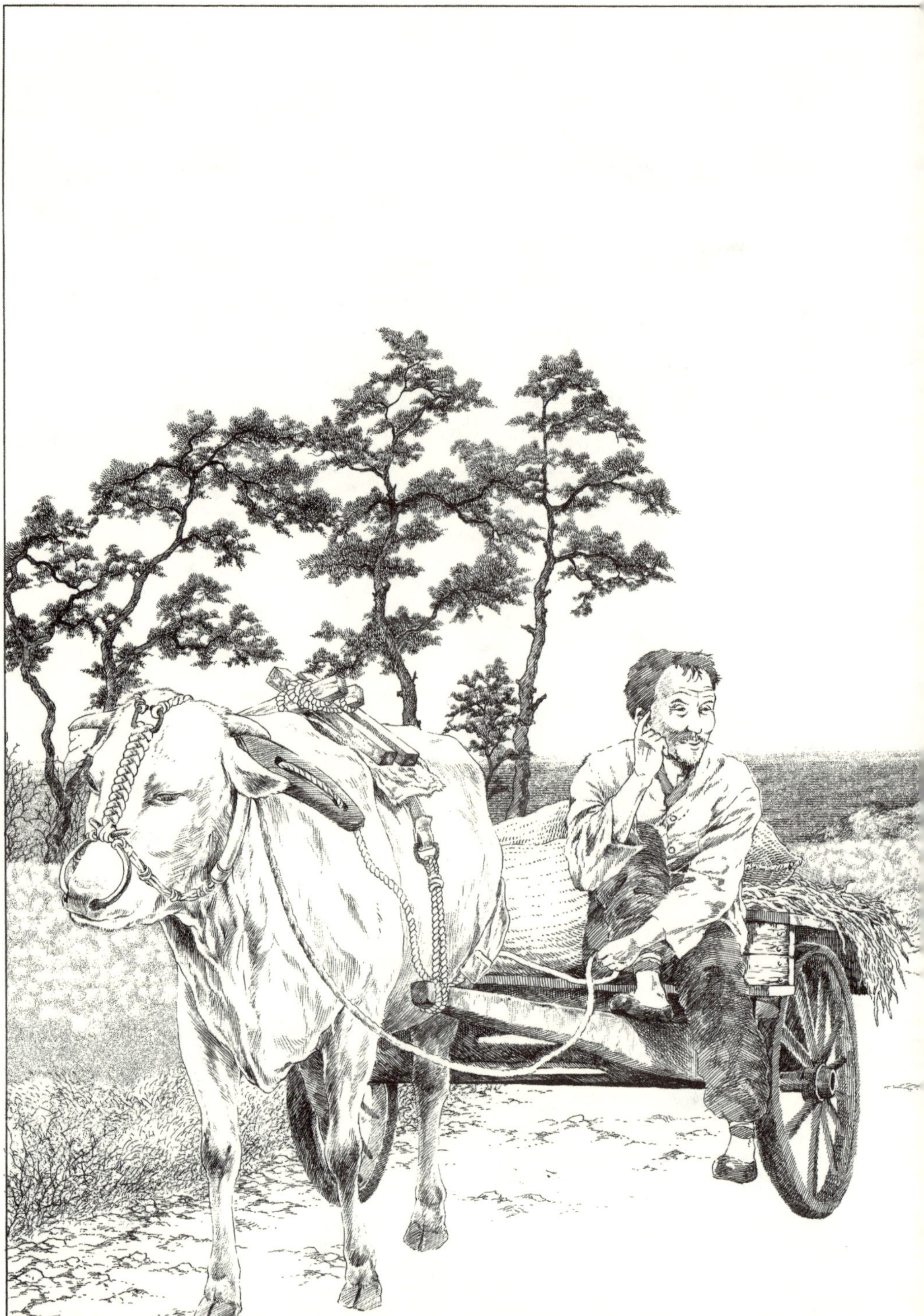

I wish I could become a traveling salesman and travel from village to village like an aimless cloud.
We'd been looking forward to going to that market for so long, now that it's over, I don't want to go home.

MUMBLE MUMBLE

MUMBLE MUMBLE

What's going on? Why is there so much tension in the air? It wasn't like this when we left this morning.

MUMBLE MUMBLE

How strange.
I think something happened while we were at the market.
I wonder what?
I think I'd better head home.
There's no one at the tavern either...
I'm back!
Welcome back, thanks for going to the market.

What's going on, Mom? People around the village are acting strange. Did something happen?
Oh, they're probably worked up about that young vagrant who's been spotted around the village.
I see.
When you saw him, did he look suspicious to you?
It wasn't just me who thought he looked suspicious, it was the entire village.
That reminds me, on the way to the market we saw a man lurking around elder Lee's house.

"Ehwa, did you by any chance take some money without telling me?"

"Mom, how could you ask something like that?!"

"Well it's just that some of our money has gone missing."

"Really? How much?"

"I'm positive that I took yesterday's earnings, put it all in my money belt and hid it, but now it's completely disappeared, and I can't find it anywhere."

"Until that vagrant came to our village, I've never lost even a single coin."

But yesterday I saw your money belt in the kitchen.	What?!

So I put it inside the cabinet.

Is that really true?

Oh, thank goodness!

I was so convinced that someone had taken it.
Shame on me.
I almost falsely accused someone of stealing money!
Ehwa!
Ehwa!
What's the matter, Bongsoon?

There's a terrible fuss over at elder Lee's house right now.
Why? What happened?
Was it the vagrant? Did he actually go and steal all the bride's jewelry and clothes?
That's not it.
Oh God, they practically killed him!
Who?!

What happened?!
That vagrant got a terrible lynching.
Oh, my goodness...
Just because he was caught stealing?
That seems pretty excessive!
That's not it, I tell you.
Then what is it?
It wasn't because he was stealing.

What?

That vagrant crept inside the new bride's room.

They say that he was a servant at her parents' house.

Why did he creep into the new bride's room?
They say he forgot his station in life and had fallen in love with her.
And after she got married, she moved into elder Lee's house, but he couldn't forget about her and followed her here.
That's crazy! Even if he loved her, how could he do such a thing as sneak into her bedroom!
I don't understand why men can't seem to realize what is and isn't appropriate.

Even if they are butterflies, they need to know which flowers they can land on and which ones they can't.
The butterfly should know its place! How dare it try to land on a flower that's off limits?
That's why they lynched him.
So what happened to that young man?
The men in the village beat him up something terrible and threw him outside the village entrance.
Is he alive or dead?
How would I know?
Where are you going?
Since when is love a sin?

He must have really loved and wanted her, to do such an outrageous thing.

Only someone who's endured the pain of waiting and the pain of longing knows how it feels.

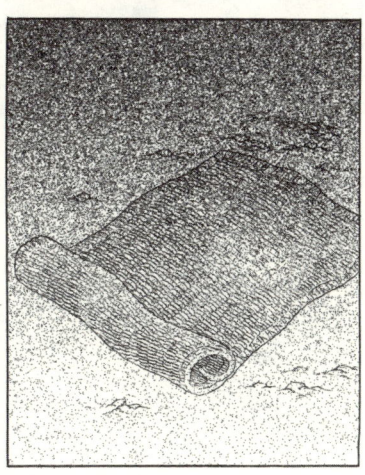

Even if that's true, what are you going to do? Mom?

Whether he's alive or not, it's a decent person's responsibility to at least hold his hand and bid him well.

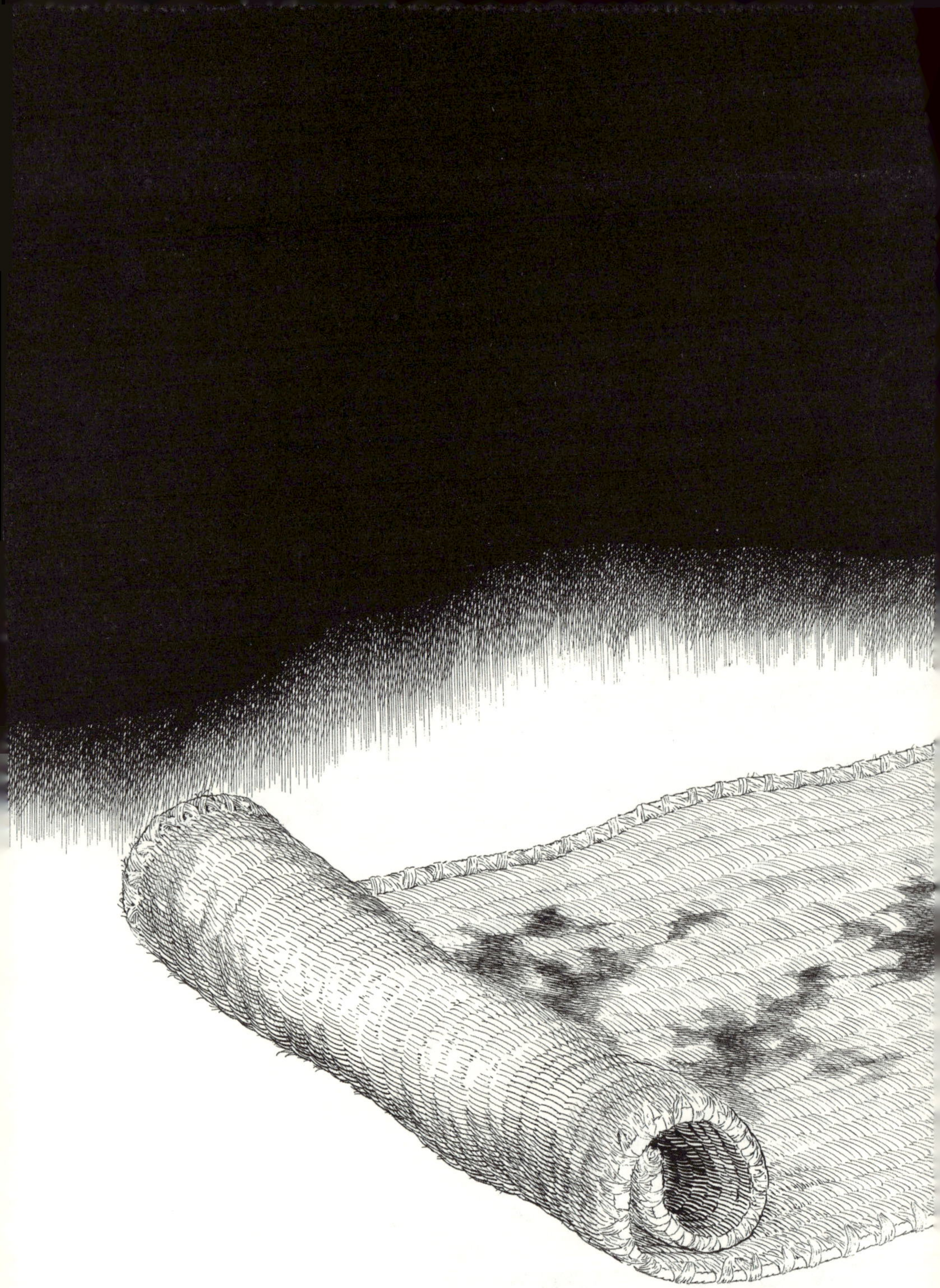

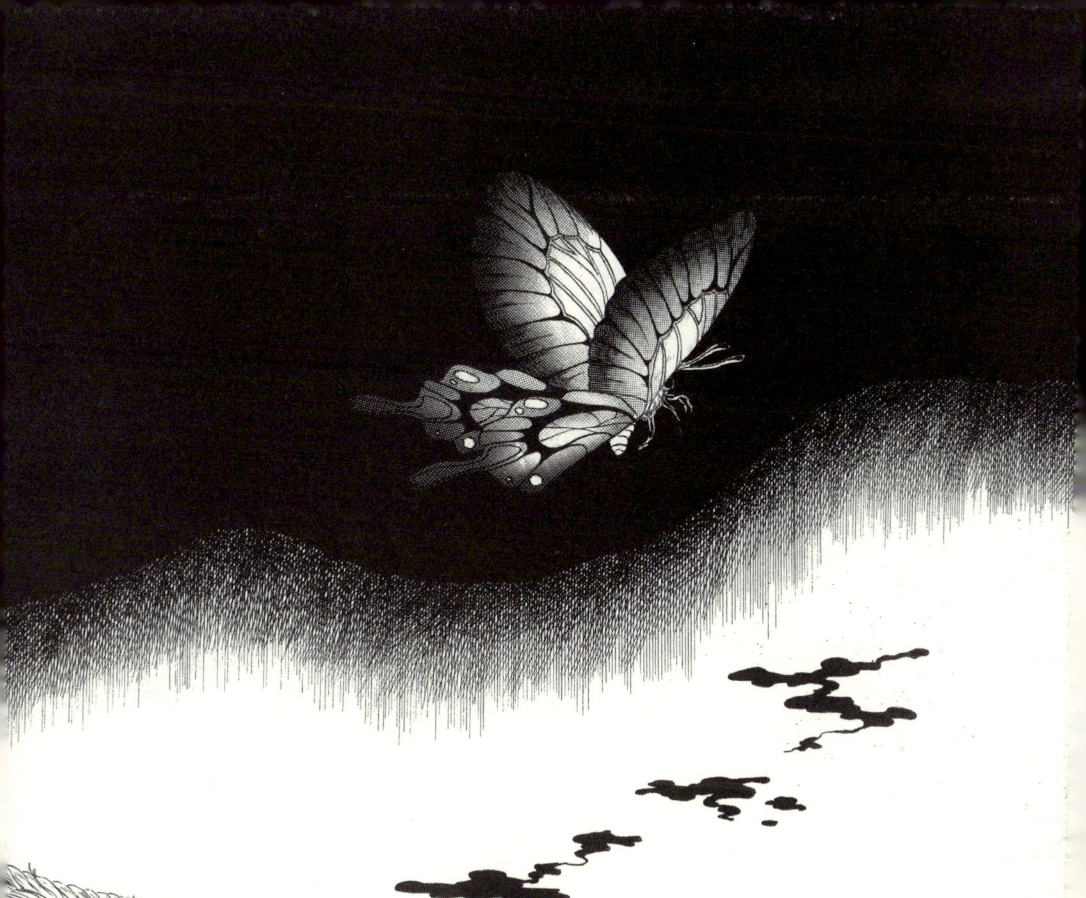

Often in Korea, when someone committed a very serious crime, they were rolled up in a mat of straw and left to die.

Yes, of all the butterflies, that young man was probably a fire butterfly.

A fire butterfly that boldly flies into the fire not knowing that he'll die. Or perhaps not caring.

But still, of all the butterflies, the fire butterfly is the happiest of all.

It's not like the other butterflies that casually fly to hundreds of flowers, only eating the nectar and flying away. They have no idea what deep love is.

Although this fire butterfly had a short life, it experienced the greatest happiness in this world seconds before it drew its last breath. It probably was the happiest butterfly of all.

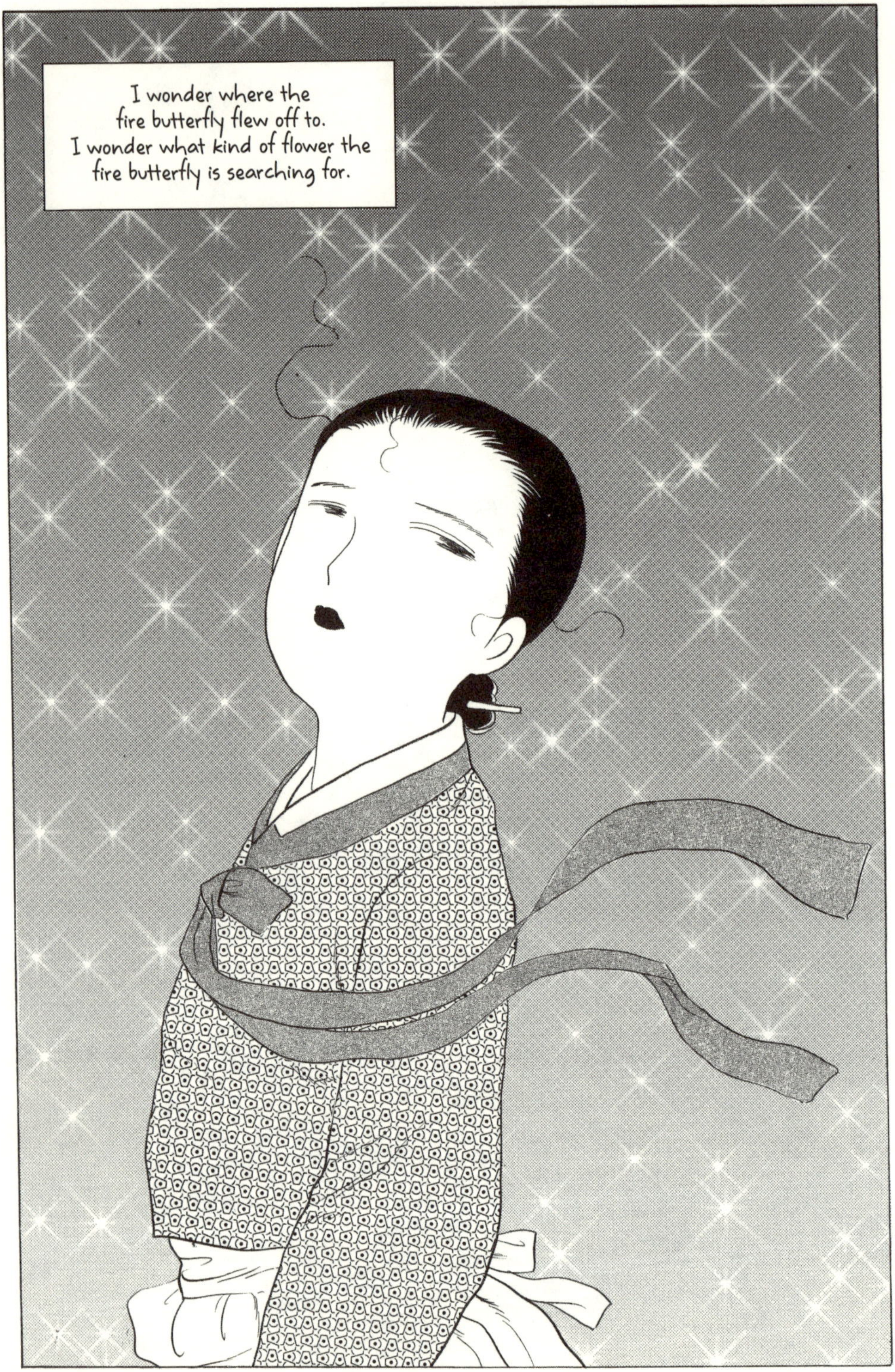
I wonder where the fire butterfly flew off to. I wonder what kind of flower the fire butterfly is searching for.

Chapter Four

PAPER MOON

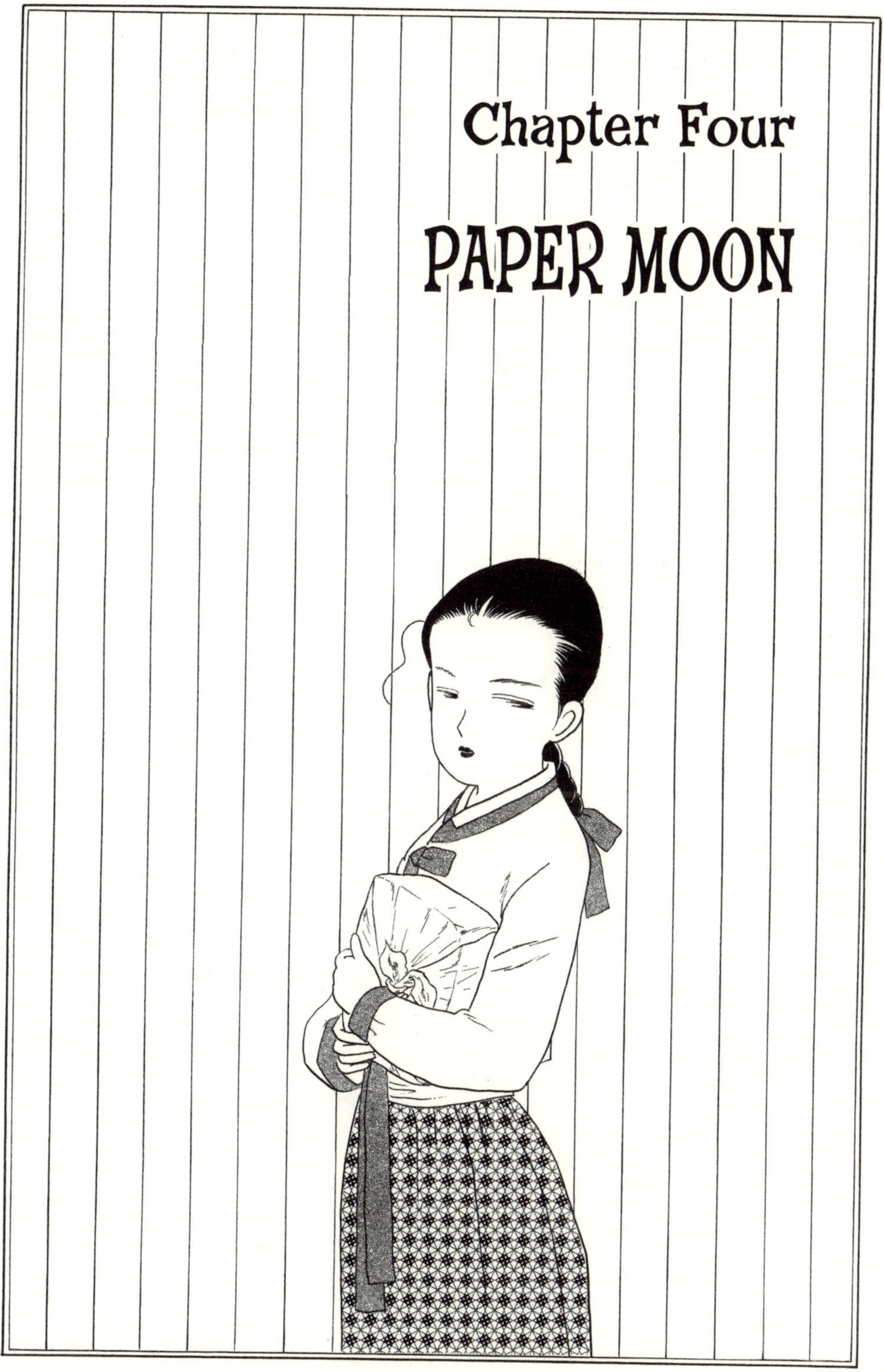

Ehwa, how old are you now?
Don't you know your own daughter's age, Mother?

Of course I know! Although I may forget my own age, I'd never forget my daughter's age.
Then why did you ask?

I'm just amazed at how you've grown. Donghae's mother came by today.
What did she want?
Heh Heh!
She came with a matchmaking request for you.
Oh my!
Thu-Thump Thu-Thump
I'm only seventeen! How can they even think of marriage for me already?
Then again, it *is* pretty flattering.

"Especially because none of the other girls my age have received matchmaking requests! I'm the first one!"

"That must mean that of all the girls my age, I'm the prettiest of all."

"By the way, who was it that foolishly asked to be matched with me?"

"It was the acupuncturist's son. The younger one."

He's said to be quite a good looking young man, and he's had some education. I just told her that you were too young for marriage yet, and gently sent her away instead of giving her a direct no.
Thu-Thump
Thu-Thump
You should have told her I wasn't interested, since it's not because I'm young that I don't want to marry.
Why did a marriage request come for me from such a respected household?
Because my daughter is the prettiest of all the girls in this village, of course.

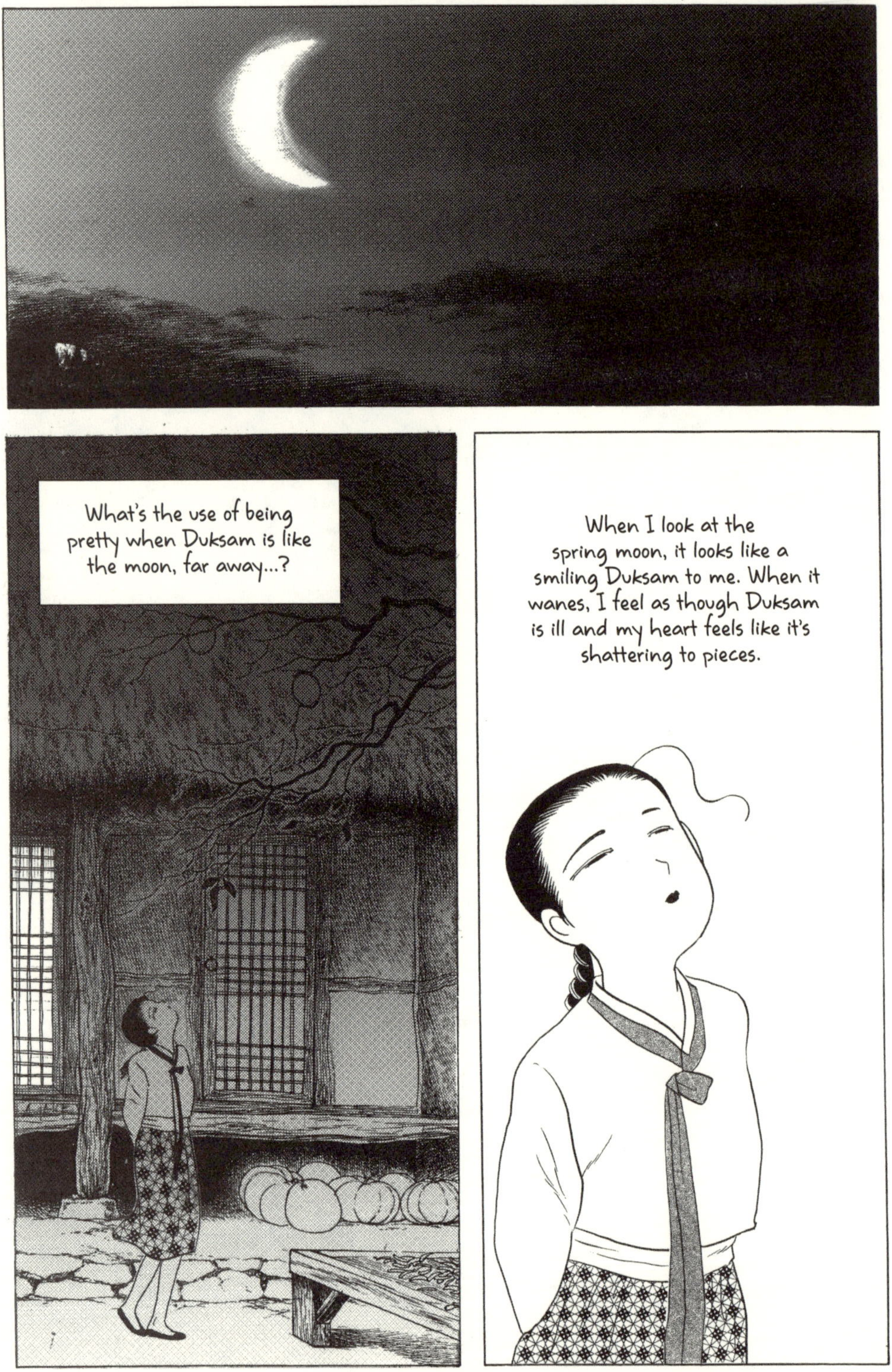
What's the use of being pretty when Duksam is like the moon, far away...?
When I look at the spring moon, it looks like a smiling Duksam to me. When it wanes, I feel as though Duksam is ill and my heart feels like it's shattering to pieces.

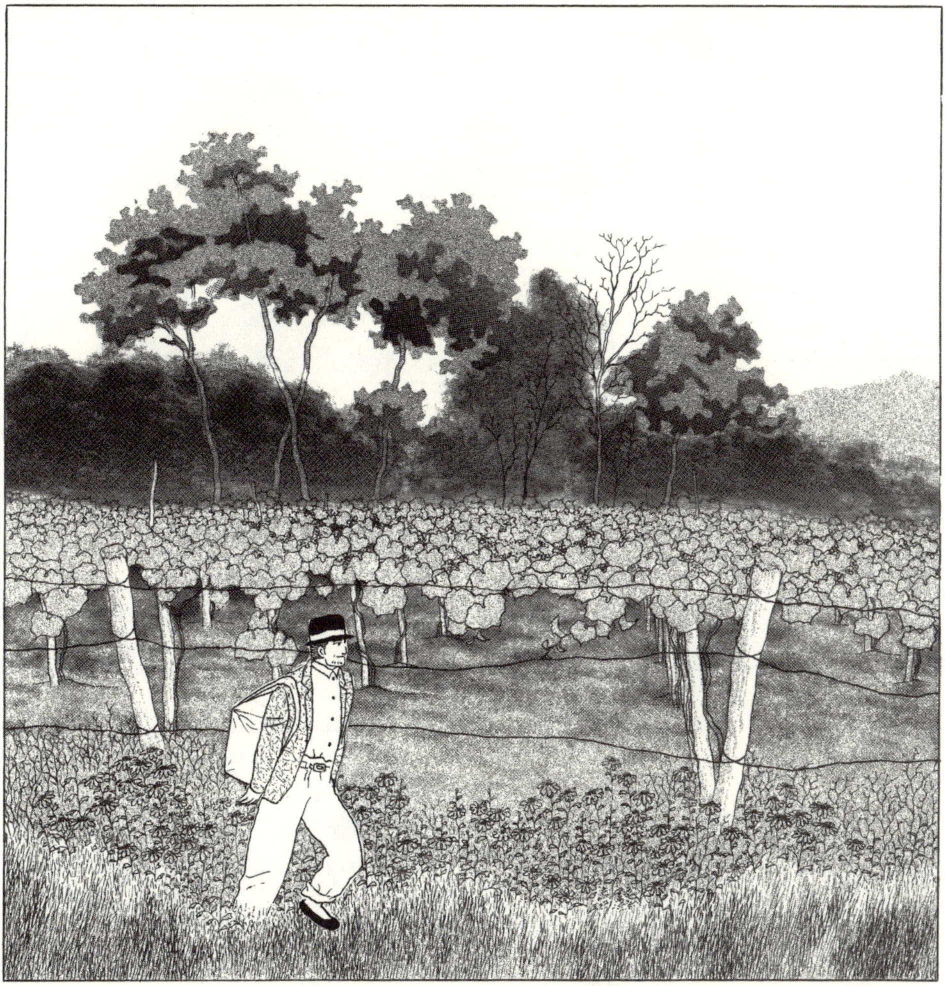

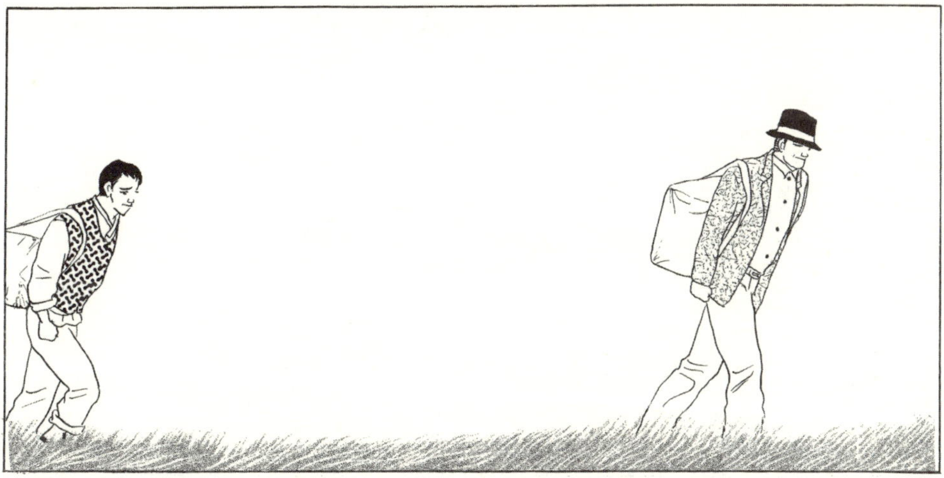

The market is far and yet you're in such a hurry. Why the rush?
Huh? Oh, it's you. The picture man.
How do you know who I am?
I've seen you at the markets.

How did you ever learn such a wonderful talent? I've always been so envious of you.
Swish, swish and a letter appears! Swish, swish and a flower blooms within the letter and a bird sings! Just when I think you've drawn a mountain, a waterfall appears.
You're the only one with the talent of making the sun and moon rise at the same time.
It's not much of a talent, and hearing you praise it leaves me at a loss for words.
But then again, what's more amazing than a person's hand?

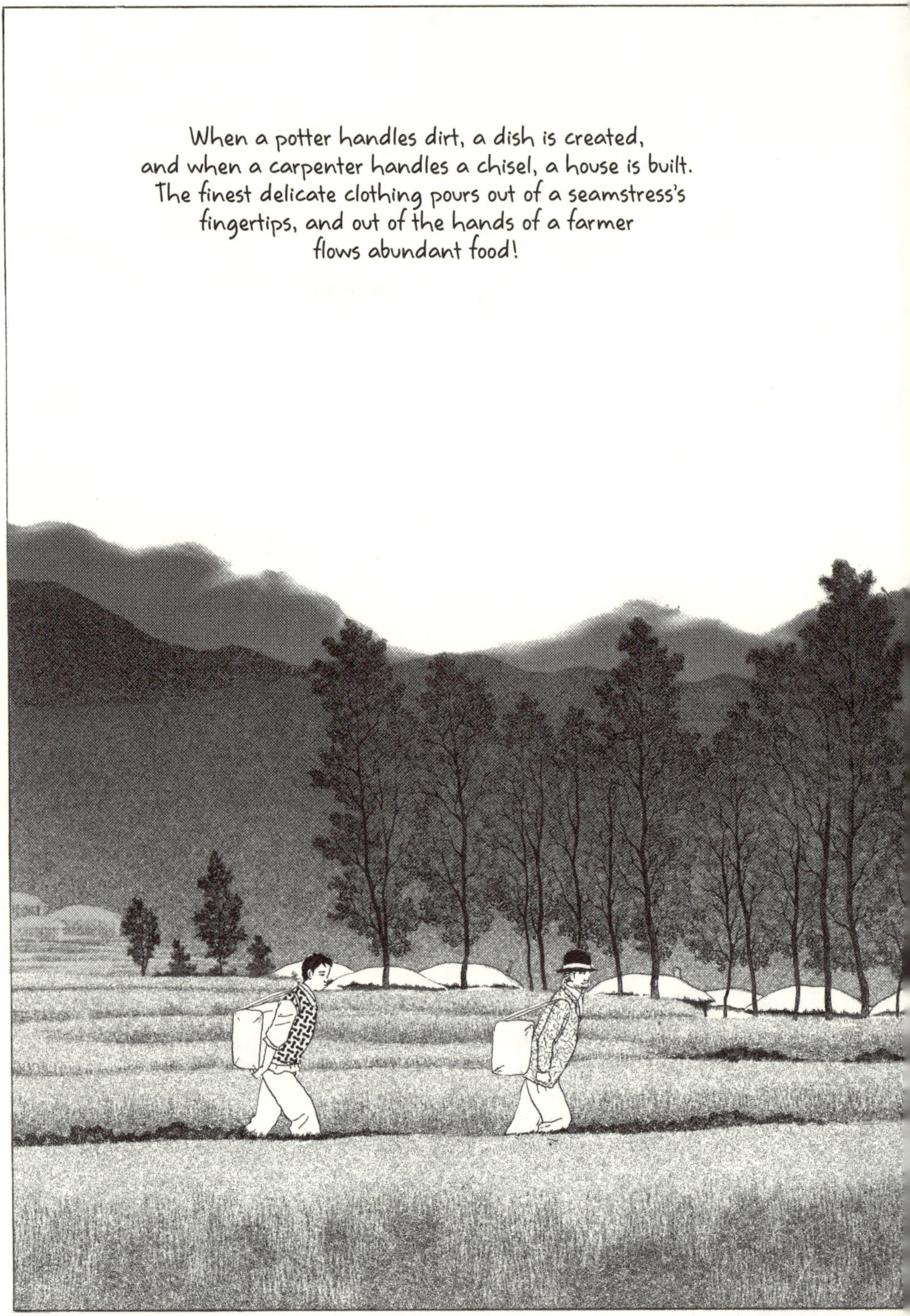
When a potter handles dirt, a dish is created,
and when a carpenter handles a chisel, a house is built.
The finest delicate clothing pours out of a seamstress's
fingertips, and out of the hands of a farmer
flows abundant food!

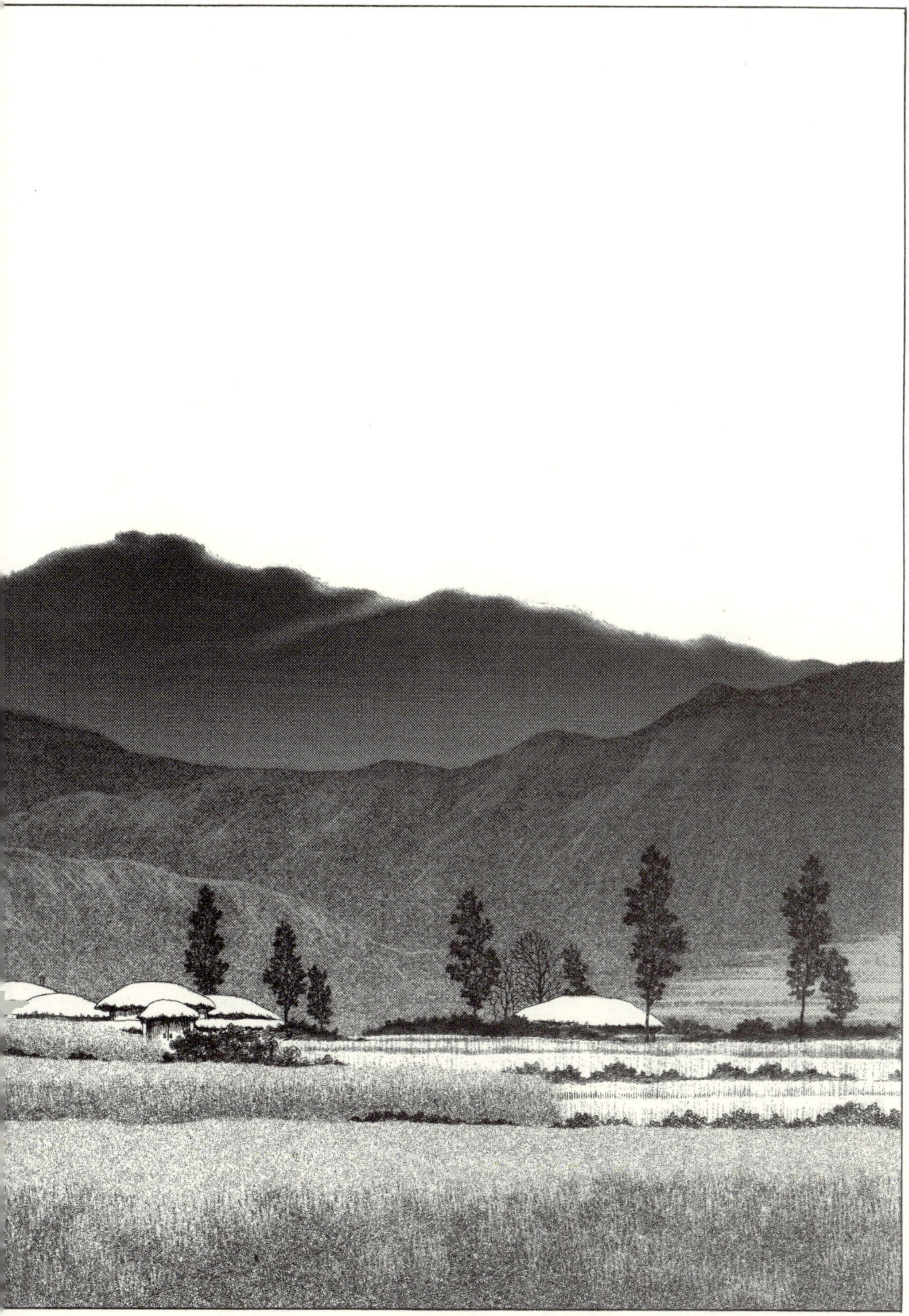

Every person has their own special talent... I'm just a man that draws pictures for a living.
Yes, so they say, and that's what I believed when I went out to sea.

I got on a boat believing that I just needed to stretch out my hands and catch fish to make a lot of money.

What a young fool I was.
What happened?

I was kicked off the boat before I could even toss out a net.
Was there not a single fish in that entire ocean?
On the contrary! There were hordes of fish flapping around all over the place, and they were all money.
Then why did you get kicked off the boat?
Because I was seasick.
Seasick?
Every time a wave crashed against the boat, my entire body felt like it had flipped inside out, and I thought I was about to die.

Instead of grabbing the fish and counting the money with these hands, all they did was clench my chest in pain.
I'm sorry.
Since I don't have any land to farm, I've been trying to think of what I can sell at the markets as I've been traveling.
That's a great idea! As a farmer, you're tied to the land around you. Your entire life, that's all you'll ever see. But as a salesman, you're free to roam about, and each market is a new adventure.
You must have made a lot of money.
How could I make a lot of money with cheap drawings? As long as I make enough to cover the cost of paper and ink, I consider myself rich.
So you're saying that you're rich in heart, right?

No amount of money can compare to the treasure trove in my heart.
When my body gets cold, I draw a spring scene and I become warm.
When I become exhausted from the heat, I draw a waterfall and I become refreshed.
Because you have that kind of talent, a flower will bloom in your spring scenery.
Not only do flowers bloom, but butterflies appear as well!

However, no matter how much I may practice, there is still one thing that I will never draw accurately.
I find that hard to believe. What is it?
The person I long for.
She lingers right before my eyes with a smiling face, but the face that appears from my fingertips is a strange woman I don't even recognize.
That's why, since meeting her, I've always just kept her in my heart.
When I think of her, I smile.
And when I think of her again, I look toward the Namwon sky—

| Did you just say the Namwon sky? | Yes, I did. There is a person I long for who lives beneath it. |

| She's a warm, loving person, and the fragrant wind that blows from that place gently calls out to me. | I guess only gentle and beautiful women live in Namwon. |

| Why do you say that? | He said that the sun and moon both rise from Namwon. |

The hyung* who was on the boat with me said the exact same thing.

* Hyung is a term often used when a younger male addresses an older male. It means "brother."

He said that the sun was the bright laugh of a young lady in the village...	...and that the moon was her lovely, fair face.

Ha ha ha! It's not only the sun and the moon, the stars in the night sky are like a letter sent by the one you long for. You want to stare into the sky to read it all night.

On occasion, I've written a response on leaves and sent them through the river.

While other times, I've written a response on flower petals and tossed them from a mountaintop.

> I believe that the white clouds over Namwon are all the replies I've written to her. They hover there, just waiting for her to read them.

> Then are you currently heading toward Namwon right now?

> Yes, and you too?

> Yes, that's why I was walking so swiftly!

> Are you hoping to take a Namwon lady as your lover?

> Actually, no. I'm just doing an errand for the hyung I met on the boat.

> I promised to stop by Namwon on my way to my hometown to relay news and a gift for a lady.

Namwon is a large village. Which young lady are you talking about?

Do you by any chance know the Namwon Tavern along the outskirts of the village?

Namwon Tavern?

It's the tavern owner's daughter.

You mean Ehwa?

That's right.

That young lady has a flower name.*

* Ehwa means "pear tree flower."

120

I'm headed for Namwon Tavern as well.
Then the person you're longing for isn't by any chance...?

It's Ehwa's mother. People say that food from the south is tasty, but her food is the very best I've ever tasted across the entire world.

Then that means that you and the hyung I met on the boat have both been longing for women of the same household.

I guess so. I always thought of Ehwa as a little girl. When did she grow up into a fragrant flower?

With mother and daughter both blooming at the same time, it must be wonderful.

No wonder Namwon is such a fragrant place.

Where are you going?

Lately, I get nervous when the moon wanes or is difficult to see.

They say that being out upon the ocean is more dangerous than going to war.

Perhaps if I hung up some white and bright paper moons, I wouldn't feel so anxious.

It's not just the ocean that you need to worry about. A hazy, dark, night sky also brings discomfort for a man.

I think I'd feel better if I hung up a large paper moon too.

SNIP SNIP

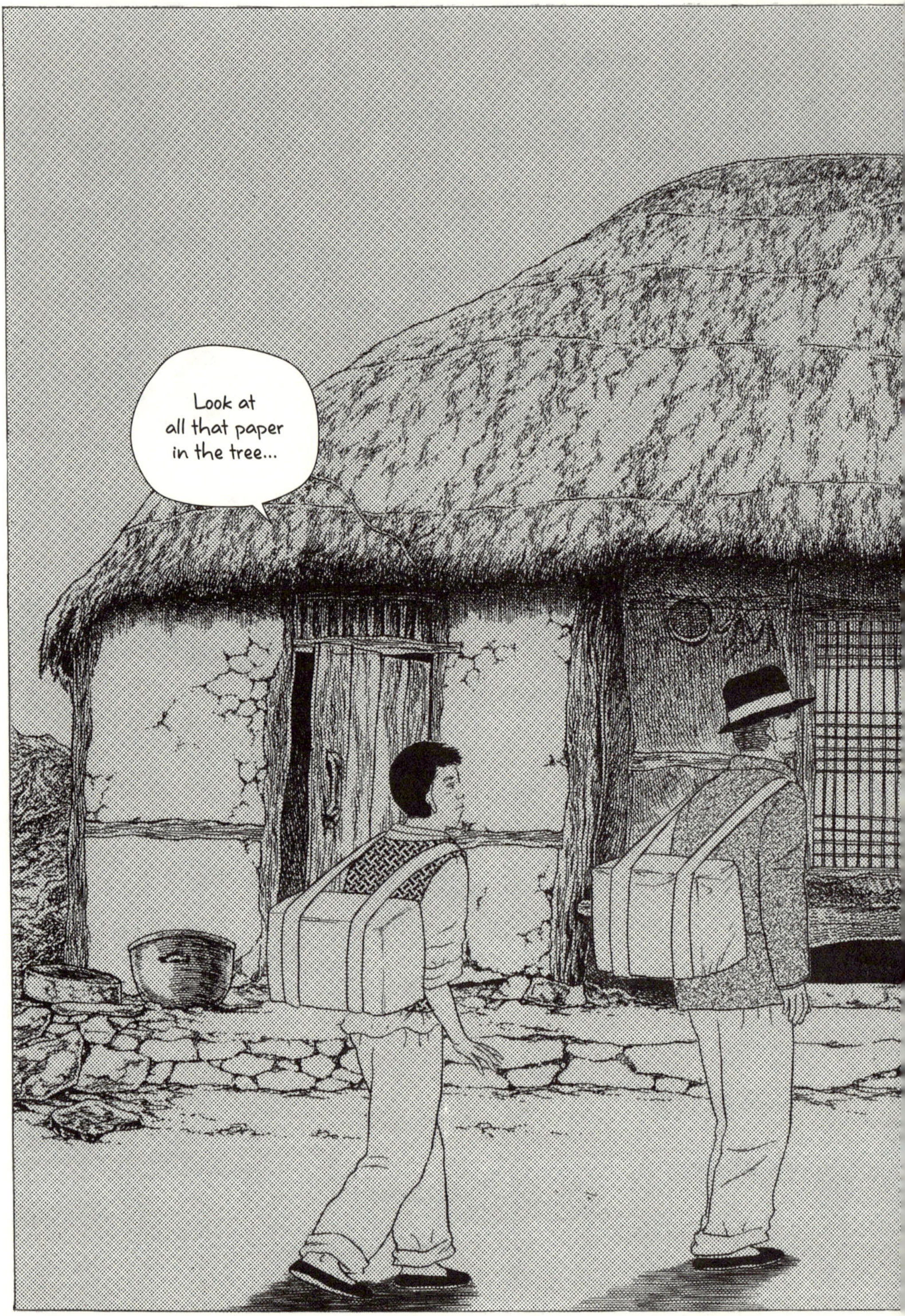
Look at all that paper in the tree...

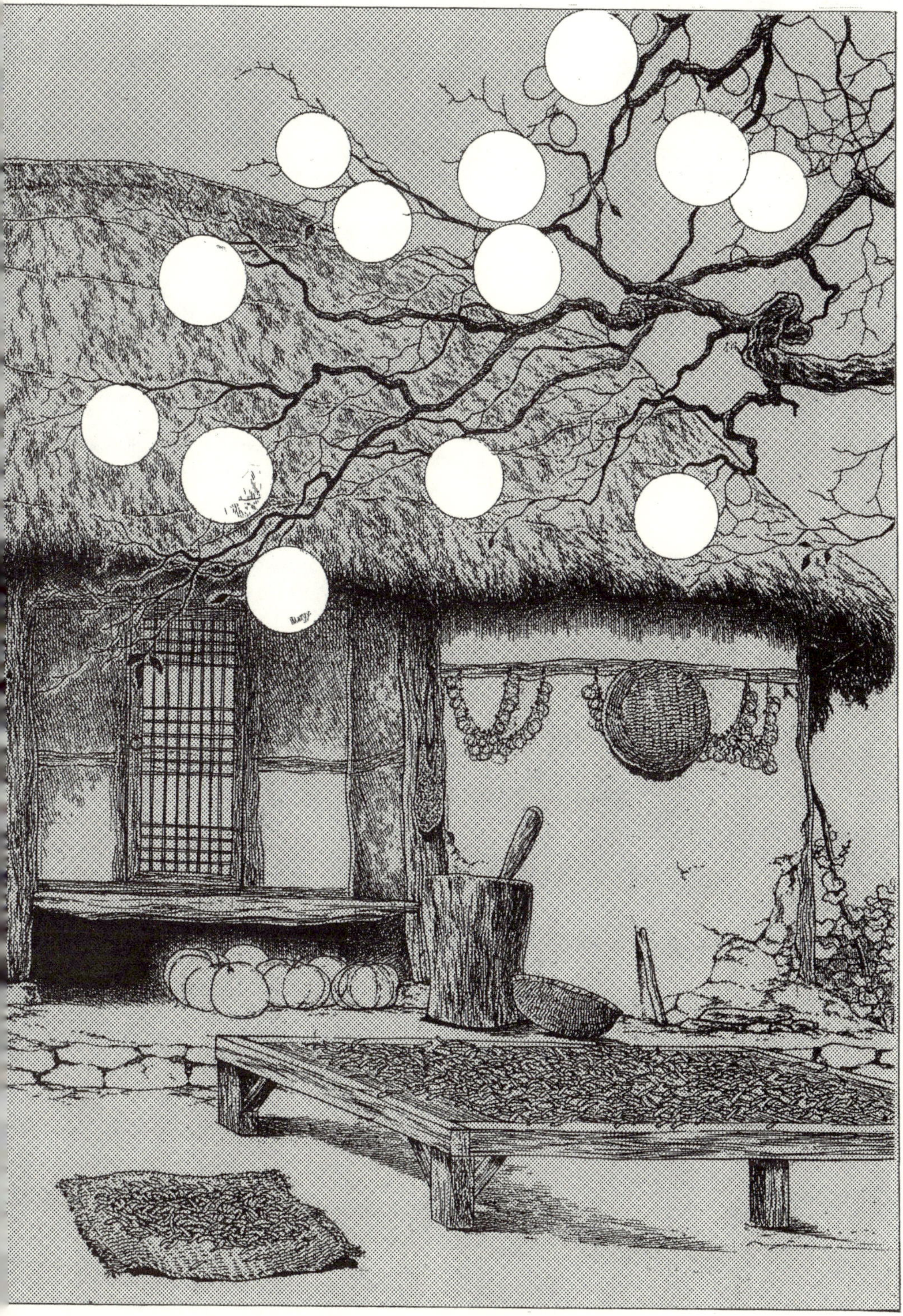

Are you in?
Oh my.
It's the picture man.
How did you get here on such a dark night?
It's not dark at all! In the yard, there were spring moons hanging from the tree guiding me here...
I could see them from far away.
I thought you might be traveling at night, so I hung up those moons for you.

Is Ehwa already asleep? We have a guest here who rode on a boat in Mokpo...
Where?
I've brought you news from a young man named Duksam.
Oh... Who are you?

There is nothing to write with on the boat, so he asked that I relay this message in person.
He said to tell you that he feeds his strength by looking toward the Namwon sky, and that he can hear singing coming from Namwon.
And he said that when he casts his nets toward Namwon, he catches lots of fish.
He asked me to ask you to look just once at the moon when it rises in the spring time... since hyung Duksam will be looking at it too.

Why does he look at the spring moon only once when I look at it day in and day out?

Especially since I look at these paper moons every day. Especially since I hung them all over the tree so that their light would shine across the lake, over the mountain and reach the sea.

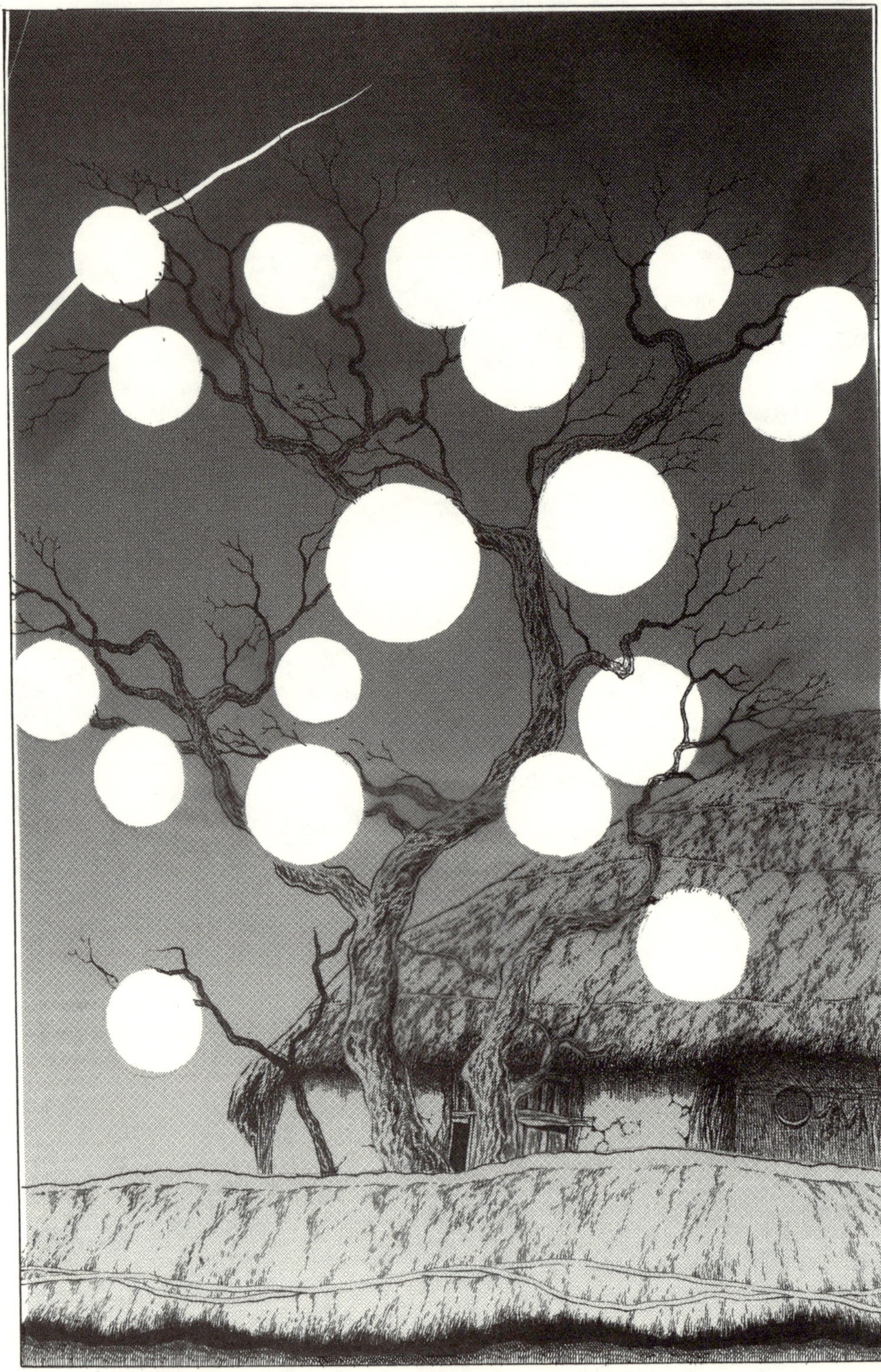

Chapter Five

NAKED LADY LILY

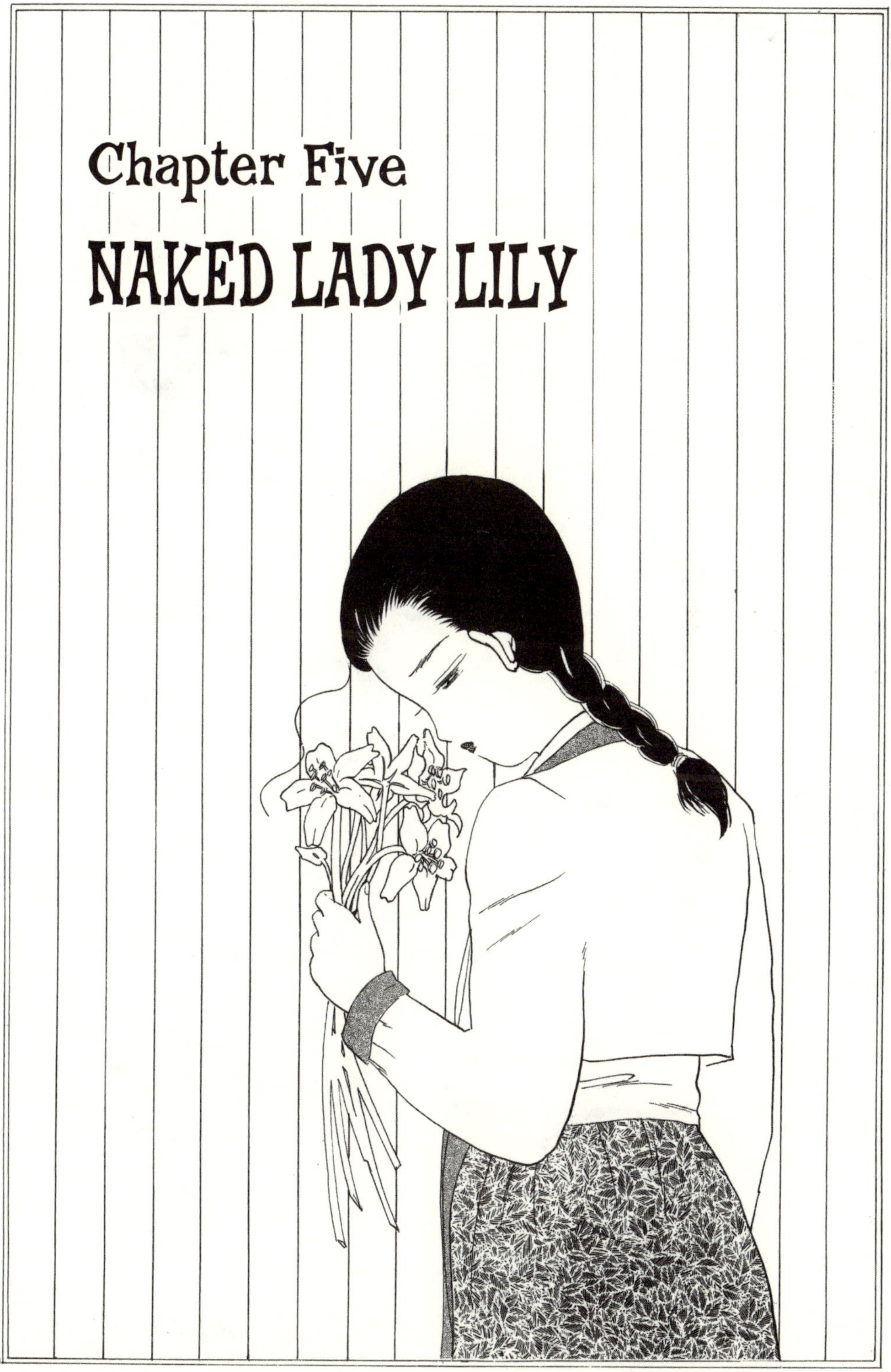

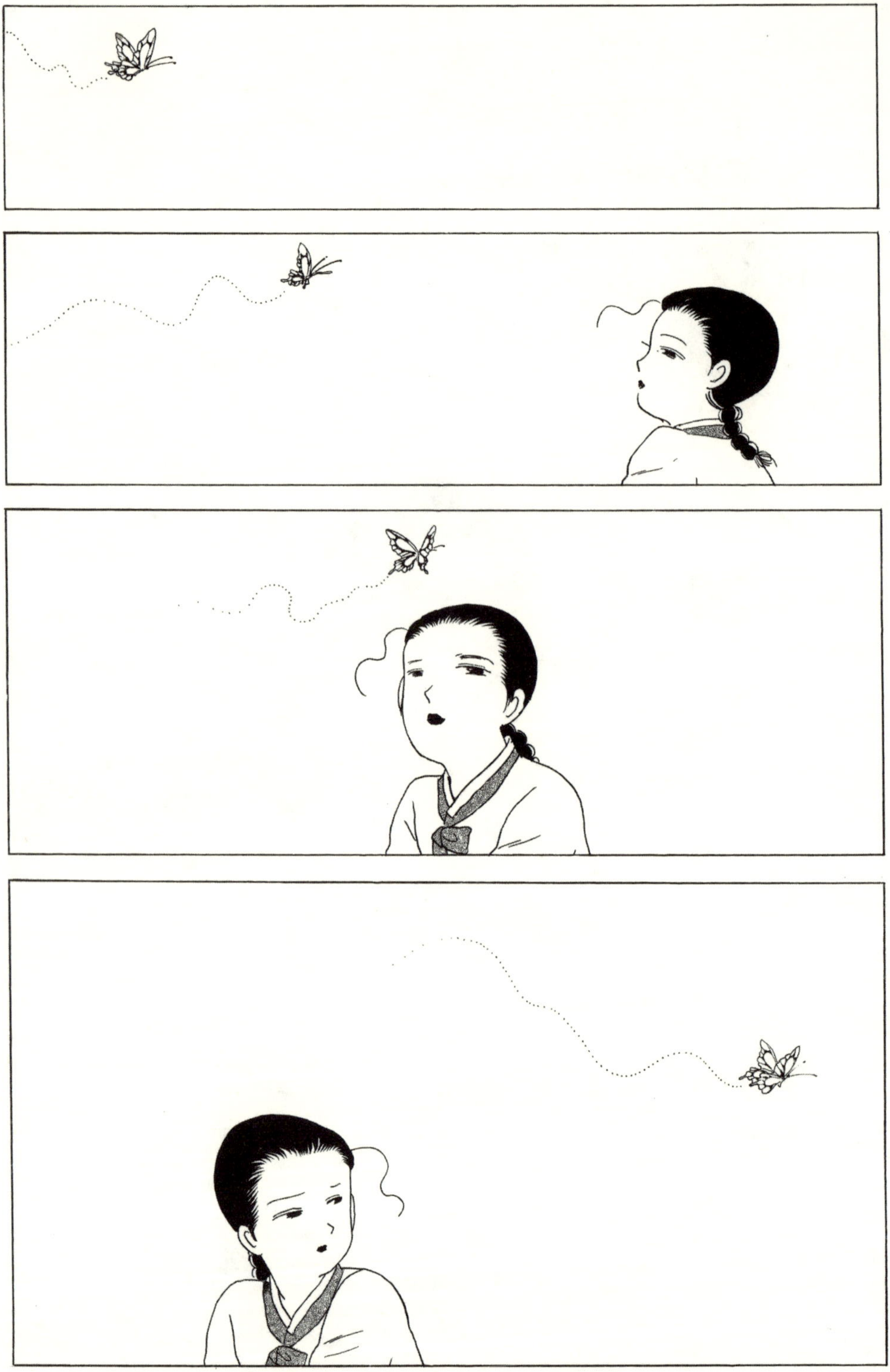

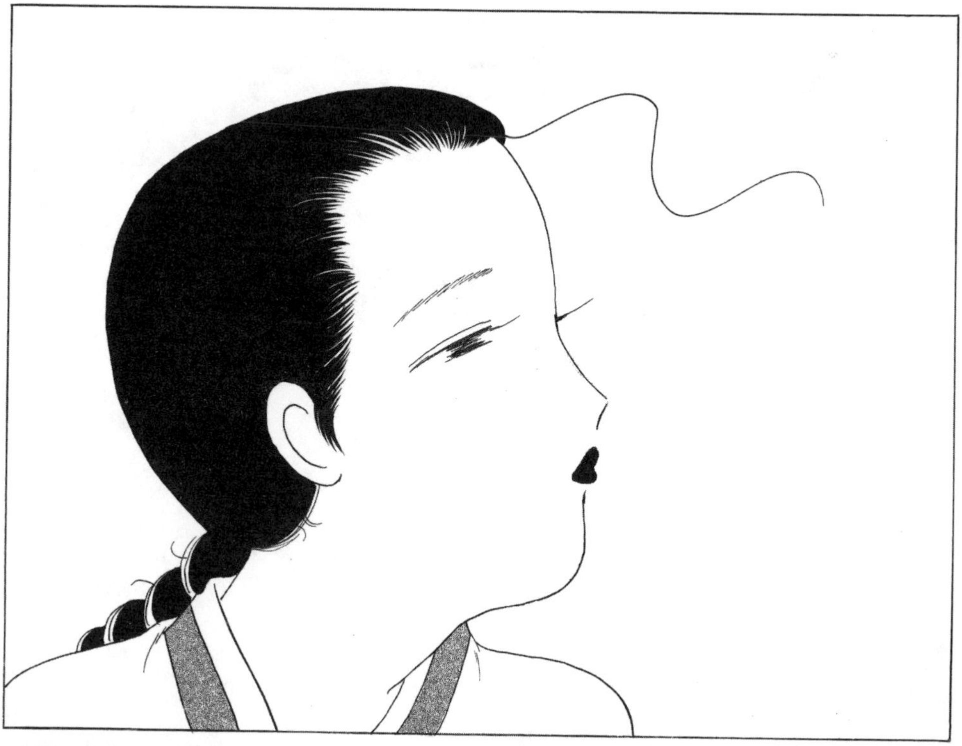

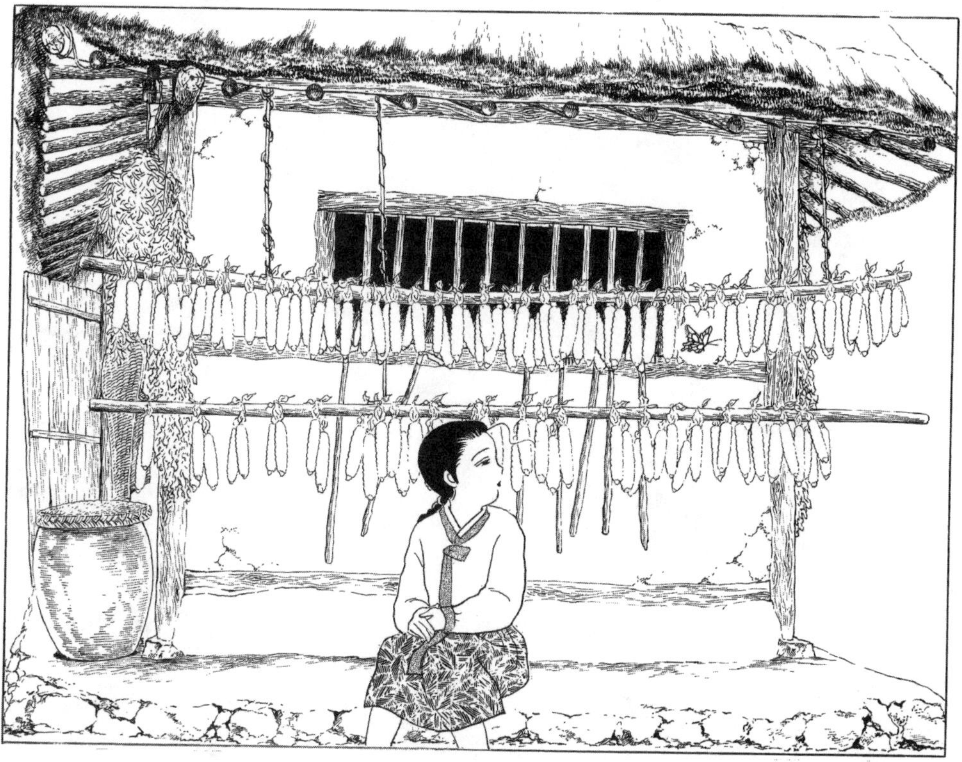

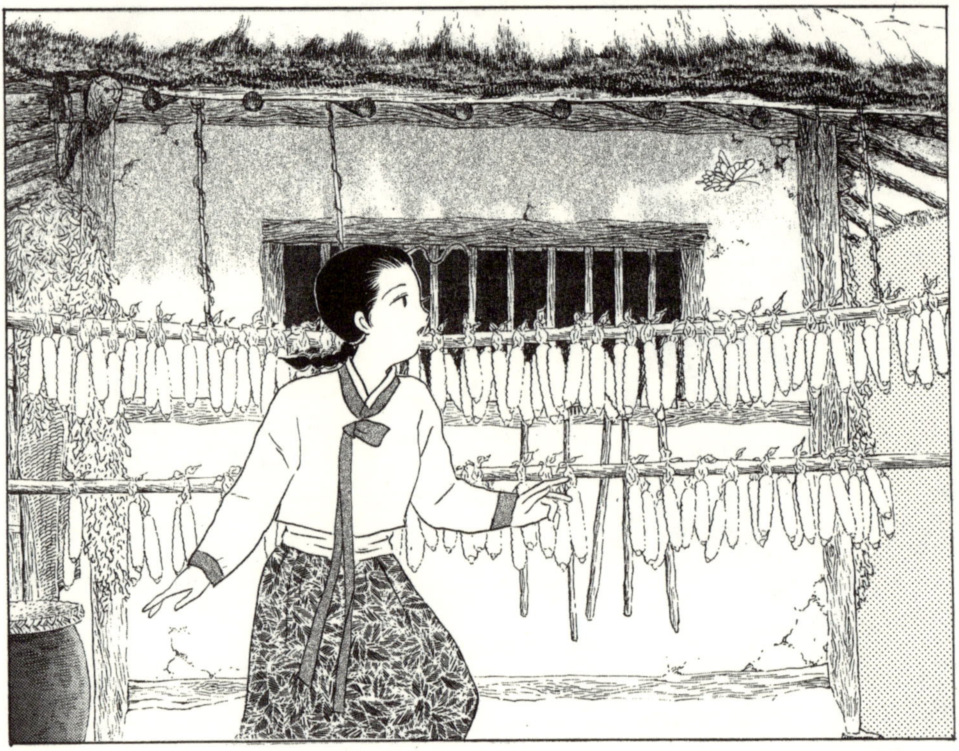

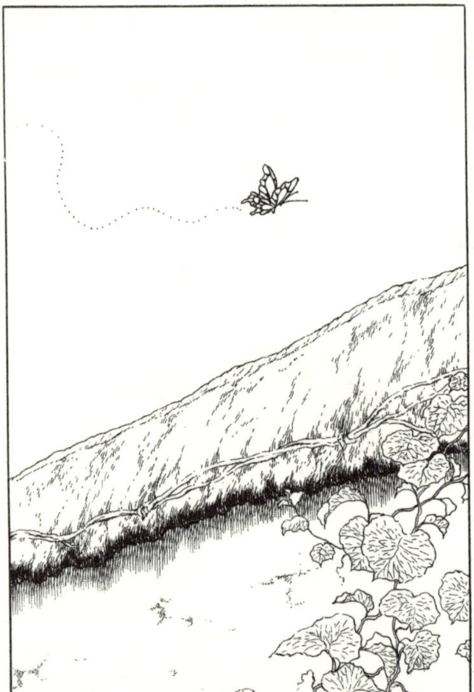

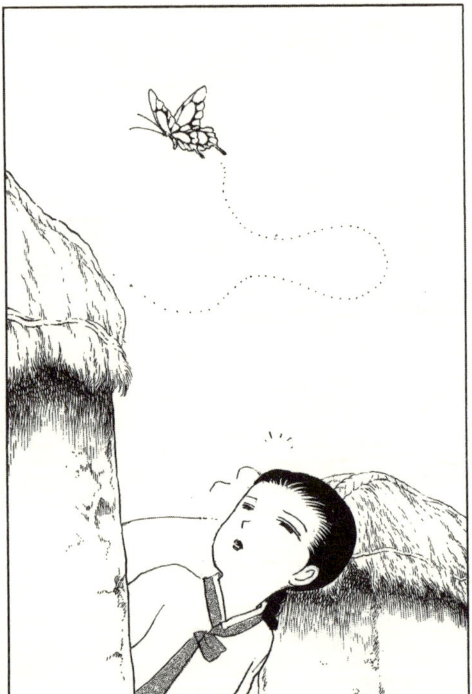

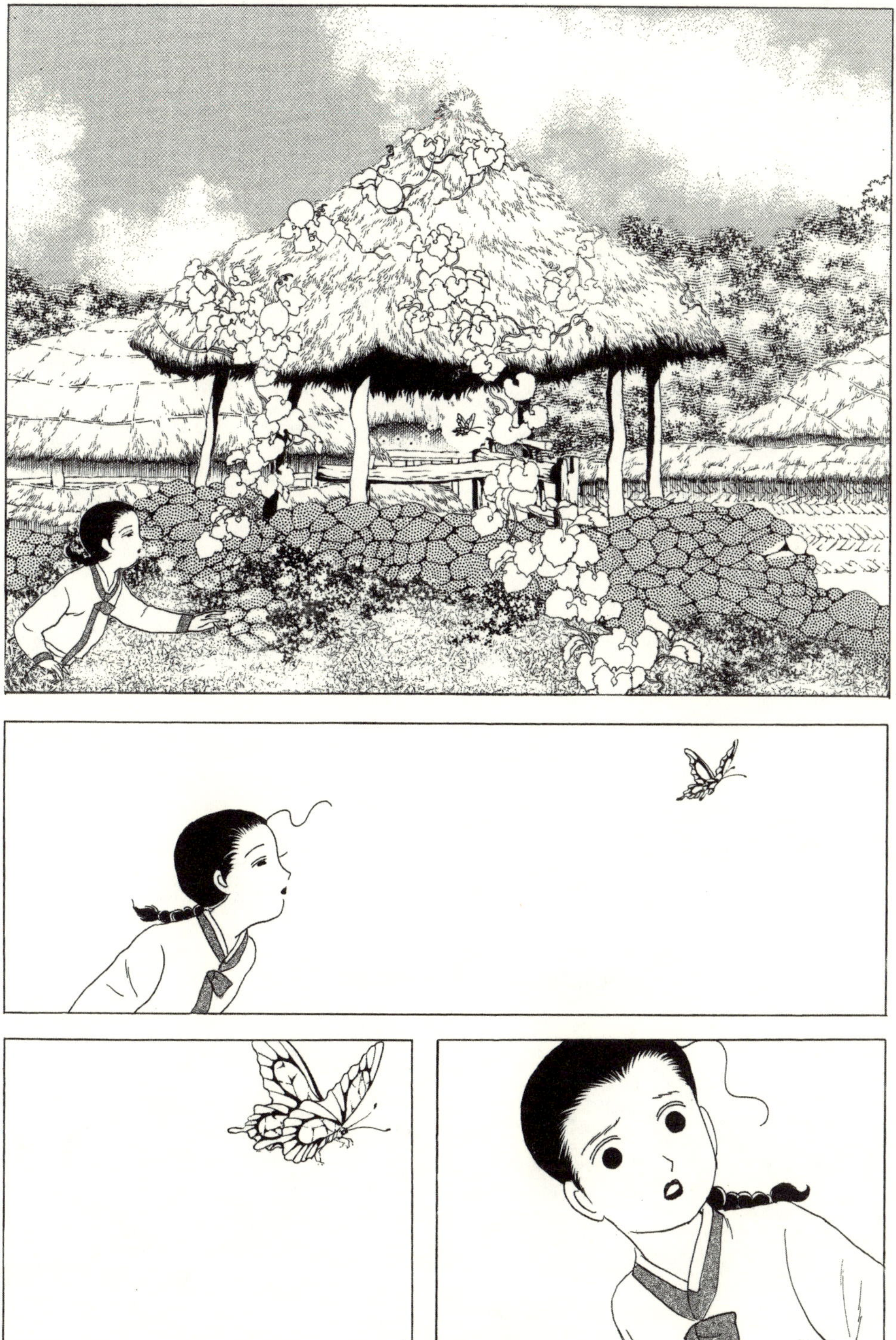

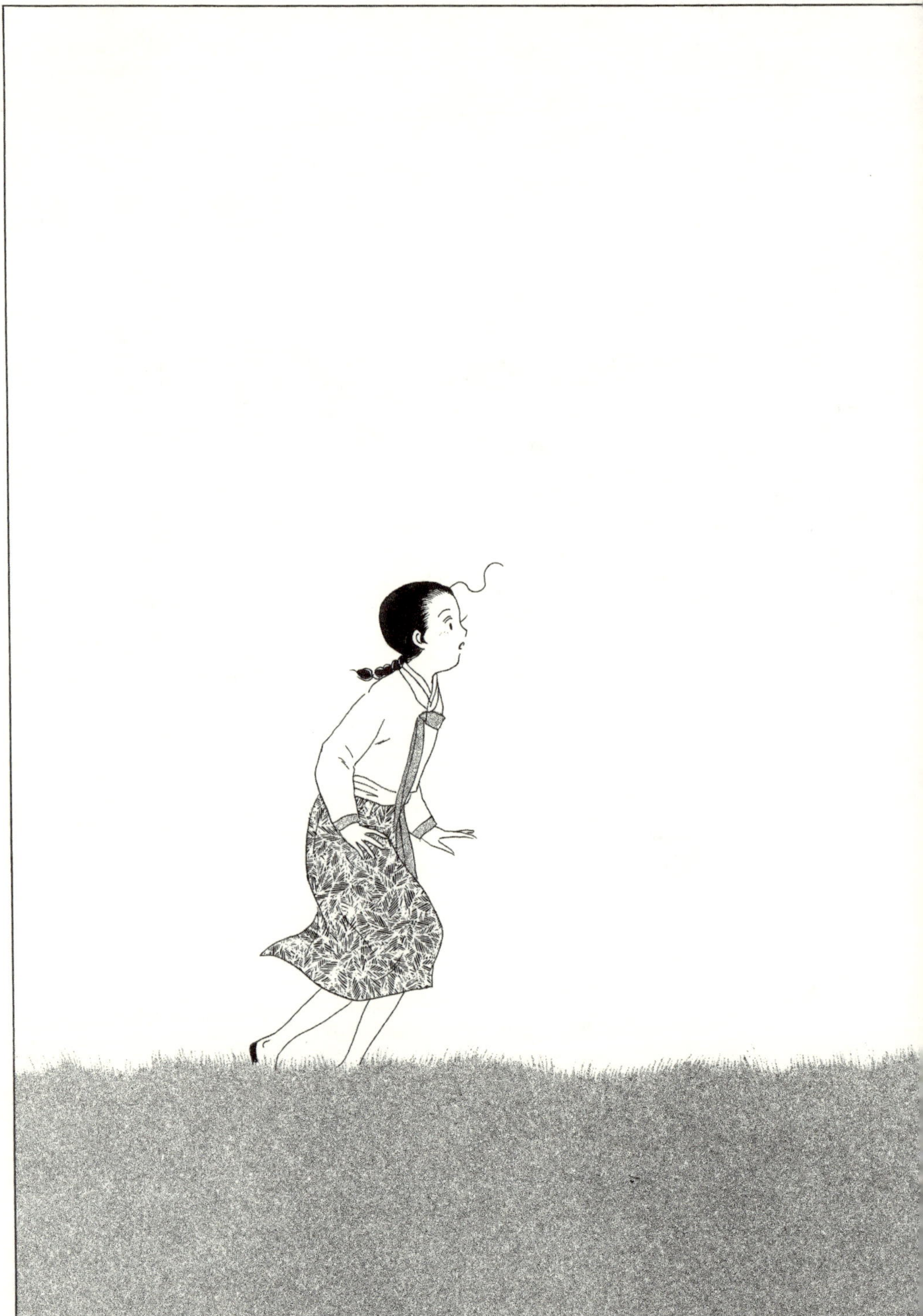

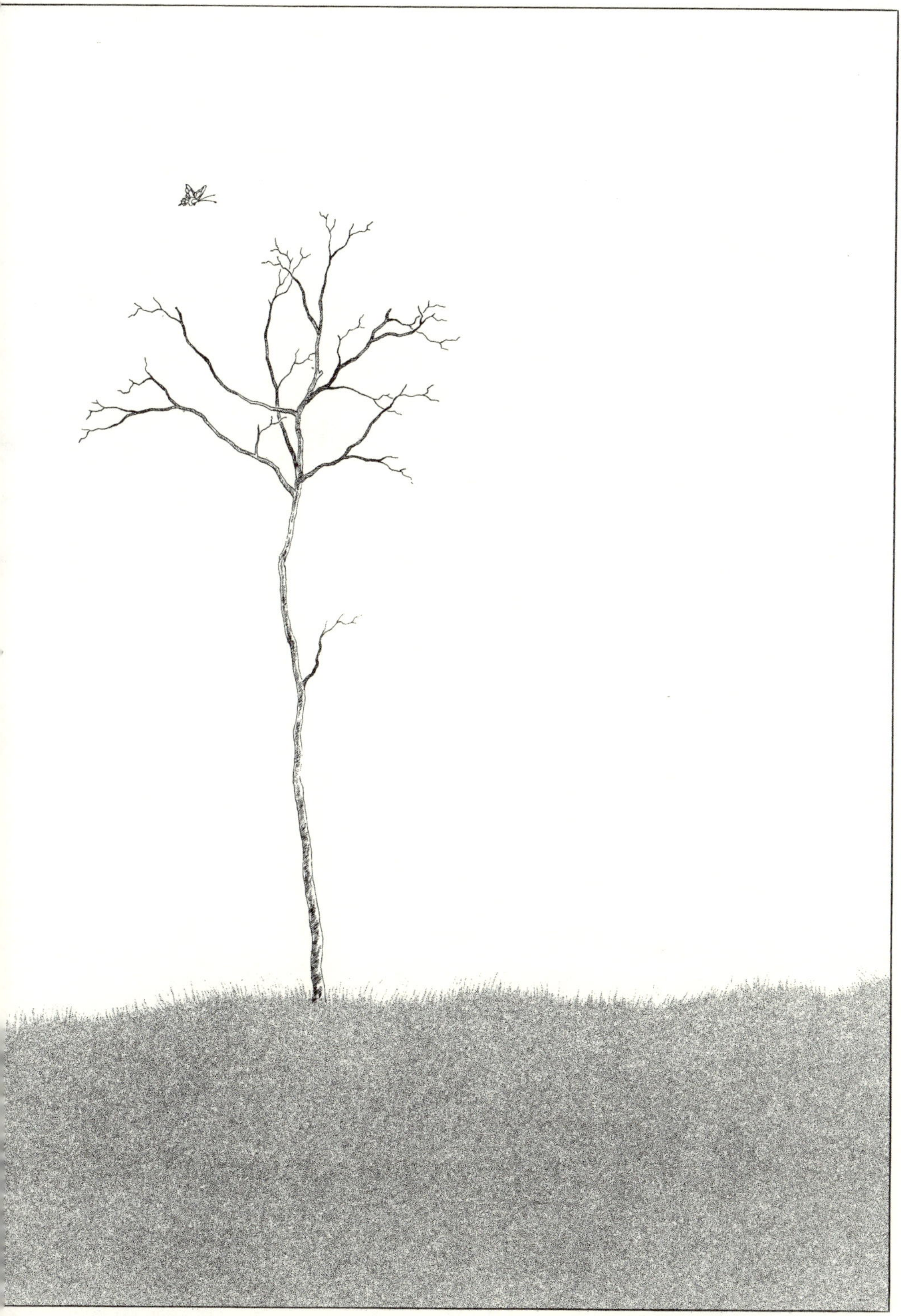

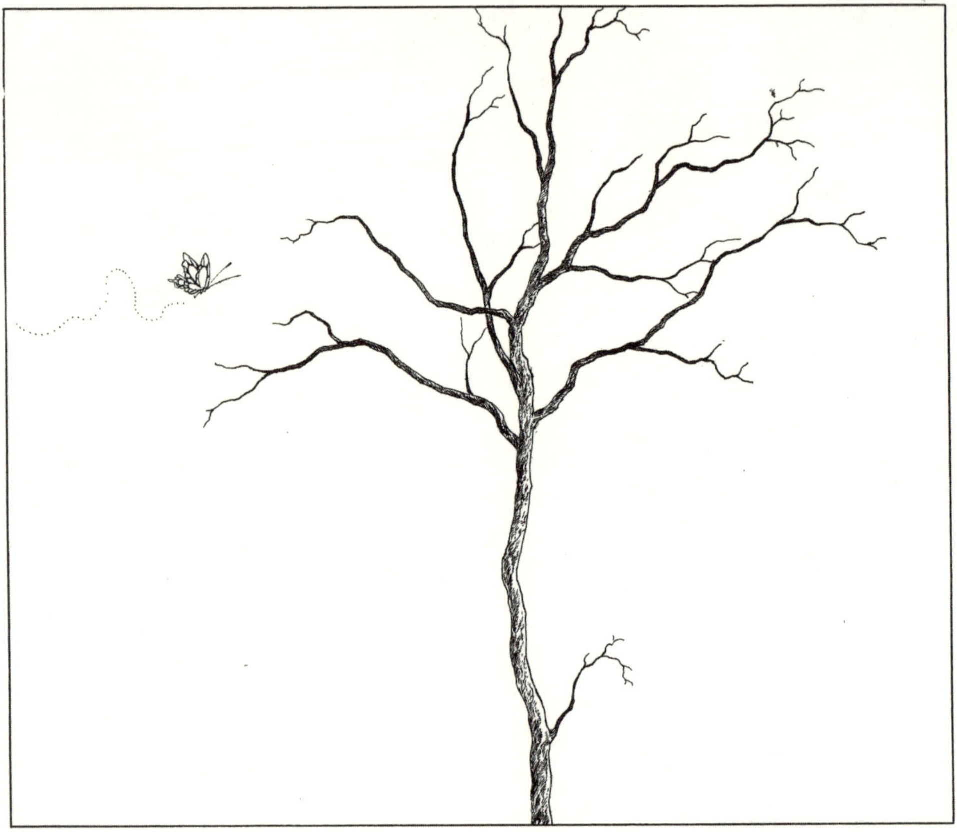

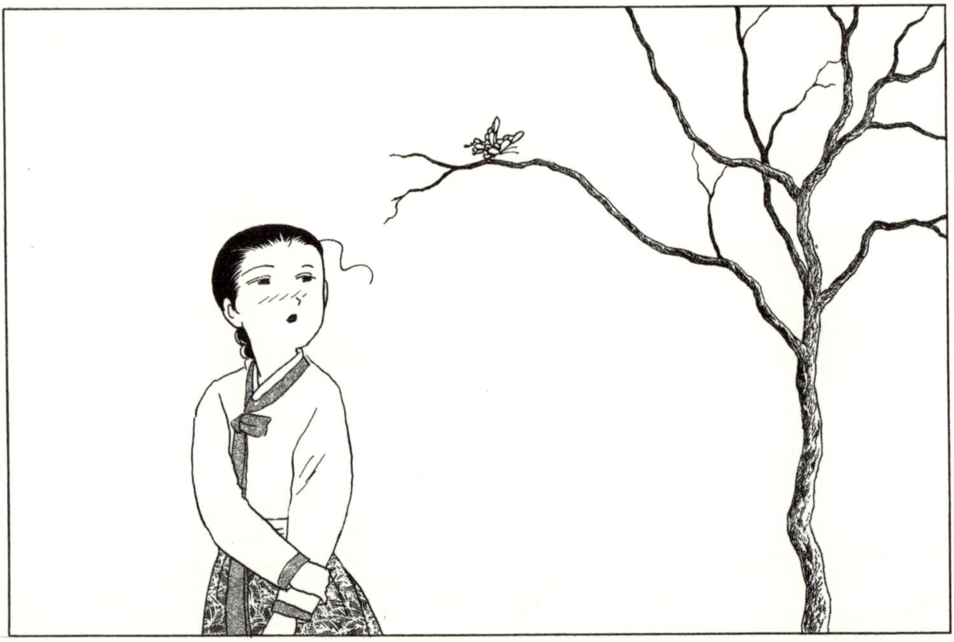

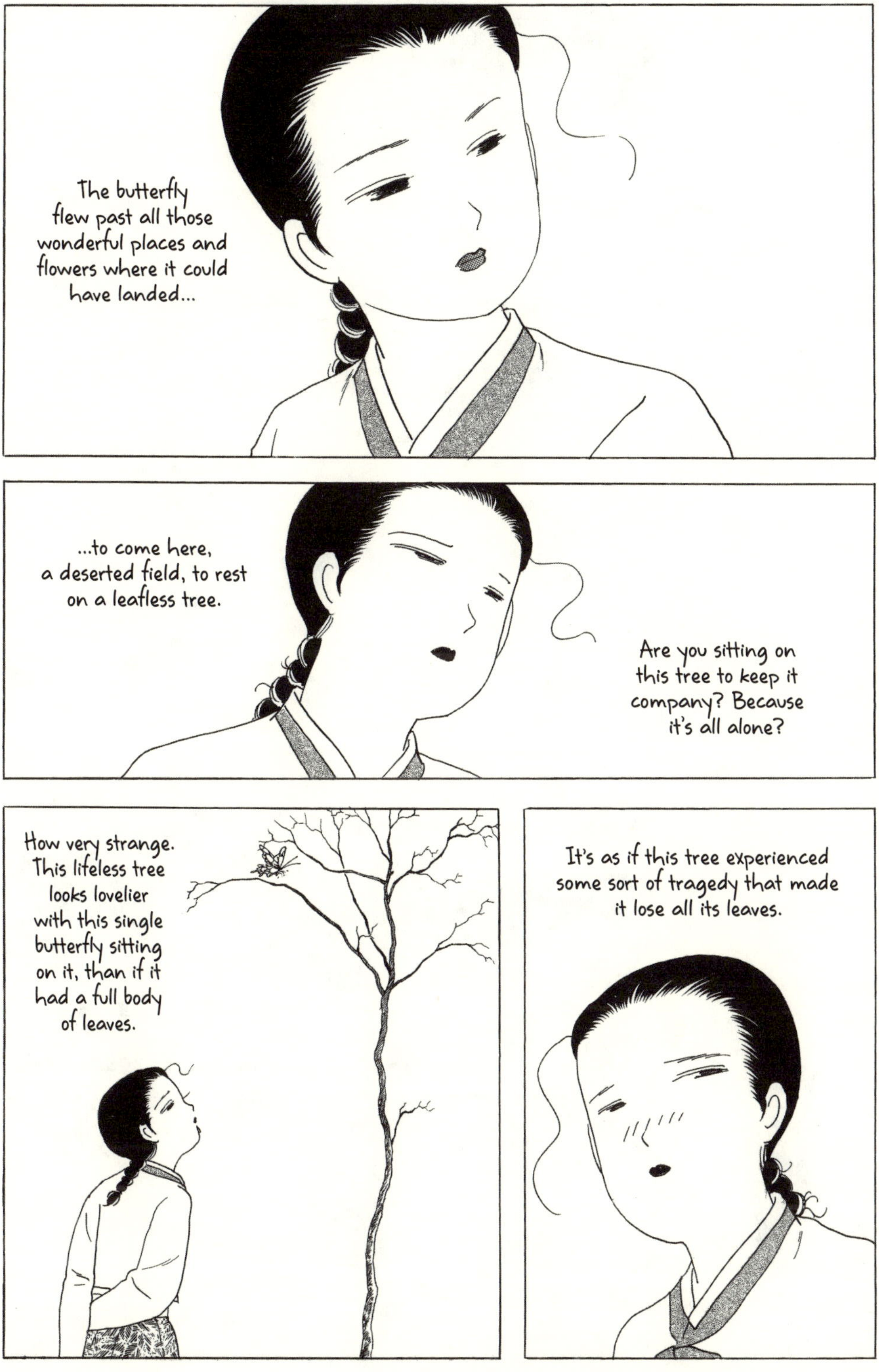
The butterfly flew past all those wonderful places and flowers where it could have landed...
...to come here, a deserted field, to rest on a leafless tree.
Are you sitting on this tree to keep it company? Because it's all alone?
How very strange. This lifeless tree looks lovelier with this single butterfly sitting on it, than if it had a full body of leaves.
It's as if this tree experienced some sort of tragedy that made it lose all its leaves.

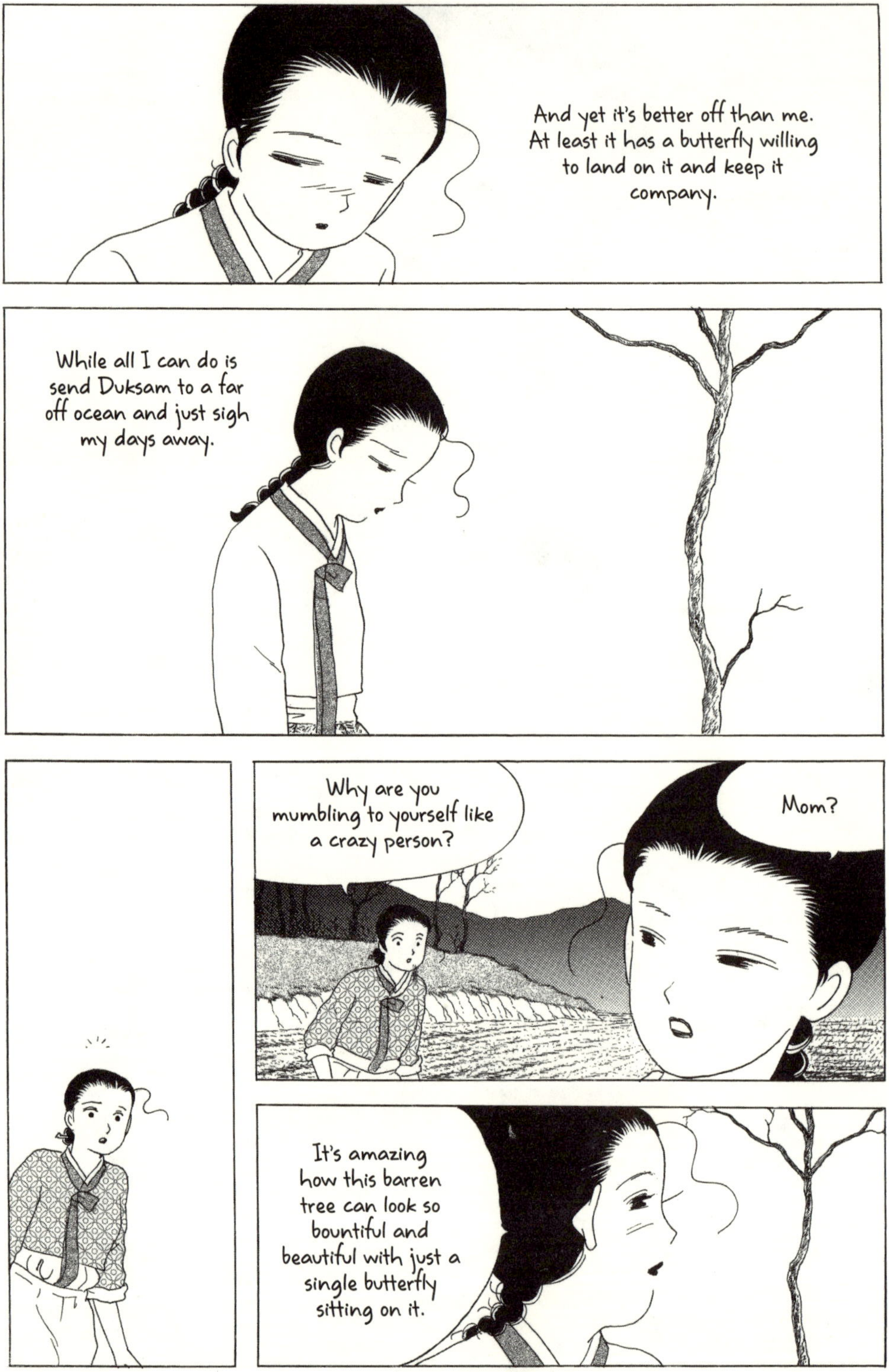
And yet it's better off than me. At least it has a butterfly willing to land on it and keep it company.
While all I can do is send Duksam to a far off ocean and just sigh my days away.
Mom?
Why are you mumbling to yourself like a crazy person?
It's amazing how this barren tree can look so bountiful and beautiful with just a single butterfly sitting on it.

What's the point of dressing a street peddler in silk clothes? On him, they'll look like a piece of rope hanging from a pole.
That's because these living things are showing their affection for each other.
Yet even if you clothe him with tattered rags, as long as there's feeling and warmth in your actions, then he will gain strength and look alive.
Whether it's that tree in the deserted field or Duksam in the middle of the sea, they both probably feel the same loneliness.
Maybe I should give Duksam some strength, just like the butterfly did to the tree.
I'll fly to Duksam's side like a butterfly.
Even though this land is large and wide, for a woman, this land is very small. It's unheard of for you to even think of traveling alone.

"Even if we tried to fly or run, the only place we could go is within our yard."

"Seeing how you draw meaning from a simple tree and a butterfly shows me that you are really experiencing true love."

"When you're really in love, just looking at a small pebble can make you become teary-eyed."

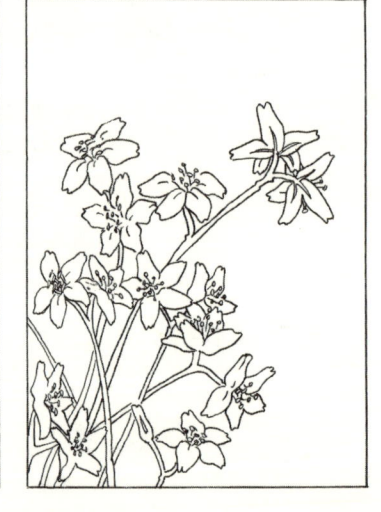

"But where is this fragrance coming from?"

"I tell her that her eyes are going to become teary-eyed and it's her nose that becomes all sensitive."

"I'm being serious, Mom. Don't you smell flowers?"

"Hmm... Huh. You're right."

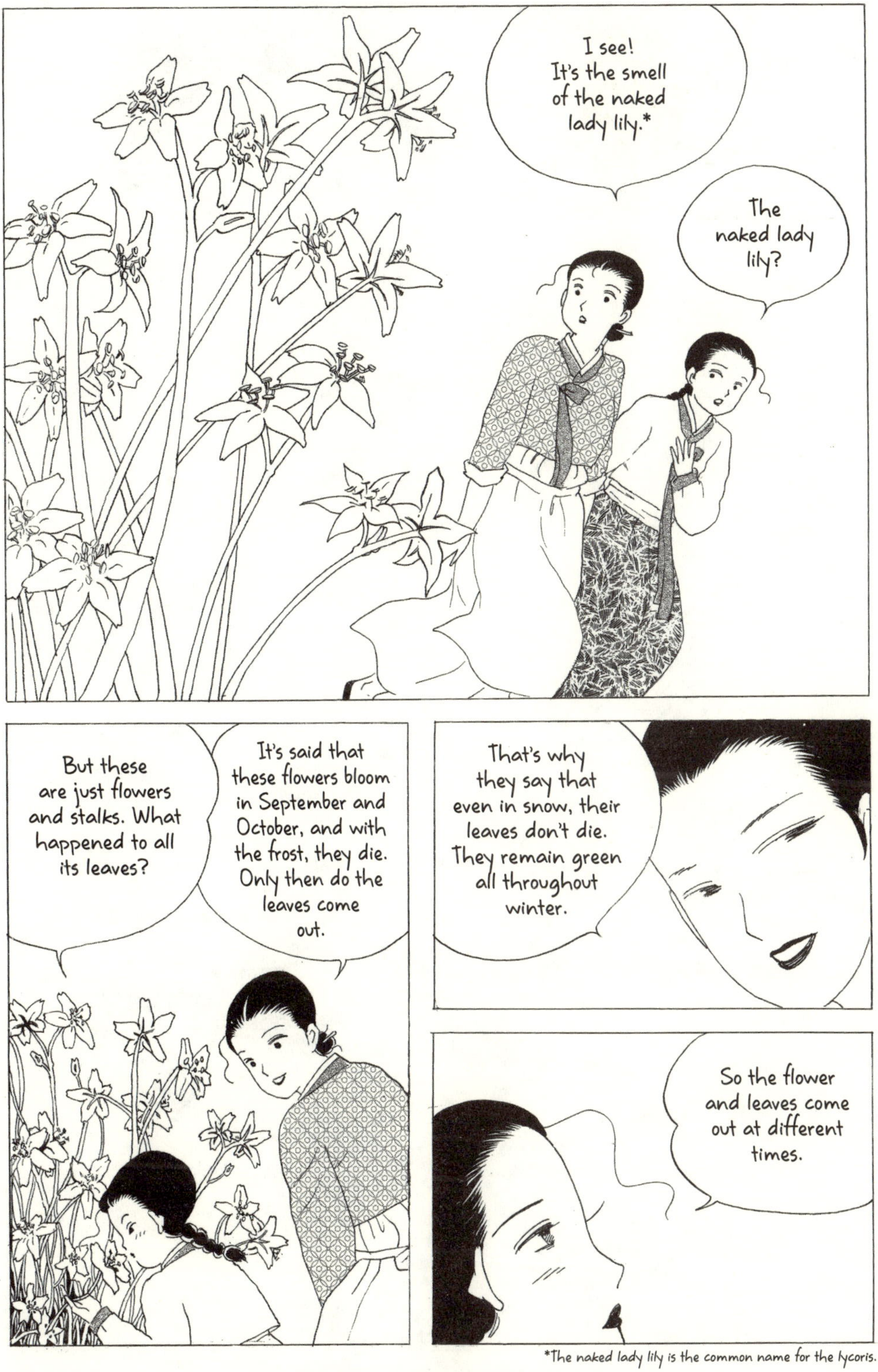
I see! It's the smell of the naked lady lily.*
The naked lady lily?
But these are just flowers and stalks. What happened to all its leaves?
It's said that these flowers bloom in September and October, and with the frost, they die. Only then do the leaves come out.
That's why they say that even in snow, their leaves don't die. They remain green all throughout winter.
So the flower and leaves come out at different times.

*The naked lady lily is the common name for the lycoris.

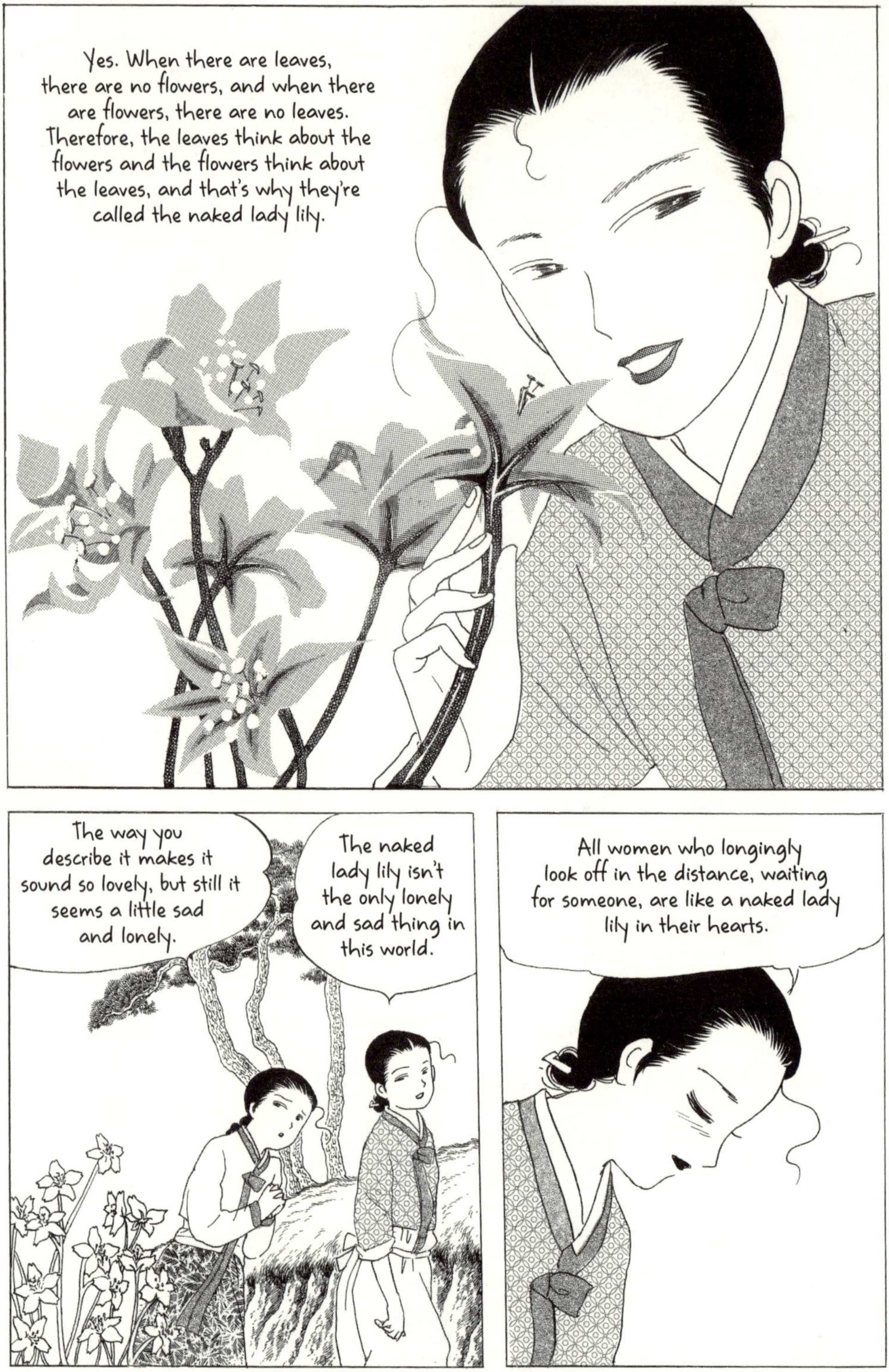
Yes. When there are leaves, there are no flowers, and when there are flowers, there are no leaves. Therefore, the leaves think about the flowers and the flowers think about the leaves, and that's why they're called the naked lady lily.
The way you describe it makes it sound so lovely, but still it seems a little sad and lonely.
The naked lady lily isn't the only lonely and sad thing in this world.
All women who longingly look off in the distance, waiting for someone, are like a naked lady lily in their hearts.

We can't go to them, nor can we see them, so all we can do is just let our fragrance loose.

I don't think I can live like that. Mom, can I go visit Mokpo and come back?

Are you planning to work on a boat too?

Do you think the ocean is like a puddle? How can you possibly find a person in such a large place?

If I search and search and still can't find him, I'll go to the top of a mountain cliff and call out his name.

My goodness! I'm worried that you'd actually go and do that.
If a woman has too much time on her hands, she begins to think of crazy and useless things.
And if that happens, it'll be you who'll be hurt and no one else.
It looks like I'll have to start teaching you how to cook and become a good housewife so that your mind will stop wandering and thinking about useless things.
Hmph.

As soon as you enter the kitchen, you need to fold up your sleeves.
Your body needs to be free and unobstructed to move around.
If you can move without hindrance, the kitchen will feel a lot larger.
You start by organizing the dishes and the seasoning containers.
If it's a mess and unorganized, you won't be able to make much of a meal.
Why are you just standing there? Hurry up and begin washing the dishes.

"Making a lot of noise while washing dishes is like grinding your teeth while you're sleeping."

CLATTER SPLASH

CLATTER CLATTER

"If you're done with the dishes, organize the kitchen and get a fire going."

"Let me rest for a bit."

"Did you come to the kitchen to have a picnic? There shouldn't be any resting whatsoever."

"To make something tasty that doesn't require cooking, you just need to season it correctly."

However, food that requires cooking depends entirely on how the fire is built.
If the fire is too low, then the food will be bitter, and if the fire is too high, the food will be tough.
Who cares if it's bitter or tough? Bitter, tough or sweet as sugar, once you eat it, it's going to the same place.
Nonsense. There isn't a wife alive who can cook well who isn't loved by her husband.
Who cares if I'm not loved? I can just do all the loving.
The things coming out of your mouth these days!

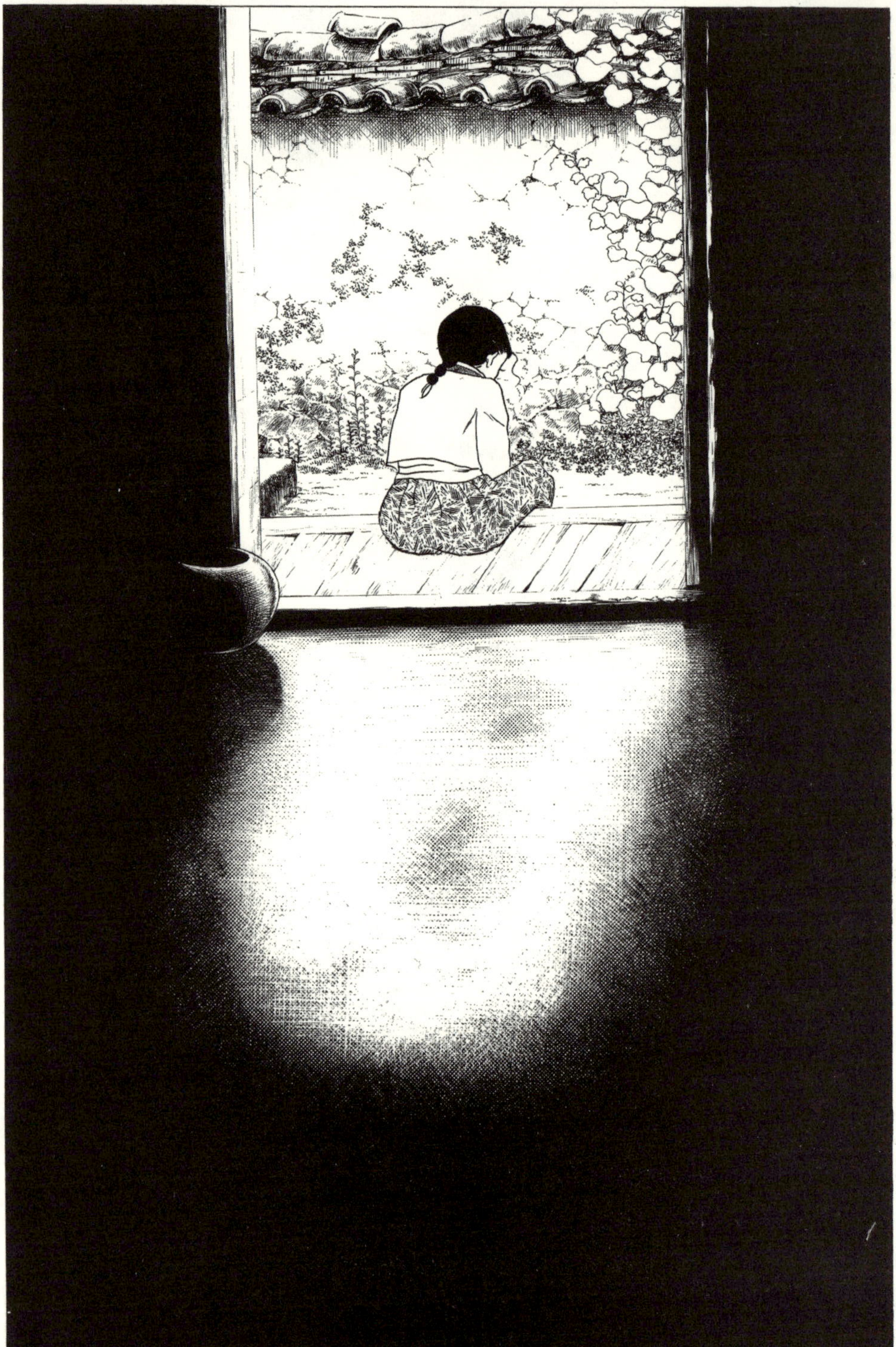

動
Why are you here in the village meeting room instead of at home? What's the matter?
I was tired of listening to my mom's nagging, so I ran away here.
Why? Did you do something wrong?
As of today, she wants me to learn to be a housewife. And she said that if I can't cook, then my husband won't love me.
By the way, what's that you're holding?
Huh...? This...? It's nothing.

"It looks like food."

"Yeah... Well, you know how Dongchul goes all crazy for millet cakes?"

"I guess my mom was right."

"What are you talking about?"

"I guess the reason why Dongchul likes you is because you're a good cook."

"Well, everyone knows Dongchul likes to eat, but the reason he likes me is because he fell in love with my face."

"Your face?"

There are three beautiful qualities in women that have been passed down from generation to generation. Do you know what they are?
I haven't even heard of them.
You'll find the answers once you look carefully at my body.
I don't see anything beautiful. Just a bunch of clumsiness.
Skin, teeth, and hand.
There are also three things that must be black for a woman to be beautiful. Can you guess what they are?
Not with you hovering over me like that.
Eyes, eyebrows, and eyelashes!

Then what three things need to be red to be considered a beautiful woman?	Lips, cheeks, and nails.
Then what three things need to be beautifully soft?	Body, hair, and hand.
Then what three things need to be short to be beautiful?	Teeth, ear, and legs.
You're really into this, aren't you?	And that's not all. You know what three things need to be skinny to be considered beautiful?

Then how about the three things that need to be voluptuous?	**I think I know, judging by how I am. Lips, waist, and ankles, right?**
Then what three things need to be small to be beautiful?	**Again, looking at myself, I'd say arms, butt, and thighs.**
Nipple, nose and head.	**...?**
Geez, you just have to have the last word, don't you?	**Your body isn't anything like any of that. But you do have a big head. That's probably how you could remember all that nonsense!**

Heh heh...
Maybe I should fry up some millet cake like Bongsoon.
I wonder if Duksam likes millet cakes.
Since he's not close by like Dongchul, I'll send the smell of the cake over the mountain and to the ocean.
I guess this is why Mom wants me to learn how to cook and take care of the house.
What she said is absolutely true—a wife who can cook well will be loved by her husband.

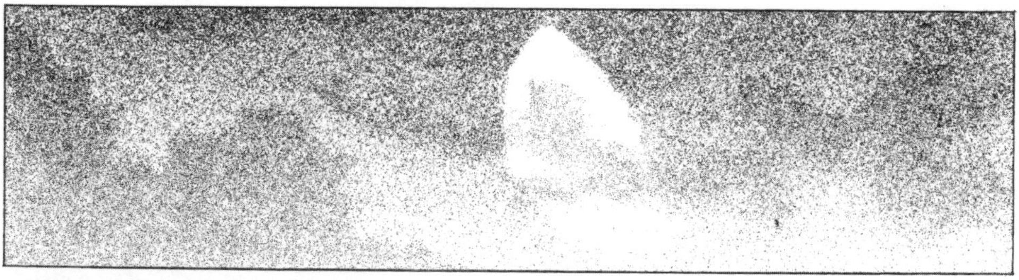

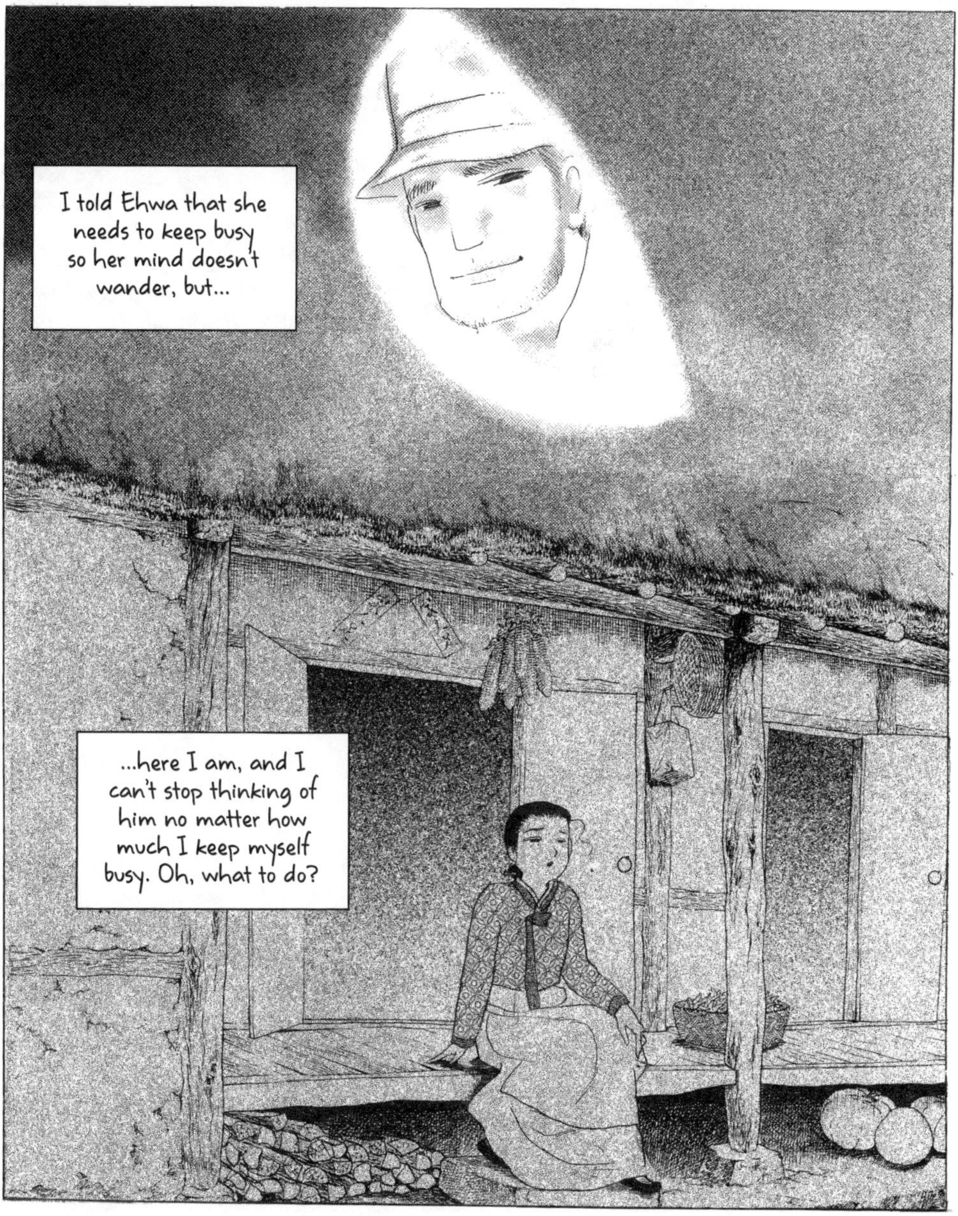

I told Ehwa that she needs to keep busy so her mind doesn't wander, but...
...here I am, and I can't stop thinking of him no matter how much I keep myself busy. Oh, what to do?

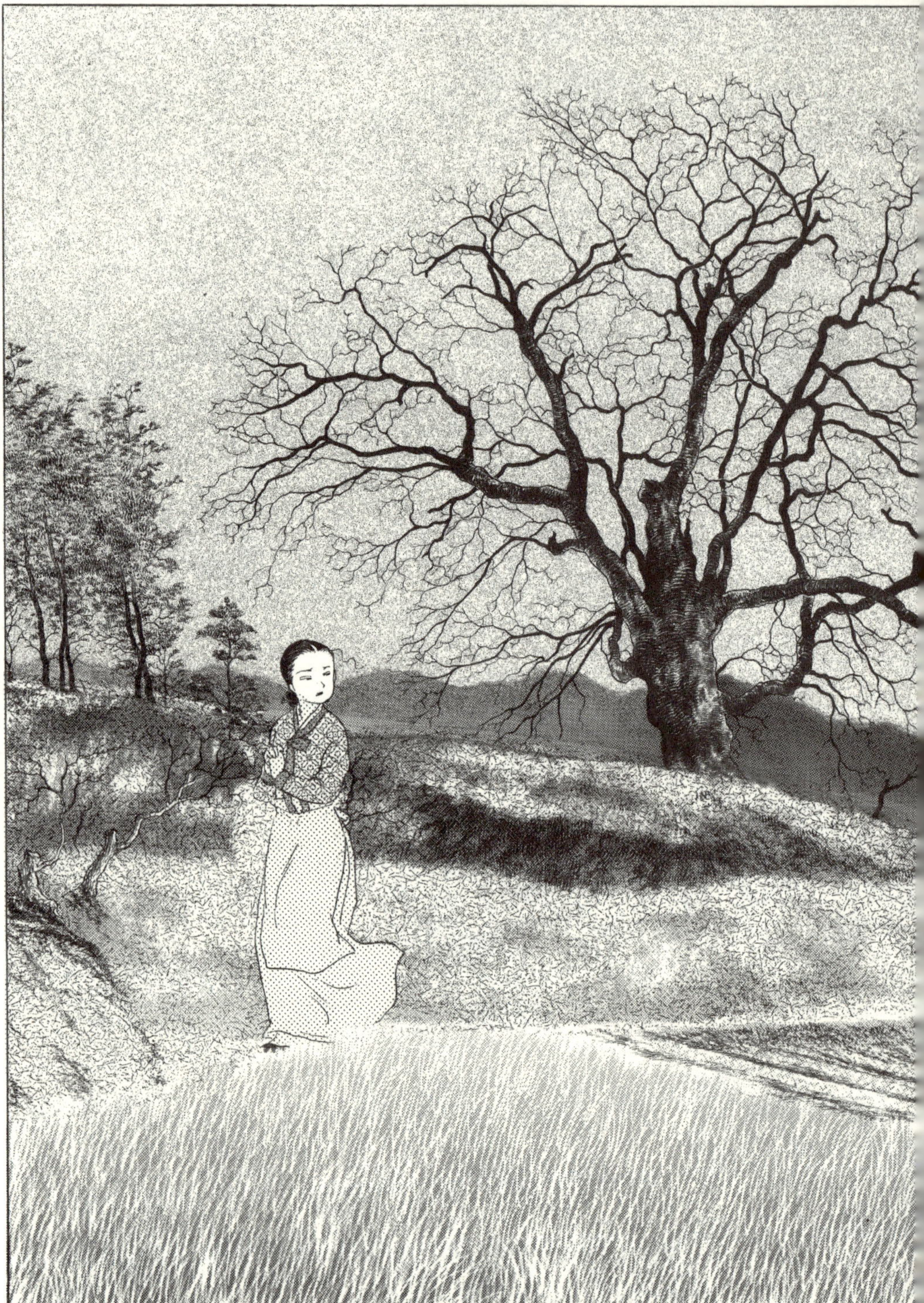

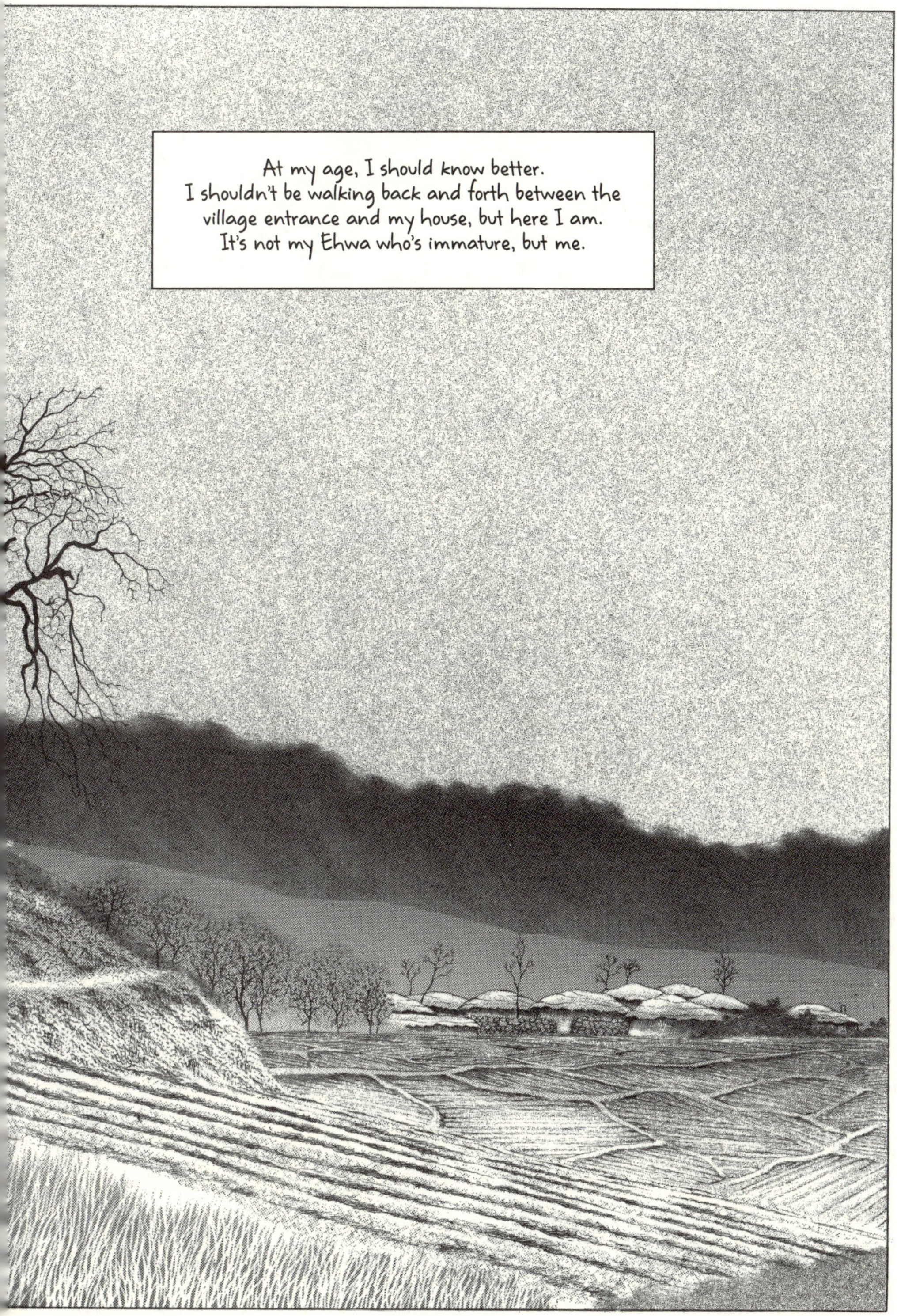
At my age, I should know better.
I shouldn't be walking back and forth between the
village entrance and my house, but here I am.
It's not my Ehwa who's immature, but me.

I always seem to get like this during the cold windy season. Perhaps it's because of the naked lady lily.

Perhaps I'll be better once the flower dies and the leaves come out.

But when the leaves come out, I'll probably long for the flower to bloom.

That's why a woman's longing is a terrible disease that can only be cured with death.

Chapter Six
FIRST SNOW OF THE SEASON

It's cloudy with no wind in sight. I guess we're in for some rain.
As if my aching back and throbbing knee weren't sign enough.

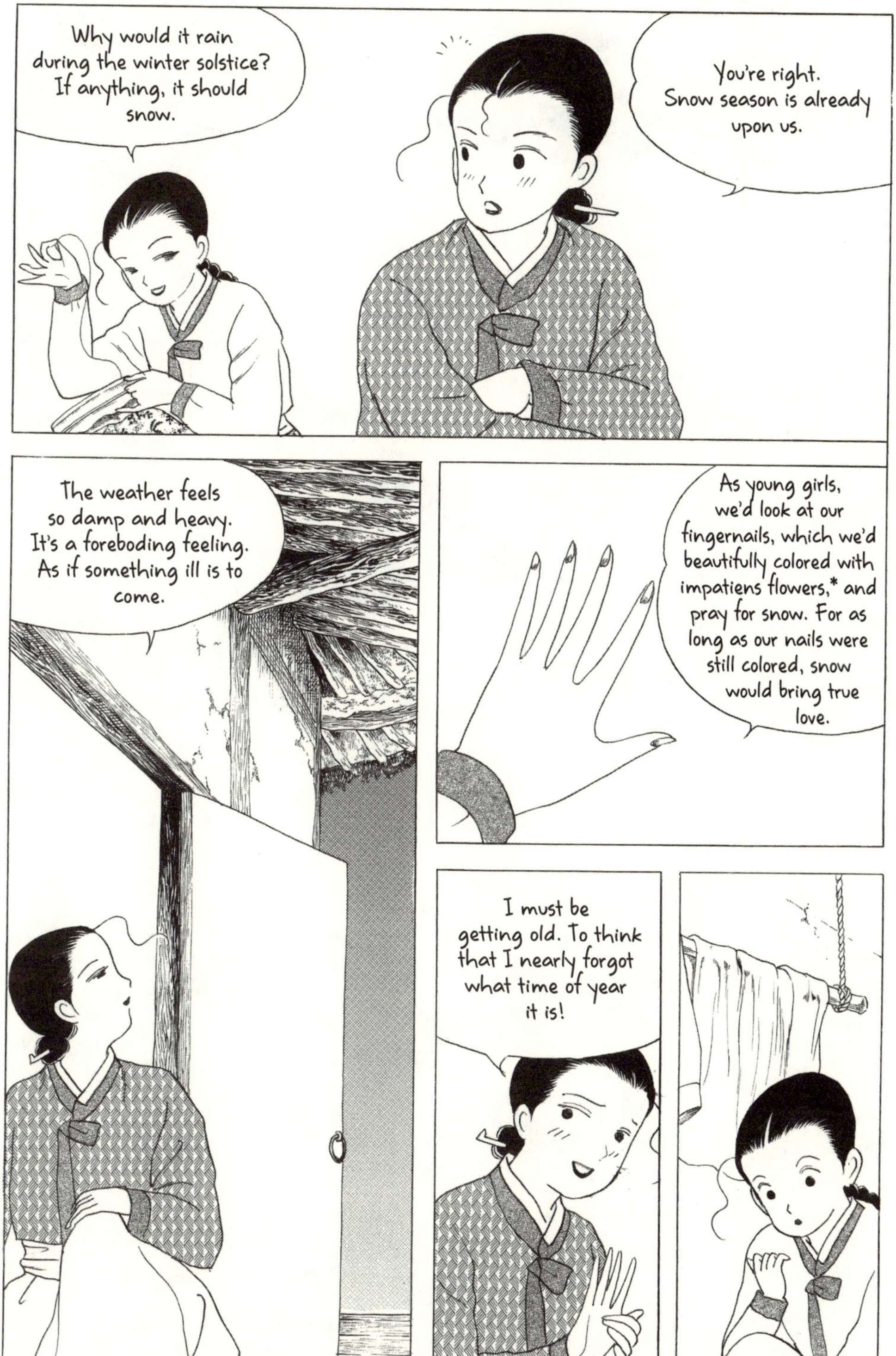

*A plant known for its effectiveness as a dye.

What is it? Is there something wrong with your nails?
It's strange. Just until a few days ago, my fingernails were still colored bright and shiny, but...
SWOOSH
...now they're as white as newly fallen snow.
Don't worry about what they look like. It's just an old wives tail and nothing to be concerned about.
Maybe, but I can't help feeling uneasy. All my life, I've colored my nails with impatiens and as long as they didn't fade before our first snow, I knew my love wouldn't be unrequited.

Look at the two of us. You hoped and prayed the color on your nails wouldn't fade, and it's faded completely.
While I couldn't care less whether my nails faded or not, and mine are as bright as azalea flowers.
You must be happy!
How nice it would be if we could live our lives based on how brightly red our fingernails and hearts are.
But I've realized over the years that men are truly blind.
Our brightly colored fingernails could serve as a beacon for them to return to us.

Although we women wave at them with our bright red hands until the first snow, they don't seem to see us, or if they do, they act like they haven't seen us. They only look when they want to, it seems.
If you know that, then why do you still color your nails every year?
That's why women are called foolish. Knowing full well that we're being tricked, we continue to color our nails until the red color begins to seep into our hearts.
It's almost as if we live to be tricked by the men and the men live to trick us.
Are you saying that Duksam is tricking me right now?
It's not because he's Duksam, but because he is a man.

Women are like the moss rose that likes to grow and remain within the yard, but men are like the persimmon tree that stretches and extends out over the fence.
When have we ever asked for anything as big as a persimmon?
When it comes down to it, all we really want is something as small as a watermelon seed.
On a day like this, we women would be completely and utterly happy just to have a man hold our cold hands and massage our aching backs. We'd be so blissfully happy we wouldn't know what to do with ourselves.
Men are never happy unless they're trying to do the impossible. It's why they roam about the world trying to conquer it.

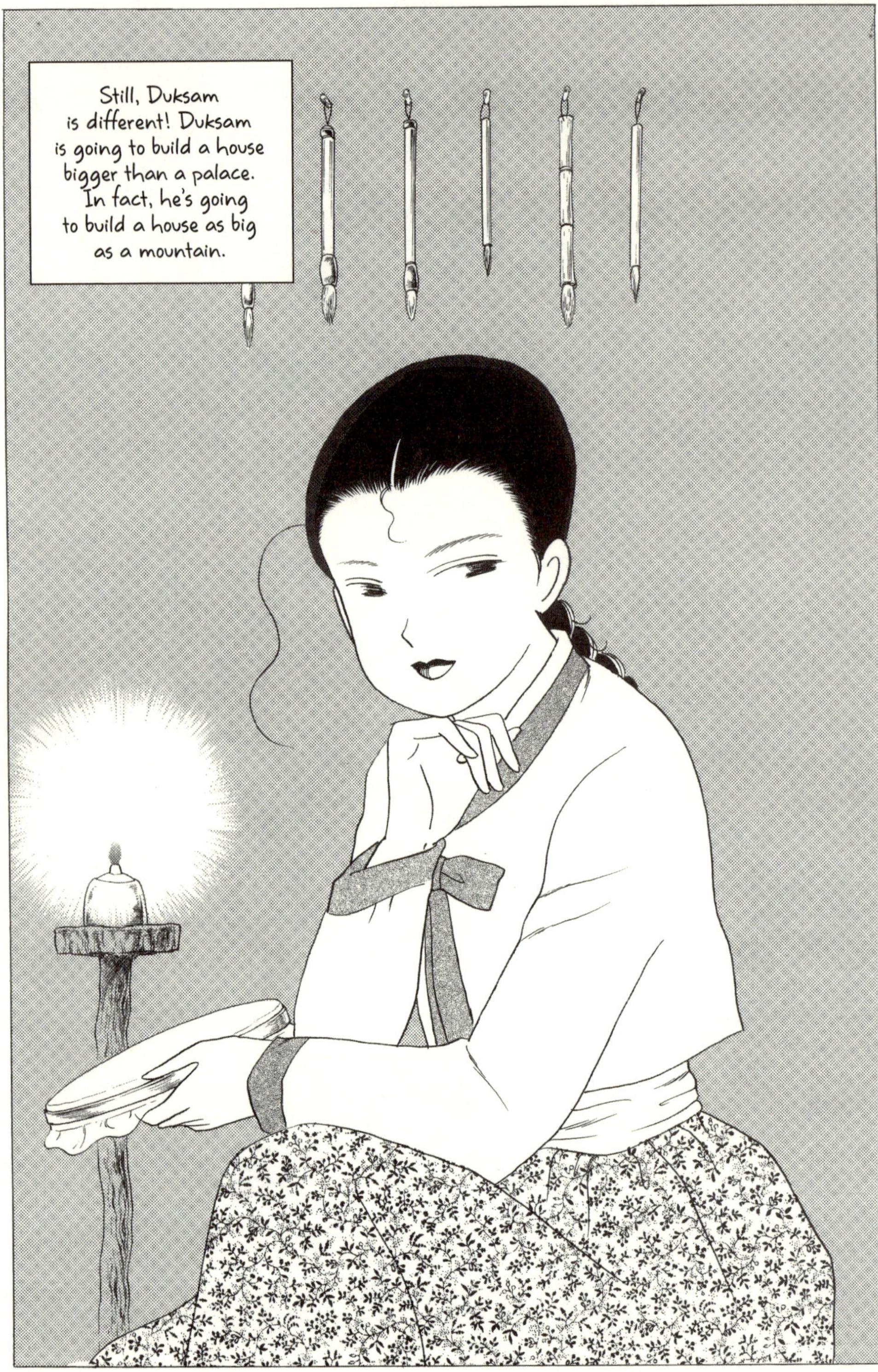
Still, Duksam is different! Duksam is going to build a house bigger than a palace. In fact, he's going to build a house as big as a mountain.

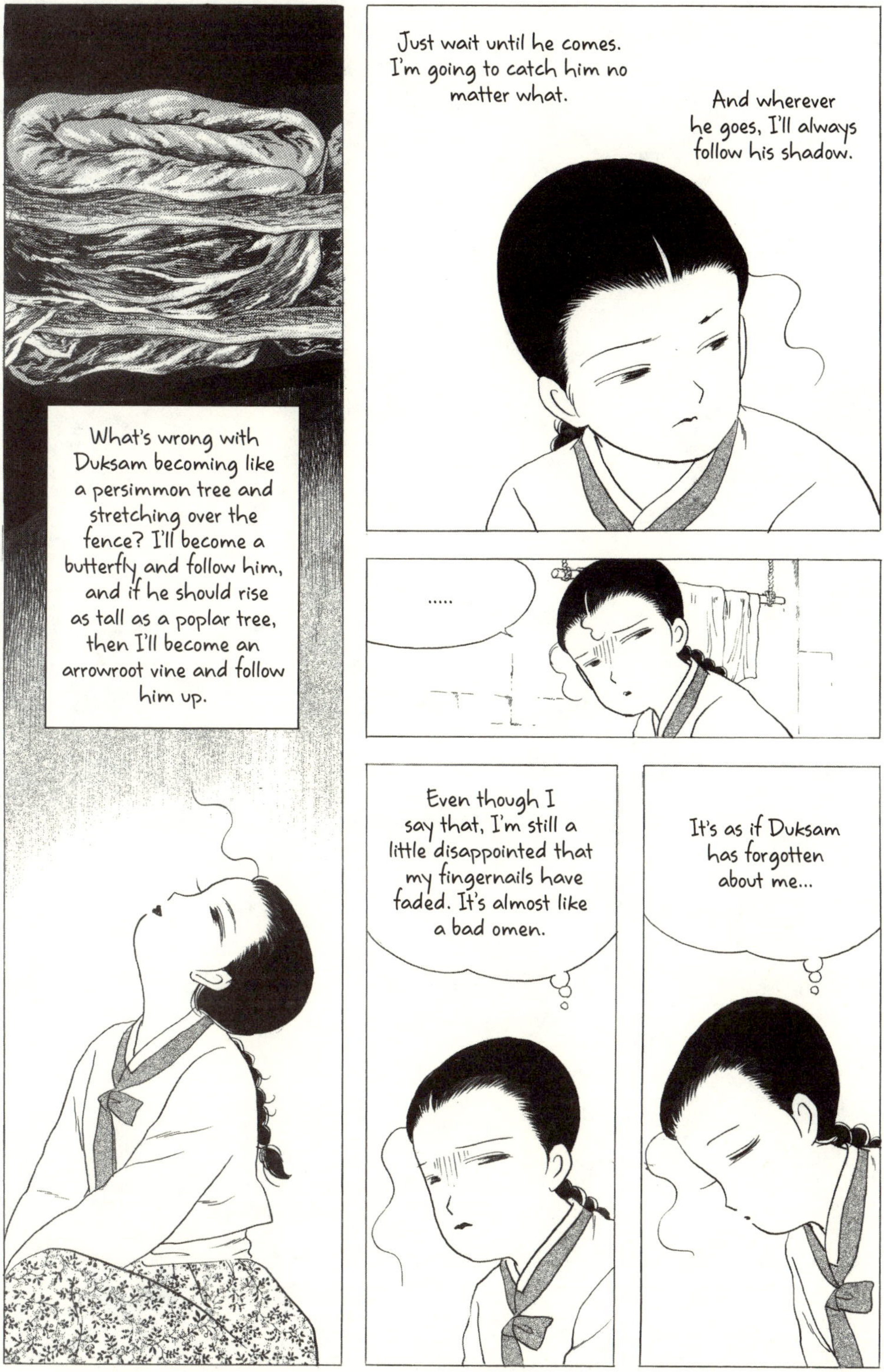
What's wrong with Duksam becoming like a persimmon tree and stretching over the fence? I'll become a butterfly and follow him, and if he should rise as tall as a poplar tree, then I'll become an arrowroot vine and follow him up.
Just wait until he comes. I'm going to catch him no matter what.
And wherever he goes, I'll always follow his shadow.
.....
Even though I say that, I'm still a little disappointed that my fingernails have faded. It's almost like a bad omen.
It's as if Duksam has forgotten about me...

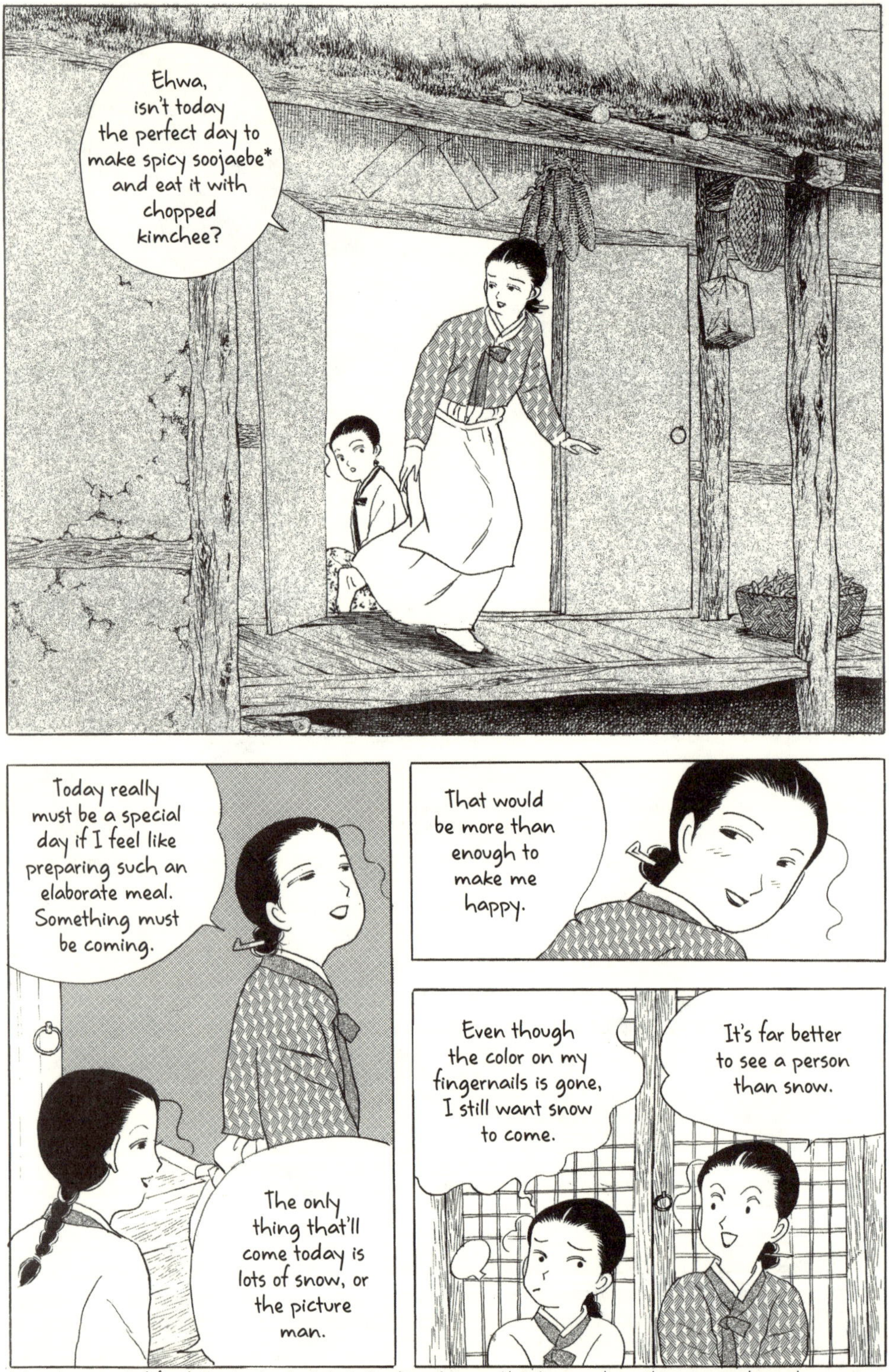
Ehwa, isn't today the perfect day to make spicy soojaebe* and eat it with chopped kimchee?
Today really must be a special day if I feel like preparing such an elaborate meal. Something must be coming.
The only thing that'll come today is lots of snow, or the picture man.
That would be more than enough to make me happy.
Even though the color on my fingernails is gone, I still want snow to come.
It's far better to see a person than snow.

* Soojaebe is a noodle (of sorts). Dough is hand pulled into thin oblong shapes and boiled in a soup base with potatoes, zucchini and green onion.

I think we should have made some extra dough.
This is enough for the two of us.
You never know. Someone just may stop by.
If someone does come, are you planning to give them overcooked soojaebe?
Why are you being so negative? I'm just saying that it would be nice to welcome a guest with food.

What to do? My Ehwa is so heartbroken because the color on her fingernails has faded. It's a shame that I can't take off my fingernails and give them to her.
Hmph!
CUCKOO!
CUCKOO!

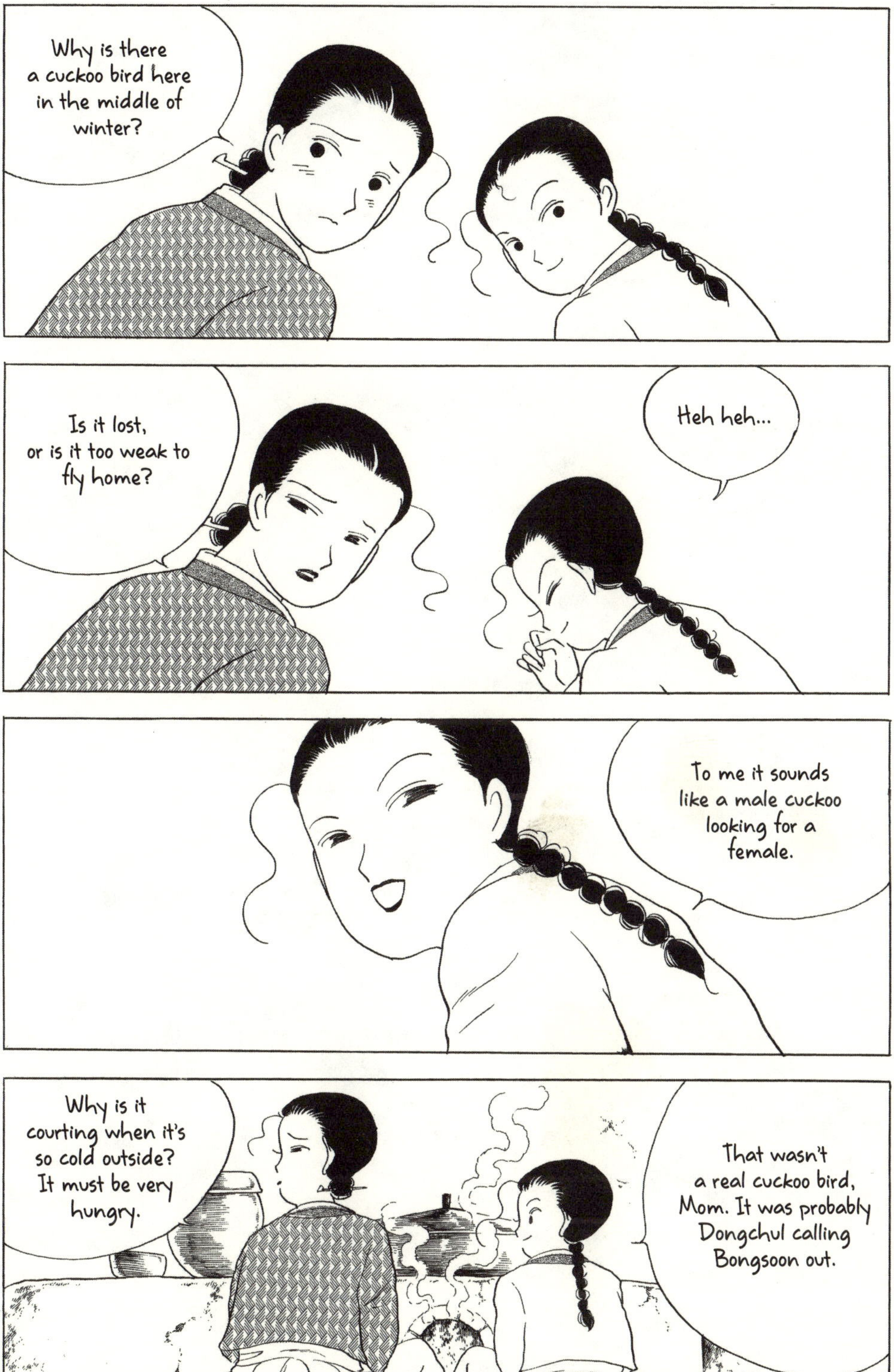

Why is there a cuckoo bird here in the middle of winter?
Is it lost, or is it too weak to fly home?
Heh heh...
To me it sounds like a male cuckoo looking for a female.
Why is it courting when it's so cold outside? It must be very hungry.
That wasn't a real cuckoo bird, Mom. It was probably Dongchul calling Bongsoon out.

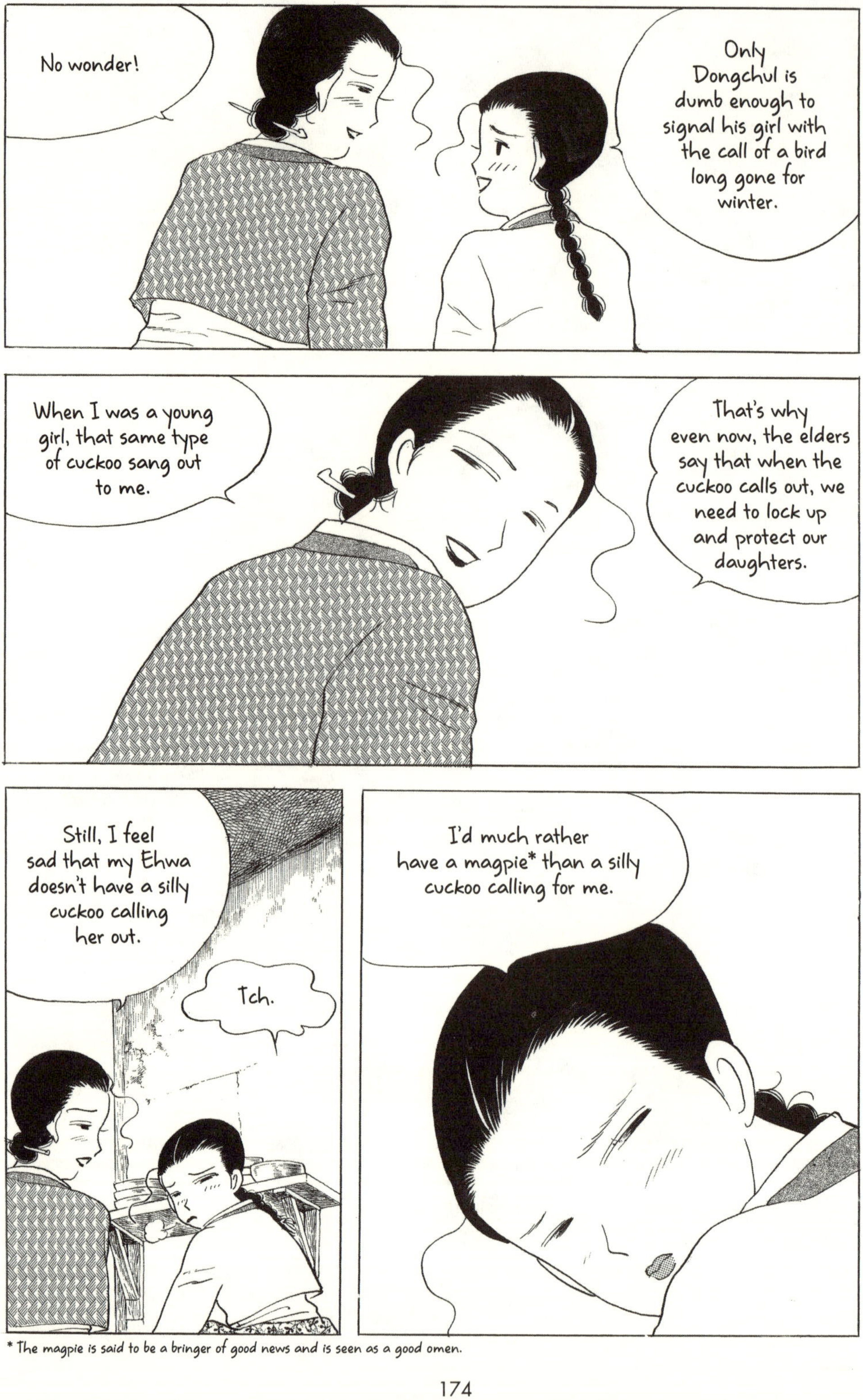
No wonder!
Only Dongchul is dumb enough to signal his girl with the call of a bird long gone for winter.
When I was a young girl, that same type of cuckoo sang out to me.
That's why even now, the elders say that when the cuckoo calls out, we need to lock up and protect our daughters.
Still, I feel sad that my Ehwa doesn't have a silly cuckoo calling her out.
Tch.
I'd much rather have a magpie* than a silly cuckoo calling for me.

* The magpie is said to be a bringer of good news and is seen as a good omen.

"Don't worry. It's said that the first snow brings even better tidings than a magpie."

"Even if there is no news, I'd be just as happy to see lots and lots of snow."

"Because only after then will the barley be in season and only after then will my daughter get married."

Thy-Thump Thy-Thump

"Huh?"

"Where are you going?"

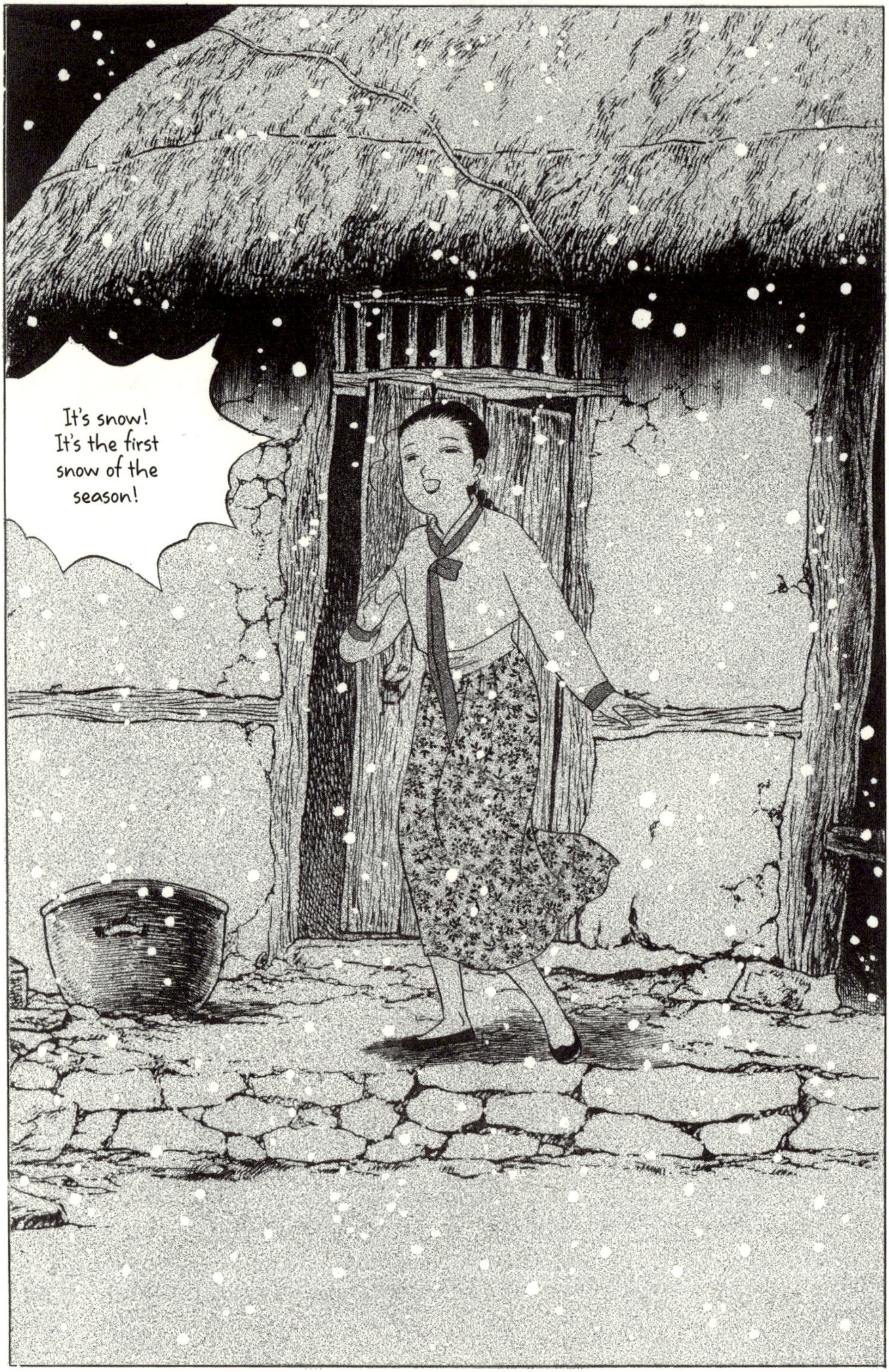
It's snow! It's the first snow of the season!

Come on, snow! Come and cover the world in your blanket!
You're saying that because you want to get married, aren't you?
That's not it.
I've been waiting for the snow so I can make a snowman as large as Duksam.

I think I'll make a snowman as big as my picture man tomorrow, as well.
CUCKOO!
CUCKOO!
CUCKOO!
CUCKOO!
Has that cuckoo still not found its mate? Why is he crying out like that?

CUCKOO!
CUCKOO!
CUCKOO!
That doesn't sound like Dongchul.
Who could it be that's looking for its mate in the middle of the night?

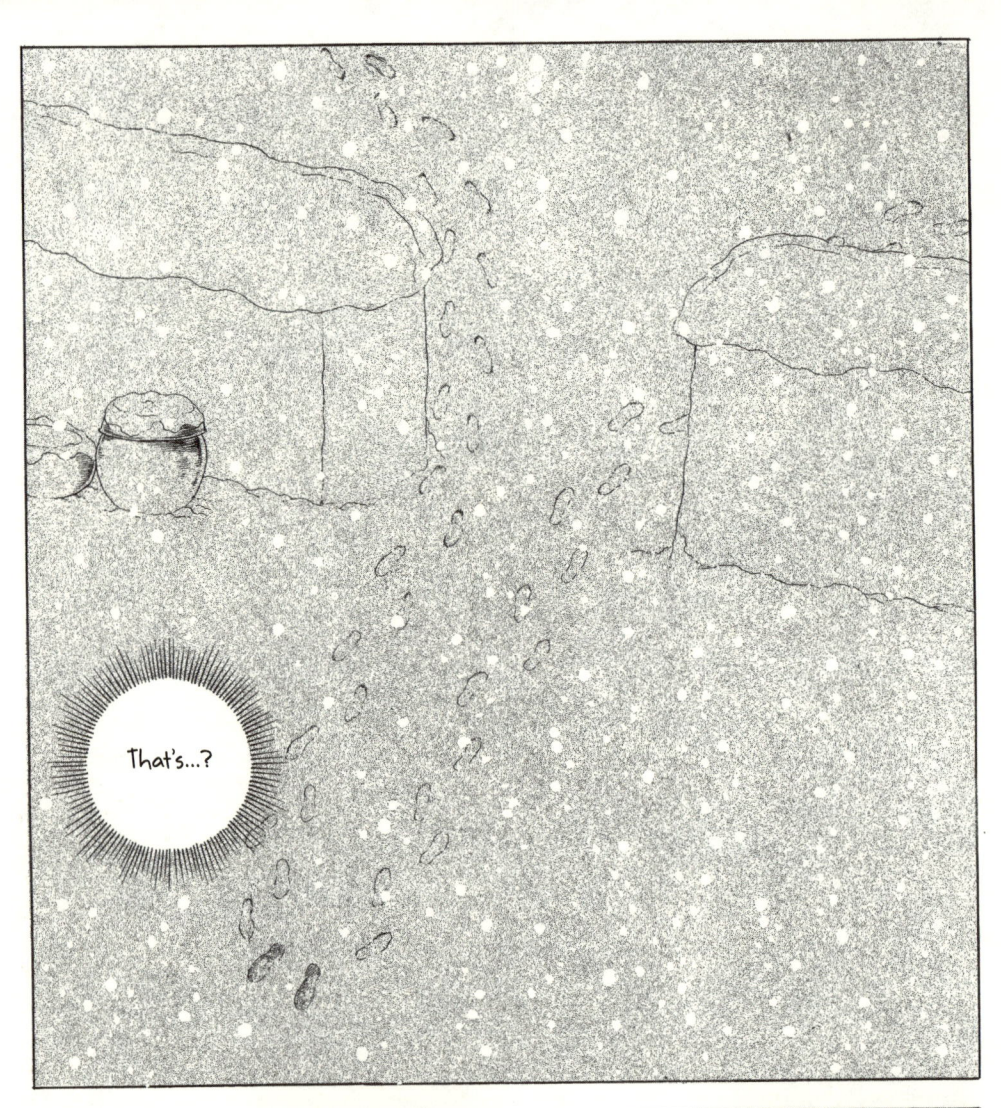

That's...?

It looks like someone came to our house!

The footprints are large. They're definitely a man's. But who could it be?

Why did he come into the middle of the yard, and what was he looking for?

He went this way...

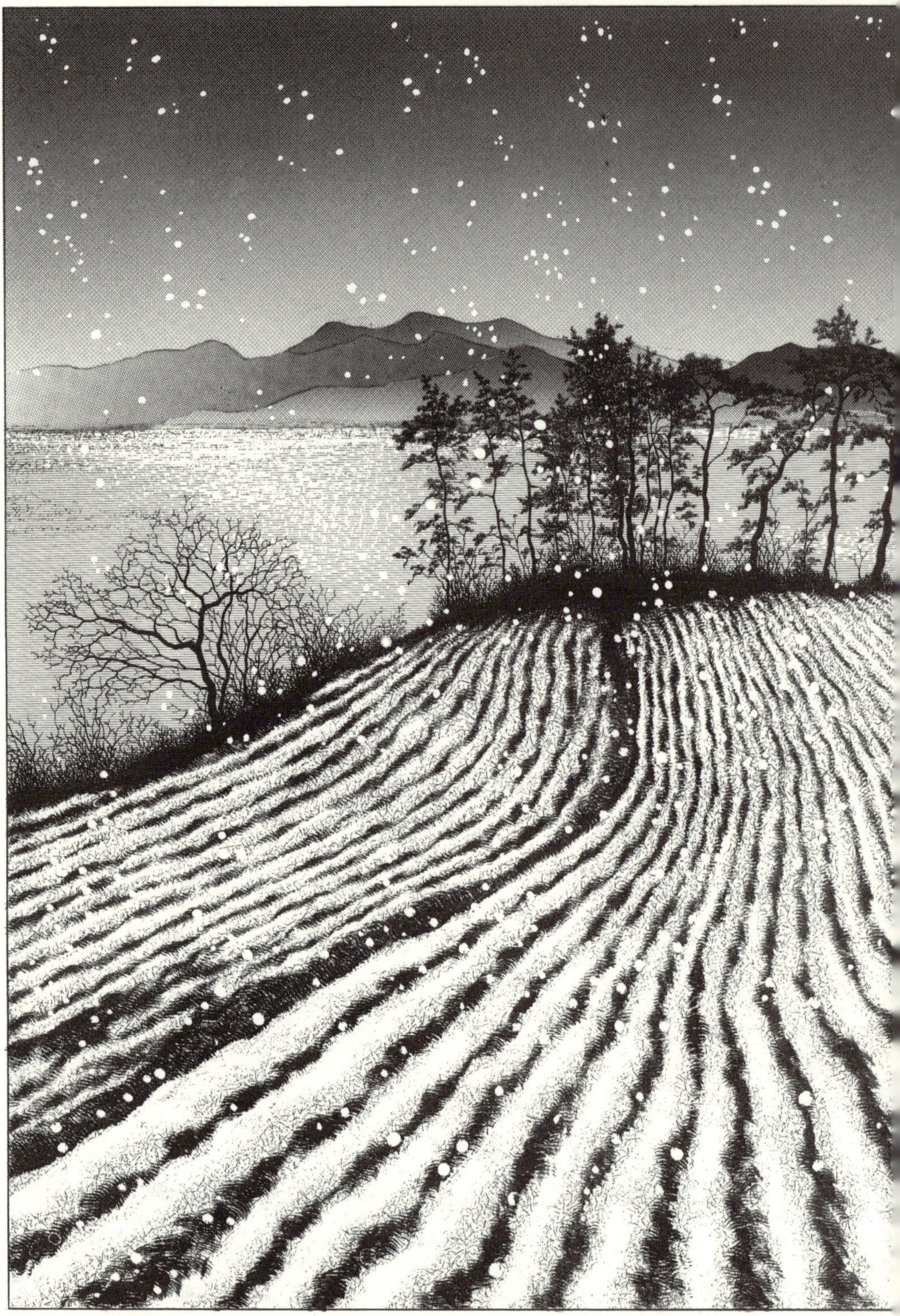

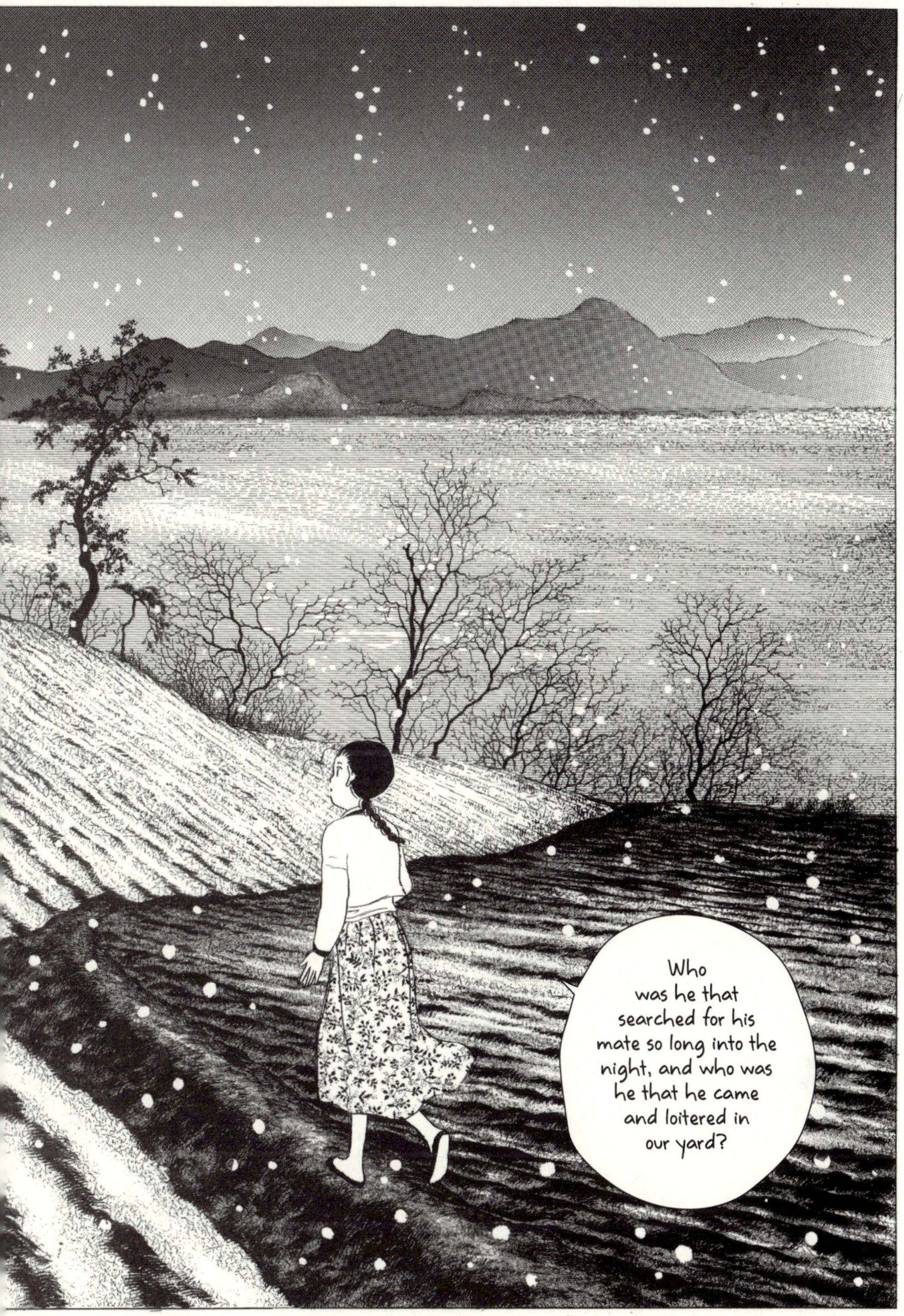
Who was he that searched for his mate so long into the night, and who was he that he came and loitered in our yard?

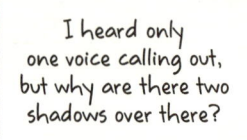

I heard only one voice calling out, but why are there two shadows over there?

It's Duksam!

And the owner of the flower shoes is you.

Idiot... There are no cuckoo birds in the middle of winter.

The cuckoo is a bird that sings only in the dead of summer. As soon as the cold winds blow, it flies away and doesn't return until spring has arrived.

Still, you understood and came out, right?

I did.

Whether it was the cuckoo or the cicada that sang in the middle of snow, I'd still have understood and come out.

I was planning to come back with the cuckoo in March, but I missed you, so I came back early.

I was planning to come back as a butterfly with the arrival of spring, but I couldn't wait any longer, so I came back in winter.

Though the ocean was large, it couldn't possibly quench my longing to see you, so I ran back here.

And yet, compared to the way I felt just sitting and waiting, you had it better.

Will you wear these flower shoes and follow me?

Though I may not have gold or silver, when you wear these shoes, flowers will bloom where your steps fall.

I'd go even if it wasn't a flower path, and I'd go even if it wasn't fertile soil. I refuse to sit and wait any longer.

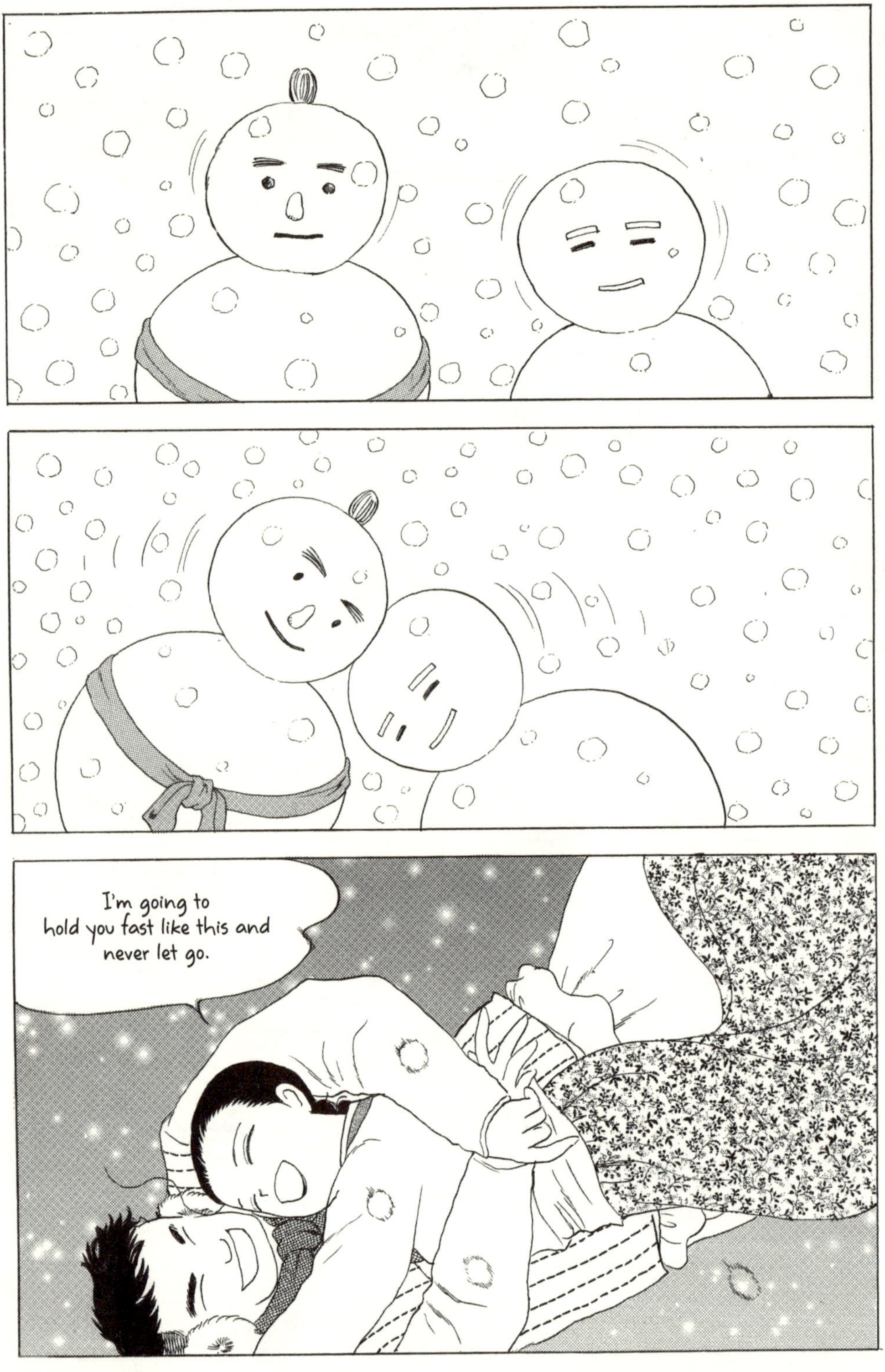
I'm going to hold you fast like this and never let go.

I guess there really is a cuckoo that sings in the dead of winter.	Though people say the cuckoo's song is beautiful, it's not as beautiful as a winter cuckoo's song.	Maybe this is why the first snow of the season is considered to be a good sign.

Silly girl! I told her we should have made extra soojaebe dough just in case we had an unexpected guest, but she just had to be difficult and contradict me. Now what are we going to serve him?
And you never know if another person might unexpectedly drop by.
I'd better get back first and at least begin boiling some water.

Chapter Seven

GUEST

동화

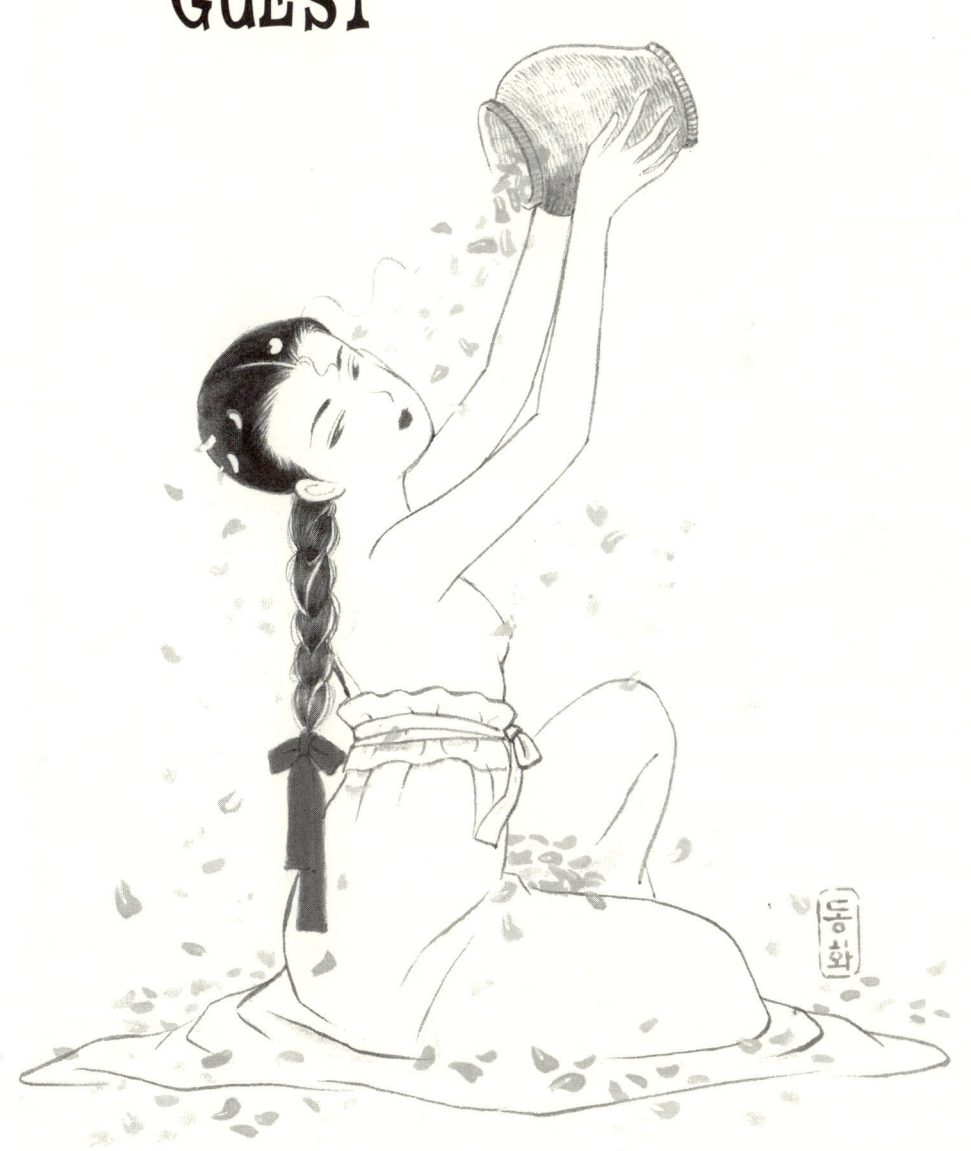

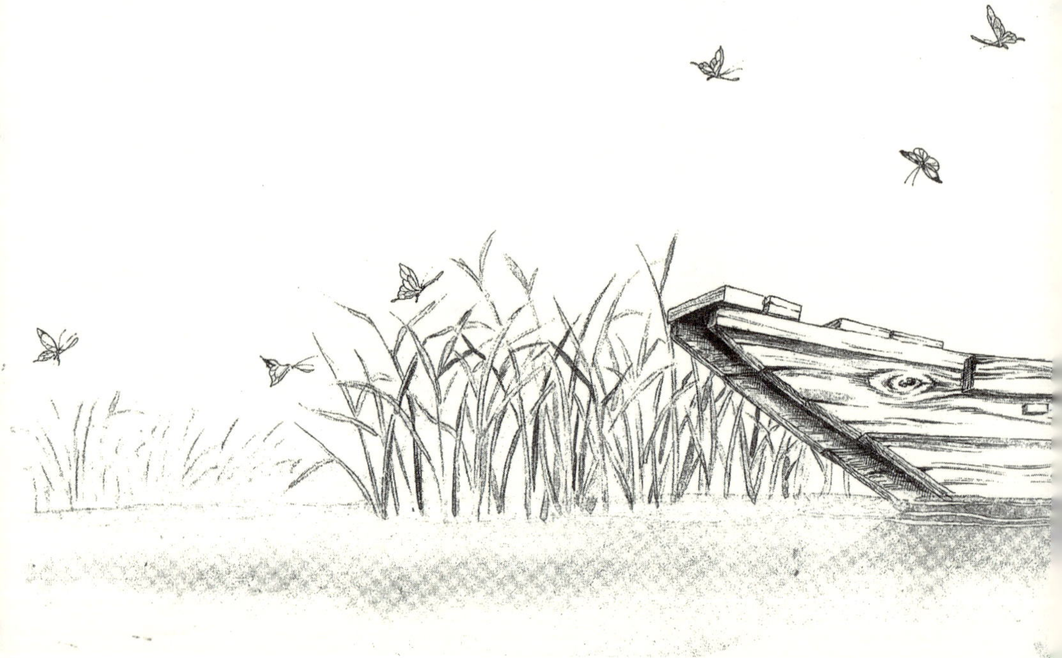

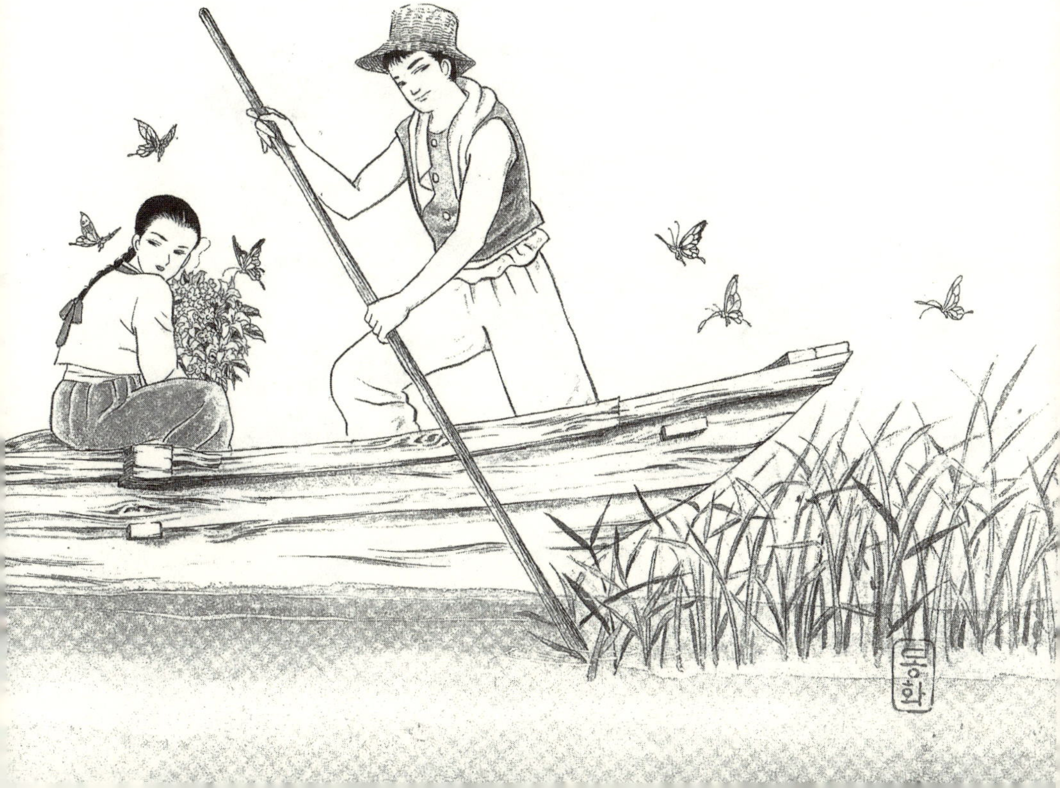

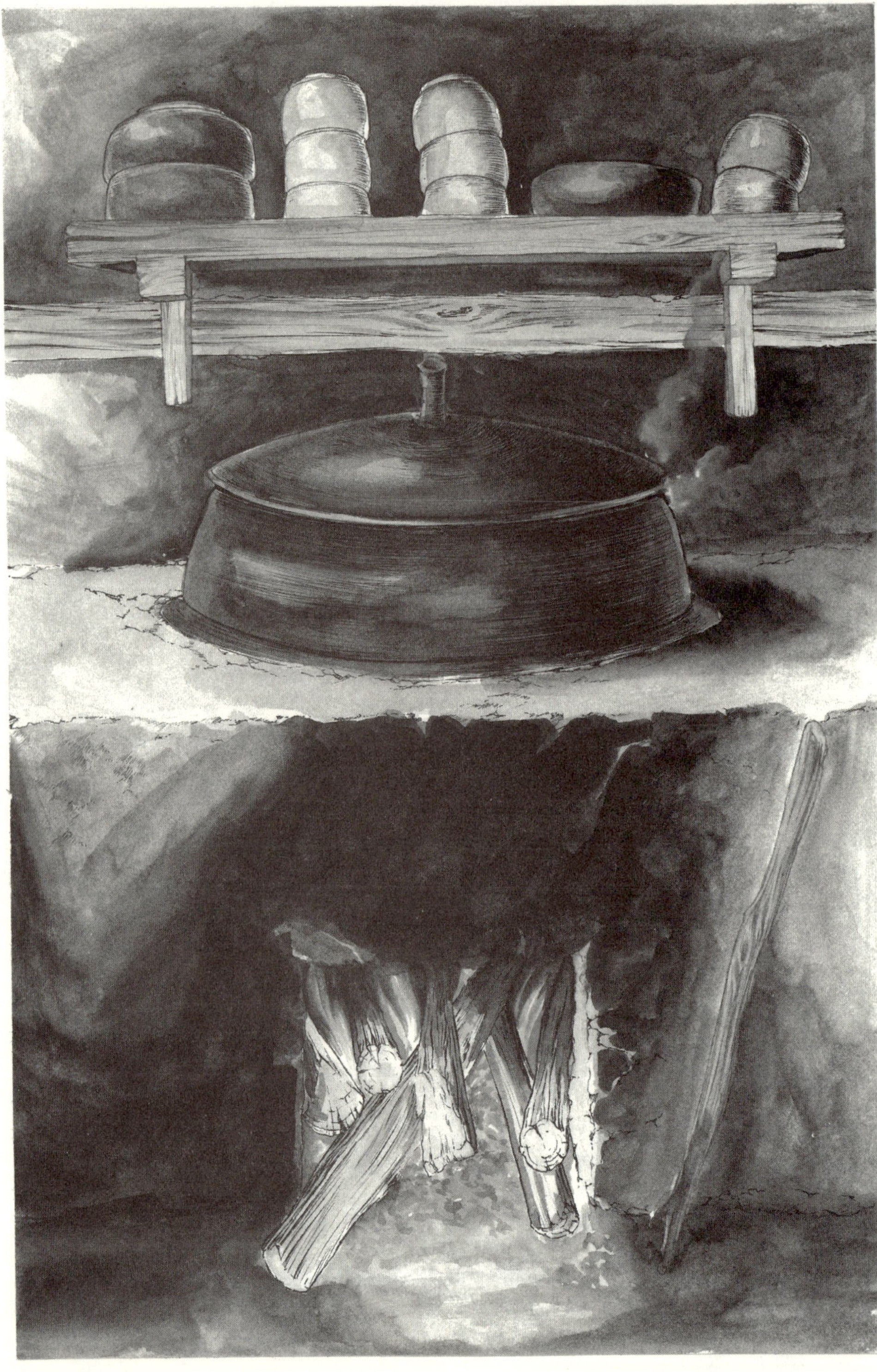

BUBBLE BUBBLE

Ah, hot!

I've gone crazy. Why did I grab that hot lid with my bare hands?! I'm not even paying attention to what I'm doing.

WHOOO

Hmm... It looks like instead of making soojaebe, I'm making glue.

And here I was just putting more logs into the fire...

Why am I like this right now? Why am I so restless and fidgety?

Anyway, why aren't those children back yet? The soojaebe has long since boiled over and even the pot is now about to melt.

Wait a minute... Did I just say "children"?

Children?

Ha! All this time, I've been referring to Ehwa as a child and now that I'm saying children, I feel as if I have lots and lots of kids.

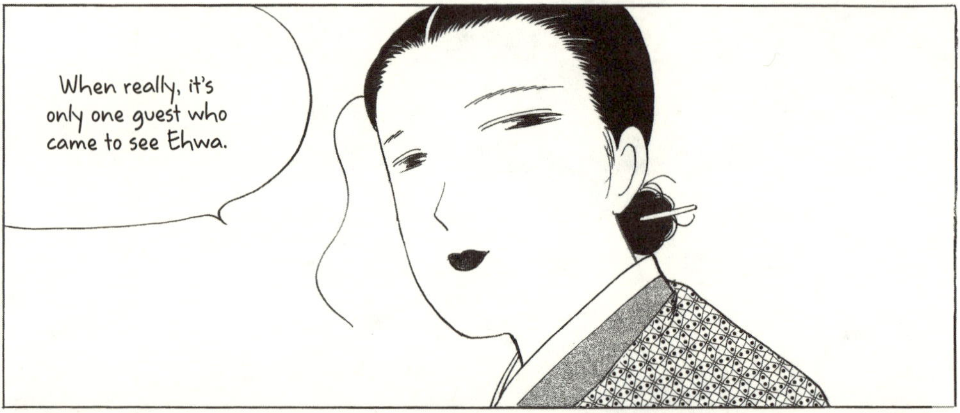
When really, it's only one guest who came to see Ehwa.

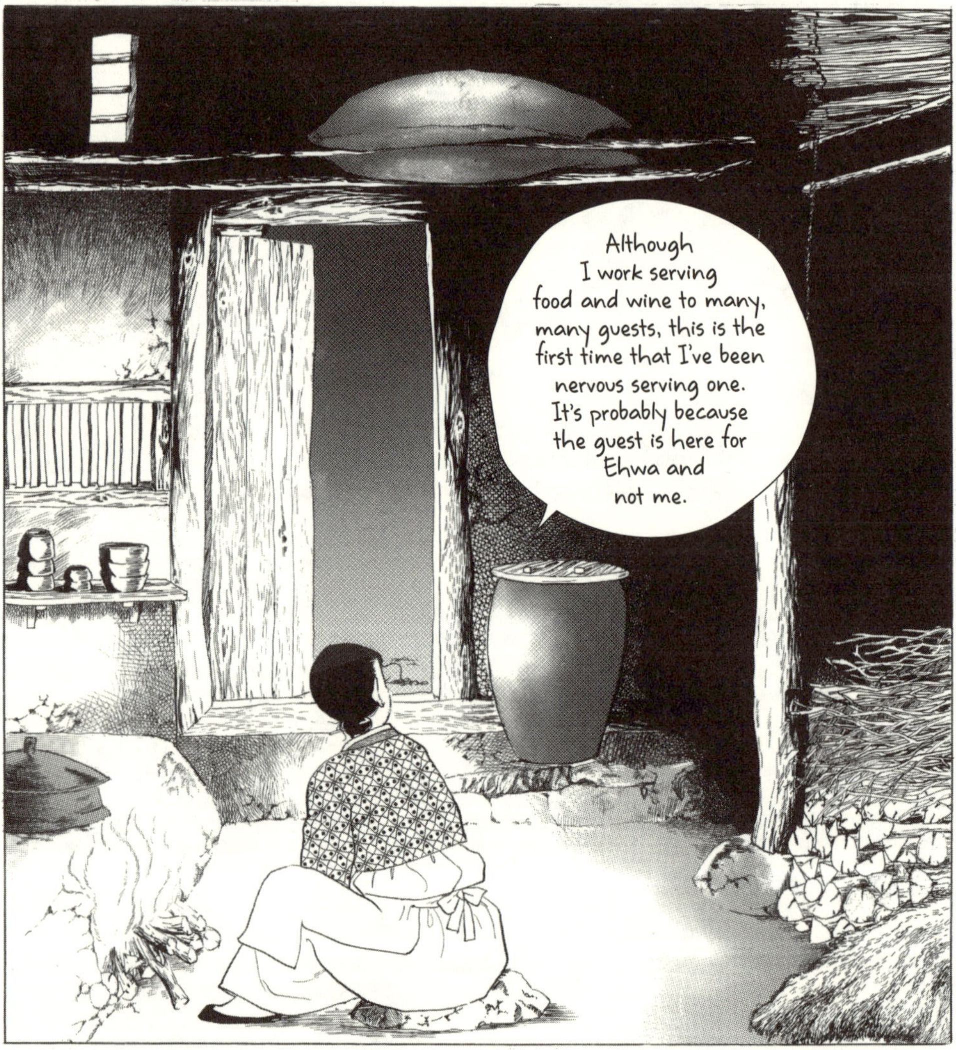
Although I work serving food and wine to many, many guests, this is the first time that I've been nervous serving one. It's probably because the guest is here for Ehwa and not me.

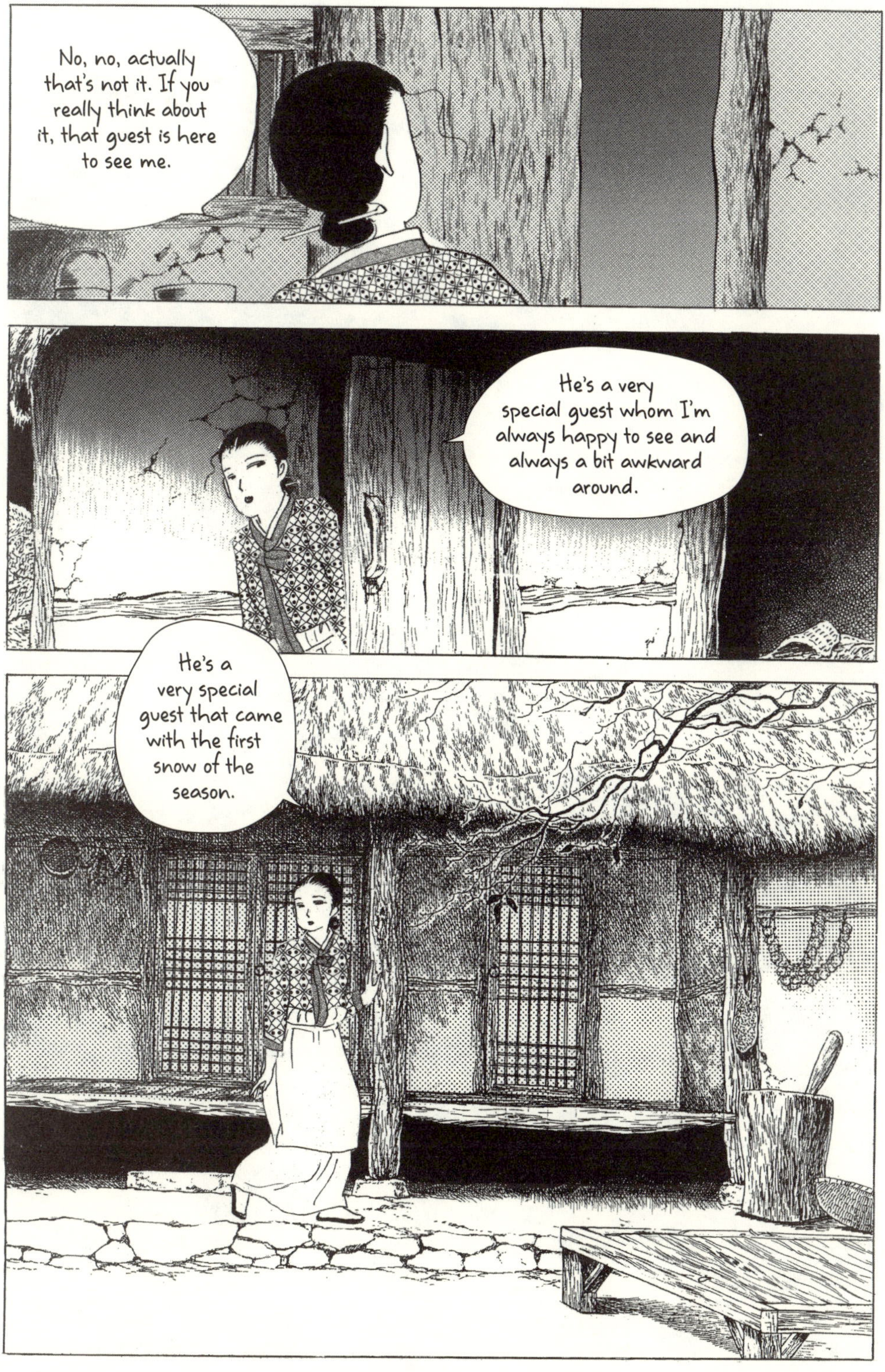
No, no, actually that's not it. If you really think about it, that guest is here to see me.
He's a very special guest whom I'm always happy to see and always a bit awkward around.
He's a very special guest that came with the first snow of the season.

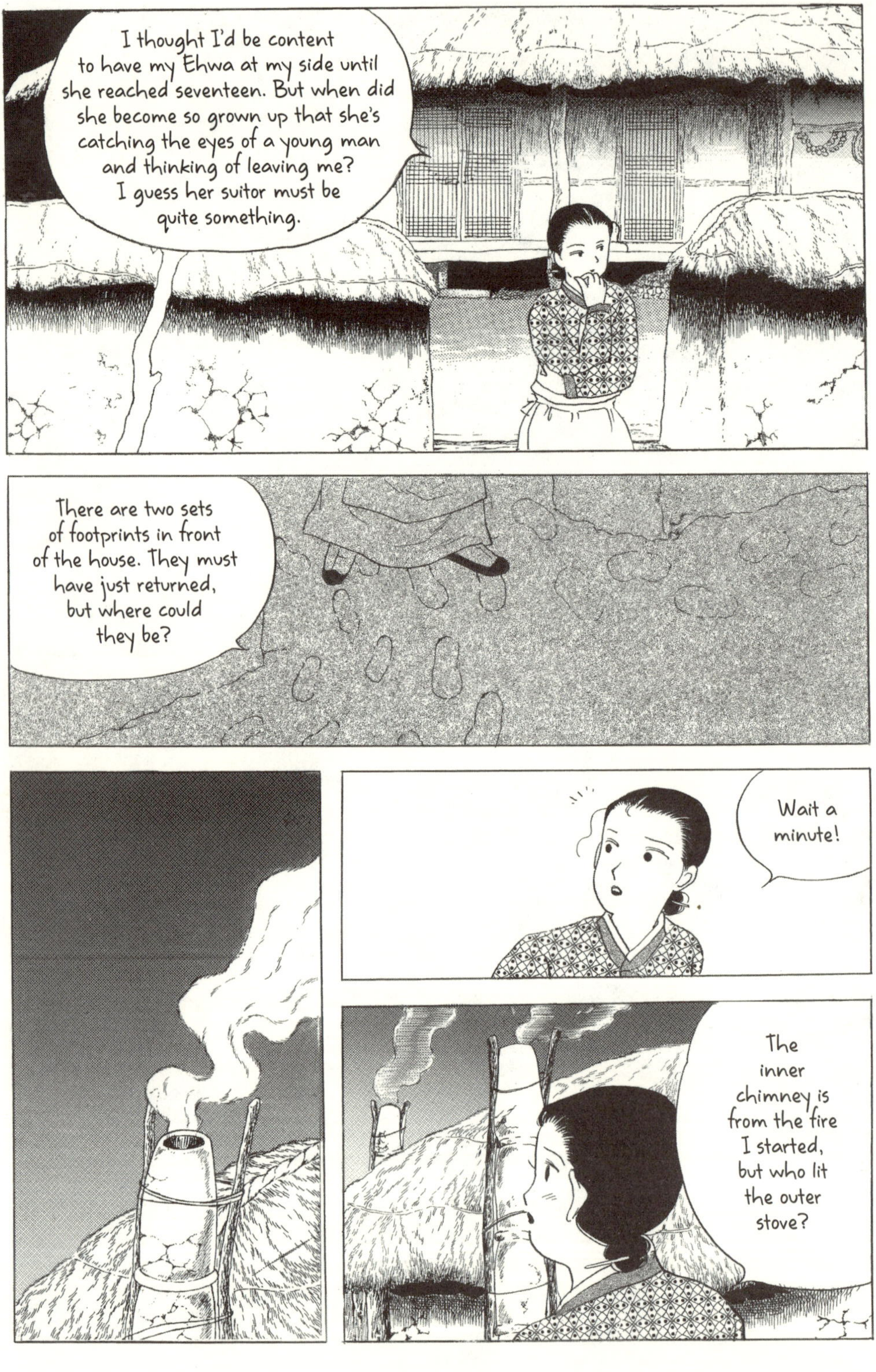
I thought I'd be content to have my Ehwa at my side until she reached seventeen. But when did she become so grown up that she's catching the eyes of a young man and thinking of leaving me? I guess her suitor must be quite something.
There are two sets of footprints in front of the house. They must have just returned, but where could they be?
Wait a minute!
The inner chimney is from the fire I started, but who lit the outer stove?

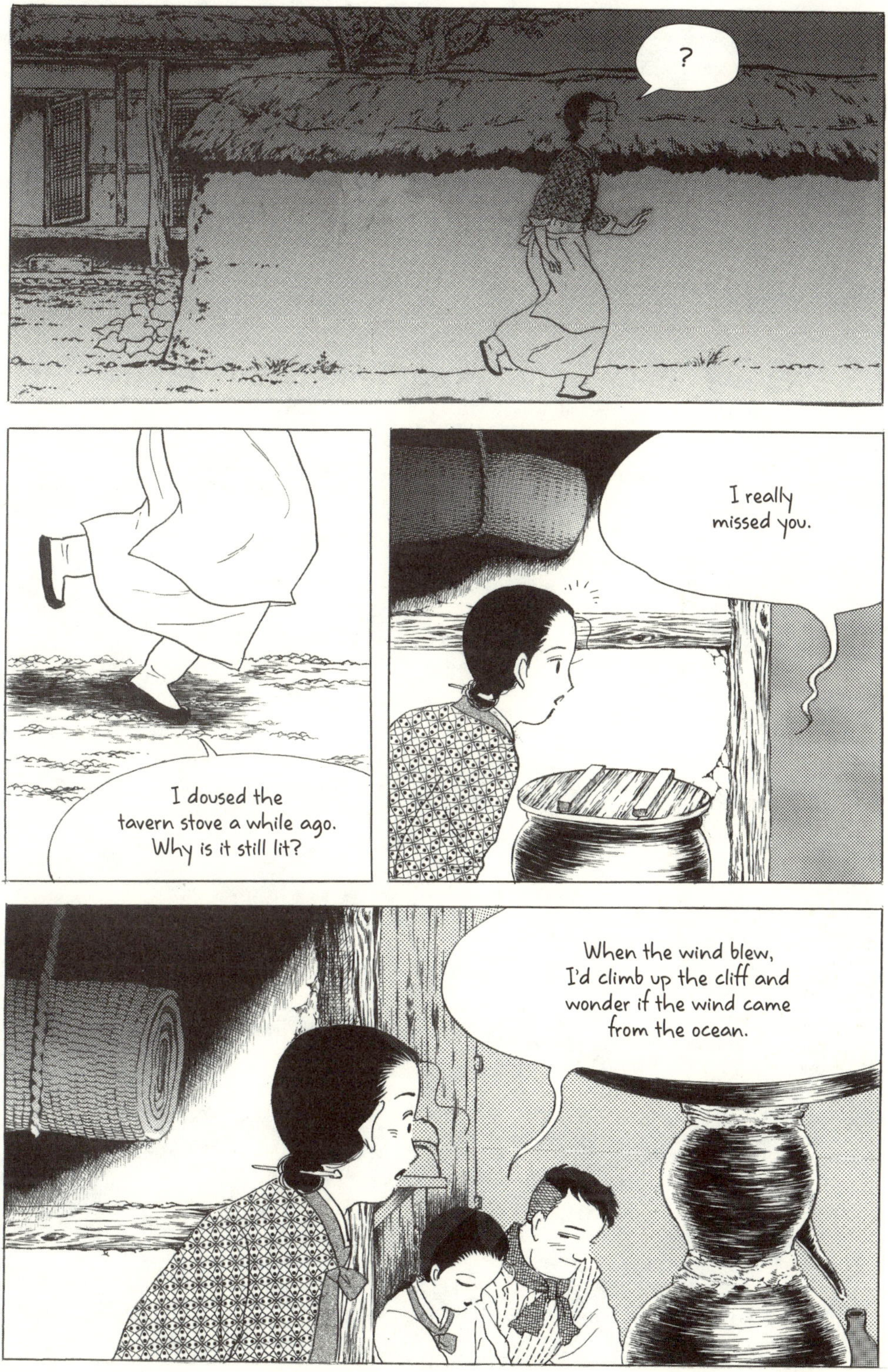
?
I doused the tavern stove a while ago. Why is it still lit?
I really missed you.
When the wind blew, I'd climb up the cliff and wonder if the wind came from the ocean.

And I'd sniff the wind in hopes that it carried your scent with it.
When it rained, I'd listen to see if it brought news of you, and then I'd wash my tear-stained face with the raindrops.

The ocean was terrible, but the waves crashing on the boat at night were even more frightening.
Whenever it was scary like that, I'd say your name and the waves would calm, and my heart would calm too.

I knew that the more fish I caught, the sooner I would see you again. And so I began to fish day and night.
Every time I pulled in the net, I imagined I was running my fingers through your hair. I never got tired, so I kept pulling and pulling.
I think you've caught me in that net.
Pfft.
They say a good fisherman never lets go of the fish he has caught.
Occasionally, there are fish that get caught on purpose.

On a night like this, I feel like going out to sea. I want to call out your name as the waves crash.
Like me.
What are you doing outside in this cold?

Duksam came back, so I lit the stove in order to make him some hot soup and rice.
And here I thought it was a cuckoo looking for a mate, but I see now it is a special guest.
So how can you think of serving just soup and rice to a special guest like him?
Although our tavern has many guests, it's your responsibility to judge which of them are for the outer home, and which are for the inner home.
It's... it's all right. I was actually planning to come see you in daylight...
How can you steal anything in broad daylight?

?

Although a thief coming to steal a daughter is still a thief, it's better that you came to steal on a snowy night like this.

This way, when you go, you leave footprints so I can find you both and see that you're living well, and also, so I can stop by sometimes with some food.

You're not angry?

What are you doing, Ehwa? Invite him inside.

When did you make the soojaebe?
Mom, did you somehow know that Duksam was going to come today?
While I was making the soojaebe, so he'd have something hot to eat, I was also keeping an eye on the gate.
I was waiting anxiously for both of you to return.
I didn't know that! We decided to sit out there at the tavern until the sun came out.
Here I thought my daughter was still a little girl inside, even though her body had grown up. But it looks like you've become a woman, bringing your lover home...

When people see you, they'll say you've grown up to be so beautiful—but what will they say about me?
Now that you're an adult, it means I've become that much older.
I don't even need to look at a mirror to see that I've aged.
That's why today is both a happy and a sad day for me.
I'm the only one getting older, Mom. You're still the same. There would be no difference between you or me getting married because you still look so young.
Of all the silly things to say—

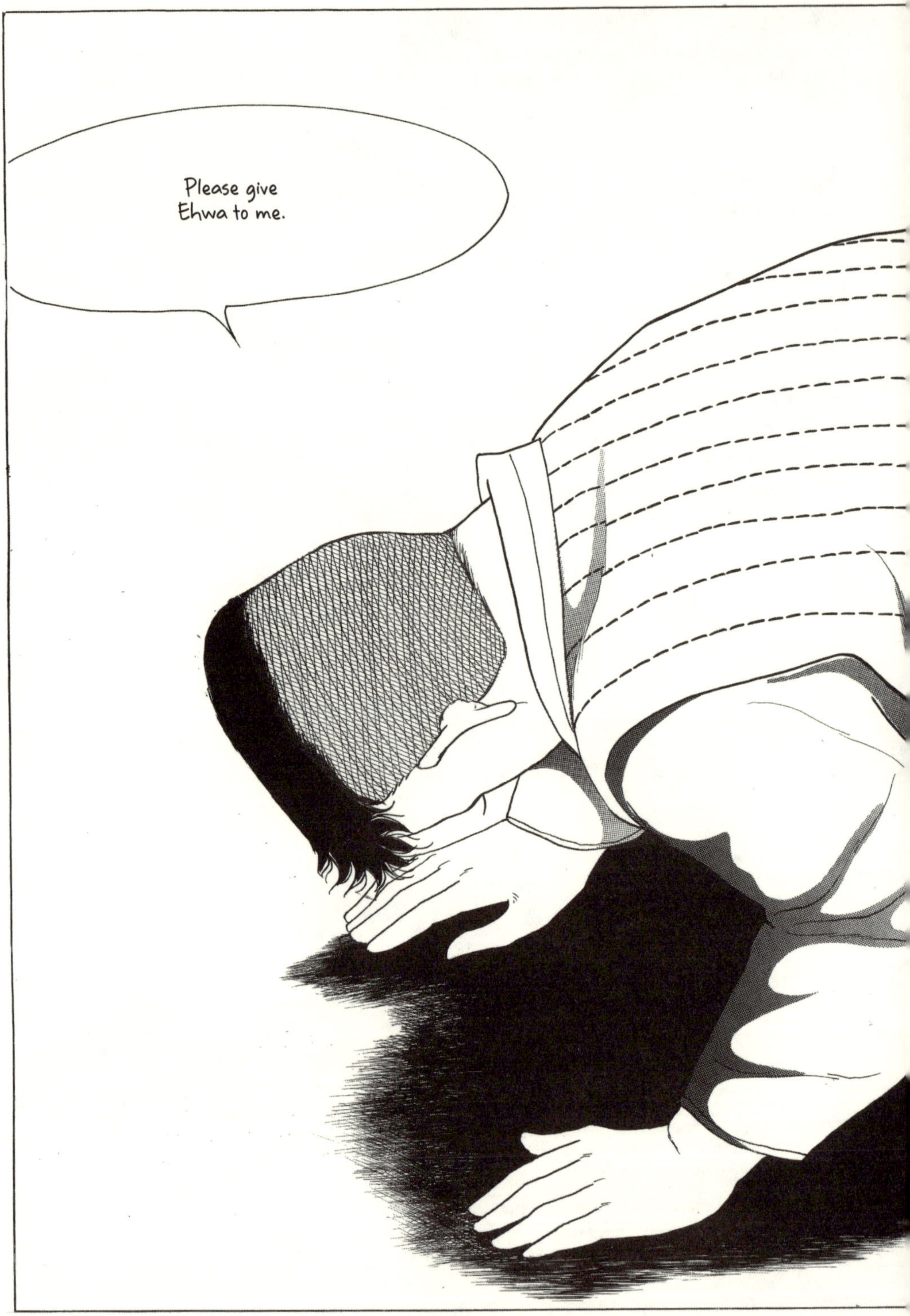
Please give Ehwa to me.

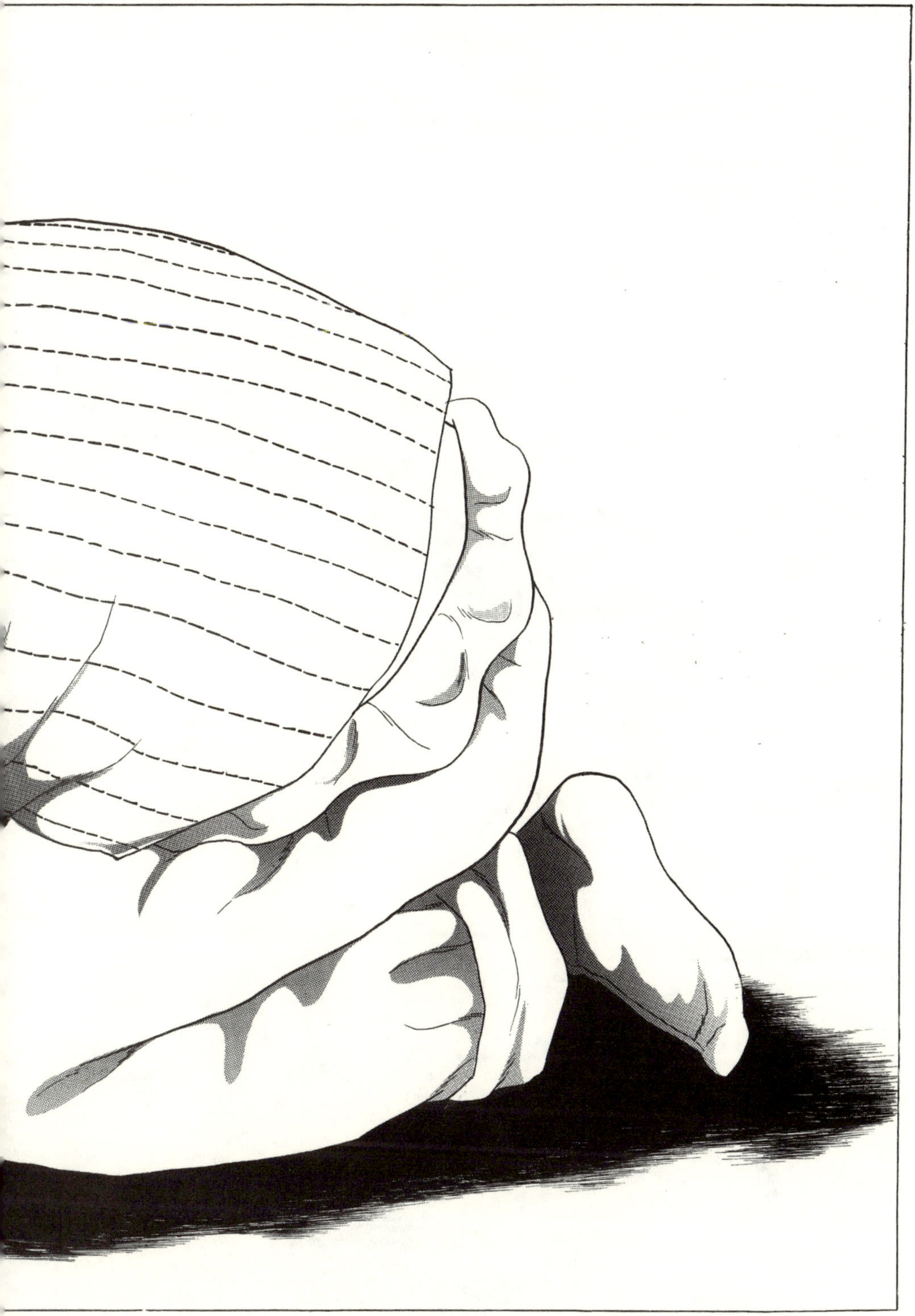

Once the sun was up, I was planning to go and bring you some camellia flowers, but I'm too impatient, so here I am now asking for your blessing.
Instead of bringing camellia flowers, I'd be just as grateful if you don't barge in on me when I'm washing my hair.
I only poured a bucket of water over your head, but you poured a bucket full of scolding over mine!
However, now that I have Ehwa, I have nothing to be sad about.
In any case, with your size, I'm not worried about you providing for my Ehwa.

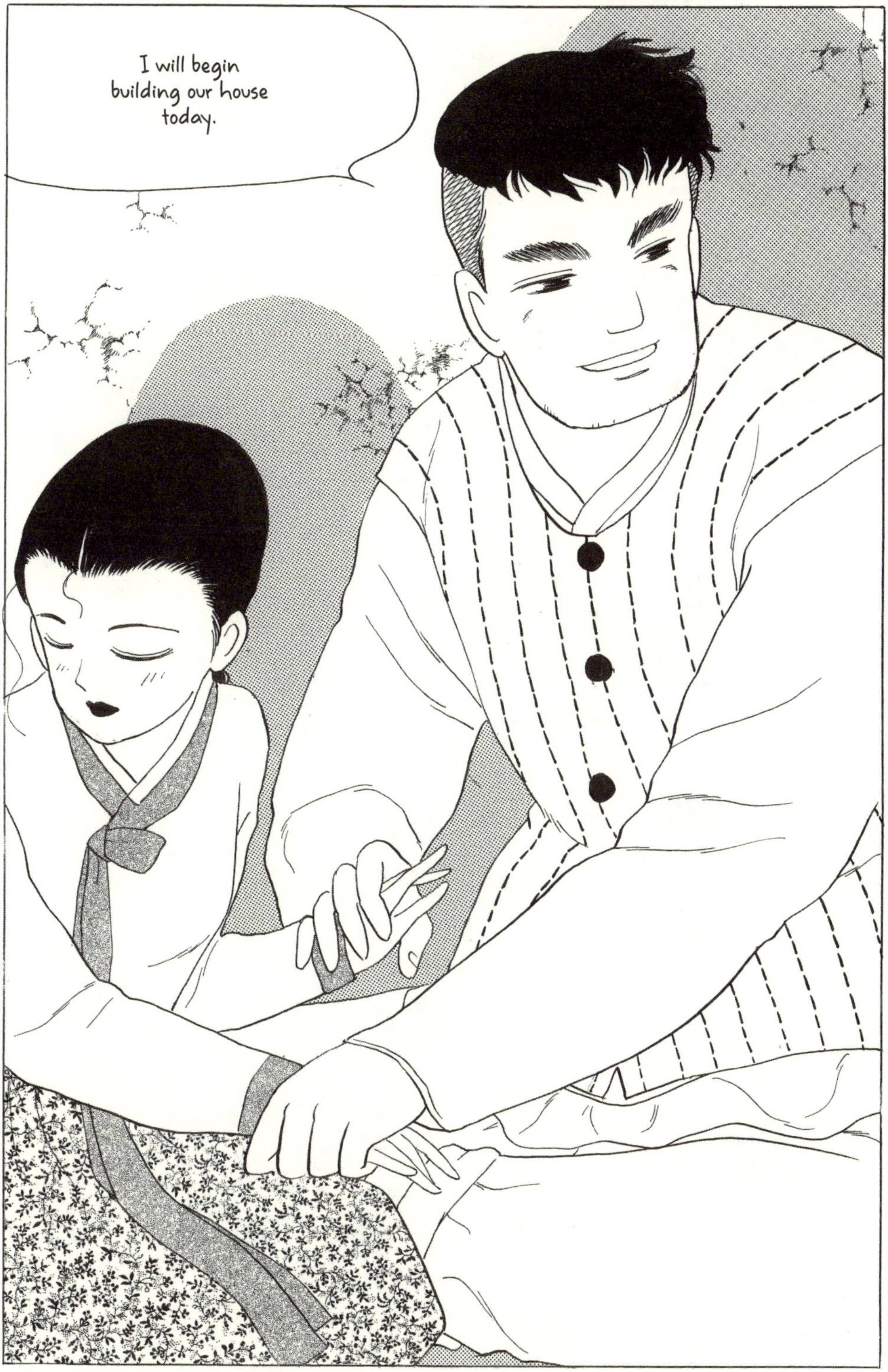
I will begin building our house today.

I will build it at the bottom of a ridge where there's plenty of sun.
Since the flowers bloom in March, I hope to marry under the apricot blossoms and the peach blossoms.
Silly fools. Do they really believe that flowers only bloom in March?
Do they really believe that apricot blossoms and peach blossoms only bloom then?

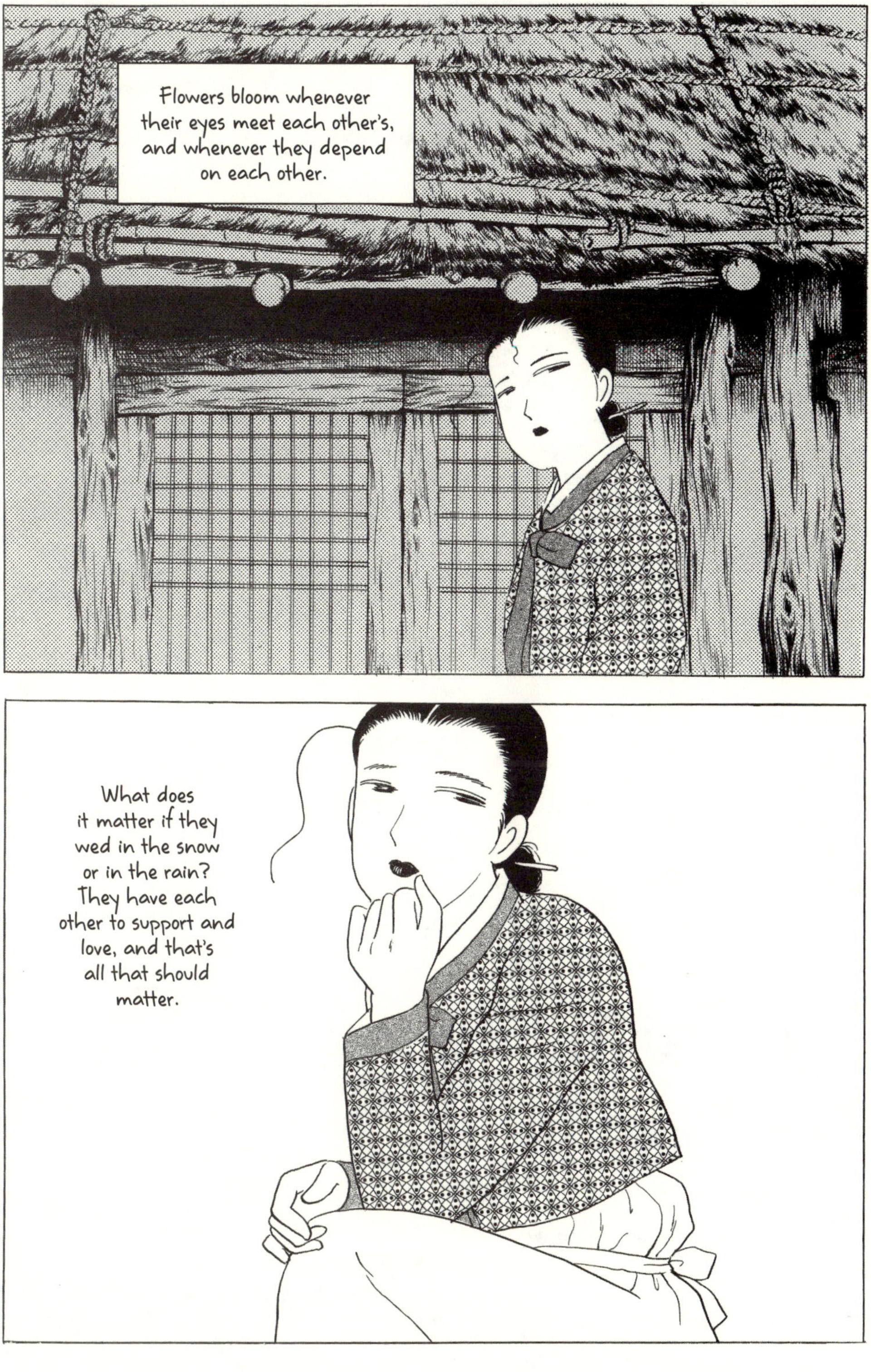
Flowers bloom whenever their eyes meet each other's, and whenever they depend on each other.
What does it matter if they wed in the snow or in the rain? They have each other to support and love, and that's all that should matter.

Mom.	Why are you coming outside in this cold weather?

Will you be all right by yourself if I get married?	It doesn't matter when you get married because I'll be sad no matter what.

Pickles taste better the longer they sit, but an unmarried woman gets crankier the longer she's single.	Still, when I look at you, I don't want to leave. I feel so sad.	It's better to arrive early and get a good seat to a show, and it's better to marry early and establish yourself.

Only foolish women complain that married life is hard. If you think about it, there is nothing better in life than getting married.

There's a shoulder you can always lean on—

There's a chest you can always embrace—

There's a face you can always stare into—

By the way, when is market day?

Tomorrow.

Perfect. Tomorrow, we'll go buy things for your wedding, and we'll also buy a few chicks.
What are you going to do with the chicks?

I'll keep them so that every time my son-in-law comes to visit I can feed him a chicken.
Ha ha...

It's snowing again. The first snow of the season brought a thief who stole my daughter. I wonder what this snow will steal from me?
You should ask your fingernails, Mom.

Yes, actually today of all days, I really miss that man's face.
I'm longing for a warm chest where I can bury the sorrow of losing my daughter.
My goodness, I really am a foolish woman! All the women in the world continue living after marrying their daughters off, and here I am making a fuss all by myself.
This spring, I'll plant gourd vines, hollyhocks and all the other flowers in the world, but I refuse to plant any impatiens.

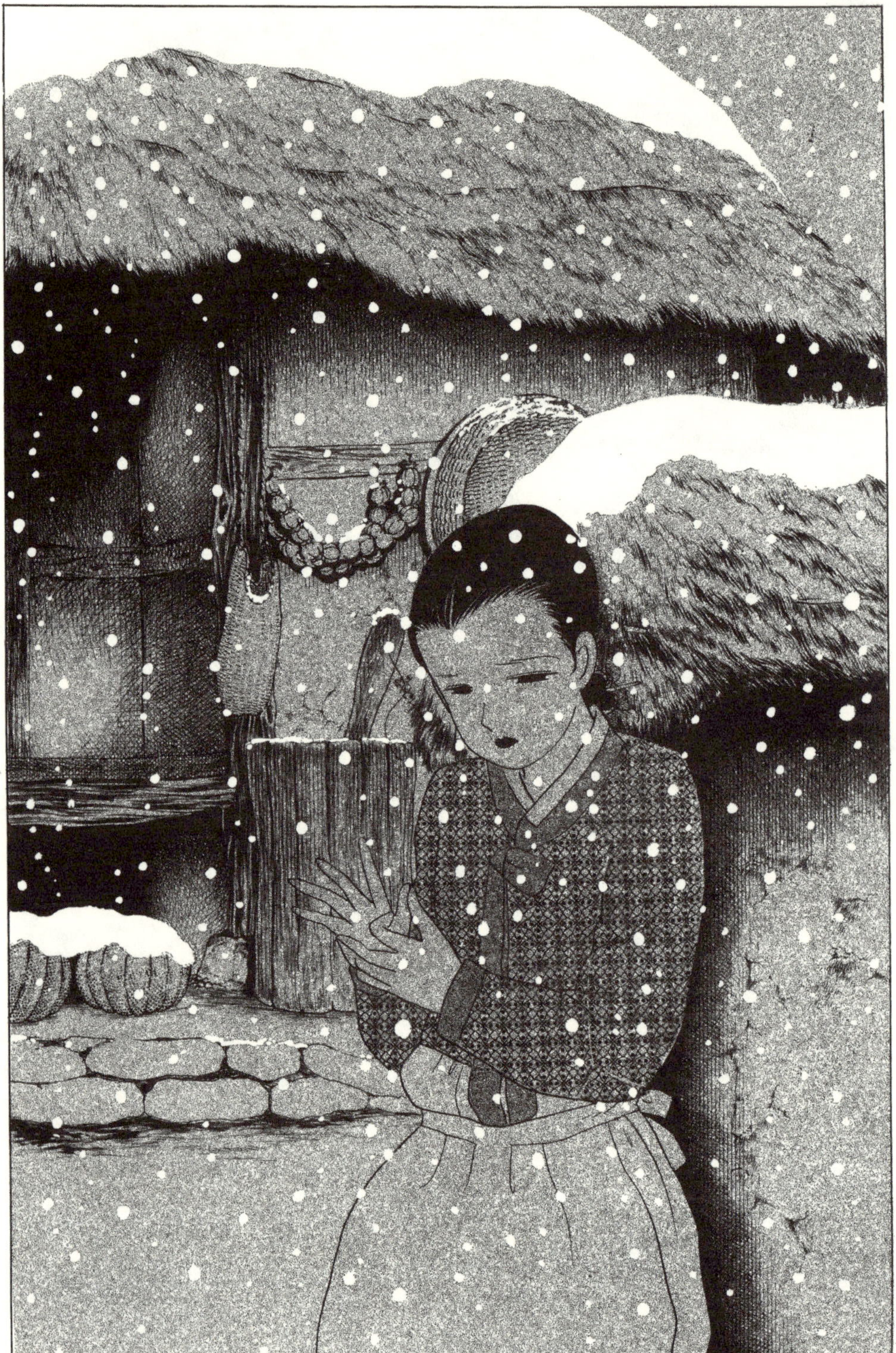

Chapter Eight

WHITE HAIR

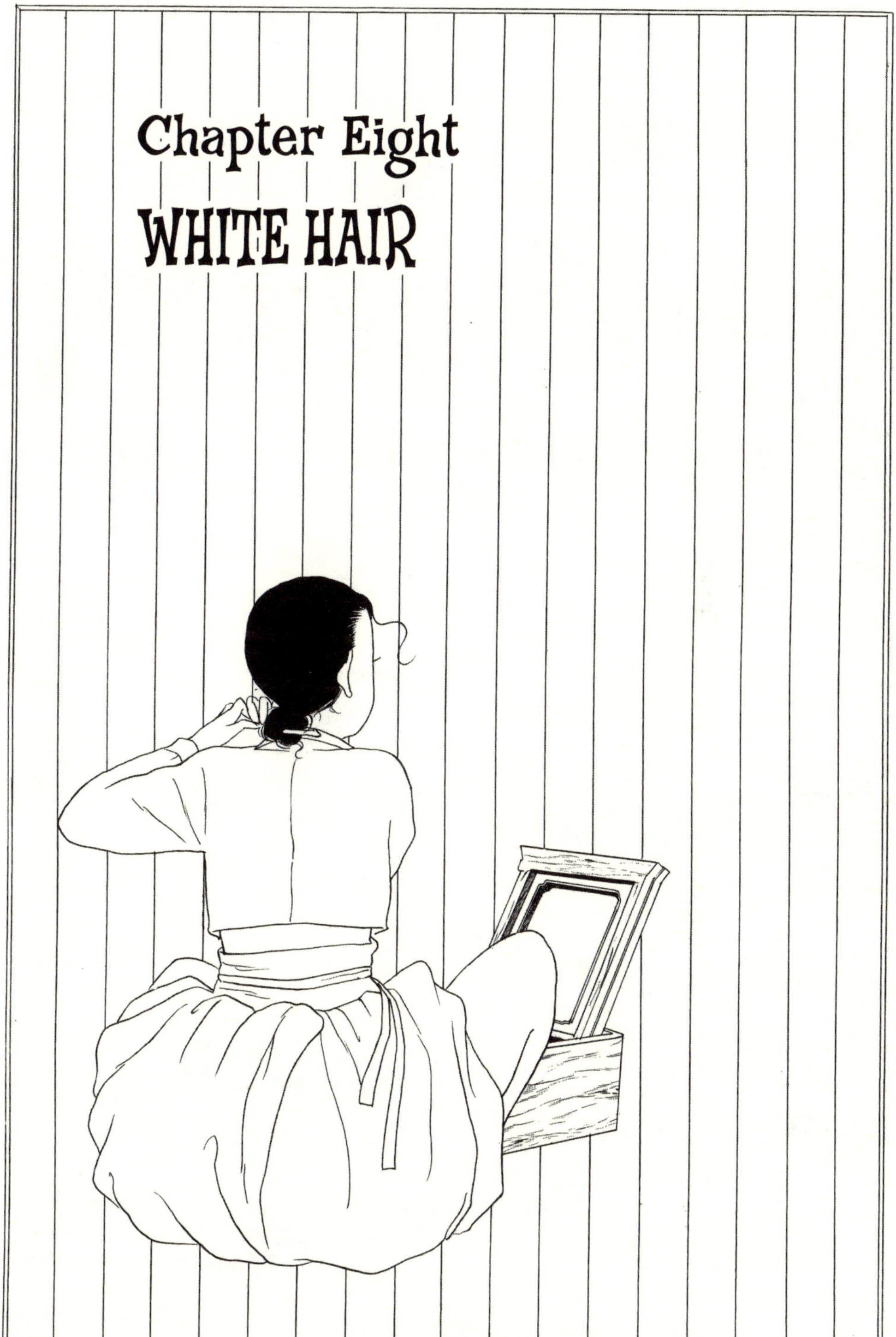

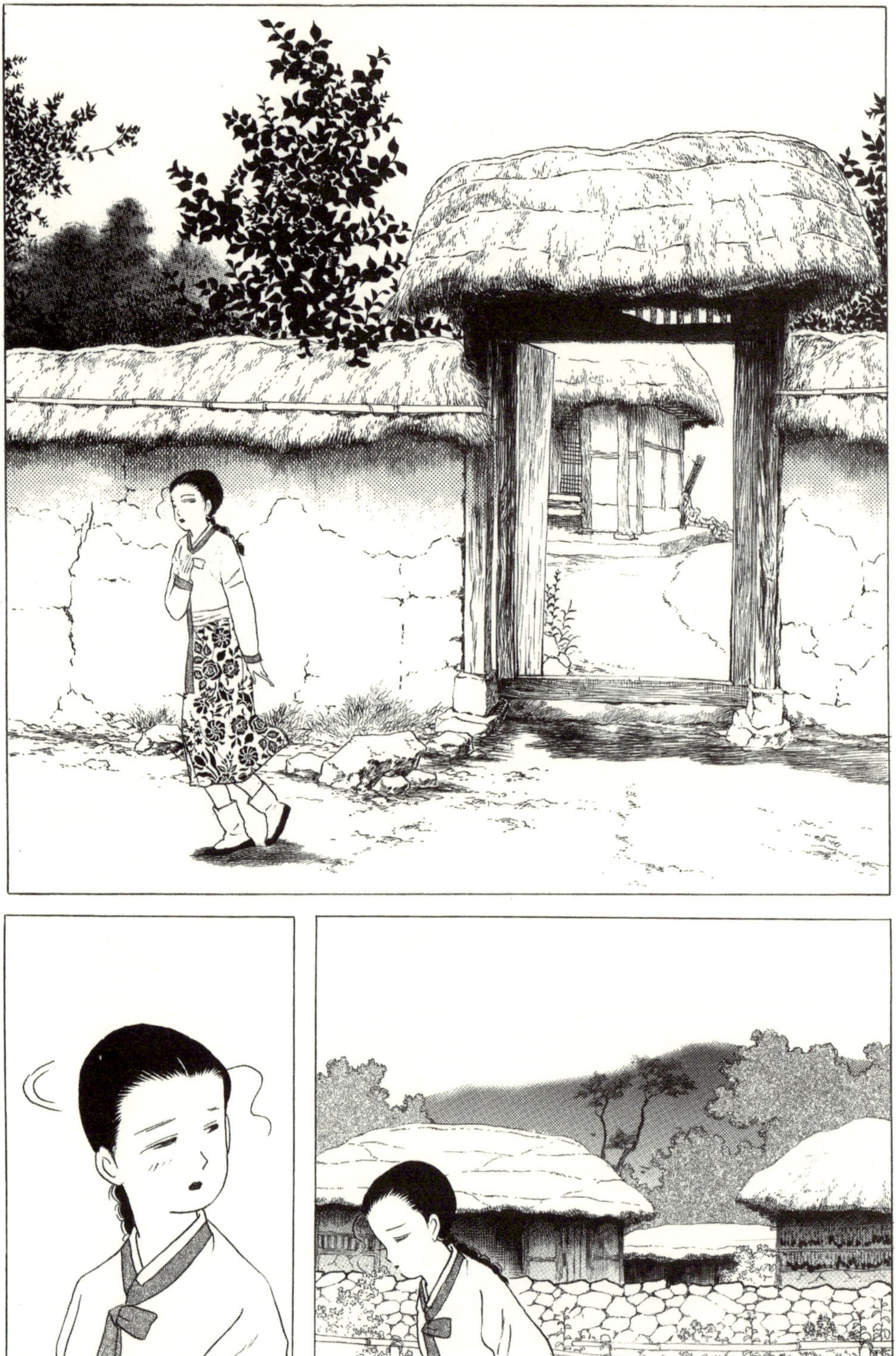

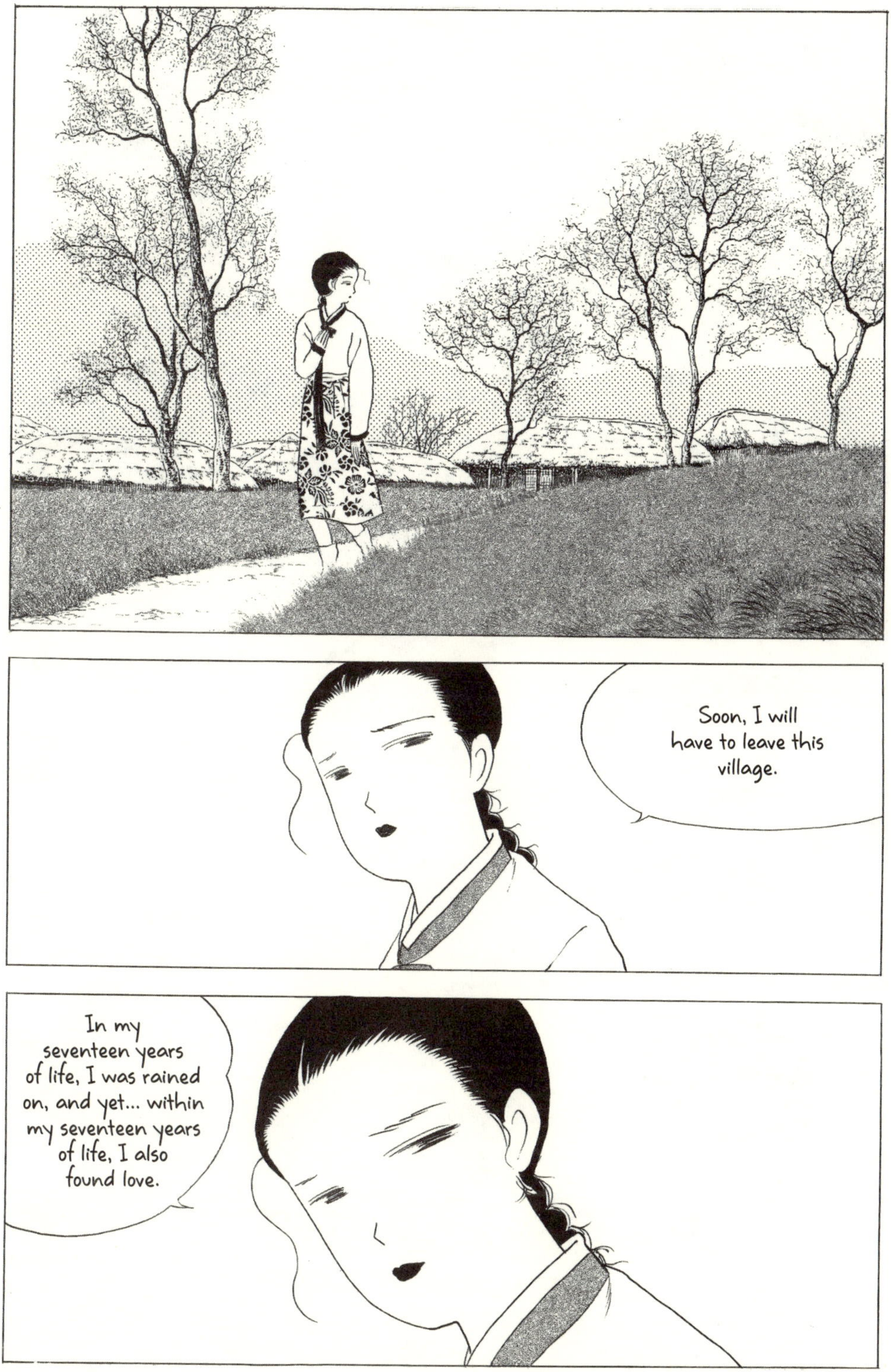
Soon, I will have to leave this village.
In my seventeen years of life, I was rained on, and yet... within my seventeen years of life, I also found love.

> After spending seventeen years of my life in this village and experiencing all sorts of things, it's time to leave.

> A butterfly lands and then flies off, leaving behind a bright and beautiful story.

Wherever a flower is in bloom, a story has already begun.

And I will have to leave all this behind and depart alone from this place.

I will leave and follow the light...
I will leave and follow the butterfly...
I will leave and follow the flower's fragrance...

I must go.

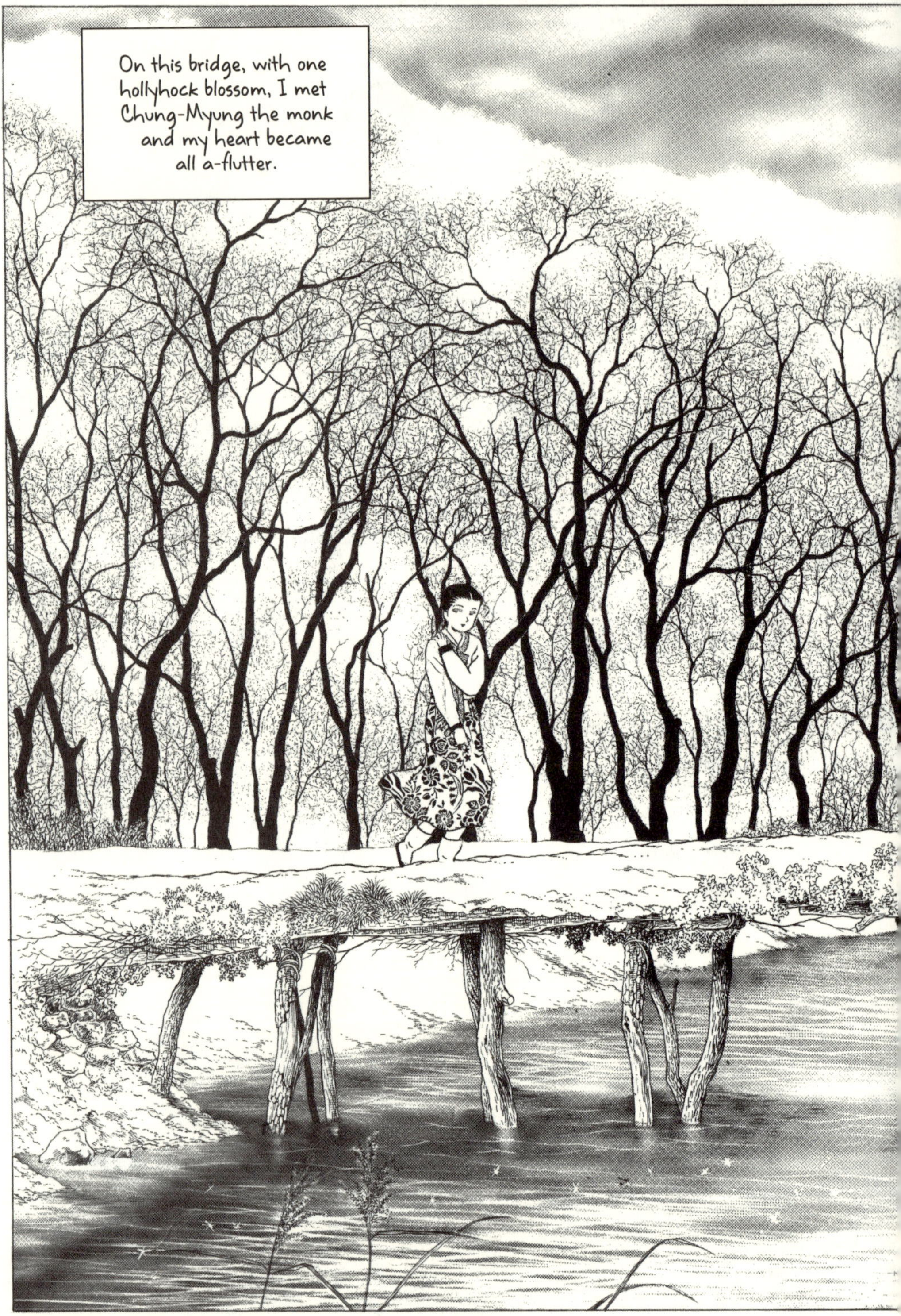
On this bridge, with one hollyhock blossom, I met Chung-Myung the monk and my heart became all a-flutter.

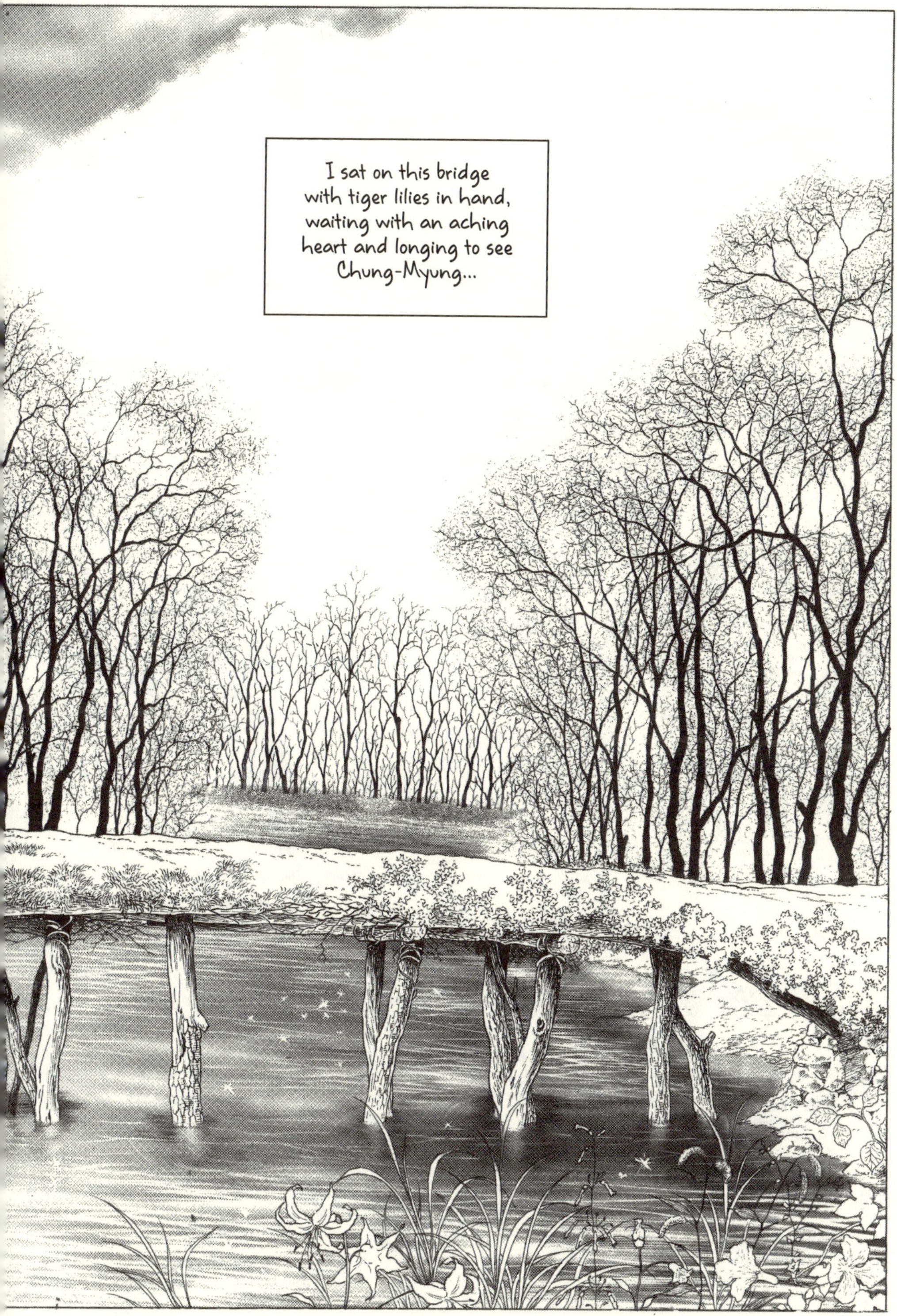
I sat on this bridge with tiger lilies in hand, waiting with an aching heart and longing to see Chung-Myung...

Because I liked a monk, I also came to like men with shaved heads, and because I liked shaved heads, I also began to appreciate the simple design of a monk's robe.
And with an anxious heart, I bloomed like a red camellia flower and waited for a butterfly, like Chung-Myung the monk, to find me.
The foolish camellia flower blooms in the snow and bruises redder and redder as it waits, then before the butterflies even arrive, it begins to lose its petals.
Perhaps that's why when I stand here, I can still smell the scent of the monk's robe wafting up to my nose.

I wonder if Chung-Myung thinks of me when he sees the hollyhock and the tiger lily?
TAP TAP TAP TAP
The sound of a wooden gong...?
I wonder if it's Chung-Myung!
TAP TAP TAP

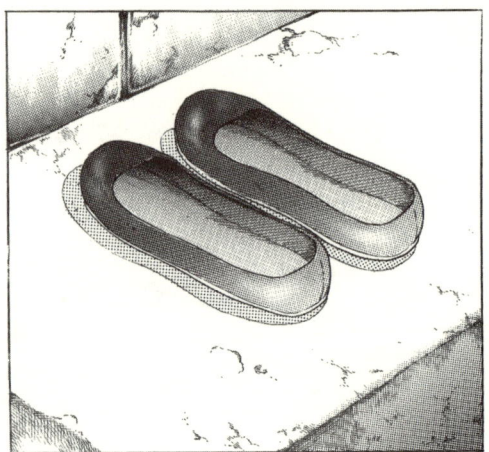

TAP TAP TAP

These shoes are so large, I wonder who they belong to. Chung-Myung's shoes used to be so tiny and small.

TAP TAP

Zzz...

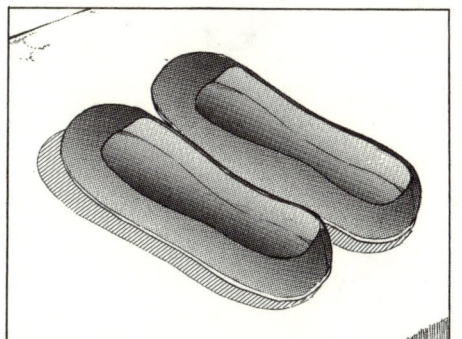

His shoes may have become a lot larger and his back may be toward me, but I can still tell it's Chung-Myung.

Although he's grown into an adult, I could still tell that dozing, rascally figure was him.

I followed the fragrant smell of a full grown flower and found myself here.
Though there are many flowers on the mountain, it is still possible for one single flower's fragrance to overpower them all.

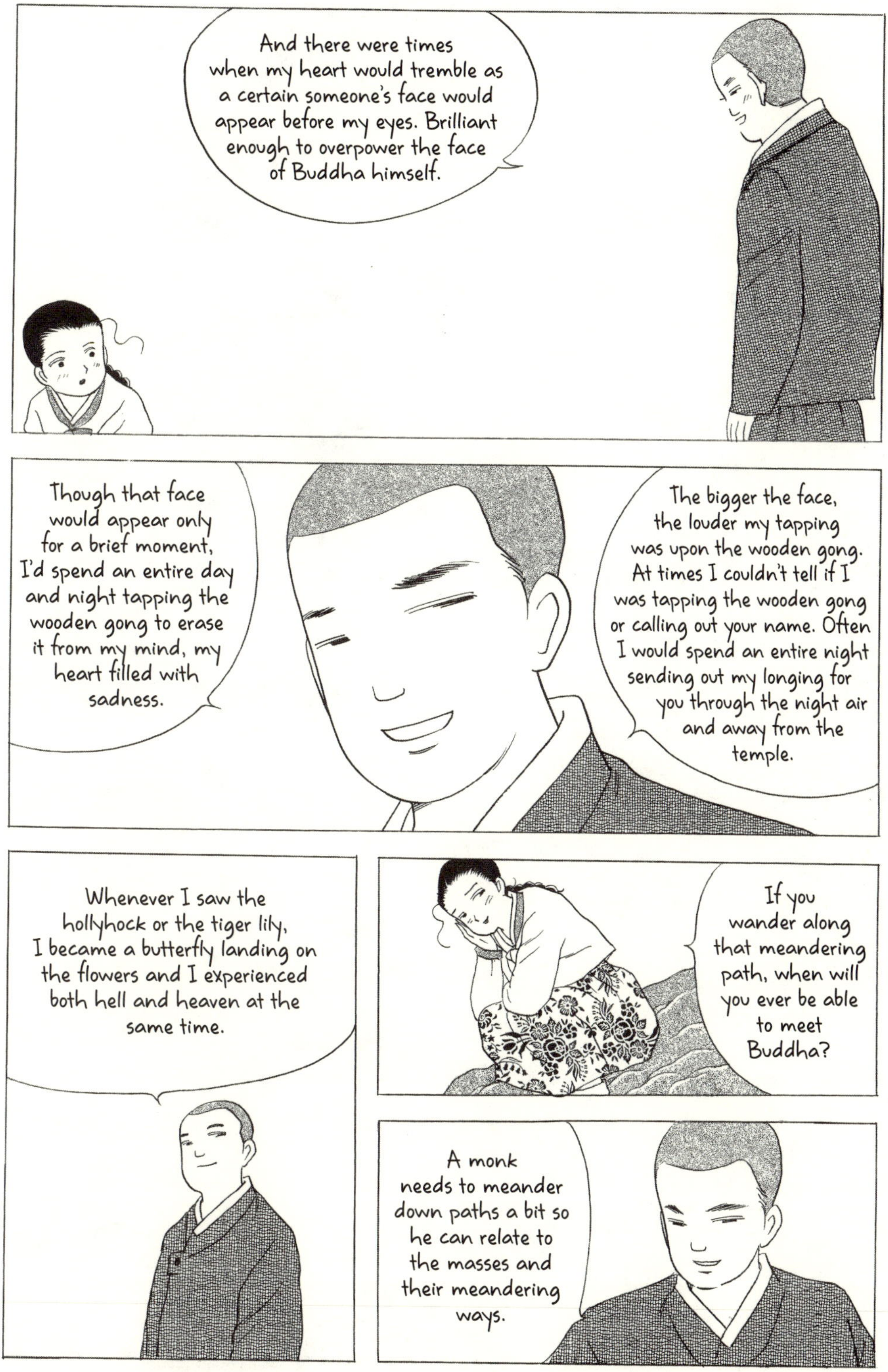
And there were times when my heart would tremble as a certain someone's face would appear before my eyes. Brilliant enough to overpower the face of Buddha himself.
Though that face would appear only for a brief moment, I'd spend an entire day and night tapping the wooden gong to erase it from my mind, my heart filled with sadness.
The bigger the face, the louder my tapping was upon the wooden gong. At times I couldn't tell if I was tapping the wooden gong or calling out your name. Often I would spend an entire night sending out my longing for you through the night air and away from the temple.
Whenever I saw the hollyhock or the tiger lily, I became a butterfly landing on the flowers and I experienced both hell and heaven at the same time.
If you wander along that meandering path, when will you ever be able to meet Buddha?
A monk needs to meander down paths a bit so he can relate to the masses and their meandering ways.

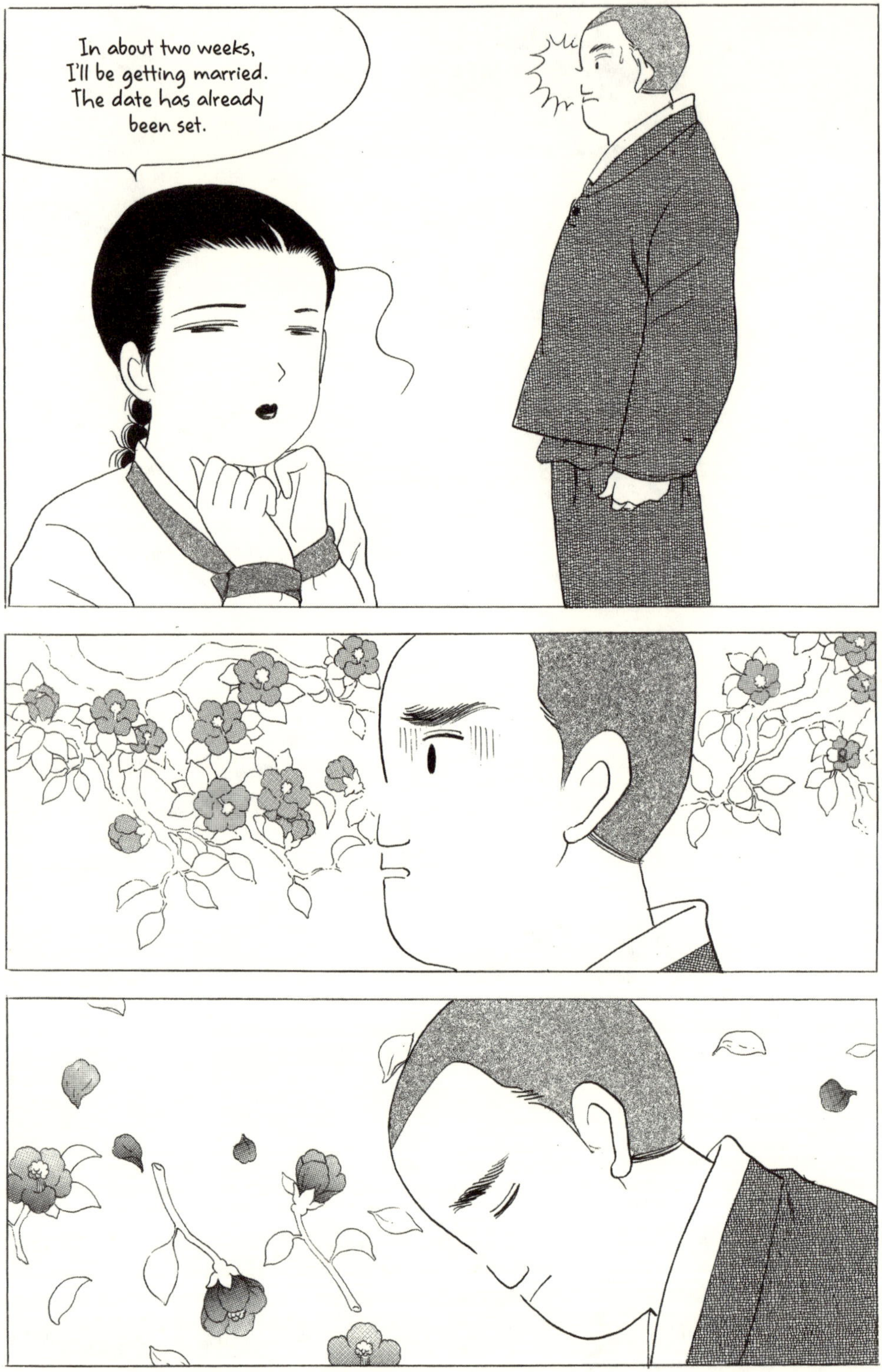
In about two weeks, I'll be getting married. The date has already been set.

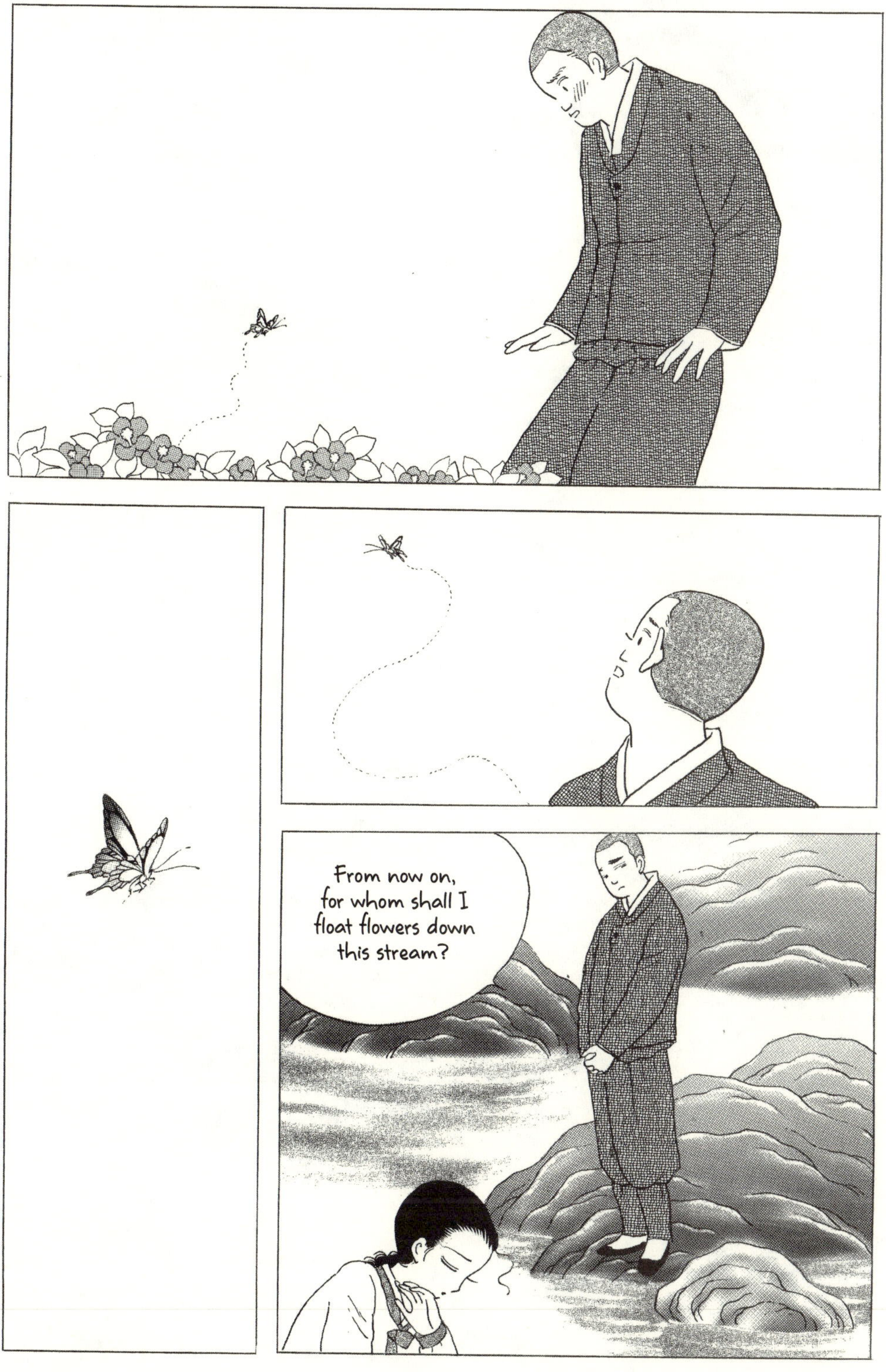
From now on, for whom shall I float flowers down this stream?

I didn't know monks cried too.

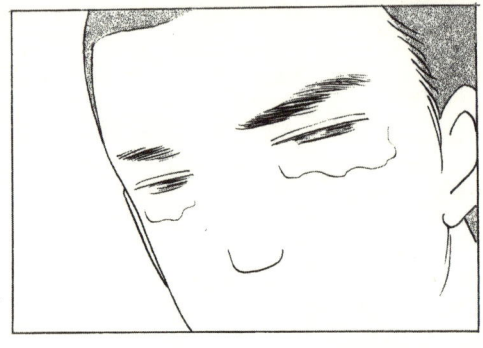

They shouldn't. That's why I'm not a full monk yet.

Still, now that I've cried a few tears, I feel as though the door to paradise has opened up a tiny bit. The one I should have been focusing on all this time was supposed to be Buddha and not you, Ehwa.

Now no matter what flower blooms before me, I will not become a butterfly and land on it.

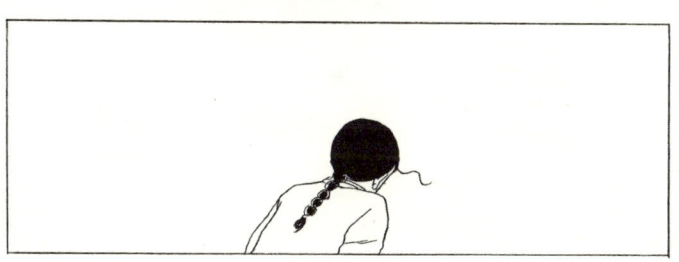

I will focus on becoming an ash-colored butterfly that lands only on the words of Buddha.

TAP TAP TAP TAP TAP

"You sly fox!"

"How did you know that young master Sunoo was back, and how did you get here so quickly?"

"He's back?"

"Aren't you here because you want to see young master Sunoo?"

"No..."

"Set wedding or not, I couldn't blame you for wanting to see him again, you naughty girl."

"I'm only here to look for our dog, Blackie! How dare you accuse me of something you don't even know anything about?!"

"Speak for yourself! You're the one up to no good! You're trying to tempt young master Sunoo even though you have Dongchul!"

"You're so rude! How can you even say such a thing?!"

Whenever this darn dog escapes, you can't find hide nor hair of him anywhere.

Blackie!

Blackie!

Blackie must be quite a dog.

How else can he escape from their house three years after they put him in the ground?

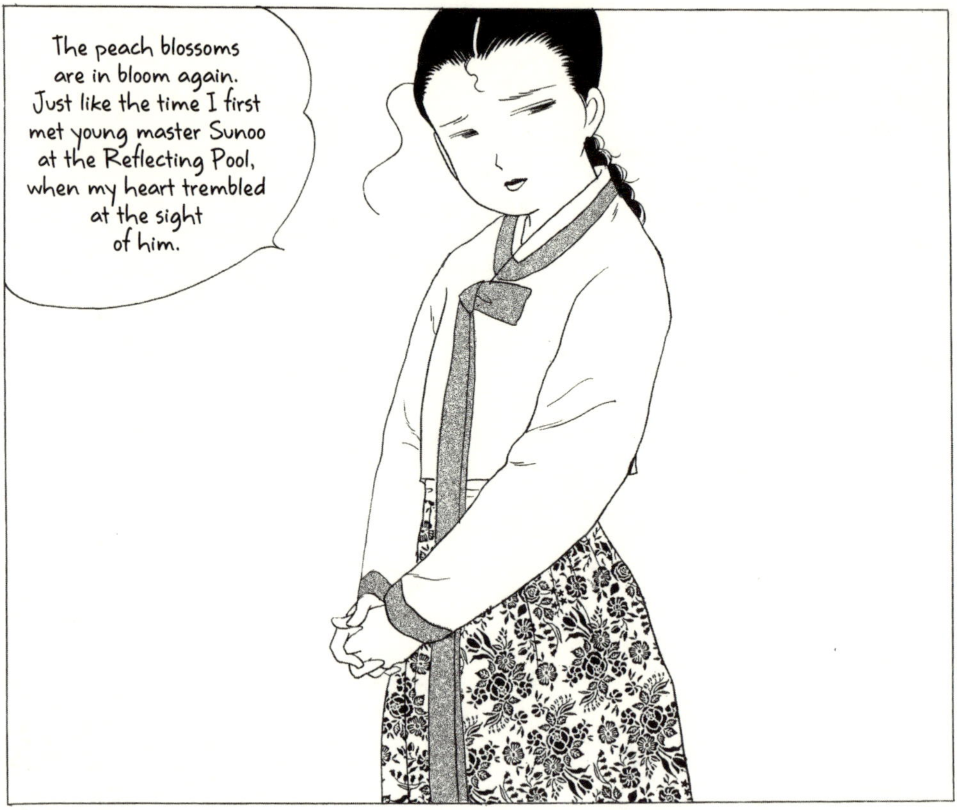
The peach blossoms are in bloom again. Just like the time I first met young master Sunoo at the Reflecting Pool, when my heart trembled at the sight of him.

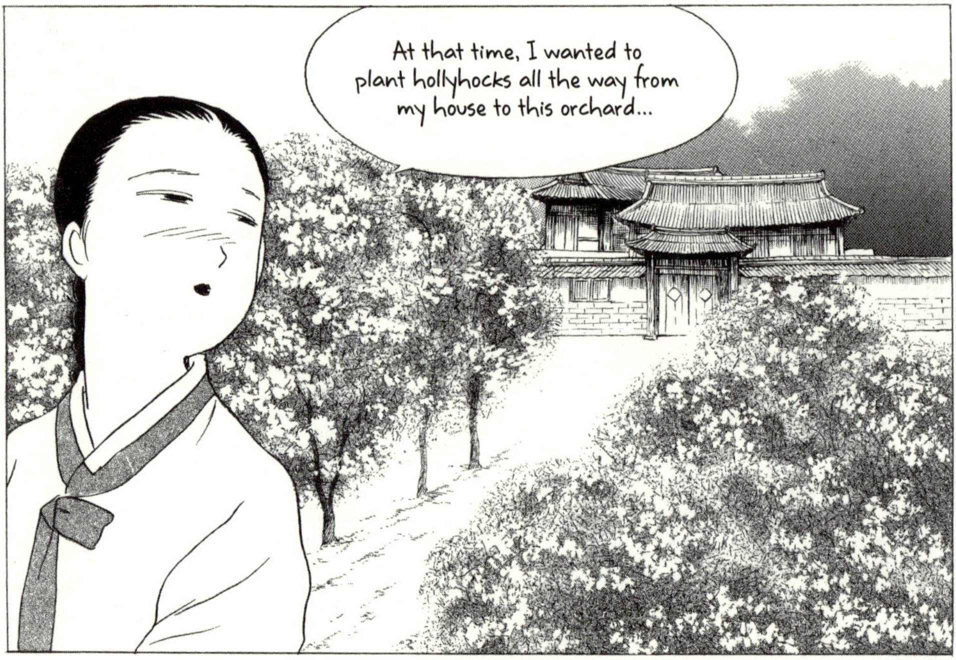
At that time, I wanted to plant hollyhocks all the way from my house to this orchard...

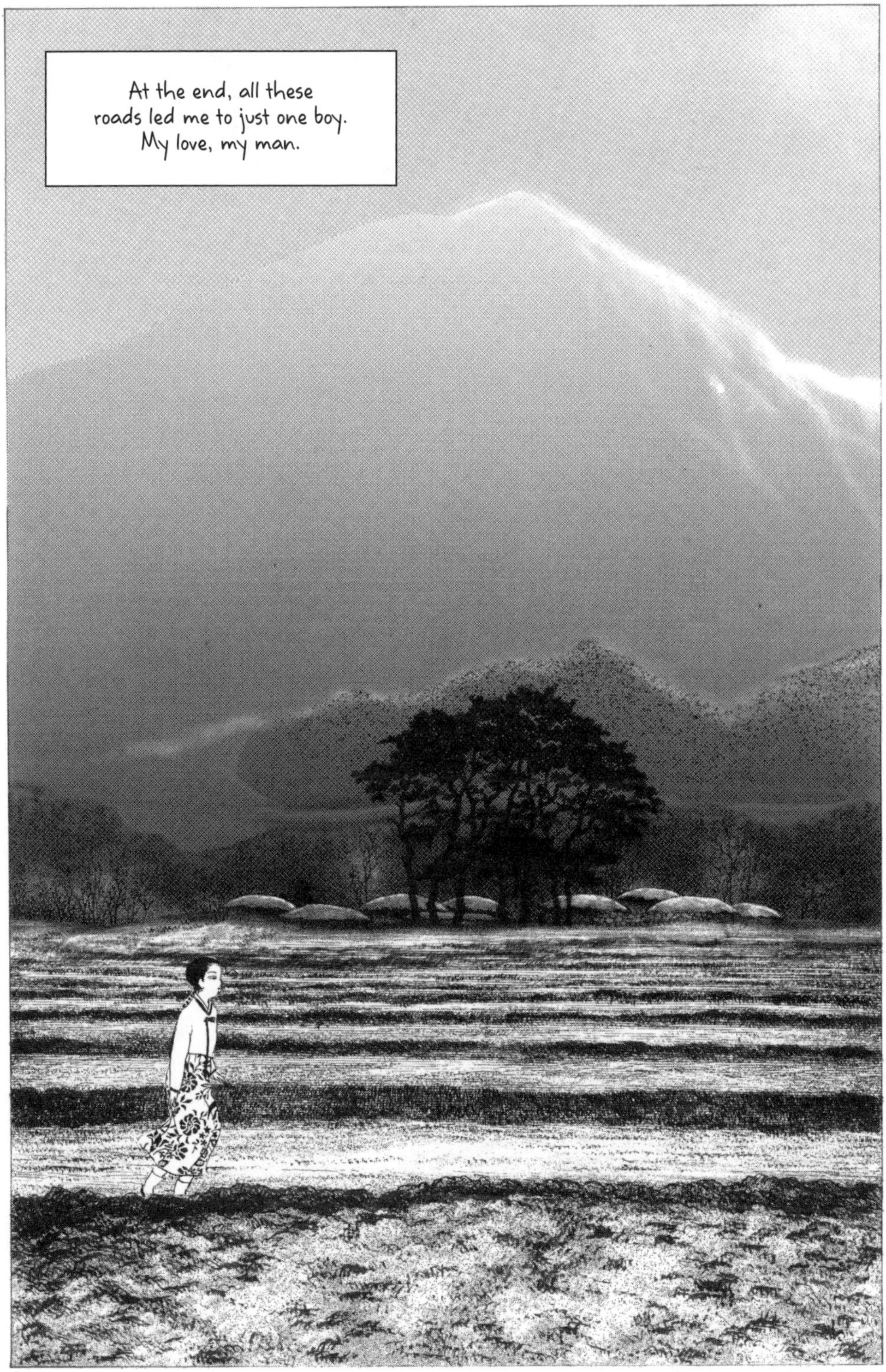
At the end, all these roads led me to just one boy. My love, my man.

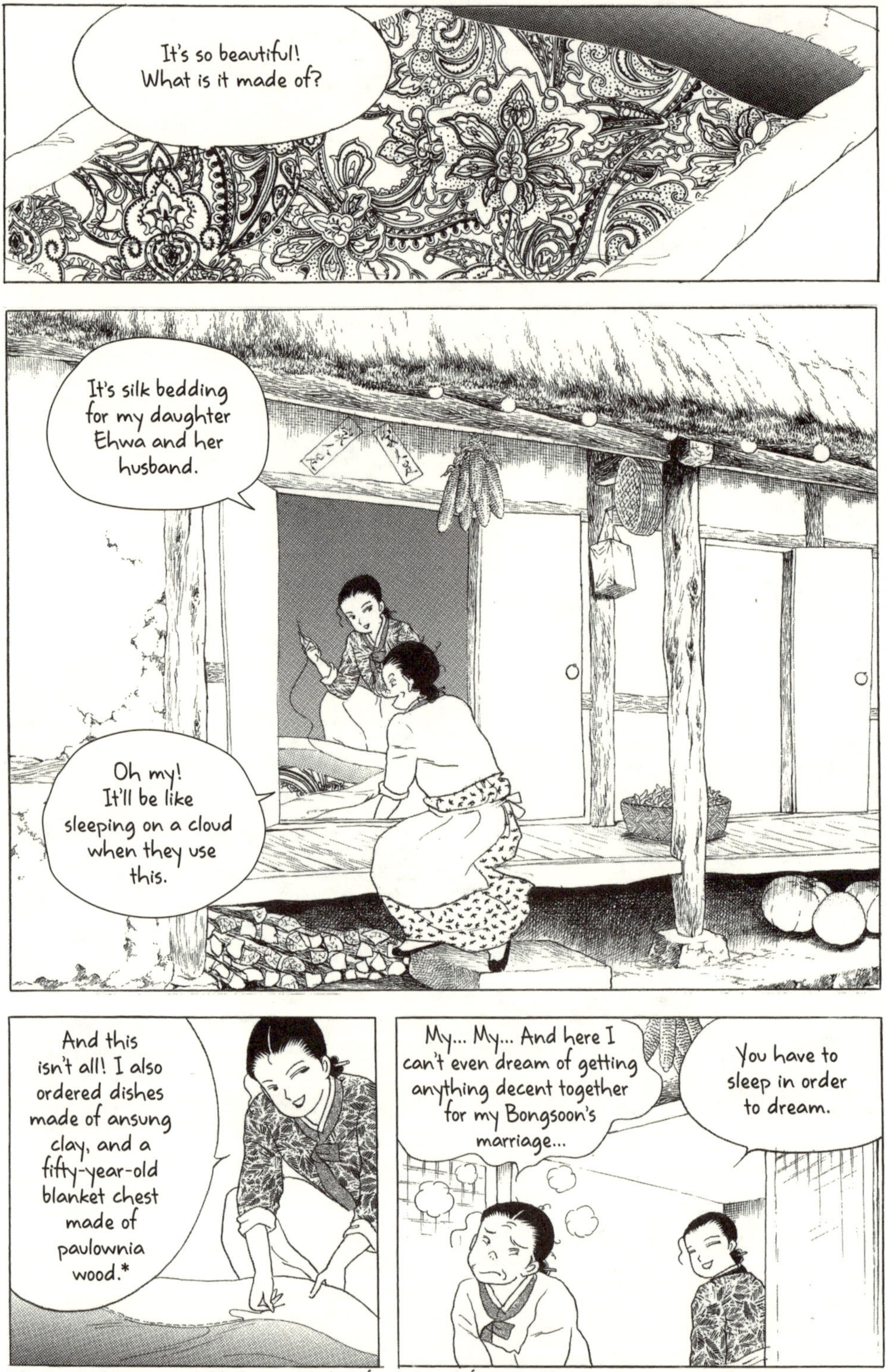
It's so beautiful! What is it made of?
It's silk bedding for my daughter Ehwa and her husband.
Oh my! It'll be like sleeping on a cloud when they use this.
And this isn't all! I also ordered dishes made of ansung clay, and a fifty-year-old blanket chest made of paulownia wood.*
My... My... And here I can't even dream of getting anything decent together for my Bongsoon's marriage...
You have to sleep in order to dream.

* Traditionally, the groom provided the house and the bride furnished it with furniture and linen.

He said that Ehwa's name means pear blossom, and since it's a flower that blooms early, he told me to watch her carefully since her eyes would open toward men sooner than other girls.

Maybe that's why you're already getting married and about to leave my side when you're young enough to have stayed with me a bit longer.

Then again, the sooner she marries, the sooner she will bear lots of fruit.

Just like how the name "Ehwa" means pear blossom and water, she will undoubtedly be drenched by her husband's overflowing love. A woman needs to be vibrant with life in order to be deeply loved.

And there's no doubt that my love as a mother is also deep and sincere. For here I am working and putting together all this to marry off my one and only child, so she will live well with her husband and be happy.

Ehwa's been gone for a while now. Where has she run off to?

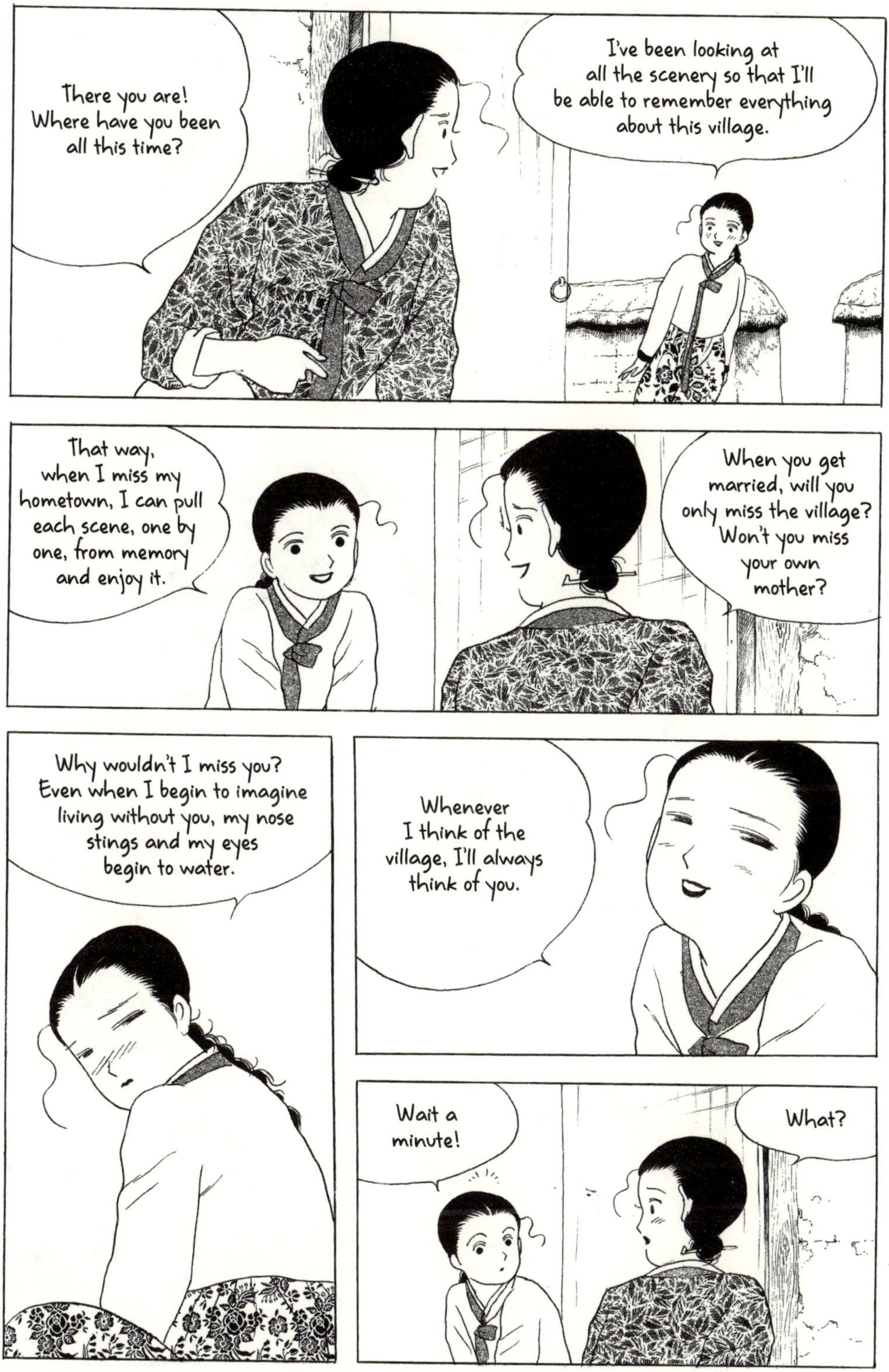
There you are! Where have you been all this time?
I've been looking at all the scenery so that I'll be able to remember everything about this village.
That way, when I miss my hometown, I can pull each scene, one by one, from memory and enjoy it.
When you get married, will you only miss the village? Won't you miss your own mother?
Why wouldn't I miss you? Even when I begin to imagine living without you, my nose stings and my eyes begin to water.
Whenever I think of the village, I'll always think of you.
Wait a minute!
What?

What's this in your hair?
What is it?
Oh, no! It's a white hair.
A white hair?
I'm horrified.

Whether it rains or snows, in my heart I have always felt like a pink azalea.. But now, all of a sudden, time feels so much more real. A white hair...

Don't worry about it. It was probably just a rogue hair.

You can hide things from the world, but you can never hide things from time.

Then again, soon I'll be a grandma, and it's not unreasonable to expect to age at least this much.

I think you got the white hair from worrying about my marriage.

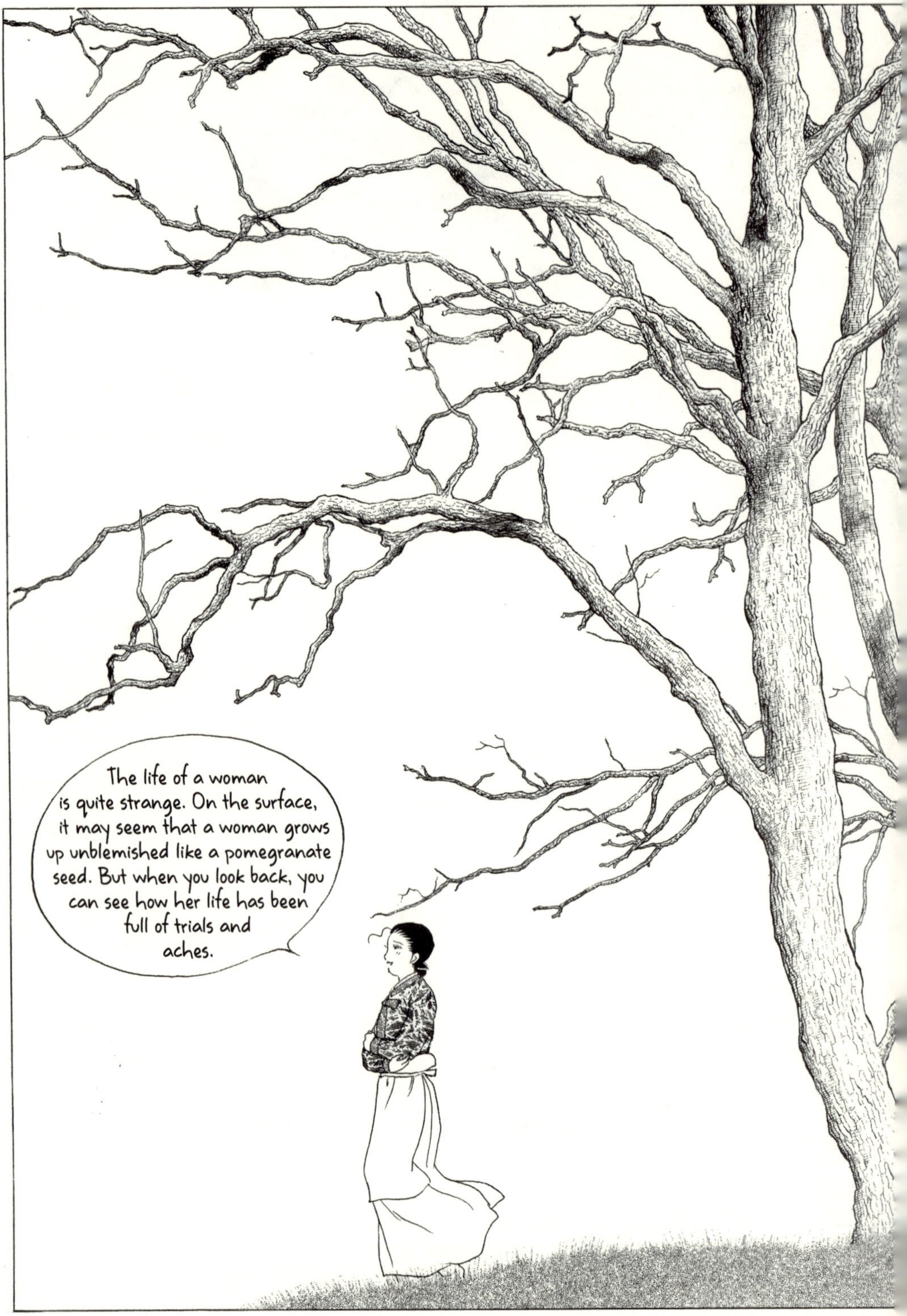
The life of a woman is quite strange. On the surface, it may seem that a woman grows up unblemished like a pomegranate seed. But when you look back, you can see how her life has been full of trials and aches.

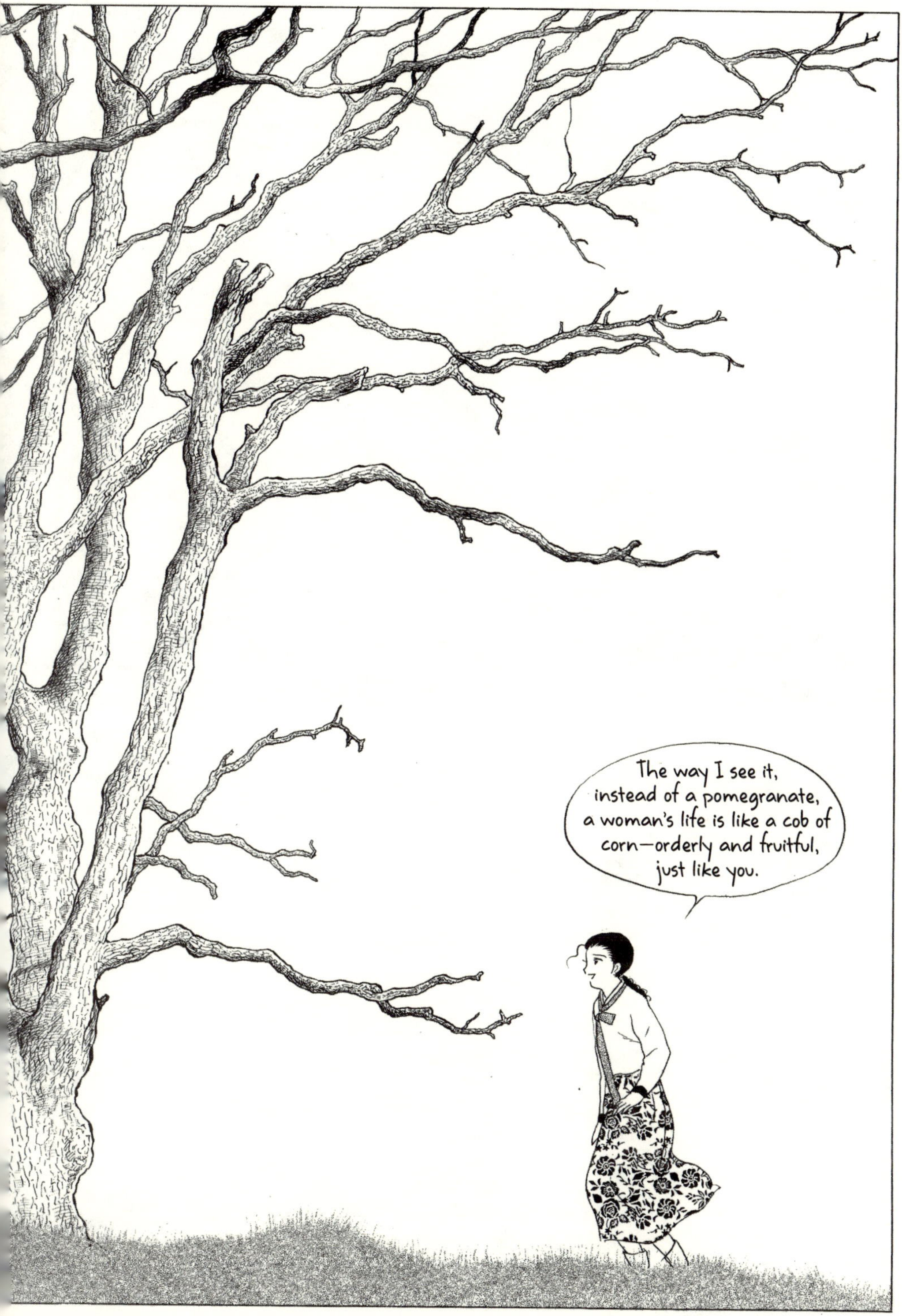
The way I see it, instead of a pomegranate, a woman's life is like a cob of corn—orderly and fruitful, just like you.

Ehwa, does your mother look becoming under this setting sun?
No... I've always thought you look more becoming in the morning sunlight rather than the setting sun.
You think so too? It may be the same sun, but I think I feel more at peace with the morning sun than the setting one.
Especially since in my heart, I still feel like a pink azalea flower.
Even though your body is like a white bellflower blossom!
Why, you!

Chapter Nine
EHWA IS GETTING MARRIED

From an egg...

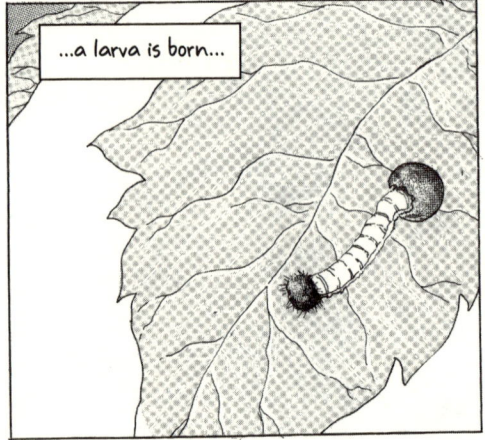

...a larva is born...

After spending winter as a caterpillar...

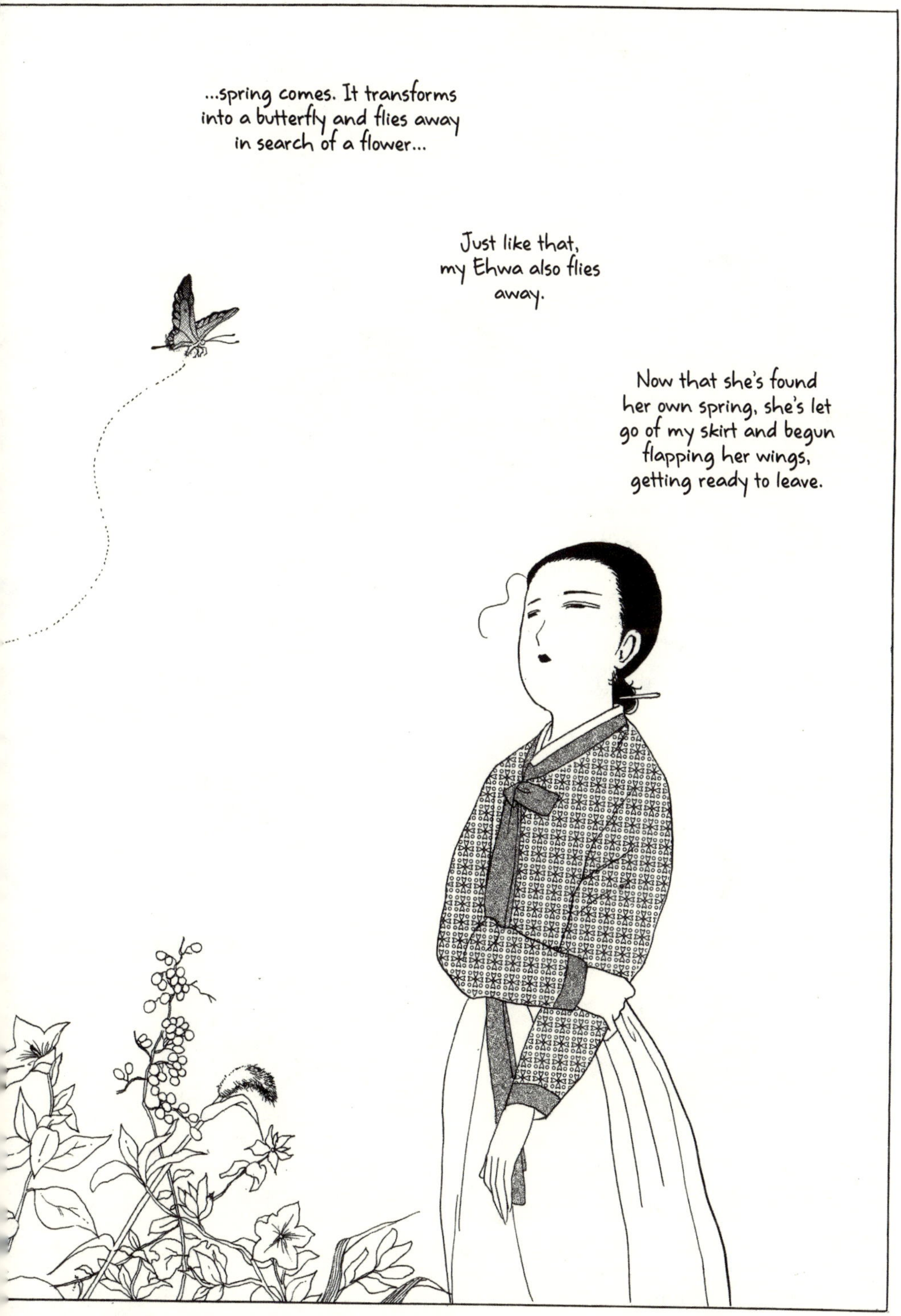
...spring comes. It transforms into a butterfly and flies away in search of a flower...
Just like that, my Ehwa also flies away.
Now that she's found her own spring, she's let go of my skirt and begun flapping her wings, getting ready to leave.

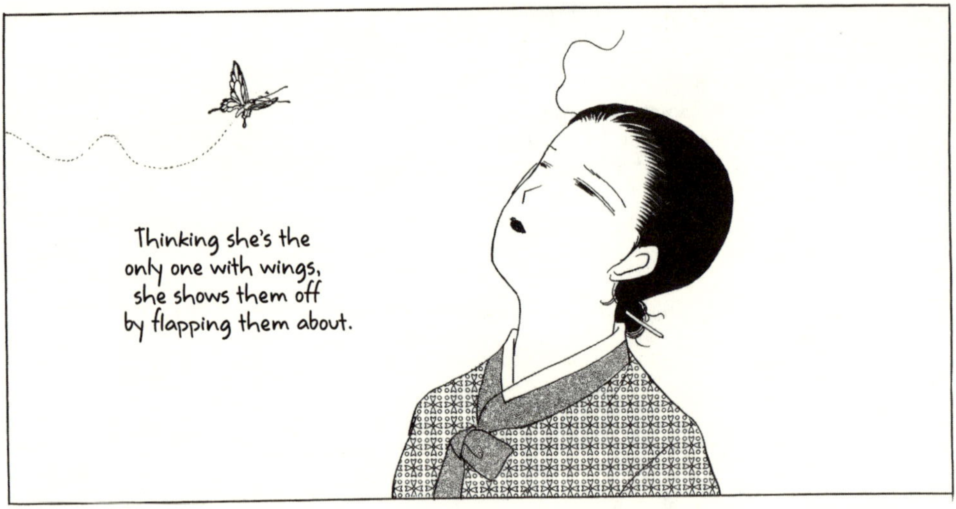
Thinking she's the only one with wings, she shows them off by flapping them about.

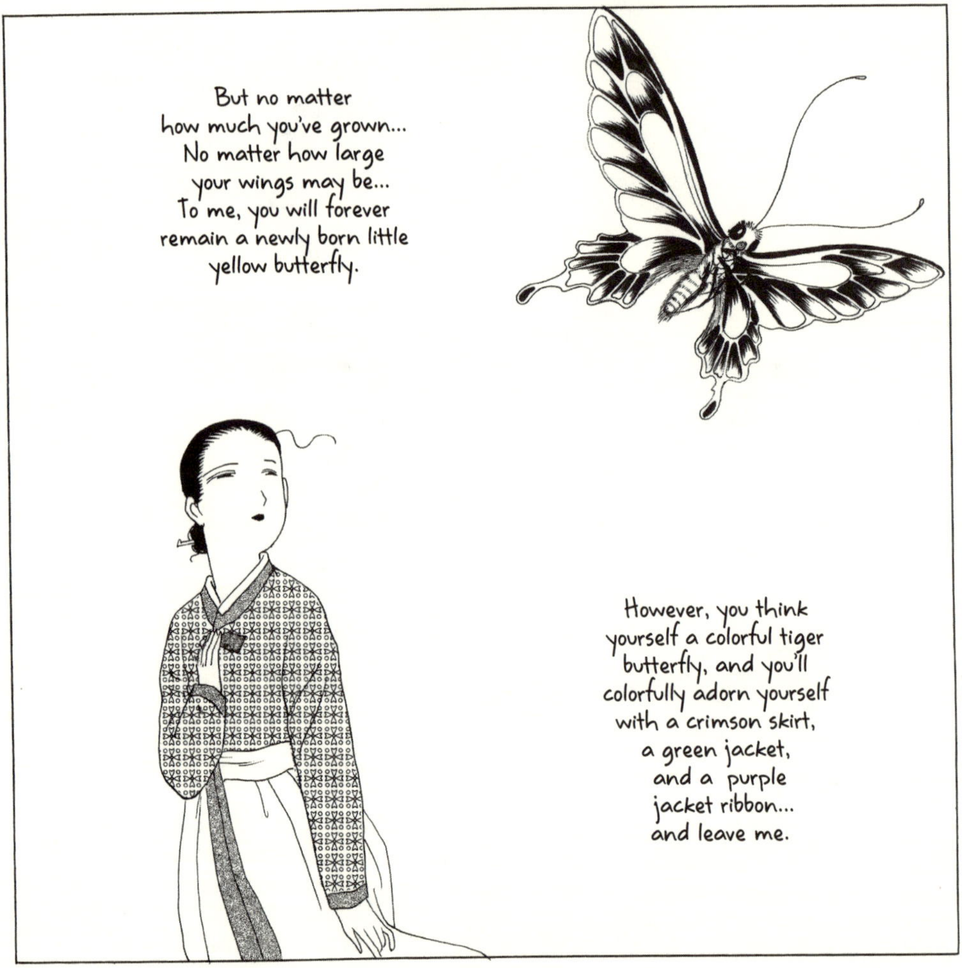
But no matter how much you've grown... No matter how large your wings may be... To me, you will forever remain a newly born little yellow butterfly.
However, you think yourself a colorful tiger butterfly, and you'll colorfully adorn yourself with a crimson skirt, a green jacket, and a purple jacket ribbon... and leave me.

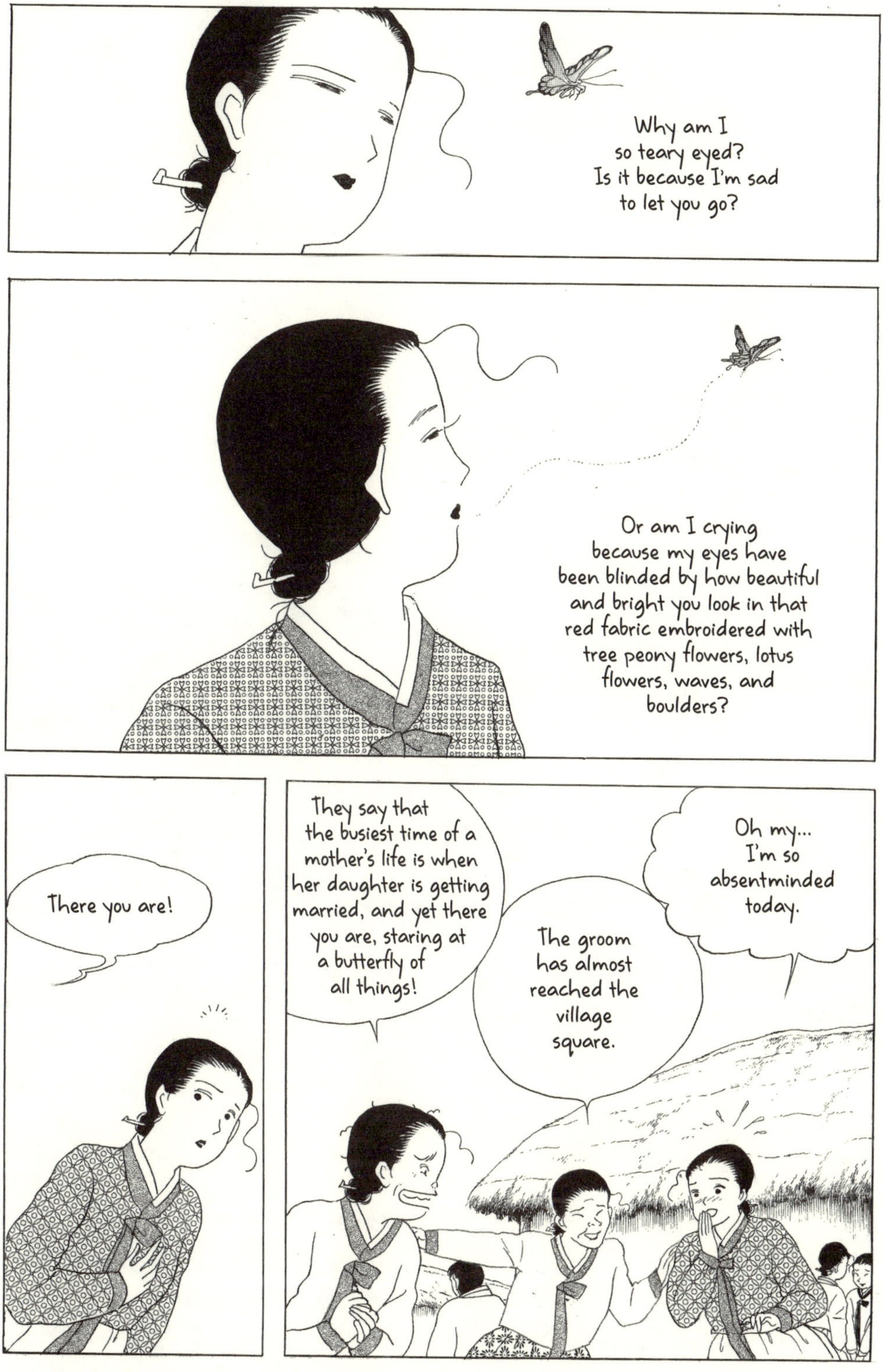
Why am I so teary eyed? Is it because I'm sad to let you go?
Or am I crying because my eyes have been blinded by how beautiful and bright you look in that red fabric embroidered with tree peony flowers, lotus flowers, waves, and boulders?
There you are!
They say that the busiest time of a mother's life is when her daughter is getting married, and yet there you are, staring at a butterfly of all things!
The groom has almost reached the village square.
Oh my... I'm so absentminded today.

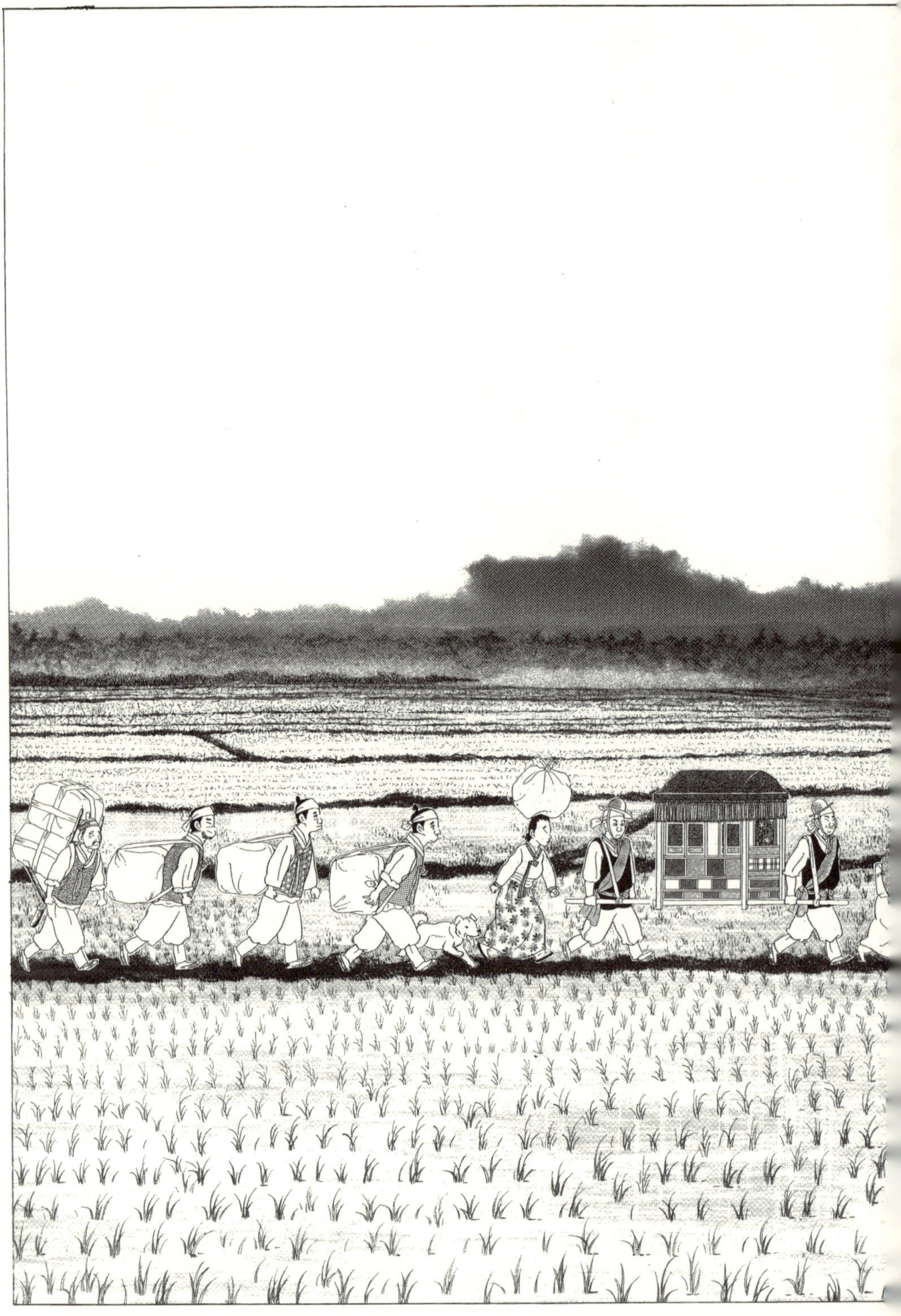

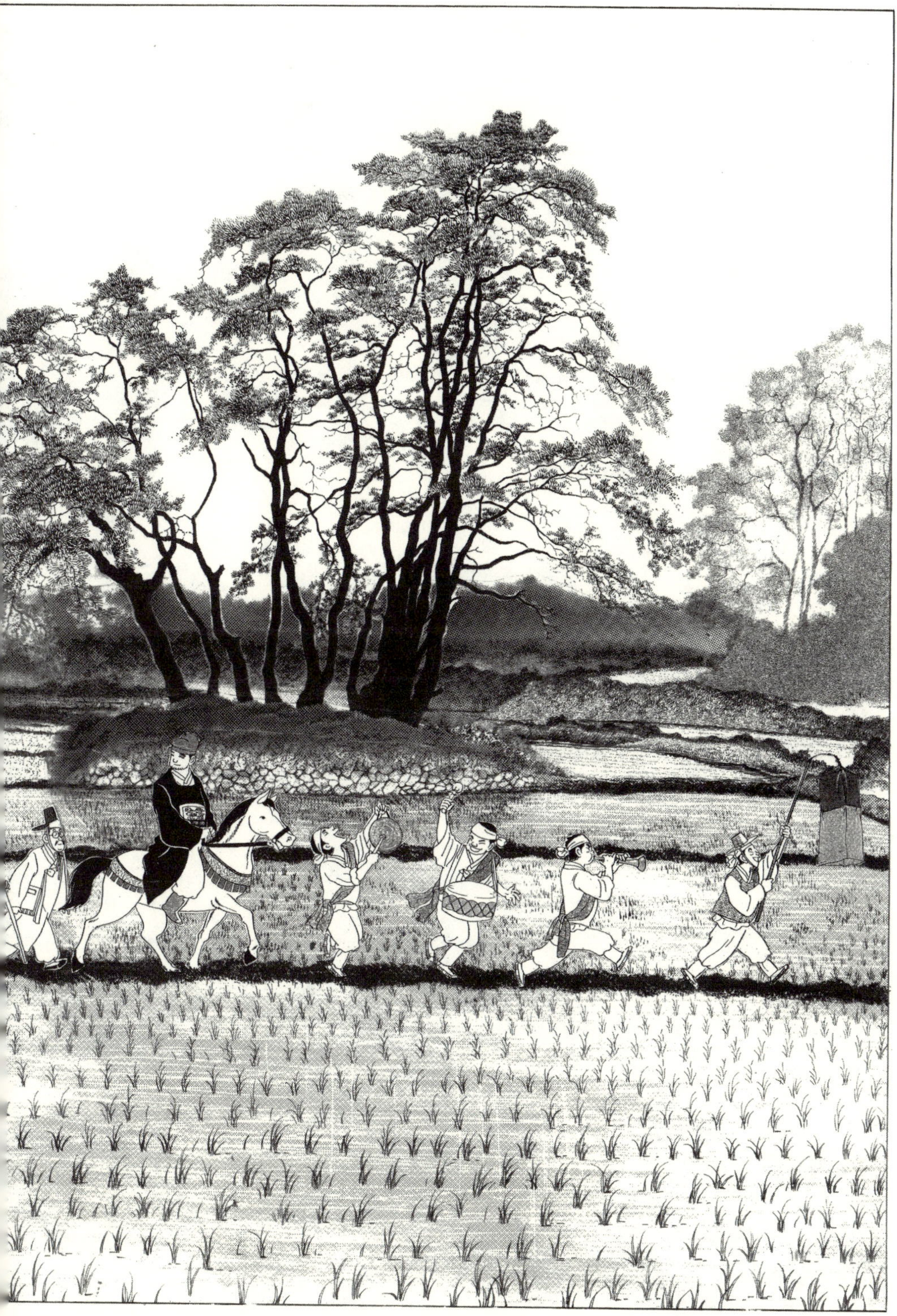

"What are we doing? They're saying the groom is already here and waiting."

"The husband you've been waiting and waiting for has finally arrived and is waiting outside for you."

"The closer he is, the shorter my journey from this house will be."

"And the sooner I'll have to leave my mother's side."

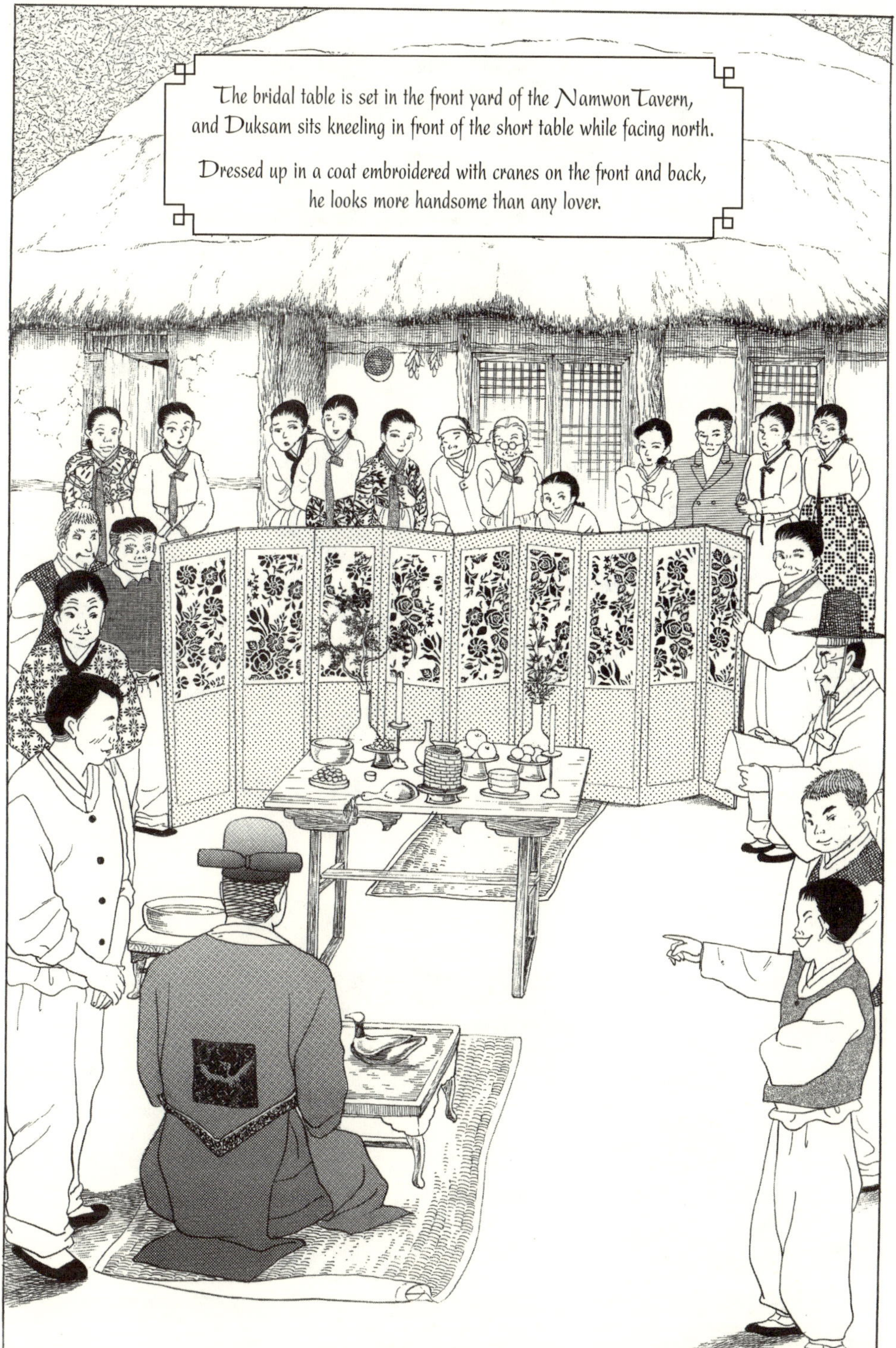
The bridal table is set in the front yard of the Namwon Tavern, and Duksam sits kneeling in front of the short table while facing north.
Dressed up in a coat embroidered with cranes on the front and back, he looks more handsome than any lover.

The groom is really a good looking man.
He looks so fine in those clothes, you'd think he came from great wealth.
Ehwa's mother is so lucky. She must be happy to gain such a strong son-in-law.
Since good fortune didn't bless her with **her** husband, it seems fair that it should with her daughter's.
We will begin with the presentation of the duck.
Young man, do you know what that wooden mandarin duck represents?

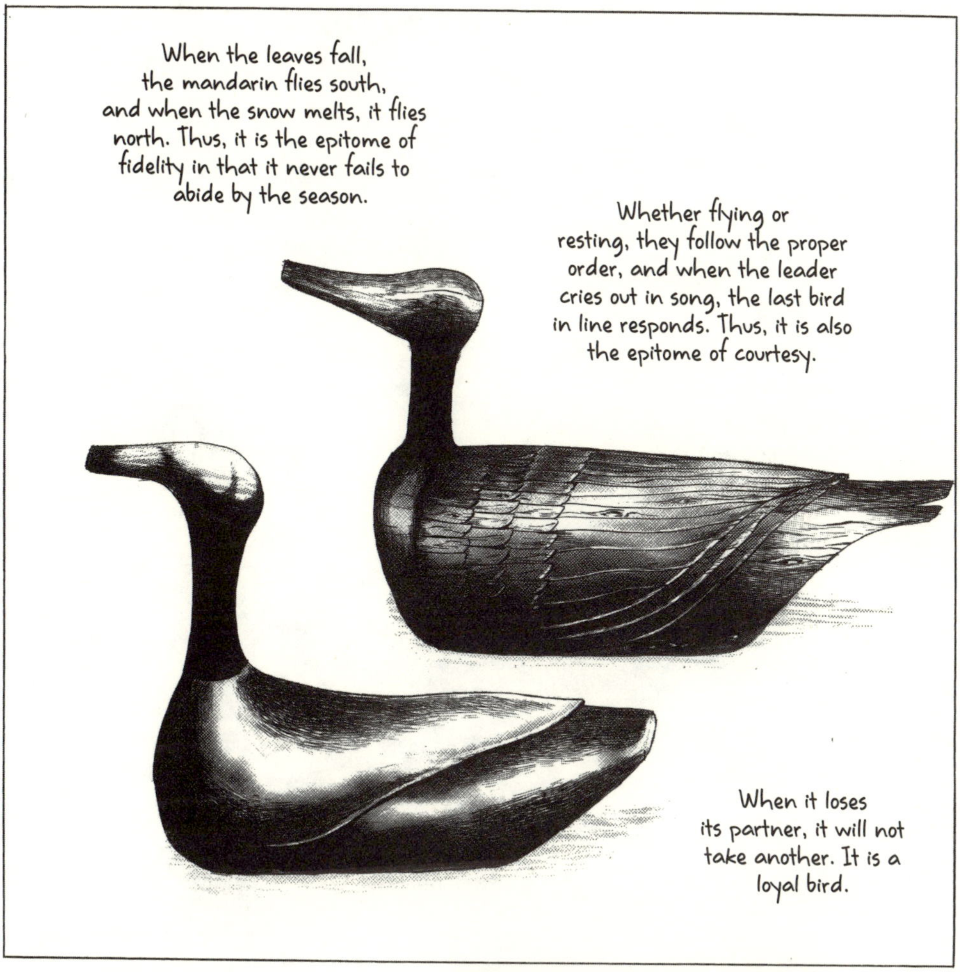
When the leaves fall, the mandarin flies south, and when the snow melts, it flies north. Thus, it is the epitome of fidelity in that it never fails to abide by the season.
Whether flying or resting, they follow the proper order, and when the leader cries out in song, the last bird in line responds. Thus, it is also the epitome of courtesy.
When it loses its partner, it will not take another. It is a loyal bird.

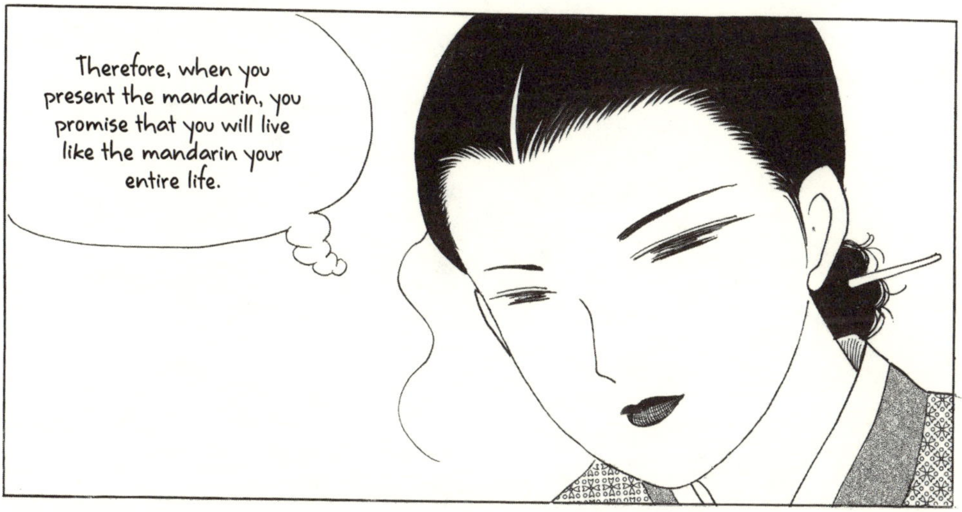
Therefore, when you present the mandarin, you promise that you will live like the mandarin your entire life.

The mandarin is a bird that truly lives for another, and yet it is not necessary for them to tell us this. They say it through their actions.
I think the groom's arms are about to fall off!
Ma'am, I believe that's your cue. Why are you just standing there?
Hurry and take the mandarin into your apron.

Ehwa's mother gets a bow from a fine looking son-in-law.
She may be blessed now, but what about tonight when she's all alone?
Then either you or I will have to make her feel less lonely.
I've tried helping her with that—she doesn't let me in!
Now that you've received his bow, go and throw the mandarin at the bride.
CLATTER
The mandarin has arrived!

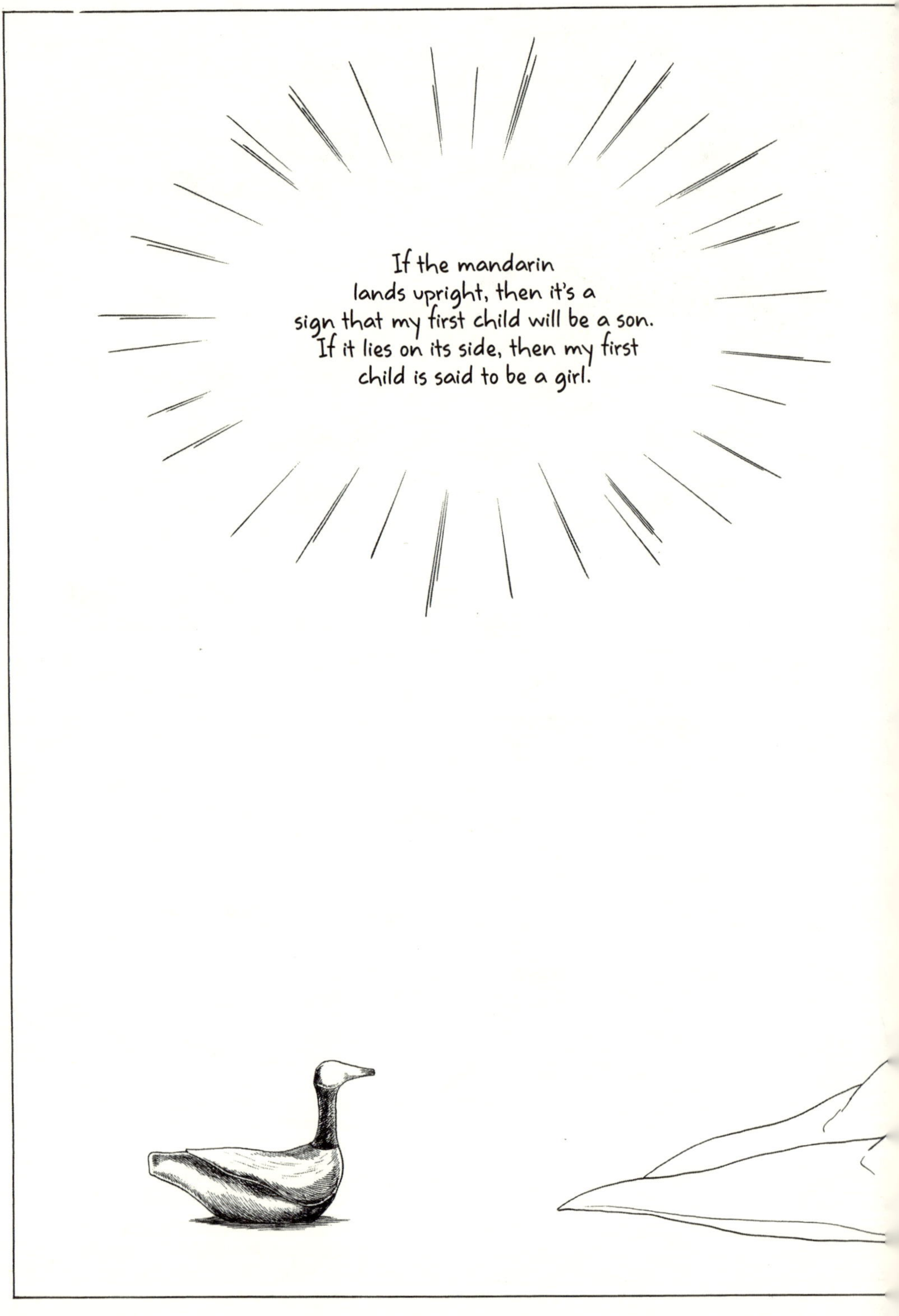
If the mandarin lands upright, then it's a sign that my first child will be a son. If it lies on its side, then my first child is said to be a girl.

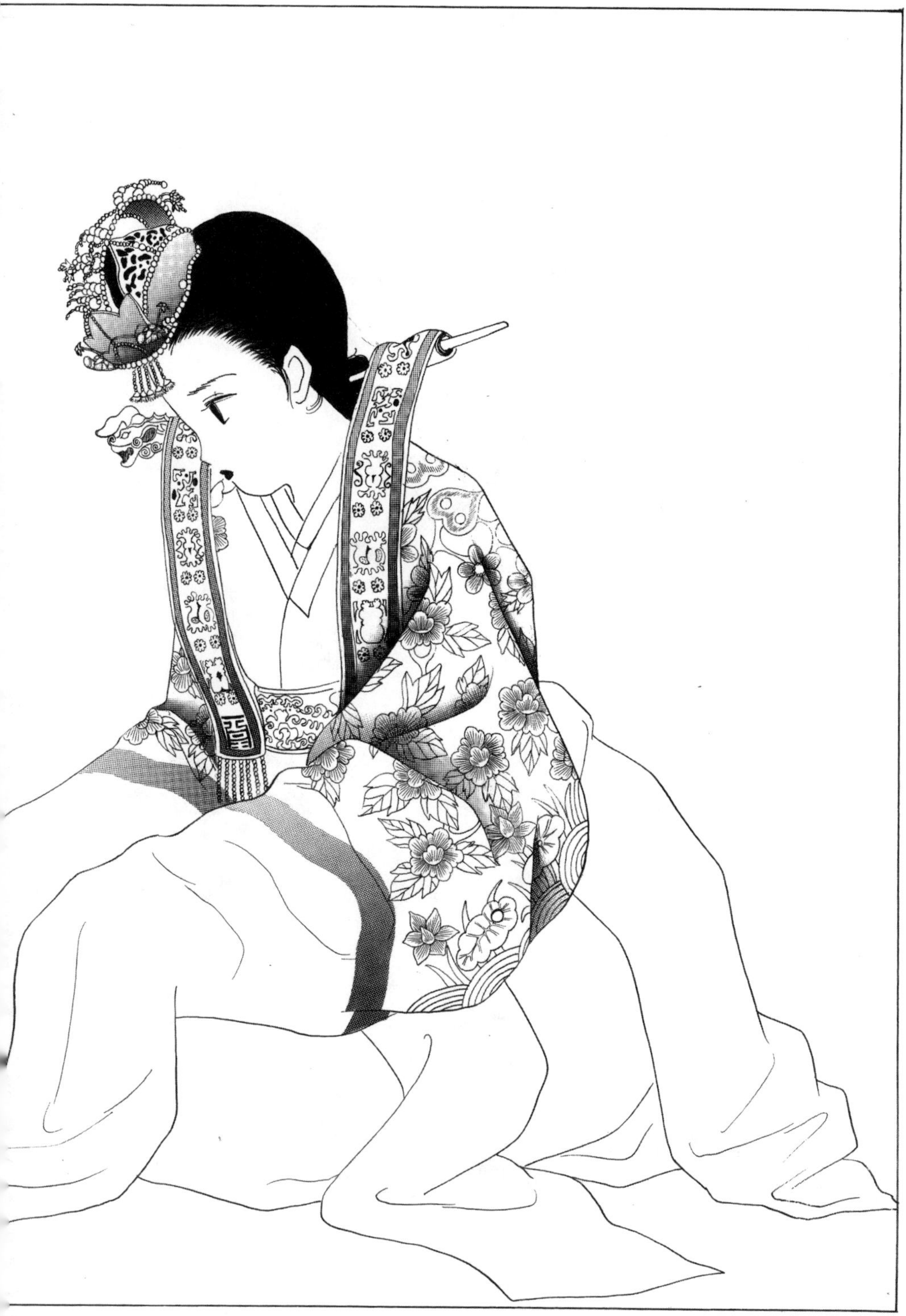

"It's sitting upright!"

"You're so lucky, Ehwa. You've already assured yourself a son, even before spending your first night with your husband."

"Ehwa, after you get married, you know what you're supposed to do with that mandarin, right?"

"What use is a duck made of wood? What am I supposed to do with it?"

"Actually, it has a very special purpose in your marriage."

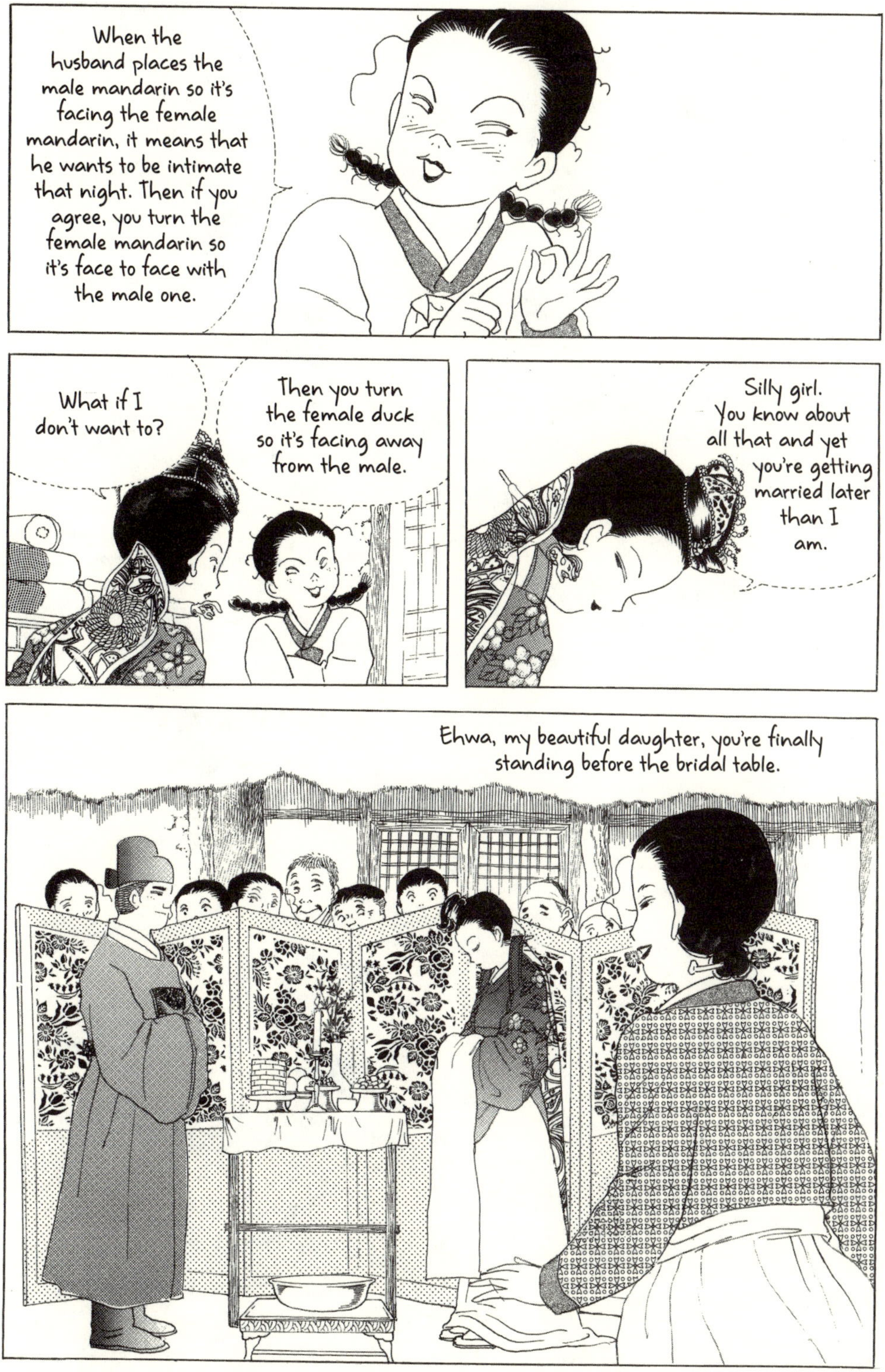
When the husband places the male mandarin so it's facing the female mandarin, it means that he wants to be intimate that night. Then if you agree, you turn the female mandarin so it's face to face with the male one.
What if I don't want to?
Then you turn the female duck so it's facing away from the male.
Silly girl. You know about all that and yet you're getting married later than I am.
Ehwa, my beautiful daughter, you're finally standing before the bridal table.

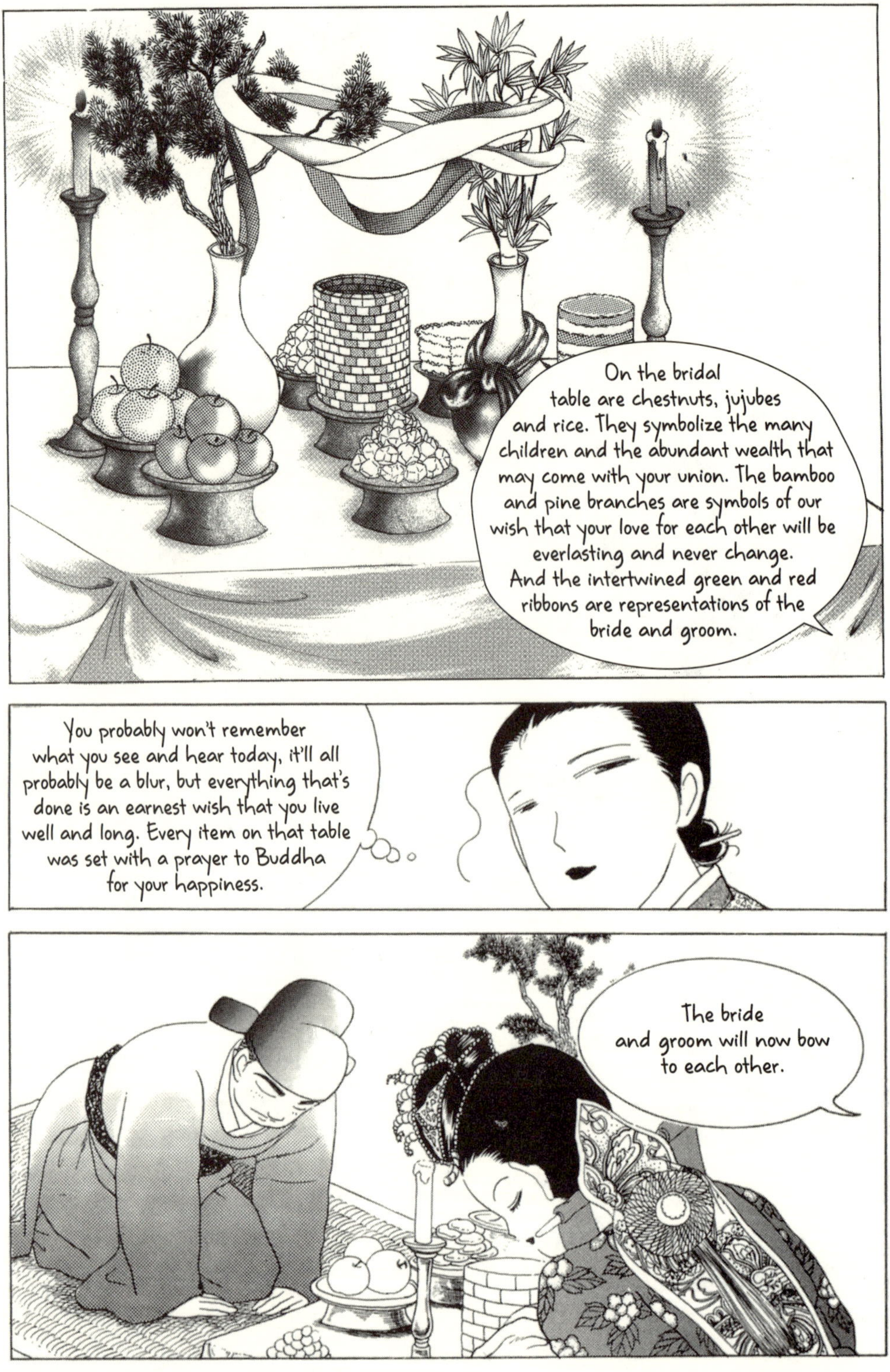
On the bridal table are chestnuts, jujubes and rice. They symbolize the many children and the abundant wealth that may come with your union. The bamboo and pine branches are symbols of our wish that your love for each other will be everlasting and never change. And the intertwined green and red ribbons are representations of the bride and groom.
You probably won't remember what you see and hear today, it'll all probably be a blur, but everything that's done is an earnest wish that you live well and long. Every item on that table was set with a prayer to Buddha for your happiness.
The bride and groom will now bow to each other.

The sharing of the wine is a symbol that you and your husband are now of one body.

At the time when I got married, I did not realize how deeply a parent wants happiness for their child. But now that I'm sending off my own daughter, I can understand that desire.

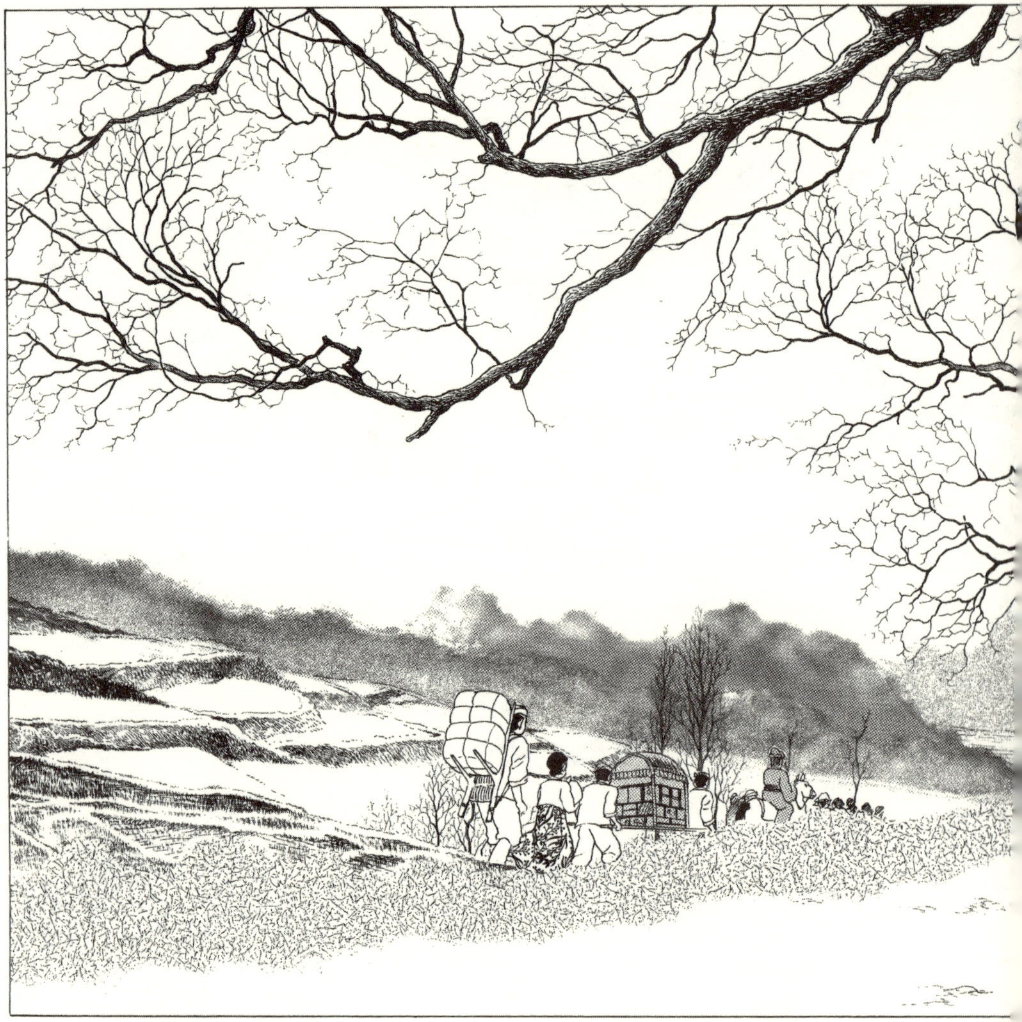

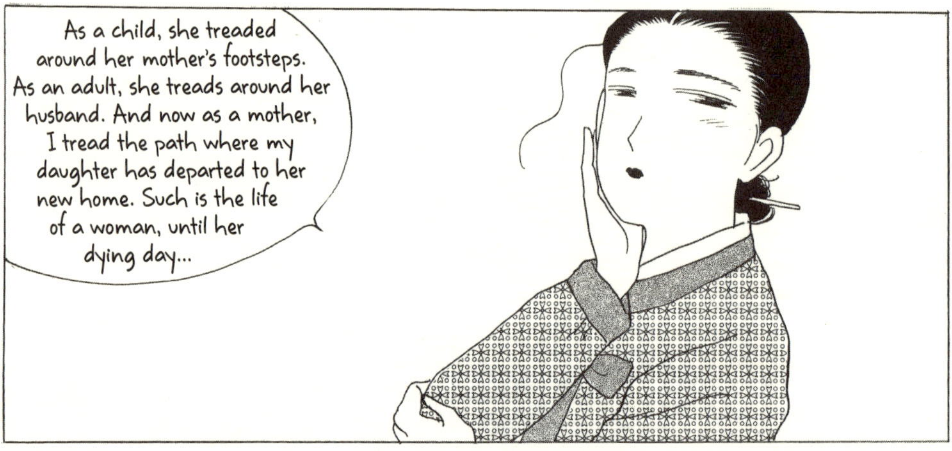
As a child, she treaded around her mother's footsteps. As an adult, she treads around her husband. And now as a mother, I tread the path where my daughter has departed to her new home. Such is the life of a woman, until her dying day...

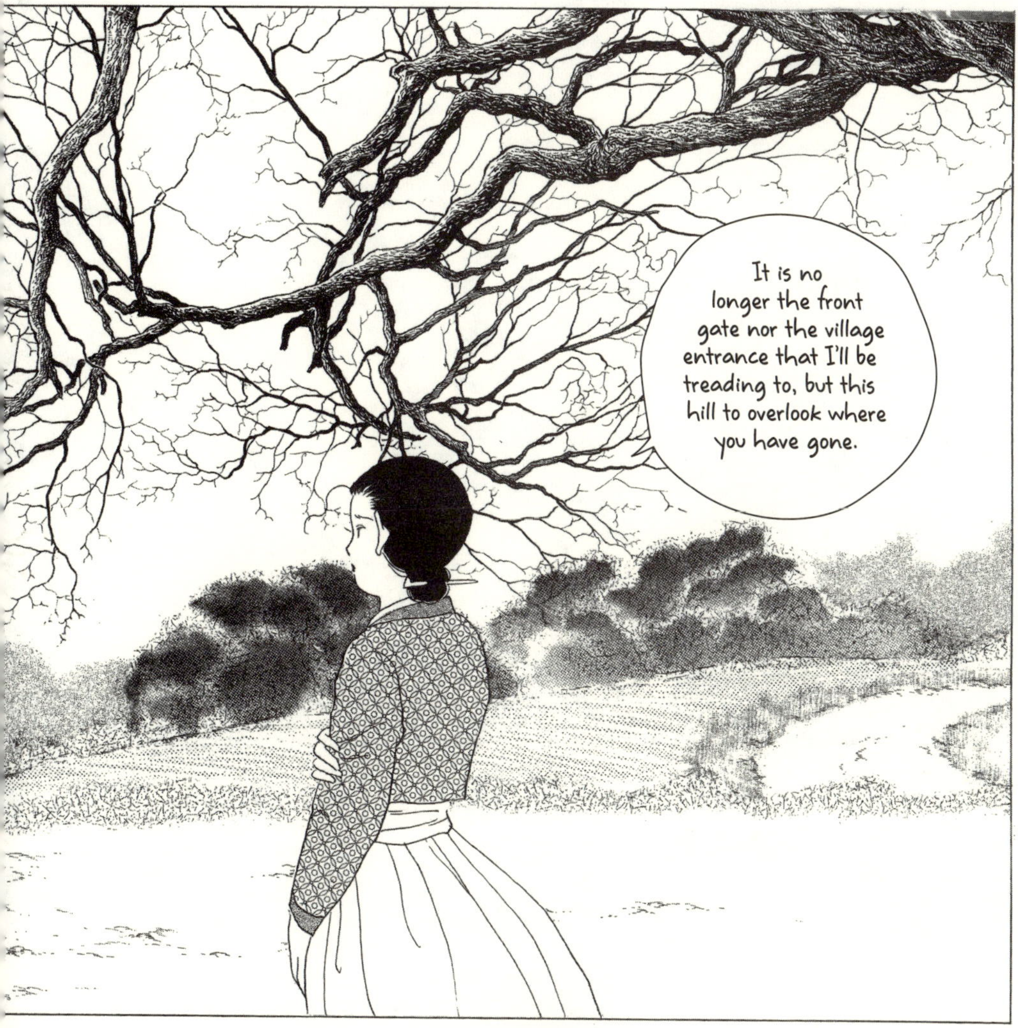
It is no longer the front gate nor the village entrance that I'll be treading to, but this hill to overlook where you have gone.

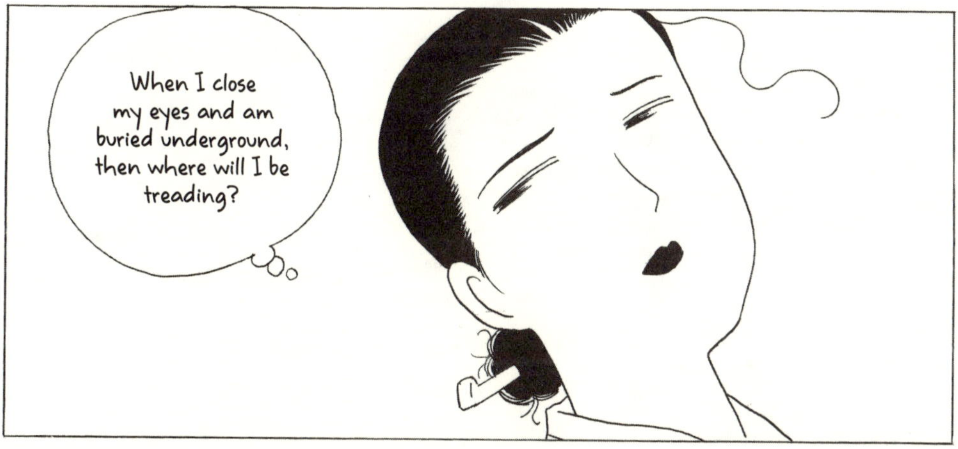
When I close my eyes and am buried underground, then where will I be treading?

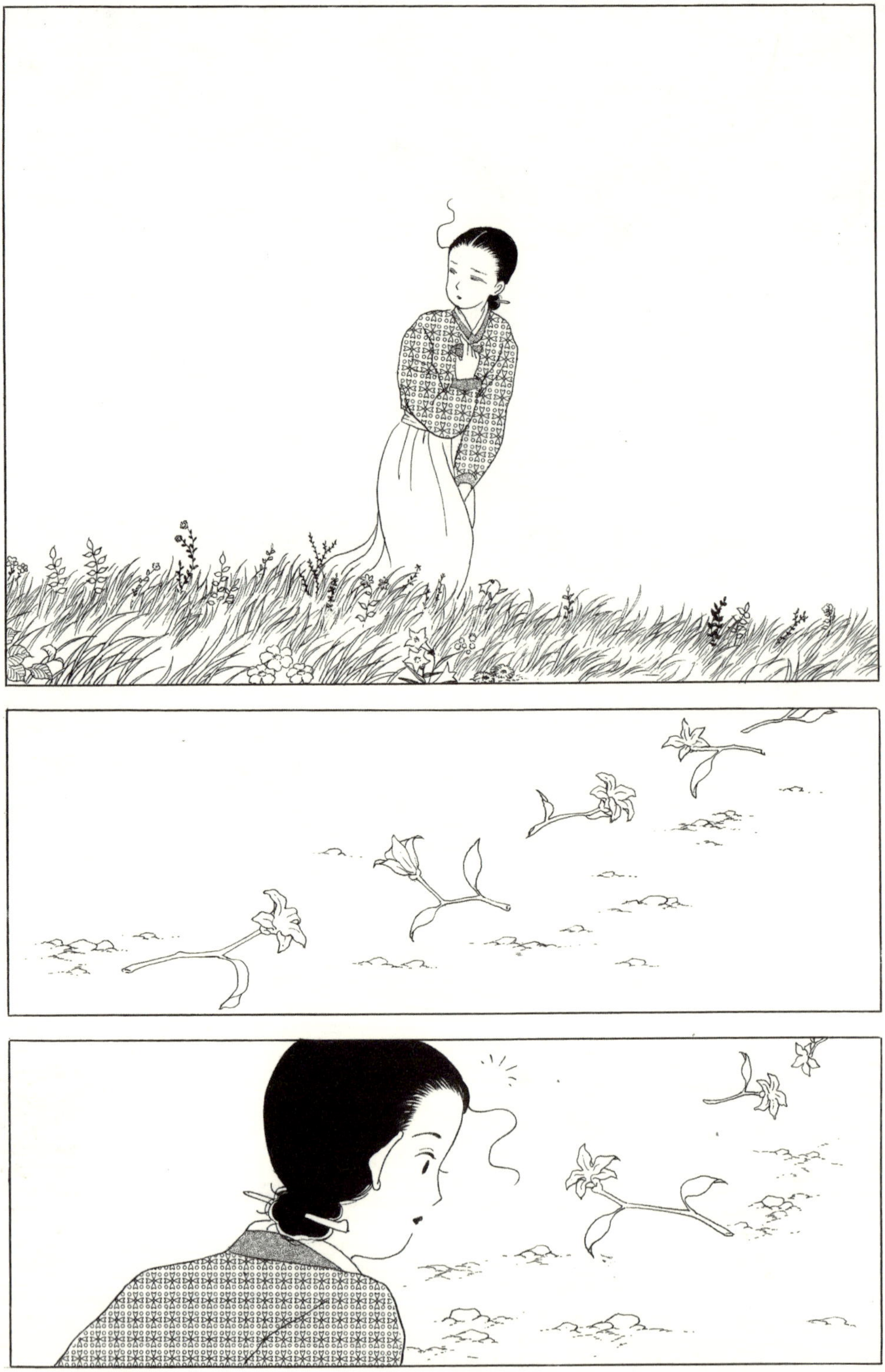

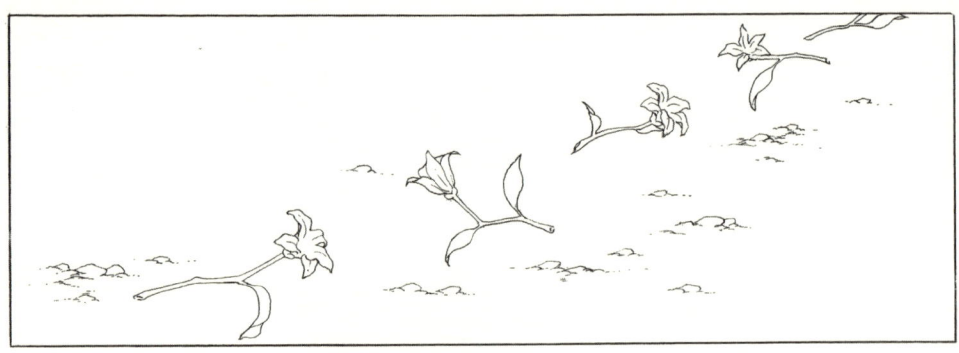

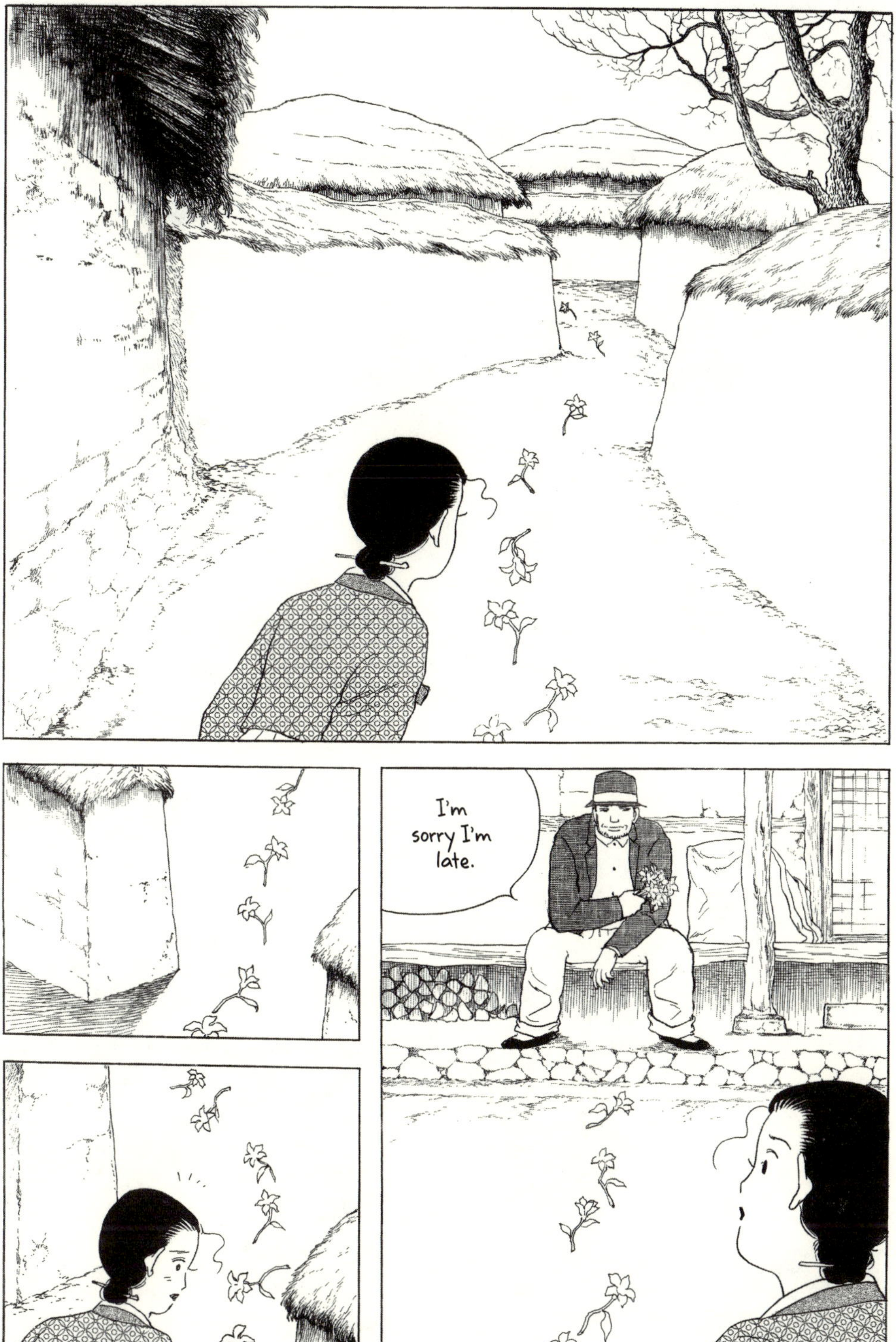
I'm sorry I'm late.

I thought there must be some happy news when I noticed that the smell of flowers was unusually strong this spring. I came rushing here and found that it's Ehwa's wedding day. Unfortunately, I also see that I was late.
If you were going to drop flowers upon the ground, you should have done it along the path that Ehwa took and not along this empty road.
The one who needs consoling is you, so why would I toss flowers along Ehwa's path?
I placed the flowers all the way up to your house because I thought you would be lonely.
I realized today that a daughter is born twice.
For nine months, a mother carries and nourishes her daughter in her stomach, then gives birth to her. It's a happy occasion, but the mother is left feeling sadly empty inside...

But I realized today that, after raising her within my love and embrace and sending her off in marriage, this day is just as sad and leaves me just as empty as the one when I first gave birth to her.
Only after a parent has let go of their child will the parent truly be an adult.
Living creatures leave their nest when ready. But the ones sending them off still anxiously and unnecessarily spread out their hands to catch them.
But my Ehwa is a naïve girl who doesn't know anything. If I knew this was going to happen, I would have kept her with me longer and taught her more.

Ha ha! If you were going to be this worried, perhaps you should have gotten married in her place.
Maybe you're right. Maybe I should start chasing after them right now.
Instead of chasing after someone who's already left, why don't you scratch the back of the one right before your eyes?
Sitting here, with you scratching my back, just proves how old we've gotten. My back gets itchier every year.
Then what shall we do? I don't think you can carry your pack and continue to be a traveling salesman if you're like this.

"I can withstand the aching back, but I'm at my wits' end when it gets itchy."

"Anyway, as it is, I don't have any more room to hang your brushes."

"Meaning I should take this opportunity and stay put?"

"When you're a traveling salesman, the road you're on has no end. Therefore, your journey ends wherever you last stop."

"If I'm going to stop, why would I stop just anywhere?"

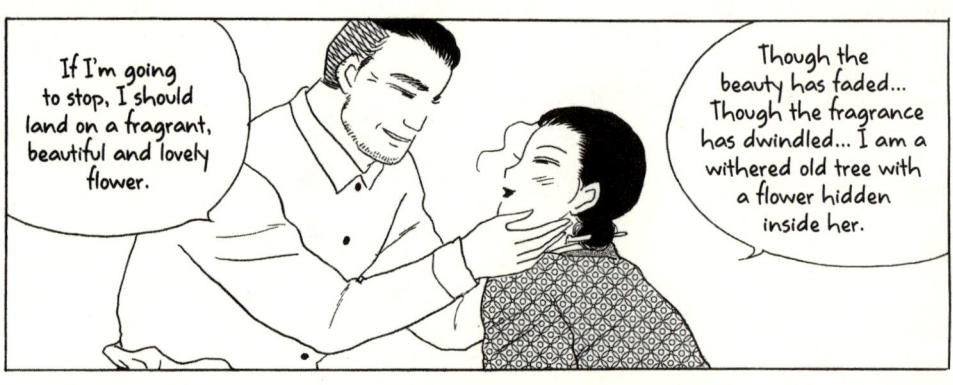

"If I'm going to stop, I should land on a fragrant, beautiful and lovely flower."

"Though the beauty has faded... Though the fragrance has dwindled... I am a withered old tree with a flower hidden inside her."

"Will you hand me one of those brushes?"

"Now that I told you I'm a withered old tree, are you leaving?"

Though the pillow is bright and bathed by the spring moonlight, An apricot blossom hides its body under the shadow of a house With a face flushed with embarrassment...

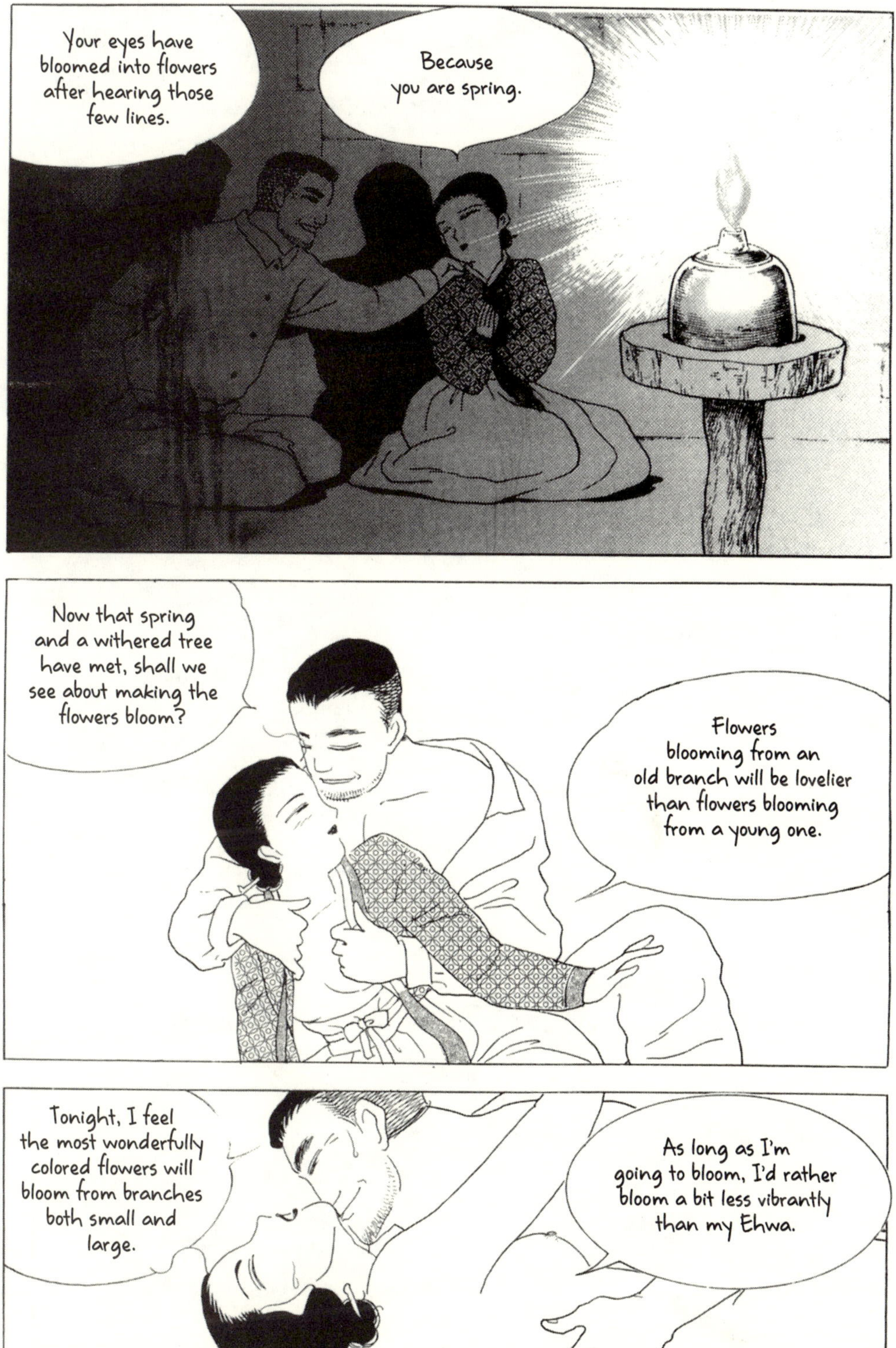
Your eyes have bloomed into flowers after hearing those few lines.
Because you are spring.
Now that spring and a withered tree have met, shall we see about making the flowers bloom?
Flowers blooming from an old branch will be lovelier than flowers blooming from a young one.
Tonight, I feel the most wonderfully colored flowers will bloom from branches both small and large.
As long as I'm going to bloom, I'd rather bloom a bit less vibrantly than my Ehwa.

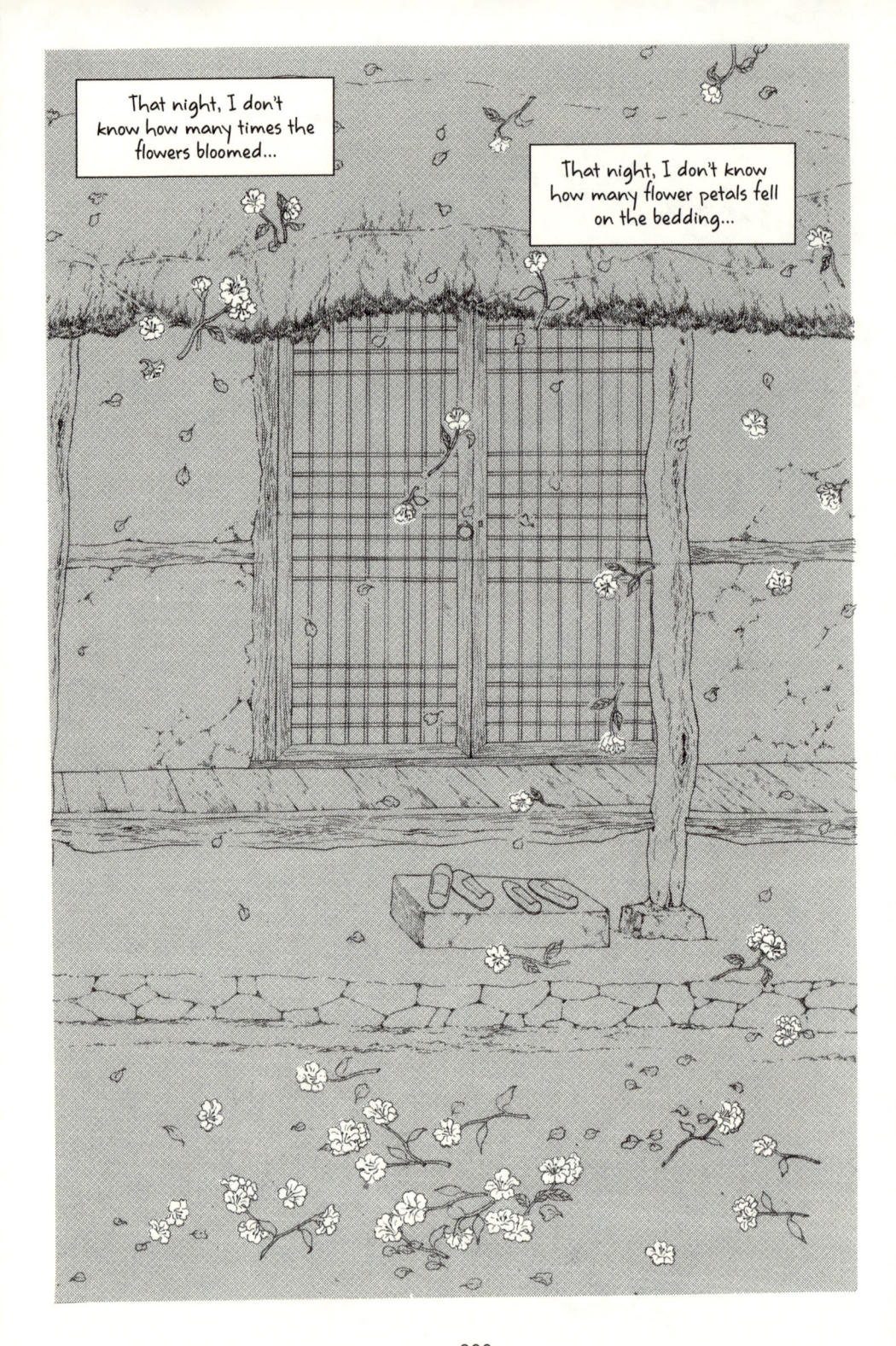

That night, I don't know how many times the flowers bloomed...

That night, I don't know how many flower petals fell on the bedding...

Chapter Ten

THE BRIDAL NIGHT

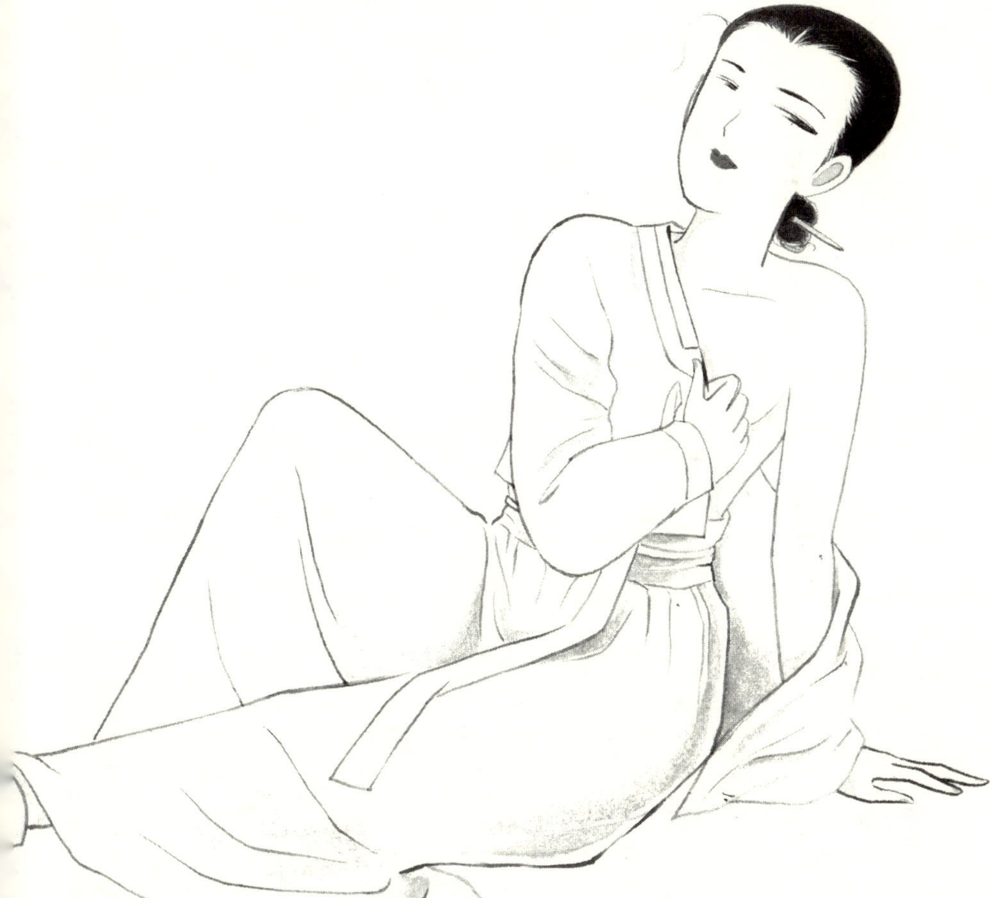

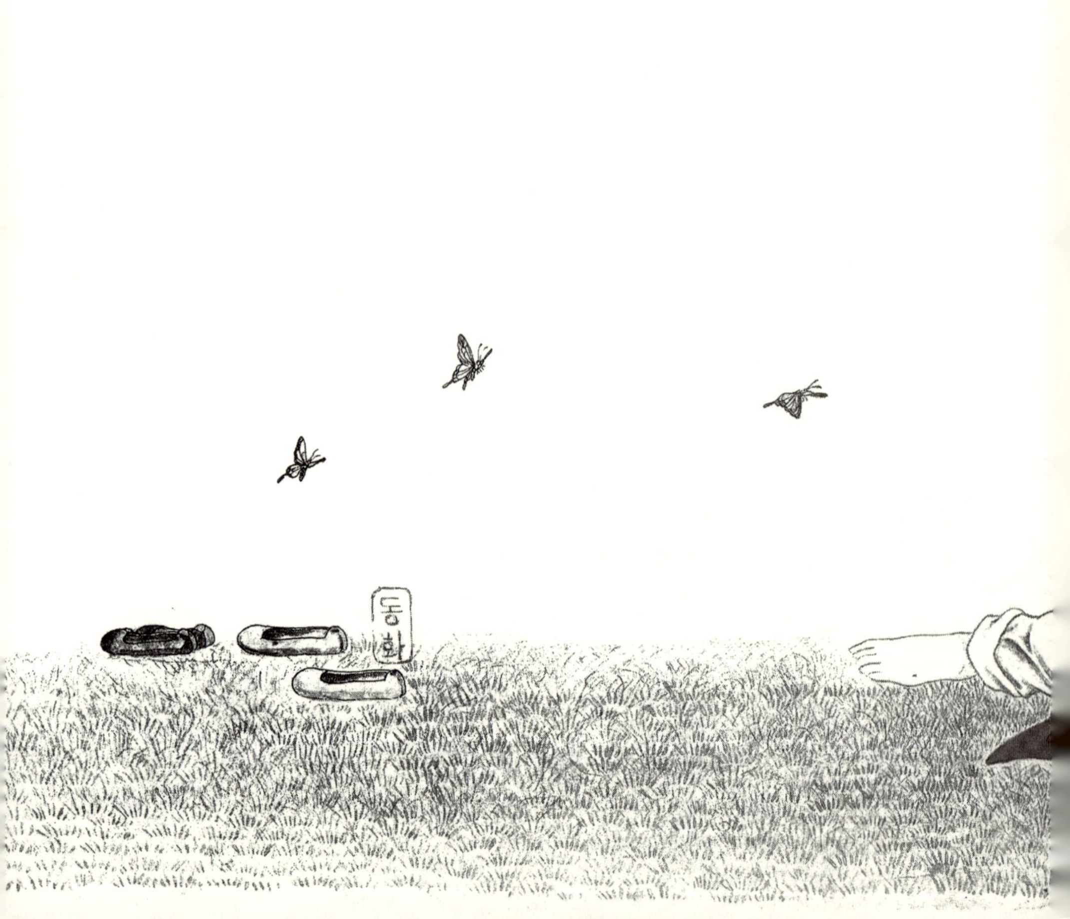
동화

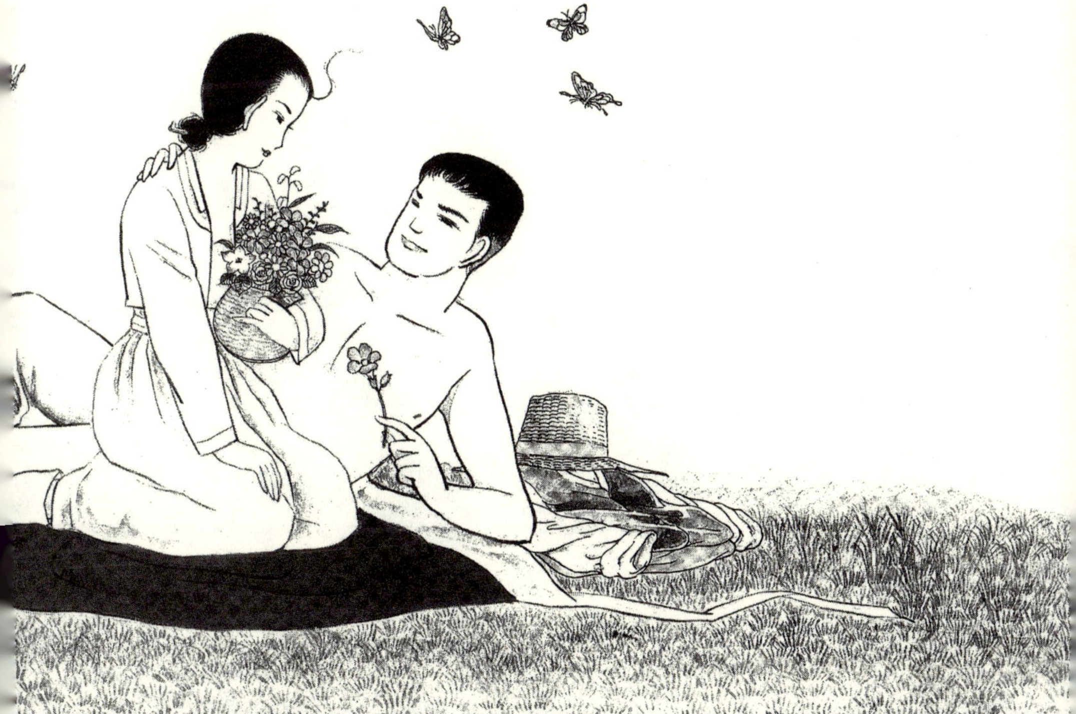

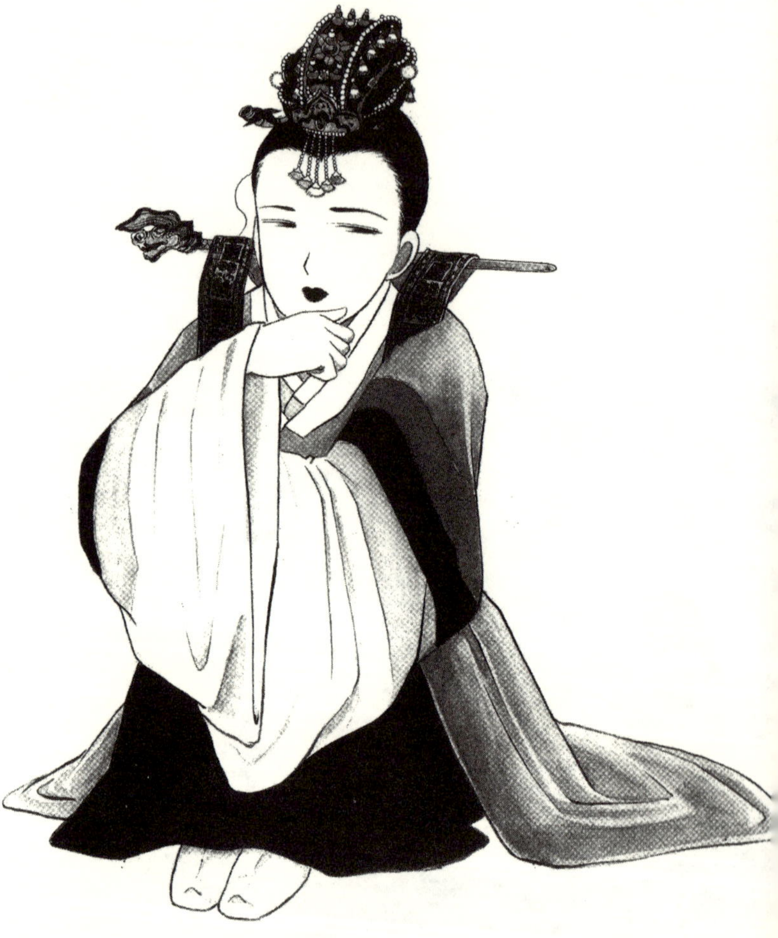

Are you planning to stay like that all night and not sleep?
Am I supposed to sleep with my bridal clothes on?
That's... that's right. Tonight, I have to remove them for you.
SWISH
SWISH
Oh my... It looks like they're finally starting.
They took so long that Hyun got bored and fell asleep!
Ooh...
I'm getting flustered just from hearing them take off their clothes.

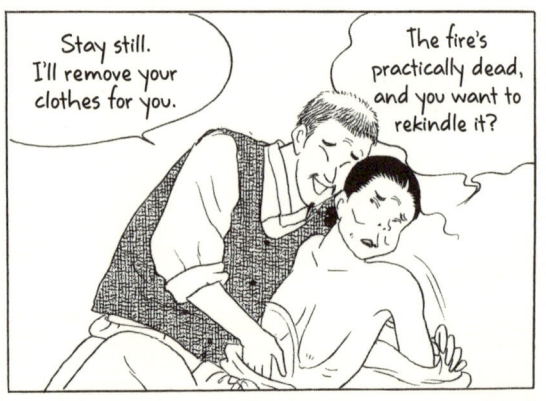

Panel 1	Panel 2
Swish, swish... Duksam must be really happy.	What was that sound supposed to be? — It's the sound of the bridal clothes being removed.

It also sounds like the snow falling in winter... And it also sounds like flowers opening their petals in March. What other sound on earth is lovelier than that?

My goodness... If you like that sound so much maybe you should get married to a new wife.

Though a glass of wine is best at the first sip, a wife is best at the very end.

What are you doing, old man?

Stay still. I'll remove your clothes for you.

The fire's practically dead, and you want to rekindle it?

Why does the noise of these clothes being removed sound like an avalanche and someone tramping through a dense forest?

RUSTLE RUSTLE

WHOOO

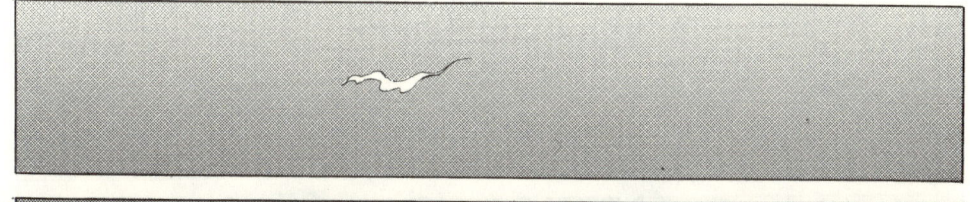

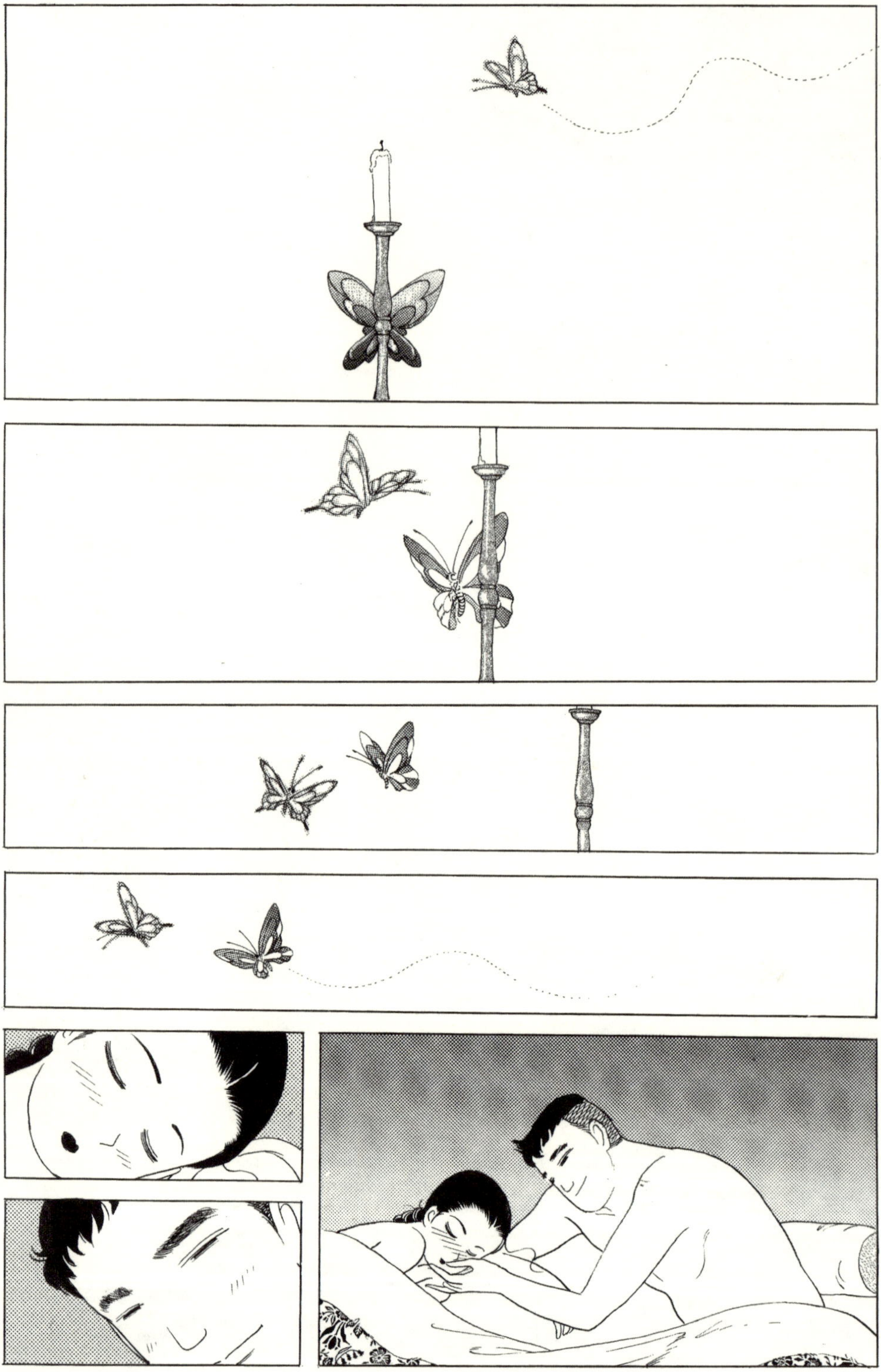

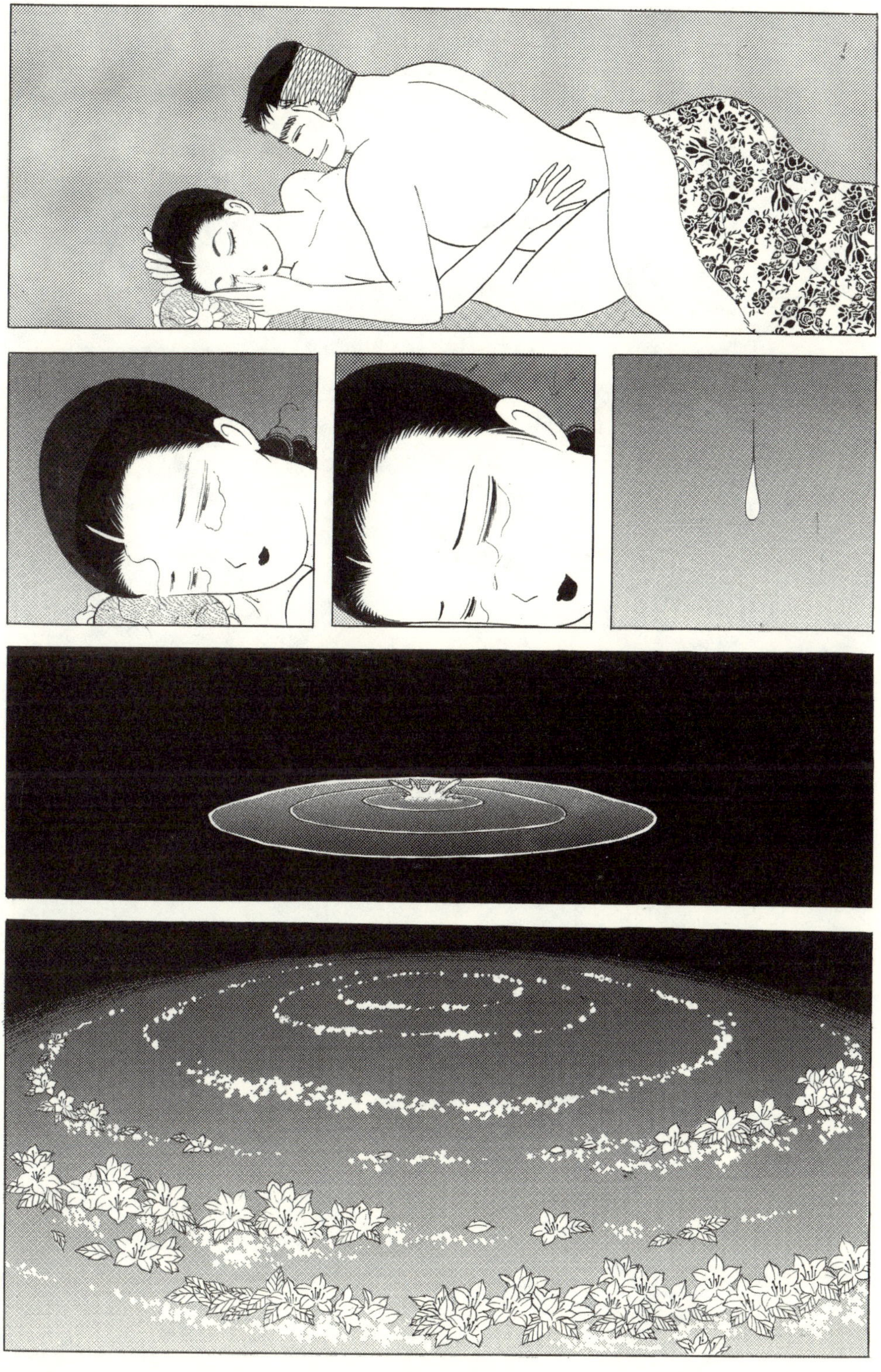

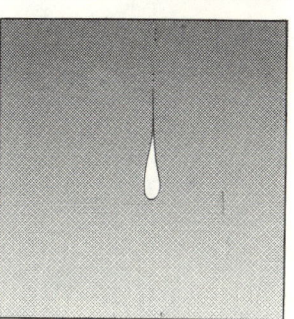

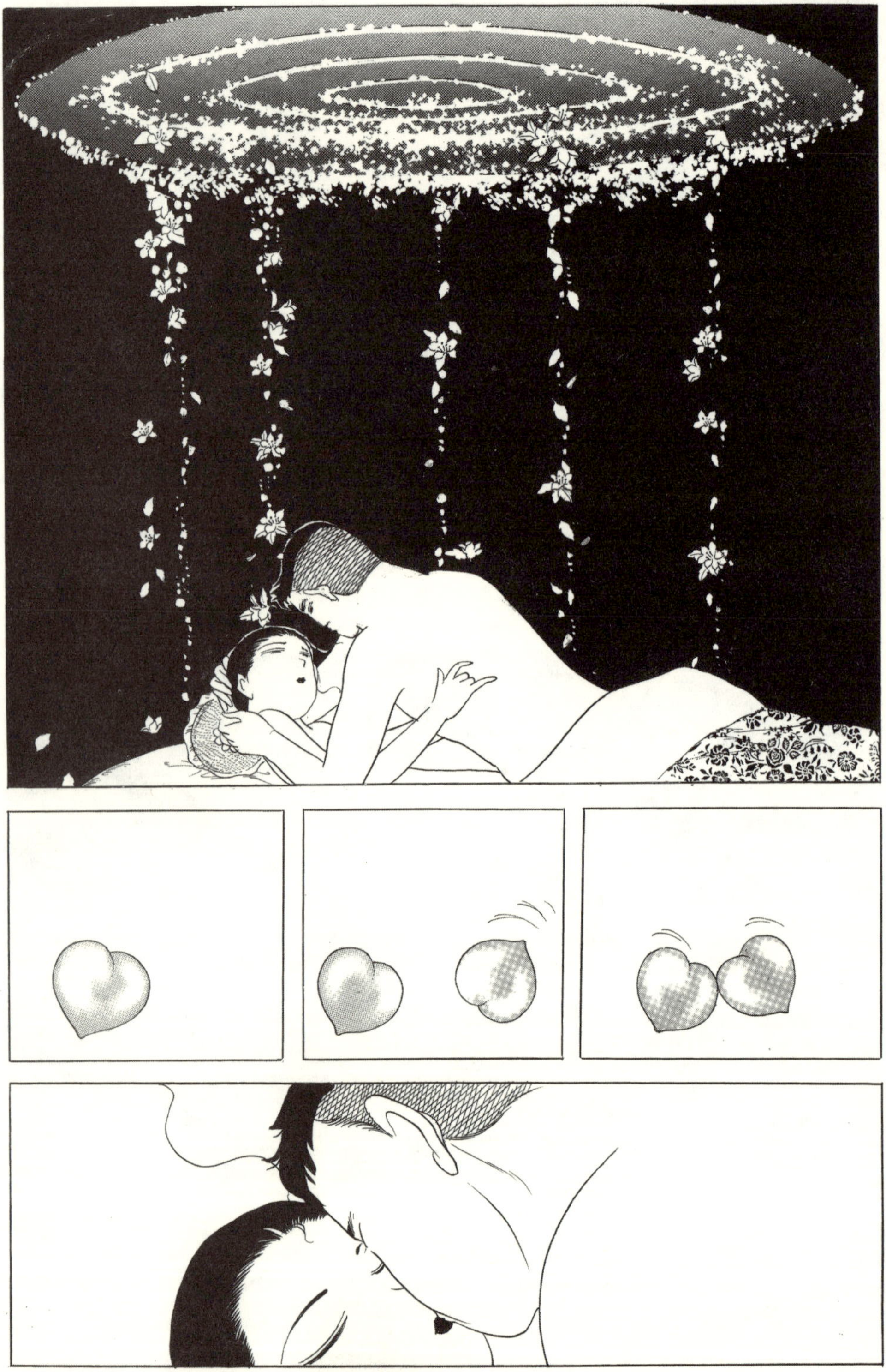

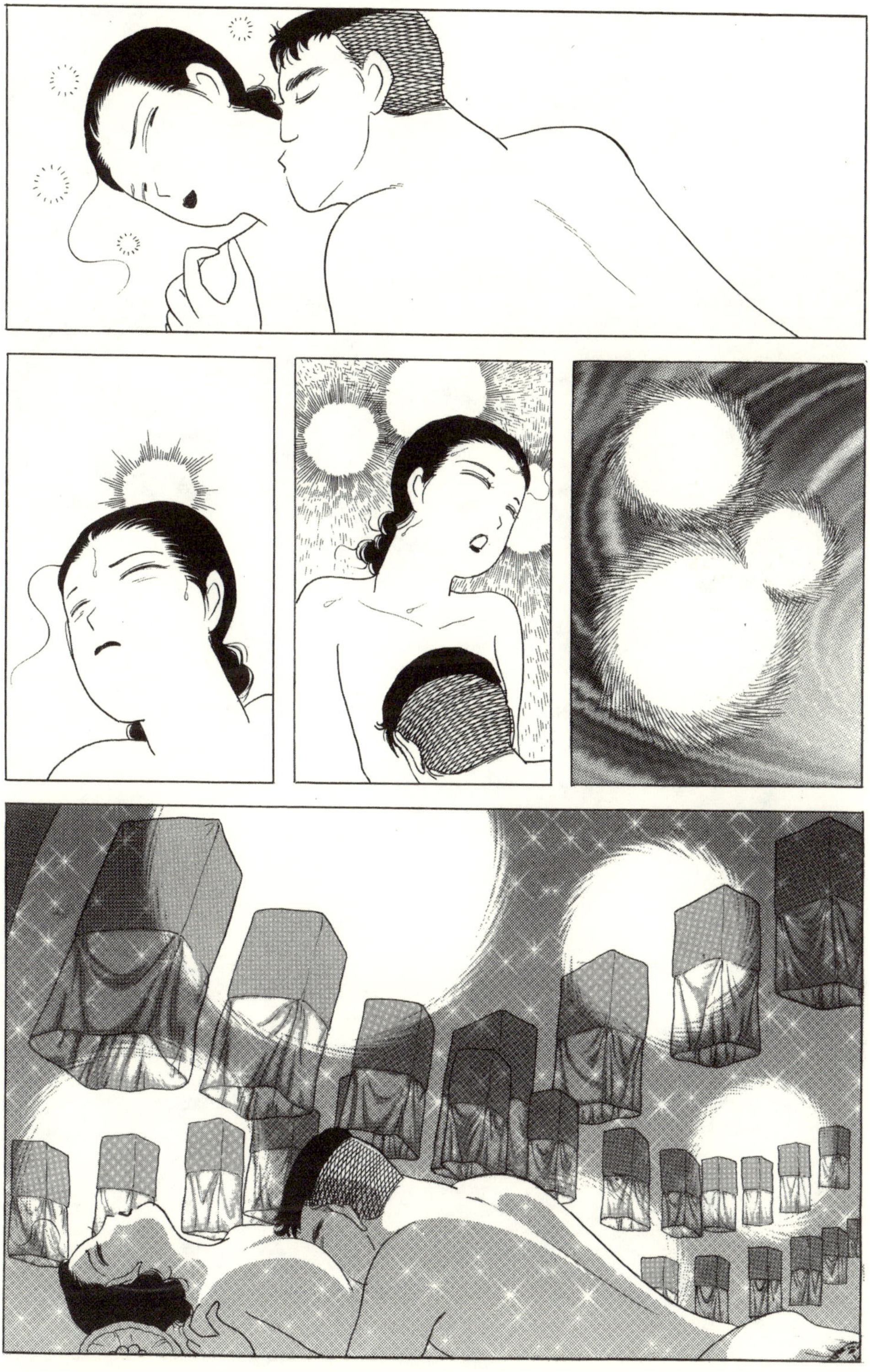

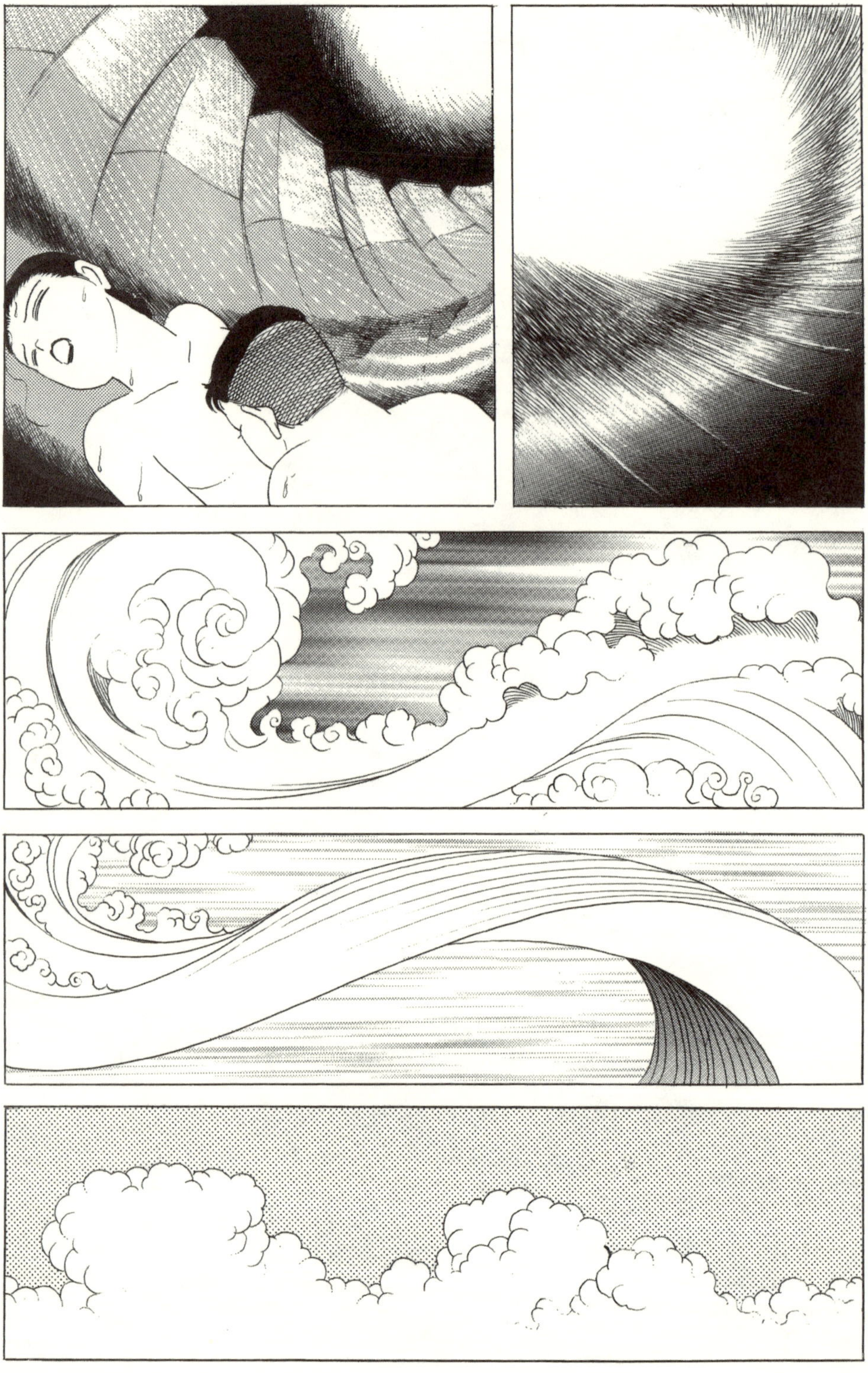

293

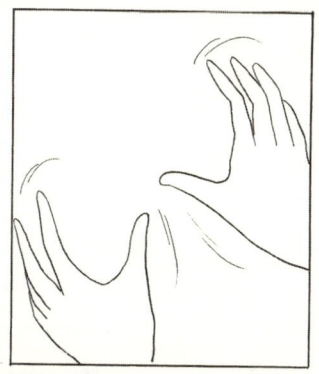

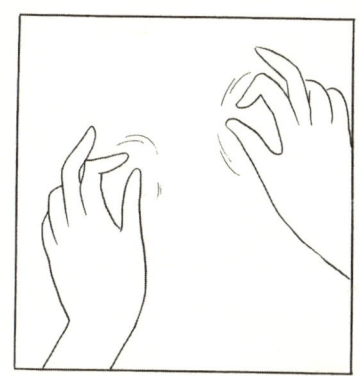

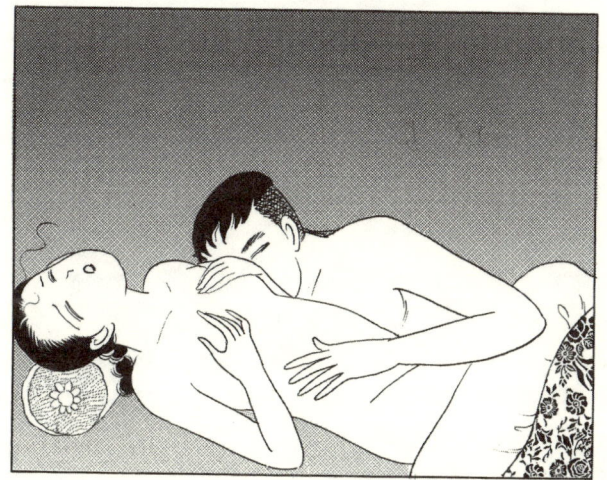

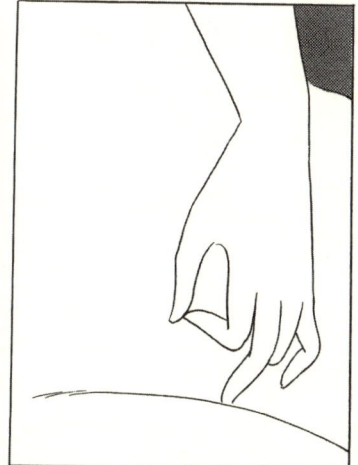

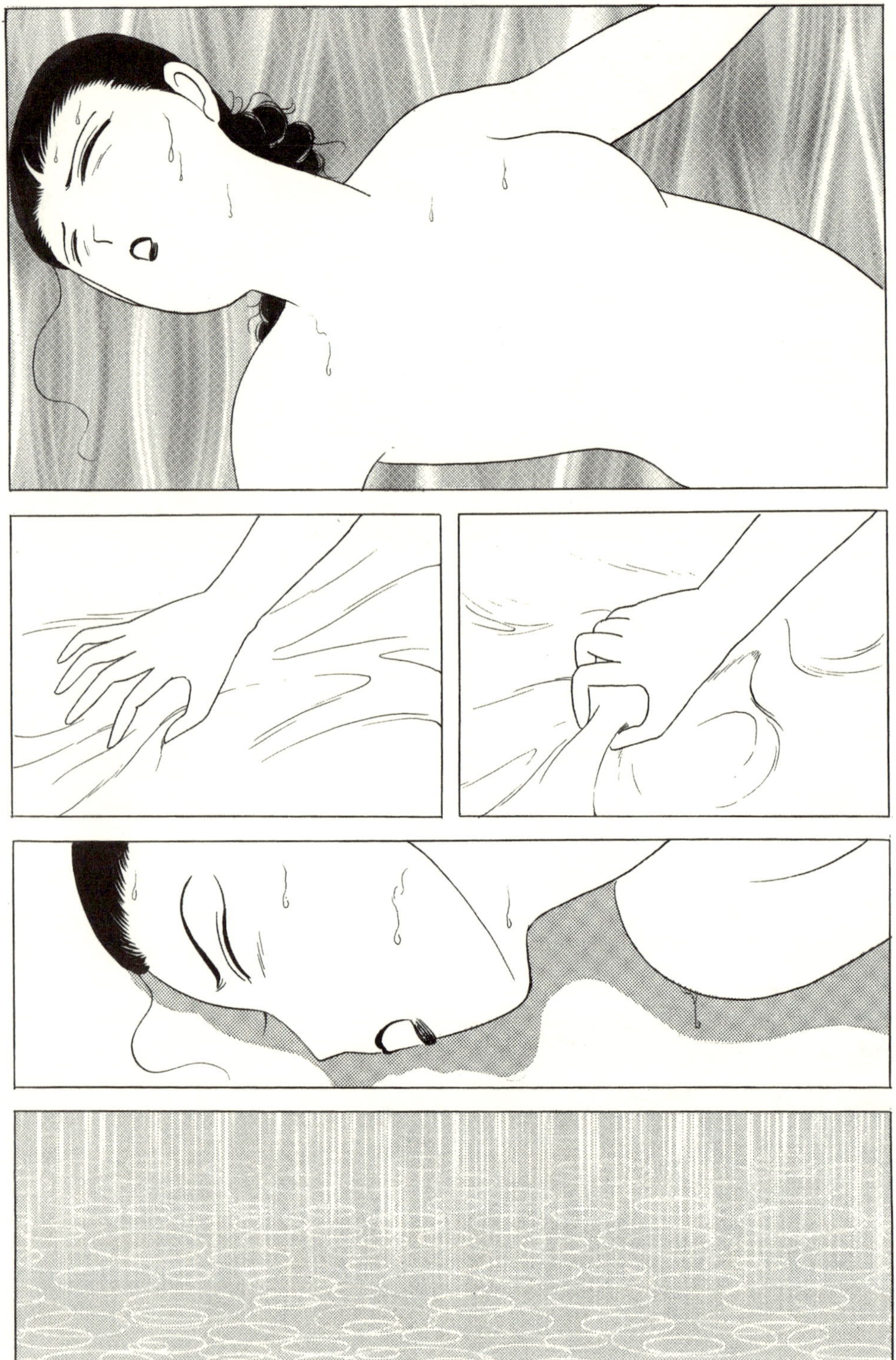

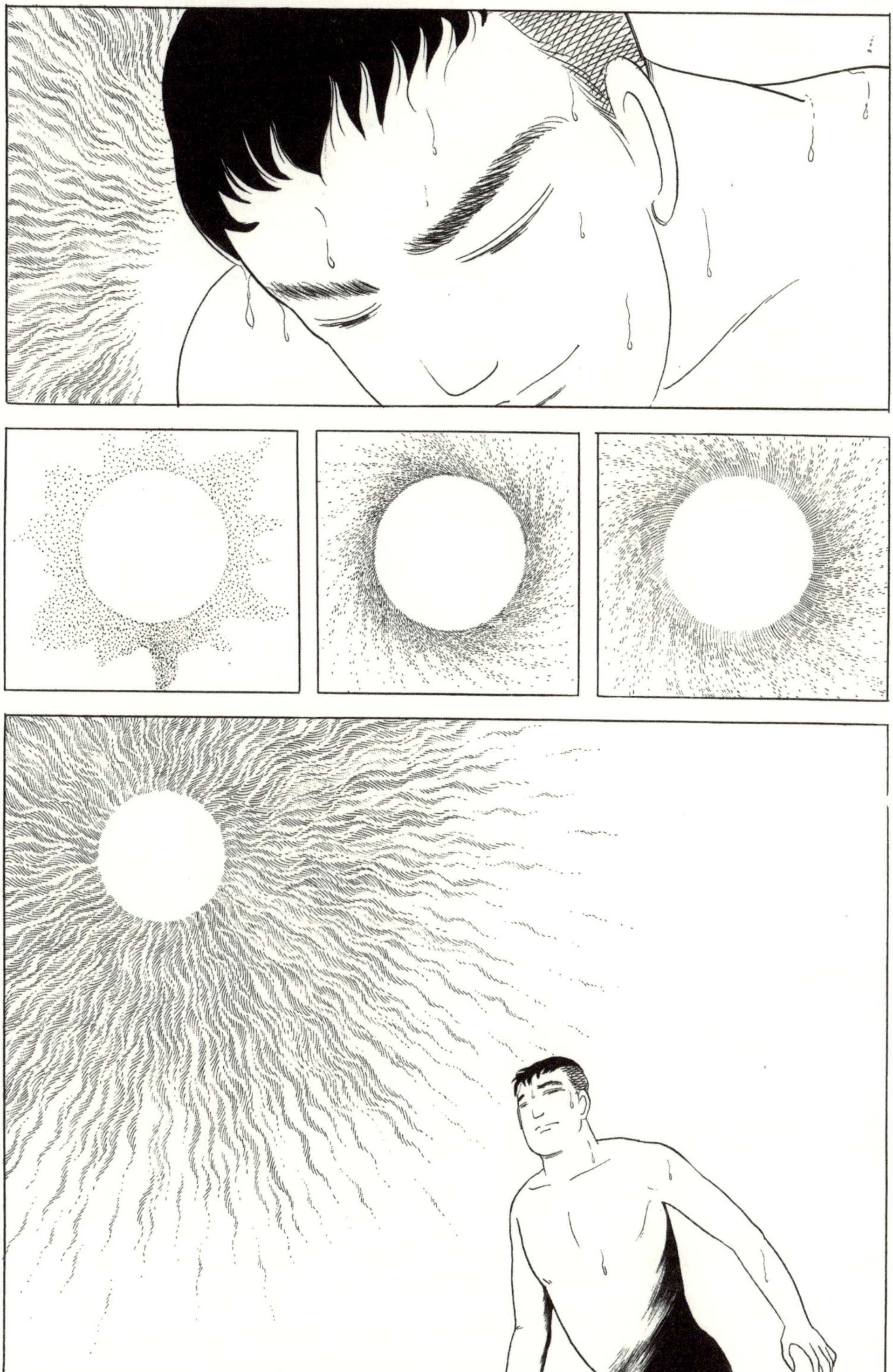

296

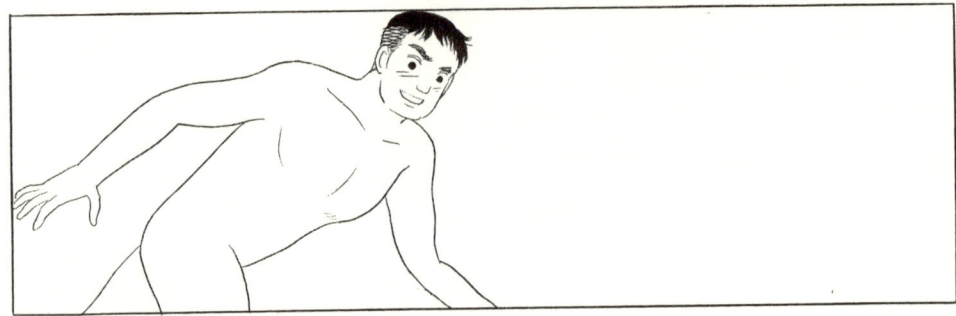

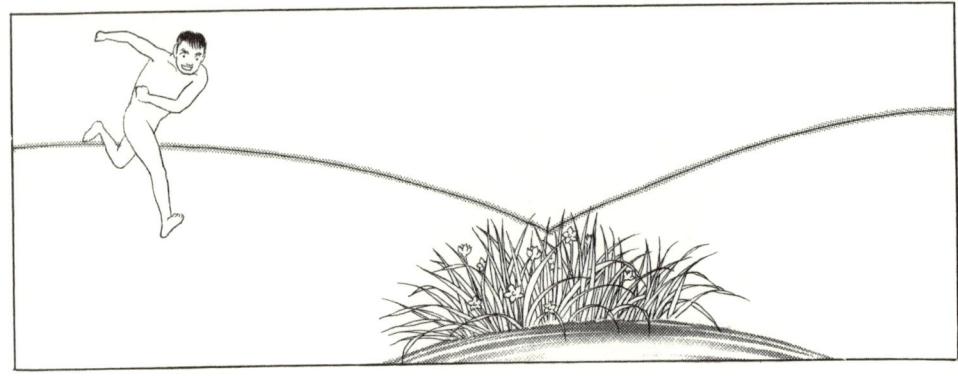

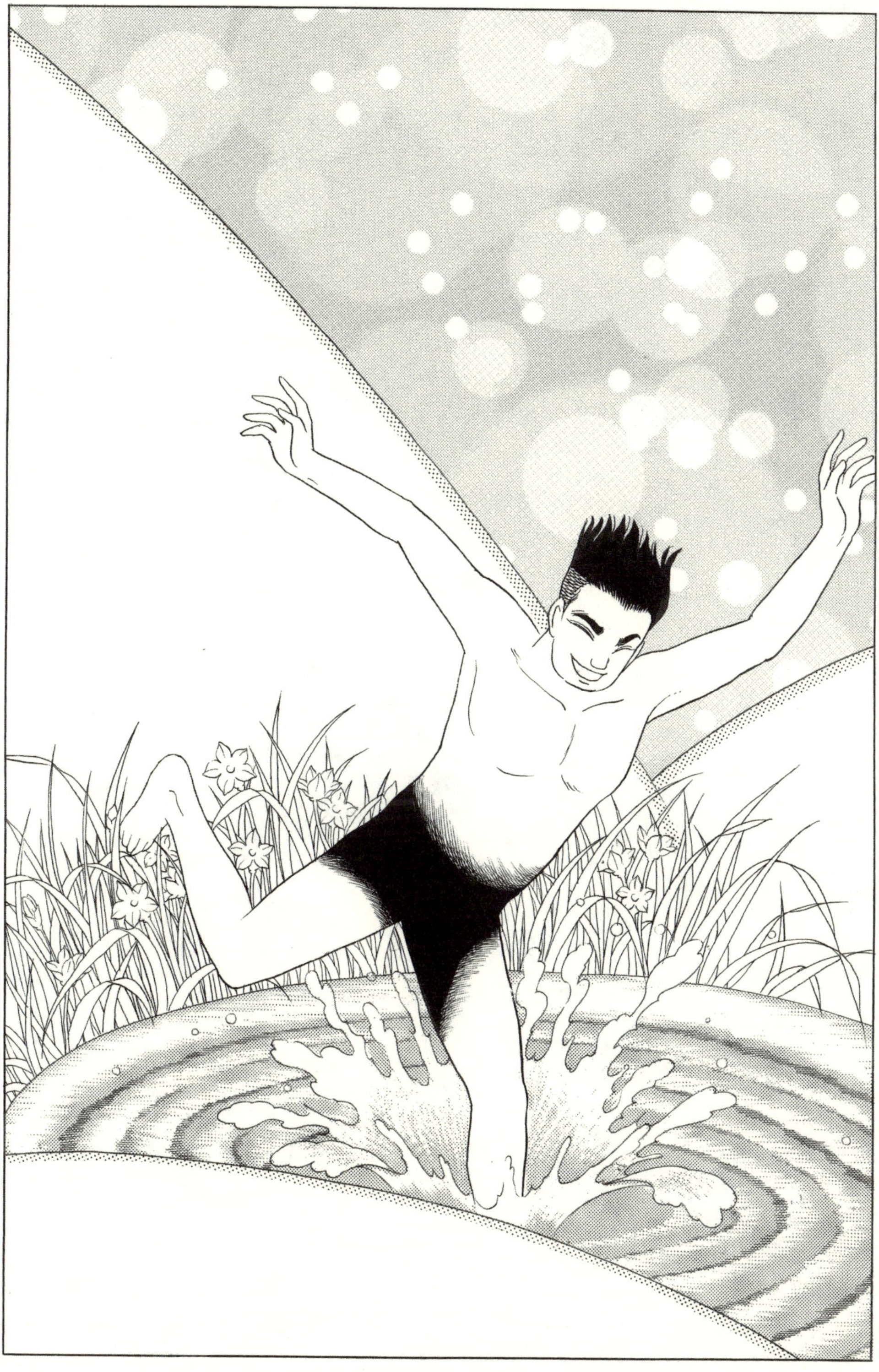

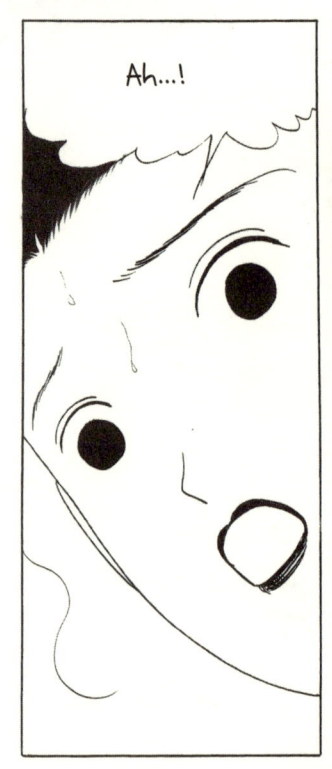

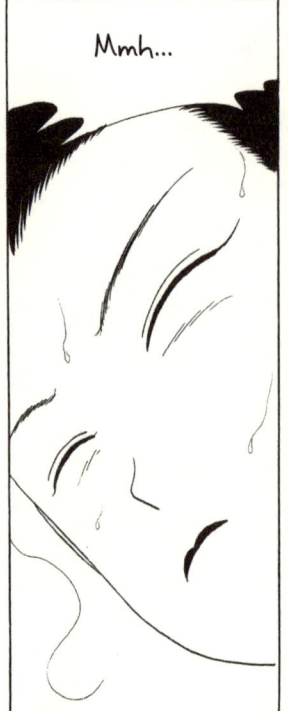

Ah...!	Mmh...

Oh my goodness!

What's with all the noise?

Is she giving birth to a child on her first night?

Aah!

I'd rather die than go through that!

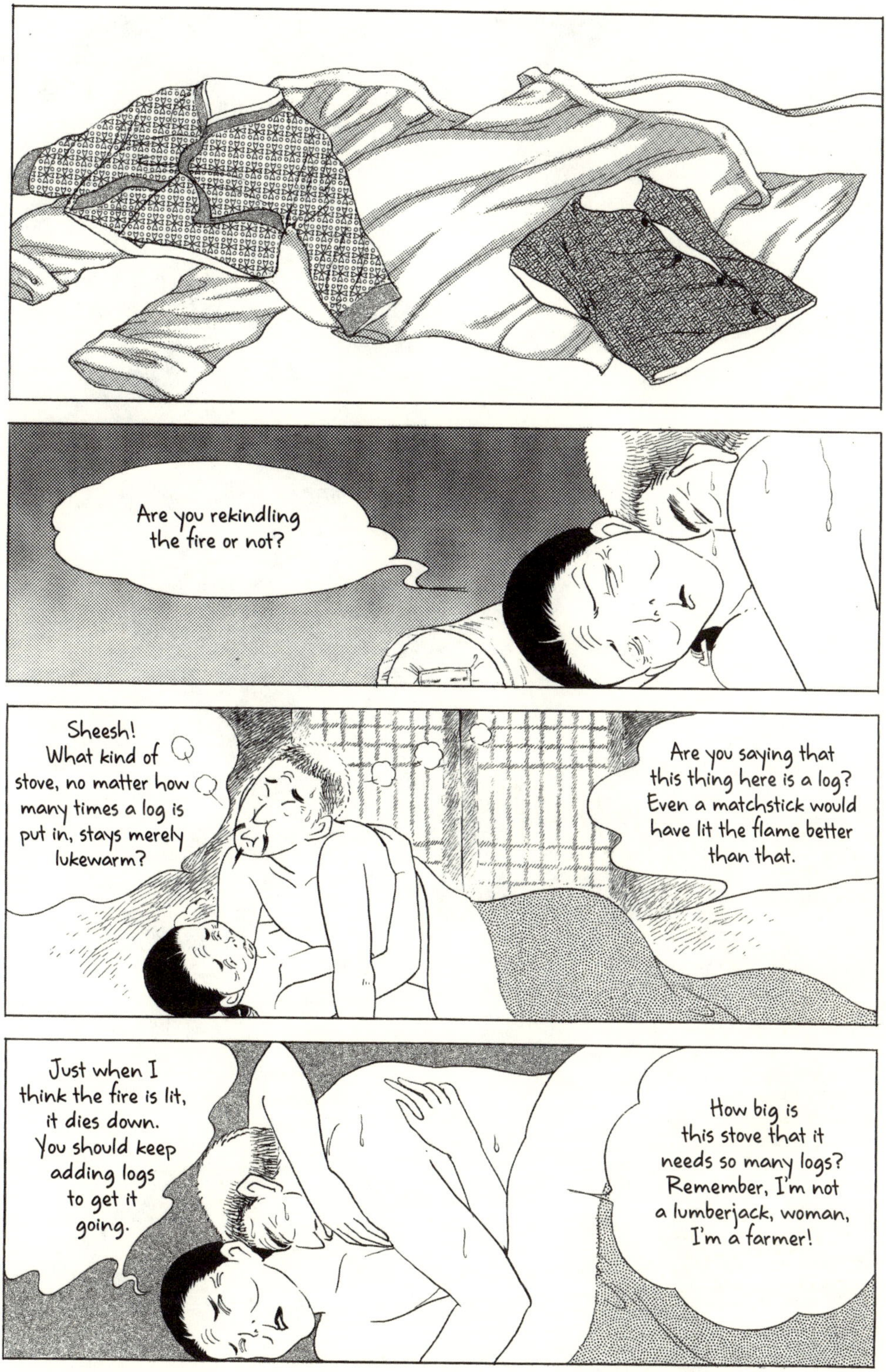
Are you rekindling the fire or not?
Sheesh! What kind of stove, no matter how many times a log is put in, stays merely lukewarm?
Are you saying that this thing here is a log? Even a matchstick would have lit the flame better than that.
Just when I think the fire is lit, it dies down. You should keep adding logs to get it going.
How big is this stove that it needs so many logs? Remember, I'm not a lumberjack, woman, I'm a farmer!

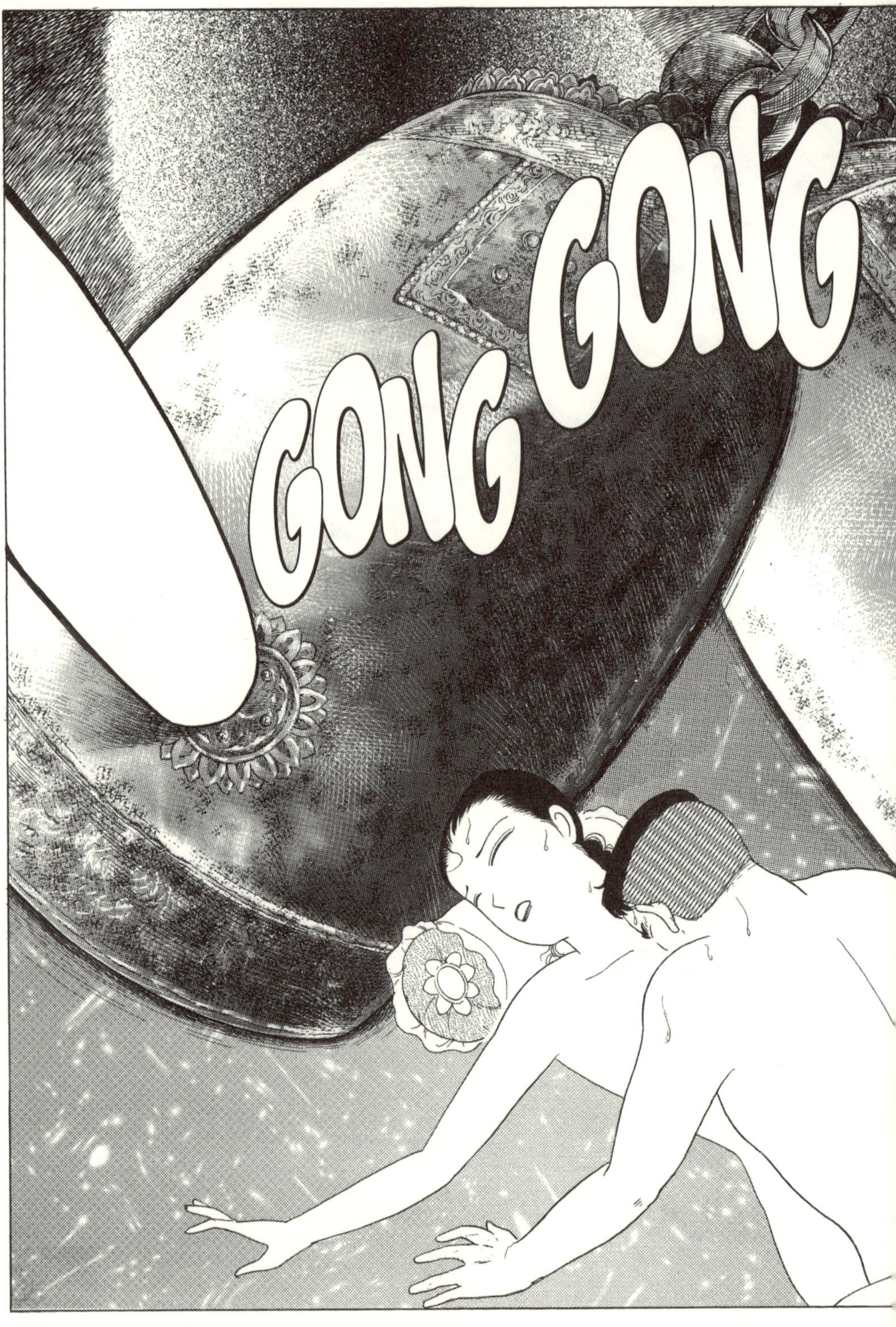
GONG GONG

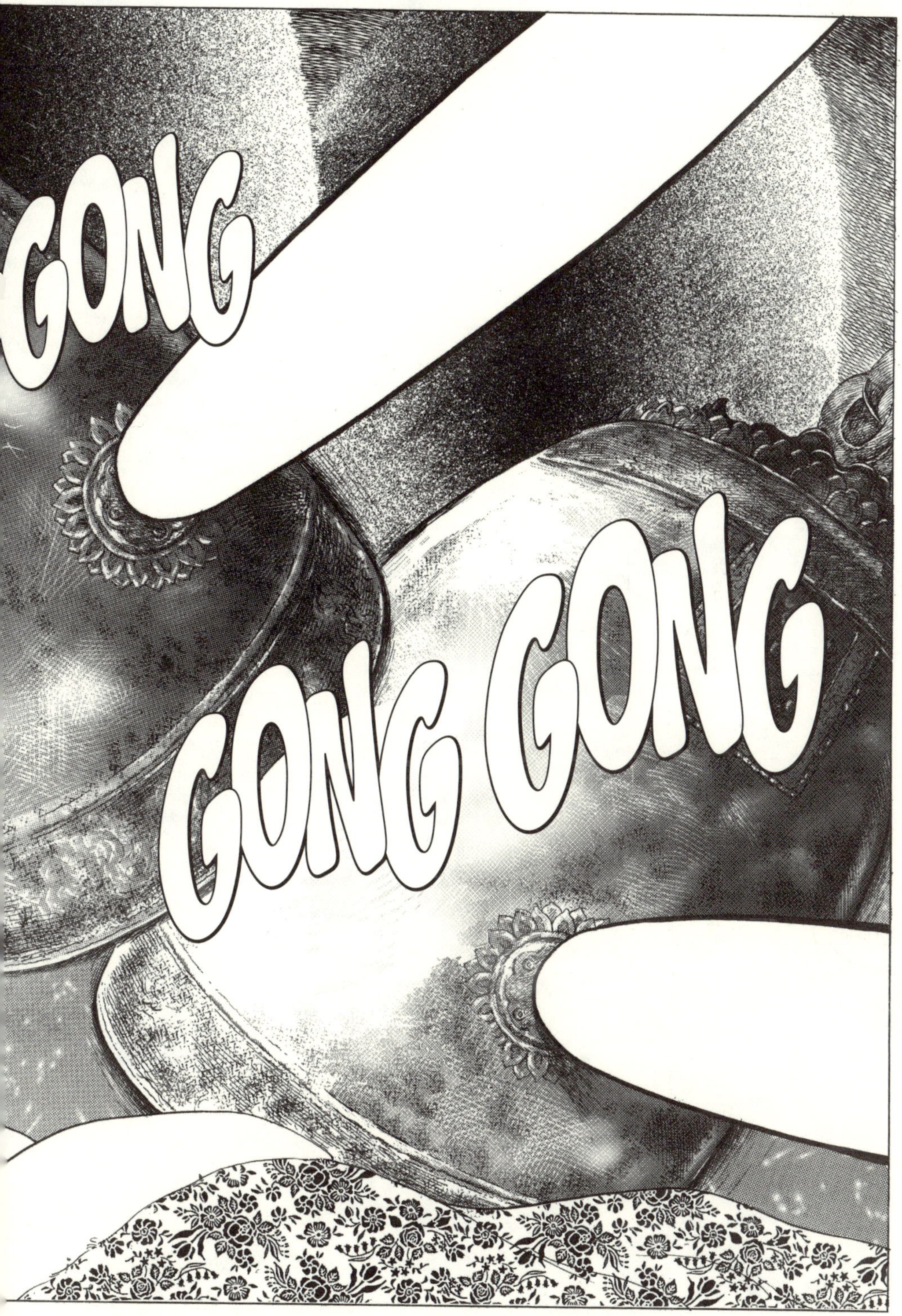
GONG
GONG GONG

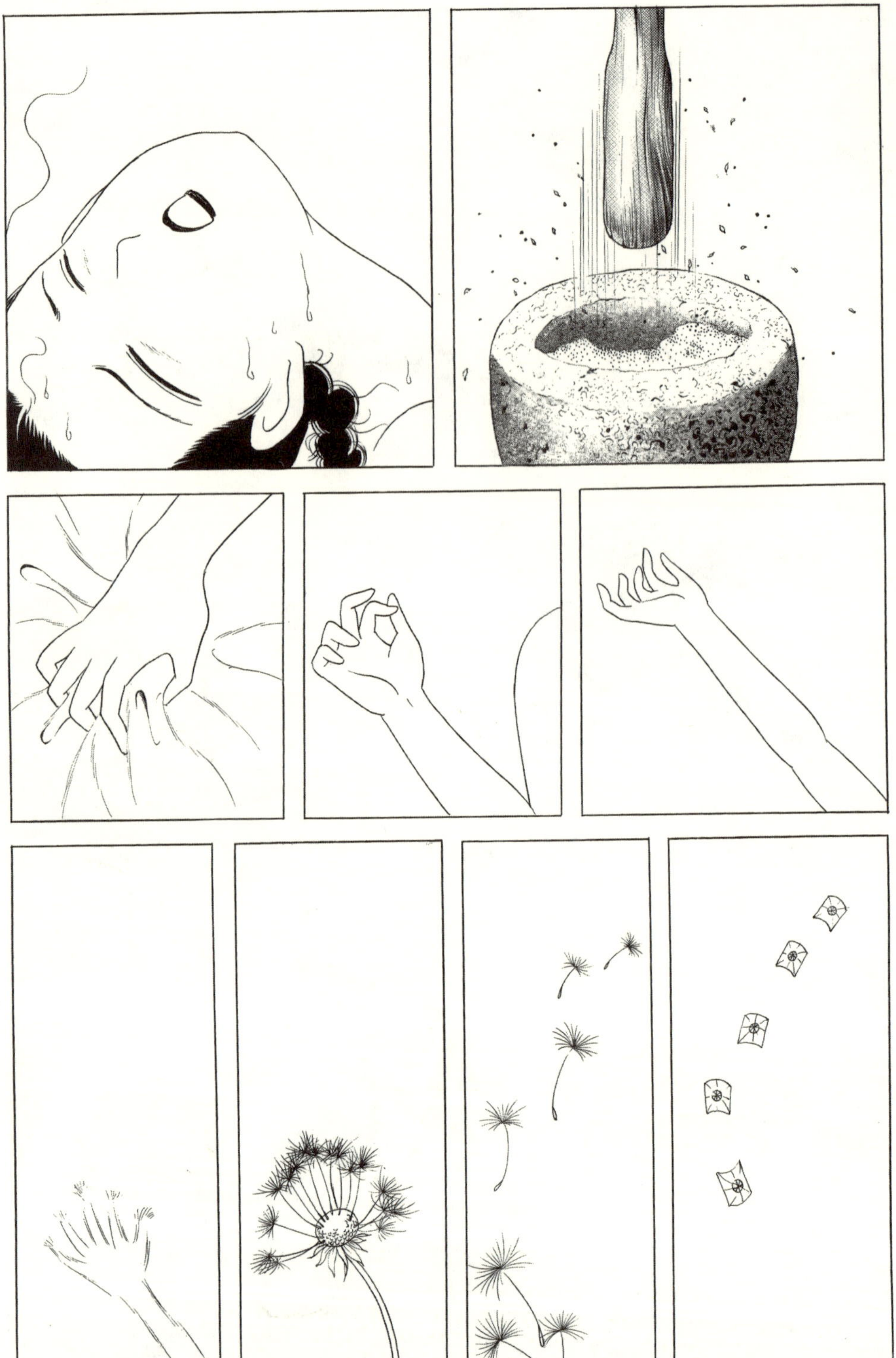

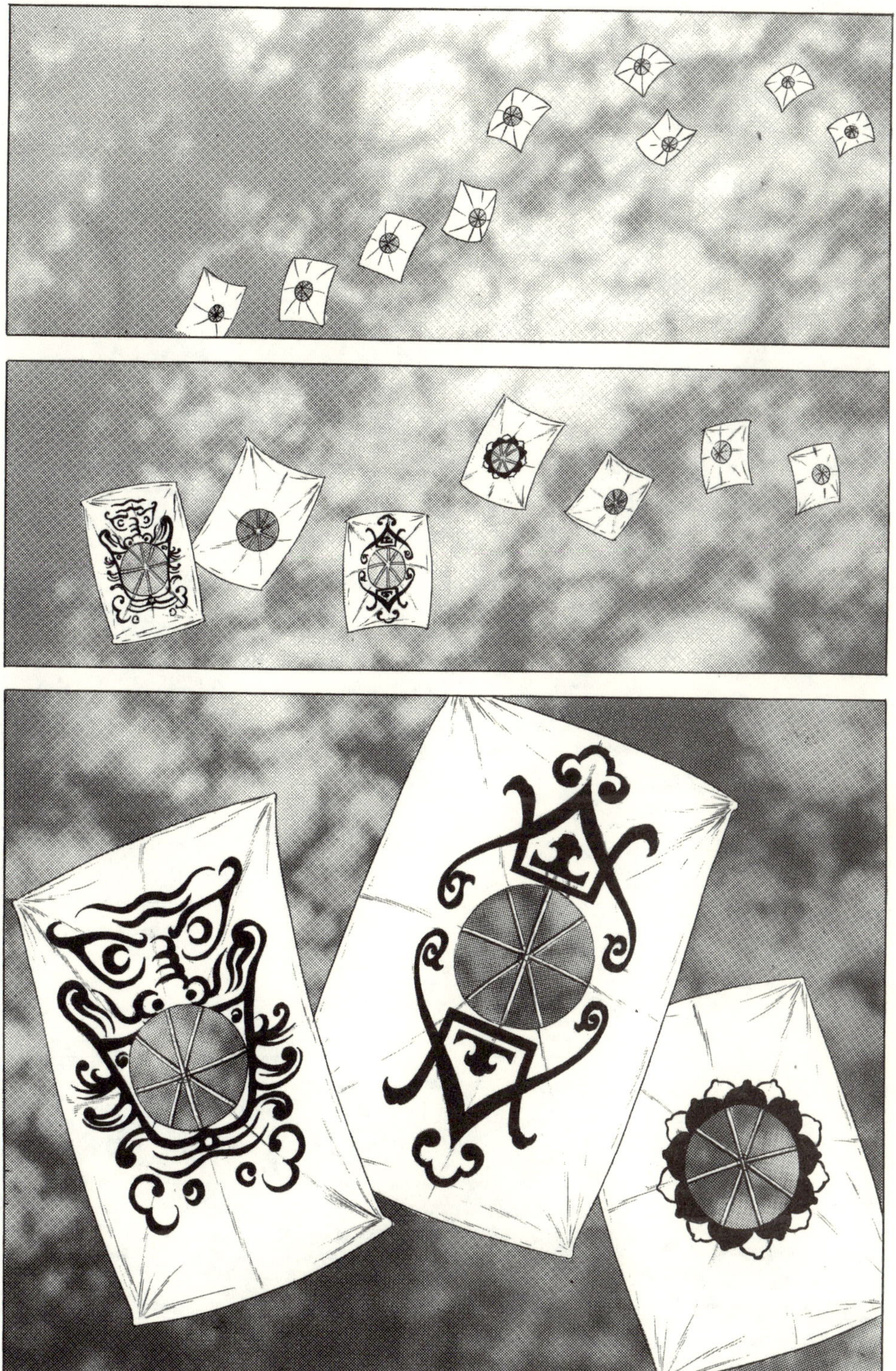

Is this your first time farming? If you use a tiny rake to lightly scratch the surface of the soil, instead of working it vigorously with a plough, you'll never be able to till the land.
This is a plough! How can you call it a rake?
How in the world can a plough be that short?
How can soil be so tough that it blunts the farming tool?
After complaining about the soil and tool, it looks as though today's farming is ruined.

KAWHOOOSH

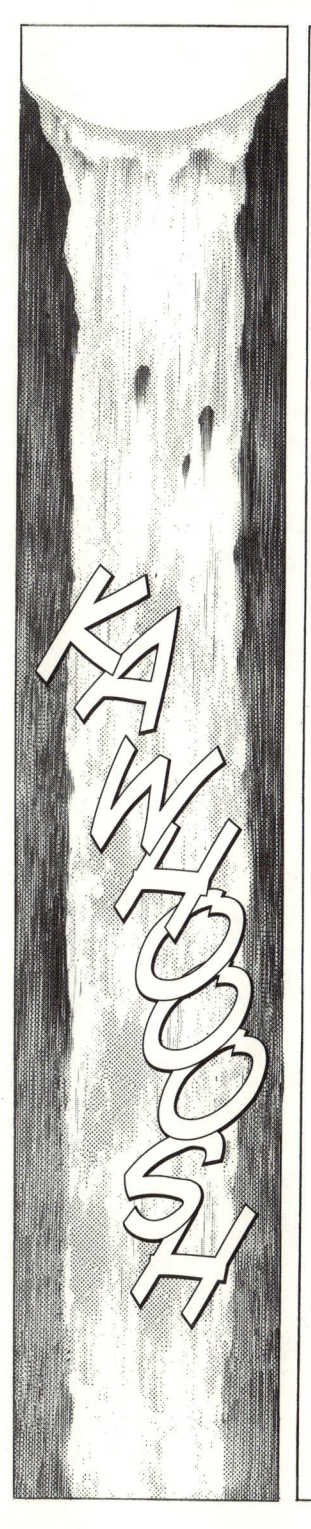

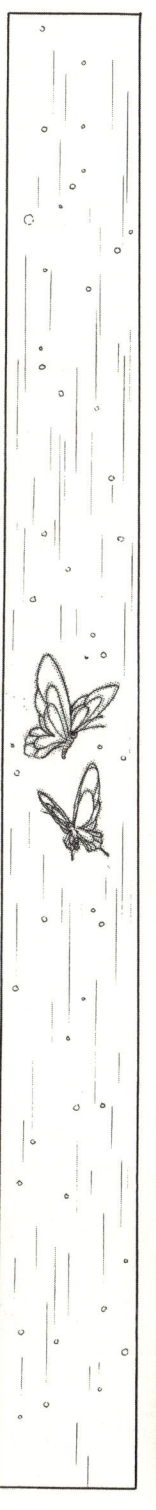

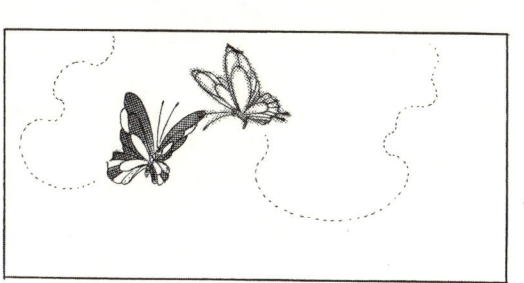

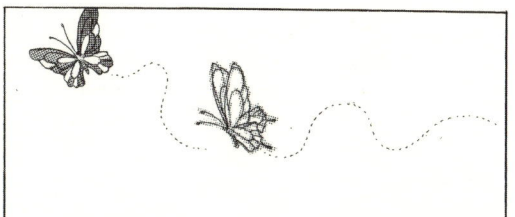

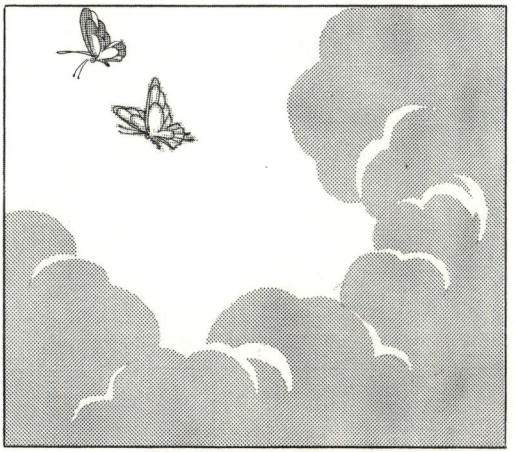

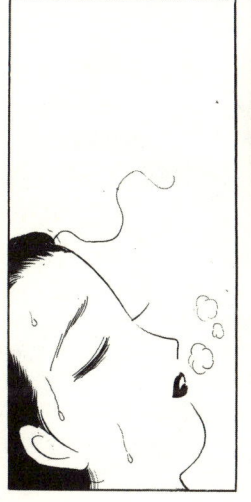

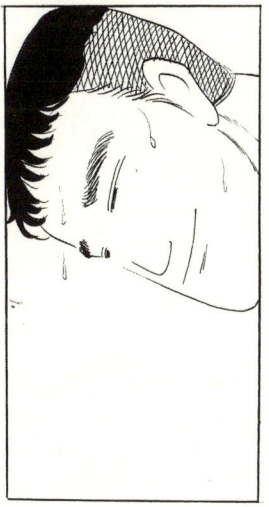

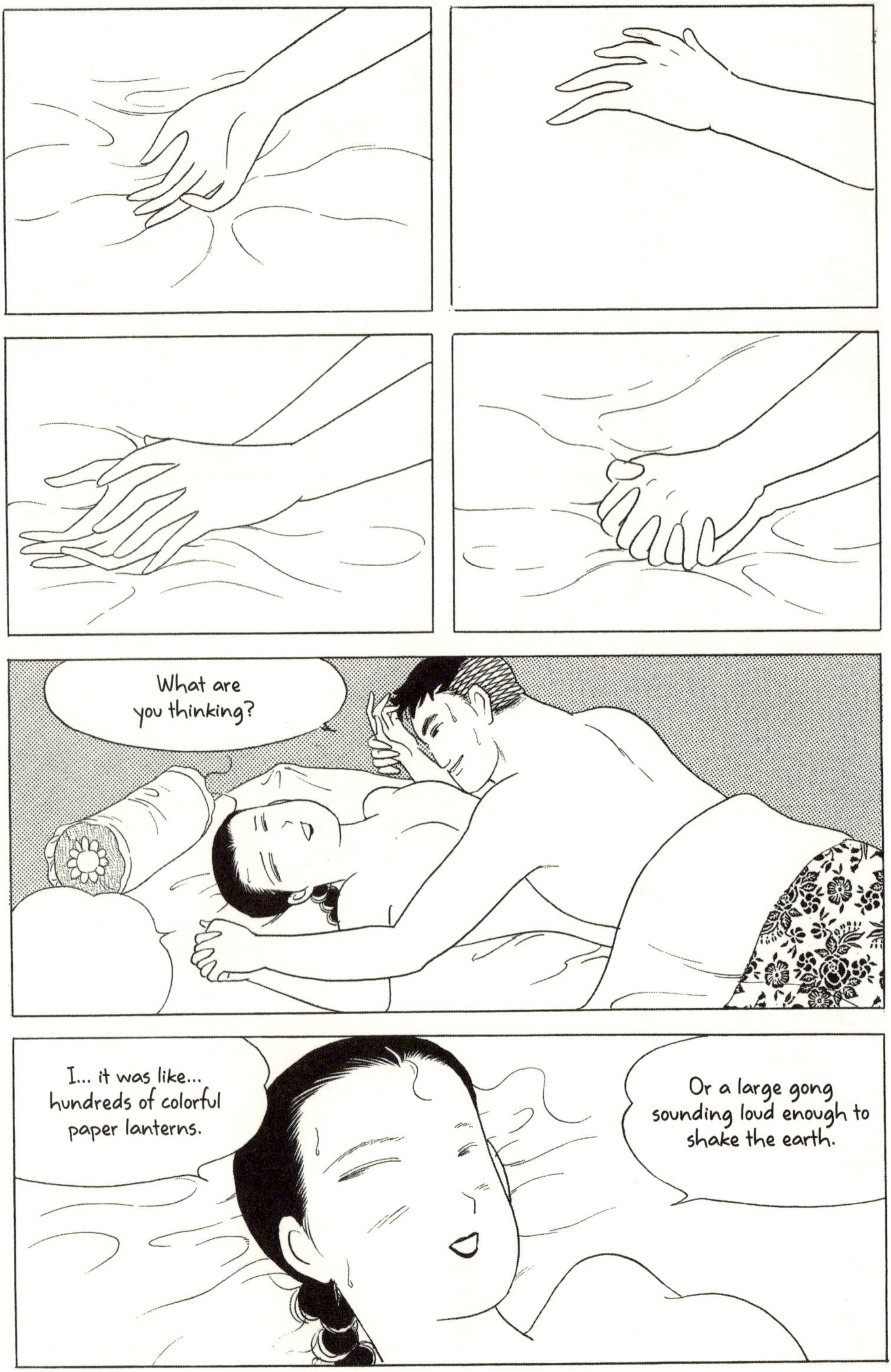

What are you thinking?
I... it was like... hundreds of colorful paper lanterns.
Or a large gong sounding loud enough to shake the earth.

I know.
I felt as if I came upon a white sand dune. It was the first time I had ever seen something so blindingly bright.
And within a pitch black forest...
...I met a small pond.
Is this what married life is like? Flowers blooming, butterflies flying, and colorful paper lanterns swaying in the wind?
As farmers, it will not be like that every day for us. We will have to face bad weather and weariness to cultivate the earth. But from time to time, the flowers and the butterflies will come to brighten our life of hard labor.

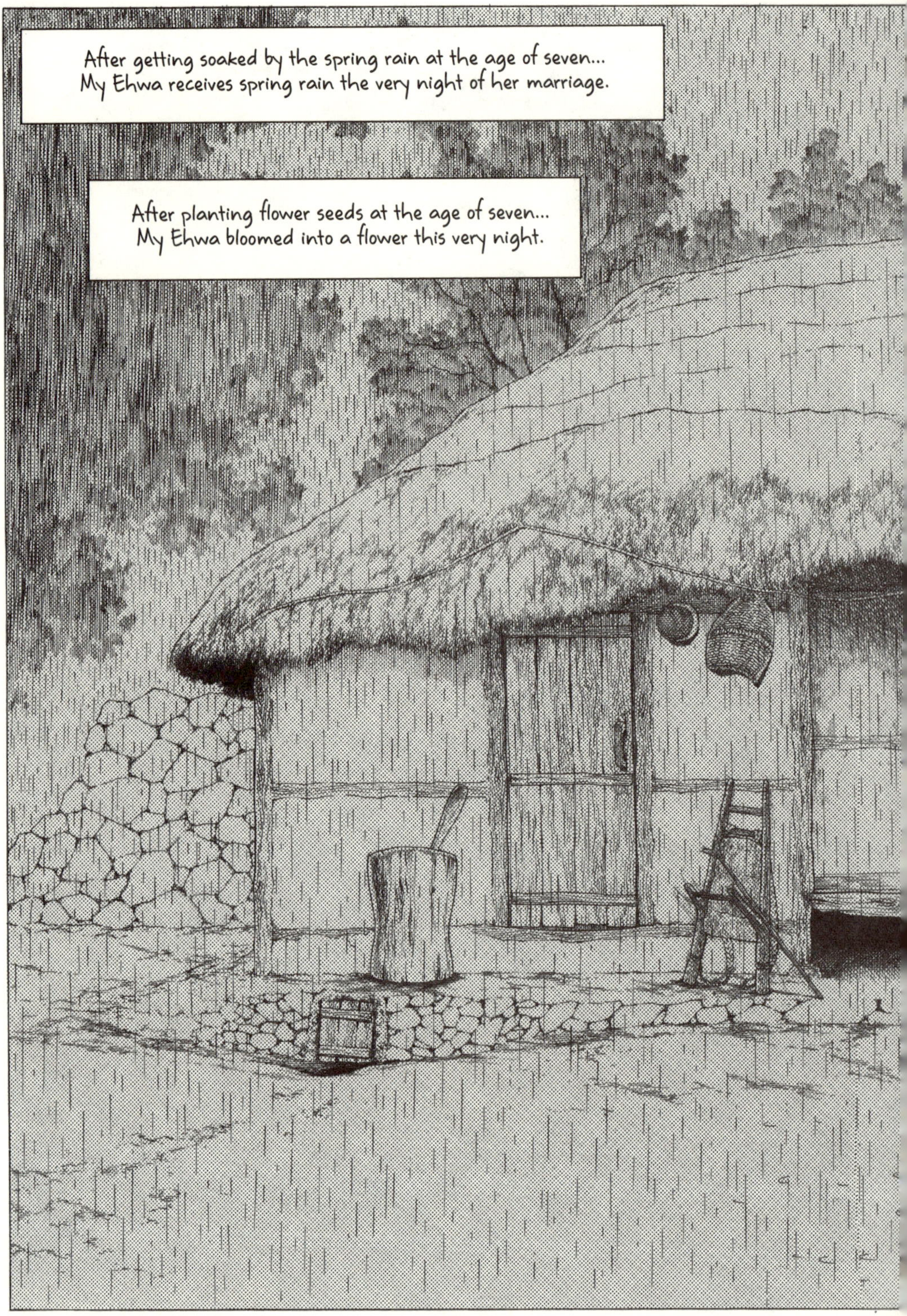
After getting soaked by the spring rain at the age of seven...
My Ehwa receives spring rain the very night of her marriage.
After planting flower seeds at the age of seven...
My Ehwa bloomed into a flower this very night.

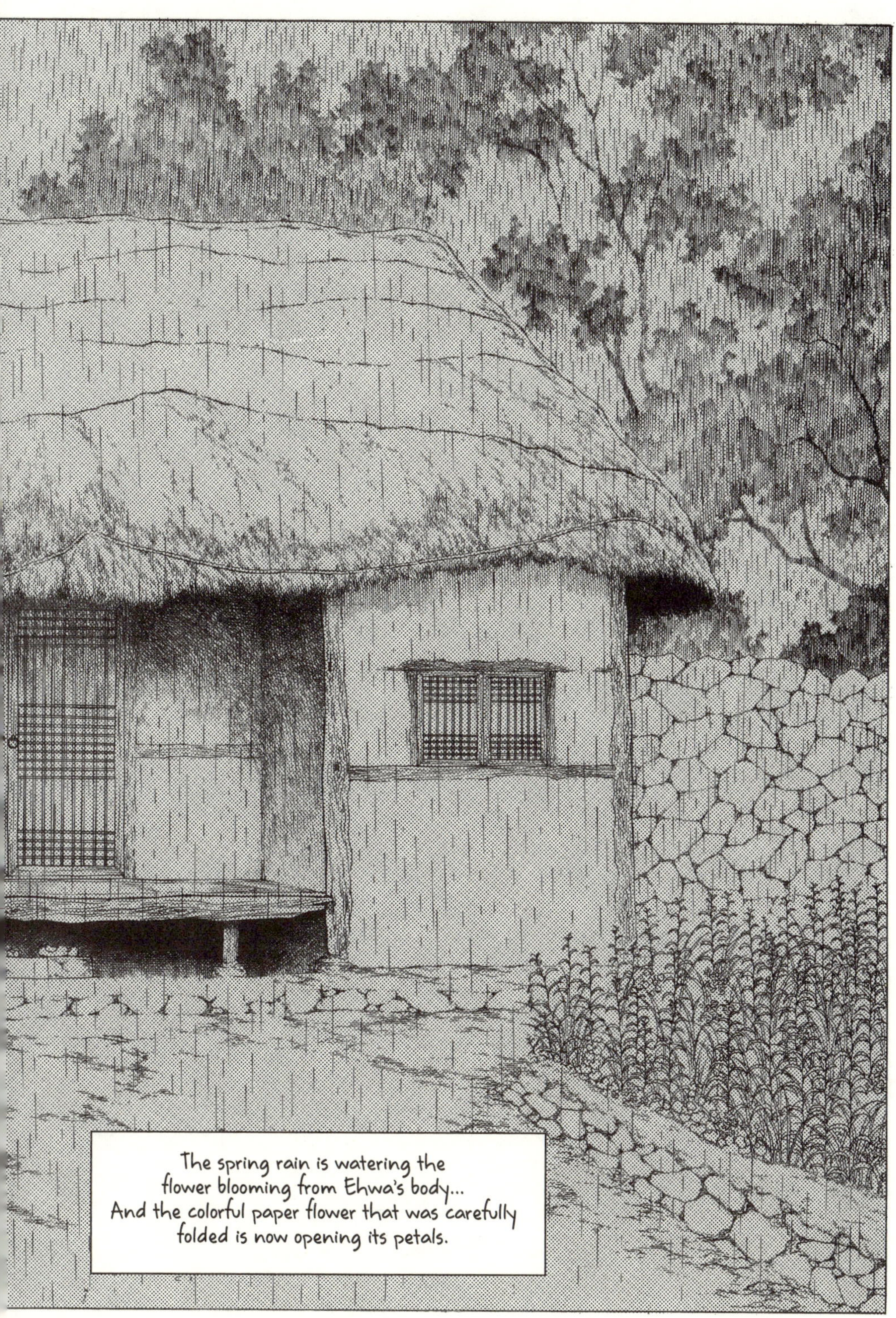
The spring rain is watering the flower blooming from Ehwa's body... And the colorful paper flower that was carefully folded is now opening its petals.

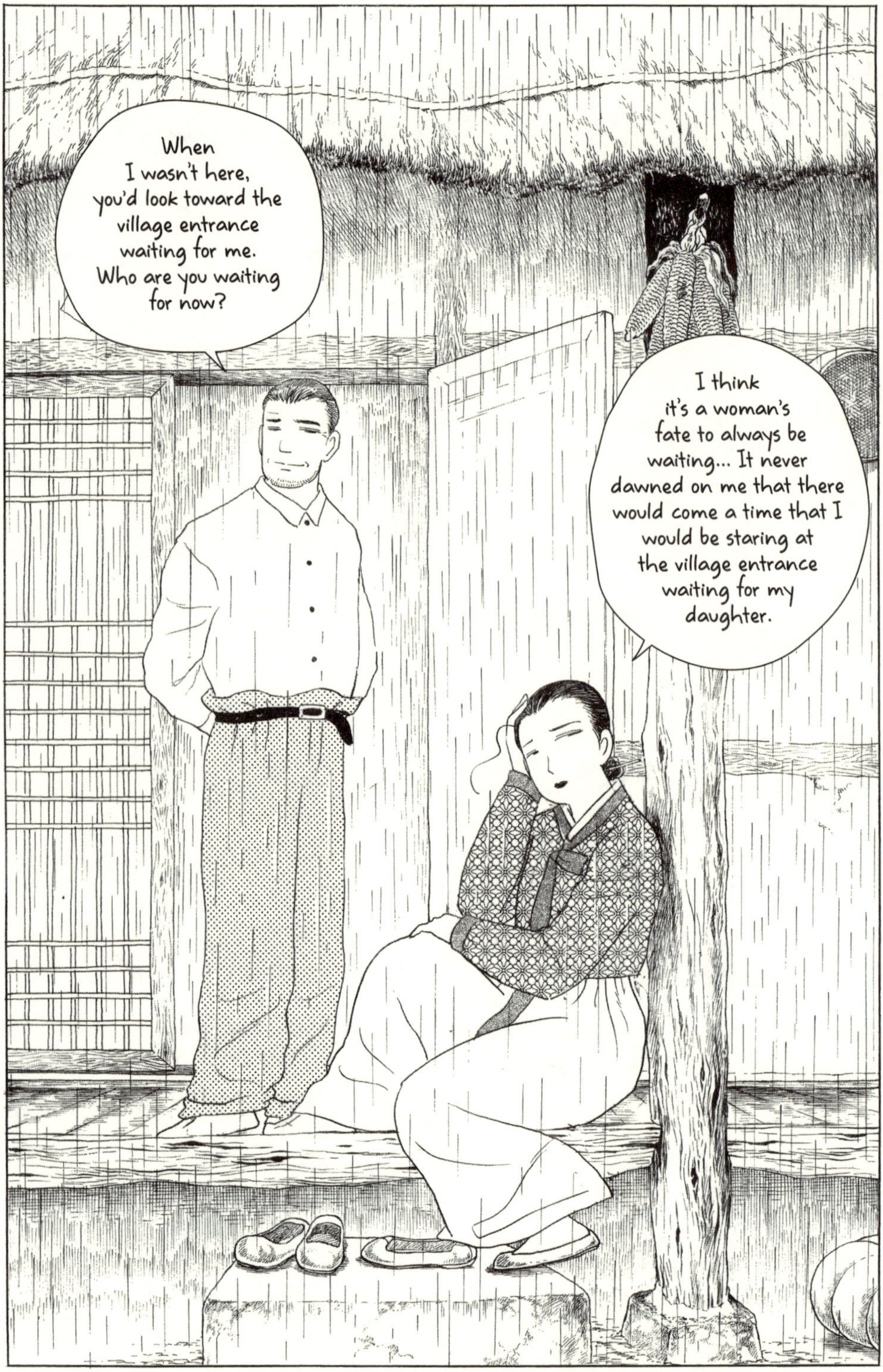
When I wasn't here, you'd look toward the village entrance waiting for me. Who are you waiting for now?
I think it's a woman's fate to always be waiting... It never dawned on me that there would come a time that I would be staring at the village entrance waiting for my daughter.

End of The Color of Heaven

THE COLOR TRILOGY READING GROUP GUIDE

ABOUT THE COLOR TRILOGY

*In a turn-of-the-century rural village in southern Korea,
a girl falls in love for the first time as her widowed mother falls in love again.*

THE COLOR OF EARTH:

Ehwa and her mother live alone in a tavern at the edge of their village. They have a quiet, wistful life together until Ehwa starts to notice boys, and her mother falls in love with a traveling pictographer who supports himself as a salesman. Over the next several years, Ehwa begins to learn about love as her mother cherishes the occasional visit from her "picture man."

THE COLOR OF WATER:

As Ehwa grows older, her feelings for the boys she meets change from crushes and vague longing to love. It is through her relationship with Duksam—and through having that relationship challenged by Master Cho—that Ehwa learns what it truly is to love. Meanwhile, Ehwa's mother contemplates what her life will be like, alone, once Ehwa marries.

THE COLOR OF HEAVEN:

The third and final volume of this series, *The Color of Heaven,* sees Ehwa rediscovering love and embarking upon marriage as her mother and the traveling pictographer decide to settle down together.

Kim Dong Hwa's delicate drawings and highly poetic language grace this three-volume epic with the light of a true master. An intimate portrait of the relationship between mother and daughter over the years, this trilogy is at once daring and sensitive in its portrayal of sexual awakening and reawakening.

ABOUT THE AUTHOR

Kim Dong Hwa is the author of many graphic novels—or manhwa, as they are called in Korea, where he lives. His books include the popular work *My Sky* and the literary piece *The Red Bicycle.*

ABOUT GRAPHIC NOVELS

A graphic novel is a long story told in the comics medium. You're familiar with comics; many of the best known are about superheroes or in the Sunday papers, and many have recently been the basis for Hollywood films. But the medium goes far beyond that. Every topic that a work of fiction or nonfiction can explore, a graphic novel can explore, too.

In discussing graphic novels, there are a few basic terms that will be good to know.

PANEL:

The images in graphic novels take place largely in sequential panels. A panel is a box that encloses the images. You can see in the three panels below that time is passing as Ehwa turns her head and sees the butterfly go by.

SPEECH BUBBLE:

When characters in graphic novels speak, their words usually appear in bubbles near their heads. You can generally tell which bubbles belong to which character because the bubble will have a tail that points to an area around the speaker's head.

I want to impress a really strong bachelor, of course!
I realized today that we need a strong young man in the house.

SPLASH
SPLASH

SKRITCH
DRIP

SOUND EFFECTS:

Sounds—dogs barking, water being wrung out of laundry, heavy breathing—are not generally conveyed in bubbles, but instead as dramatic lettering that is part of the background artwork, as you can see in the image above.

Acting like she knows everything! If she's pretty, it's because she got it from me.
She should be thankful I'm the one who brought her into this world. She's becoming so opinionated!

TEXT BOX:

Text that is not dialogue—either narration or thought—is typically conveyed in a box. Kim Dong Hwa does not use this technique very often in the Colors trilogy, instead mostly depicting thought and narration as a part of the panel without a box around it. (Occasionally, it is intentionally left ambiguous whether these words are thoughts, or spoken aloud.)

One of the most essential parts of reading graphic novels is reading the words and the pictures together: both, working simultaneously, tell the story. Look at the page opposite.

Try reading just the words on this page—then just the artwork. Then read them together. How do the art and the text work together to tell the story? What is missing without the words? Without the art?

Oh my!
Is... is that you, Duksam?
What are you doing coming here so late?
What kind of butterfly comes calling in the middle of the night?
Butterflies don't come at night—moths do! Are you a moth?

DISCUSSION QUESTIONS—
THE COLOR OF EARTH

- *The Color of Earth* opens with a scene in which men make derogatory remarks about Ehwa's mother, comparing her to a beetle. Throughout the story, this chauvinistic attitude continually comes up. What does this tell us about attitudes towards single women in the Korean society depicted in this book? What can you deduce about men's attitudes towards married women?

- The first boy that Ehwa falls in love with is a young Buddhist monk. Here are the ten precepts by which novice monks (called samaneras) are supposed to live:

    1. Refrain from killing living things.
    2. Refrain from stealing.
    3. Refrain from un-chastity (sensuality, sexuality, lust).
    4. Refrain from lying.
    5. Refrain from taking intoxicants.
    6. Refrain from taking food at inappropriate times (after noon).
    7. Refrain from singing, dancing, playing music or attending entertainment programs (performances).
    8. Refrain from wearing perfume, cosmetics, and garlands (decorative accessories).
    9. Refrain from sitting on high chairs and sleeping on luxurious, soft beds.
    10. Refrain from accepting money.

    How does Chung-Myung resolve the gap between these precepts and his passion for Ehwa? What does this say about his faith?

- *The Color of Earth* explores puberty, detailing Chung-Myung's first wet dream and Ehwa's first menstruation. How are these two events treated in the book? What can we guess about the role of sexual development in becoming an adult member of society in Korea at the turn of the century?

- Ehwa's second crush, Master Sunoo, is studying away from home. He is the only person in this book who is mentioned as attending school. What does that say about the importance—and availability—of education in Korea at the turn of the century? What enables Master Sunoo to pursue an education when others do not?

- When Ehwa learns about pruning, she decides to treat her feelings the same way farmers treat flowering trees—pruning away small blossoms to give the larger blossoms the best chance to grow healthy and strong. Have you ever done this yourself, even if you thought of it in different terms? Do you think this technique works? How successfully does Ehwa use it?

- How does Ehwa deal with her mother's relationship with the picture man? How is her ability to understand her mother enhanced or made more difficult by her own blossoming awareness of love?

- "That's why you should be careful what you do," says Ehwa on page 242, when she reveals to Bongsoon that her sexually forward behavior is no longer a secret. In the close-knit village society in turn-of-the-century Korea, the court of public opinion was clearly a component of social and economic success. Is the same true in modern-day America?

- "What is wrong with the kids these days?" says Ehwa's mother on page 264. What parts of Ehwa's life does Ehwa's mother think are wrong (or would think are wrong if she knew about them)? How are today's standards for "wrong" behavior similar to the standards of the old-fashioned Korea in The Color Trilogy? How are they different?

DISCUSSION QUESTIONS—
THE COLOR OF WATER

- Talk about the ways Ehwa's and her mother's perspectives on love are different. Which parts of their outlooks are the results of their experiences and which parts reflect the culture in which they live?

- How do Ehwa's experiences growing up affect her mother's life and perspective? Are daughters generally aware of their effects on their mother's point of view and circumstances?

• Nature is used throughout *The Color of Water:* Ehwa's life is surrounded with fruit, flowers, and vegetables. How is the progress of her sexual awakening echoed in the art depicting the natural world around her?

• How does the pastoral setting of *The Color of Water* affect the tone of the book?

• Ehwa and her friend Bongsoon are often contrasted, with Ehwa portrayed as an unknowing innocent on the cusp of adulthood and Bongsoon as an irresponsible, precocious teenager whose judgment is often compromised by sexual desire. How does Kim Dong Hwa's visual depiction of Ehwa and Bongsoon lend weight to these characterizations?

• Teenagers often draw conclusions about the adult world from what they see around them. How do the men who frequent Ehwa's mother's tavern affect Ehwa's ideas about what adulthood is?

• A matchmaker (Grandma Shaman) plays a vital role in *The Color of Water* as a go-between for Master Cho and Ehwa. Matchmakers were an essential part of marriage arrangements in Korea during this time period. How do you think this affected—or exemplified—the societal conception of married life and love?

• At the end of the book, Duksam leaves Ehwa so he can earn enough money to return to

I'll be back, Ehwa! I'm a fire butterfly, remember. I'm a fire butterfly that will always want to dance around your fire.
I'll wait for you. I'll build such a large fire that you'll be able to see it no matter how far you may be.

their village and marry her. Do you think he's made the right decision? What do you think might have happened if he stayed?

- Ehwa lives in late nineteenth century Korea. How would the life of an American girl who lived during the same period be different?

DISCUSSION QUESTIONS—
THE COLOR OF HEAVEN

- When Ehwa is out all night saying goodbye to Duksam, her mother employs a physical form of chastisement to punish her, then tells Ehwa she'll never whip her again, because Ehwa is old enough to make her own decisions and live with the consequences. Talk about the ways that parents can discipline their teenage children. When might physical punishment be appropriate?

- Ehwa's mother believes that being apart from someone you love is more difficult than going through hardship with that same person. Do you agree? What about waiting and being apart from a loved one makes it so difficult?

- When Ehwa's mother loses her money belt, she initially suspects Ehwa. Is it unfair of her to do so? What are the factors that make Ehwa's mother mistrust her daughter in this situation?

- The reaction of the Namwon villagers to the man they suspected of violating the chastity of elder Lee's daughter-in-law is to beat him and throw him out of the village, leaving him for dead. What does this say about sexual taboos and the sanctity of marriage in Korea during this time period?

- On pages 116 and 117, the pictographer (who Ehwa calls the "picture man") discusses how there are some things that his art cannot adequately represent, for example, the depth of his emotion for Ehwa's mother. Do you think this is a universal statement—that art cannot contain the emotion of real life? Do you think there are places specifically in this trilogy where the art cannot accurately represent the emotion evoked by the story?

- "If a woman has too much time on her hands, she begins to think of crazy and useless things," says Ehwa's mother on page 146, when Ehwa begins to pine openly for Duksam. Would having nothing to do be thought of the same way in Ehwa's rural, pre-industrial society as it is today? Could this social order be threatened by inactive women?

- *The Color of Heaven* places a great deal of emphasis on female beauty, describing in detail what makes a woman beautiful (pages 153-155). Ehwa is said to be in great demand as a wife because of her beauty. Does Ehwa receive special treatment from the Namwon villagers because of her appearance? How is this similar to the world we live in?

- There is a great deal of symbolism involved in the wedding ceremony, including the mandarin duck for fidelity, the chestnuts, jujubes, and rice for wealth and children, and the pine and bamboo branches for everlasting love. What symbols are involved in modern-day weddings in different cultures? Are the sentiments behind them similar? If not, why do you think that they've changed?

- The consummation of Ehwa and Duksam's marriage is depicted in highly symbolic terms. Many of the symbols used—flowers, water, bells, etc.—are common in manhwa, and used to avoid direct depictions of explicit sexuality. What effect does the extremely representational art have on this scene? Would your reaction to a more literal interpretation have been different?

- The story in *The Color of Heaven* centers around Ehwa's marriage. What will change in her life after she gets married? What will change in her mother's life?

- The Color Trilogy is a manhwa, the Korean version of a graphic novel. How does that define the way Ehwa's story is told? Are there things the author did using this form that he would not have been able to do in prose? Are there things he couldn't do? Consider especially metaphor, narrative voice, a sense of place, symbolism, and whether these literary tropes can expand to a visual dimension.

OTHER READING

BLUE, BY KIRIKO NANANAN
A finely told story of first love, awkwardness, and the infinite horizons of being a teenager.

THE WALKING MAN, BY JIRO TANIGUCHI
A series of quiet vignettes about a newly married man exploring the rural beauty of his neighborhood in Japan.

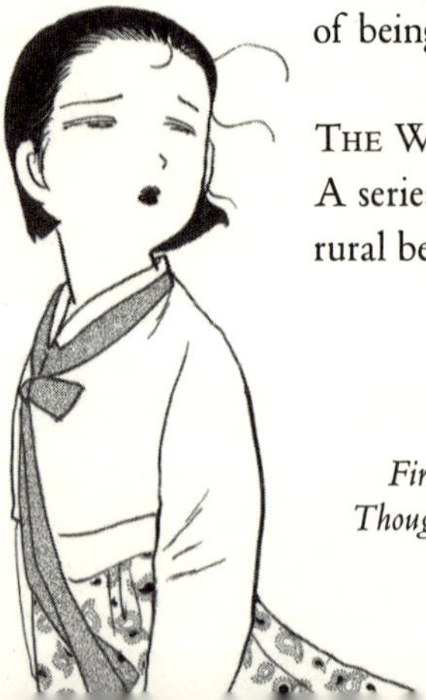

First Second Books would love to hear about your reading group experience. Thoughts, discussions, and pictures are all welcome at mail@firstsecondbooks.com.